From Ashes to Beauty

From Ashes to Beauty

John Class

Aventine Press

© copyright 2006, John Class
First Edition

Without limiting the rights under copyright reserved above, no part of this publication may be reproduced, stored in or introduced into a retrieval system, or transmitted, in any form or by any means (electronic, mechanical, photocopying, recording, or otherwise), without the prior written permission of both the copyright owner and the publisher of this book.

Published by Aventine Press
1023 4th Ave #204
San Diego CA, 92101
www.aventinepress.com

ISBN: 1-59330-337-8

Printed in the United States of America

ALL RIGHTS RESERVED

Prelude

This book has been preceded by *Alive Again*. Our main character Lev Aron is raised to life again after being killed in the first battle of Armageddon. He finds himself alive and well in a different time. He meets his family members who have survived him and enters a new way of life never dreamed of before.

He learns his marriage to Rebekah is no longer valid and soon has to learn an *agape* love, a purer love, in a higher way of life. He learns that everyone raised to life is given a home which makes him or her materially secure and independent, actually rich in having everything needful for life and the pursuit of happiness.

The world has changed. Wars have ended. The work of preparing homes and everything needful for those returning to life is the great and overwhelming challenge of those living.

Those returning who have lived noble lives with love and devotion are astonished at the happiness they feel in renewed love that had been interrupted by death. Those who had done evil find, in returning to life, that their "evil lives long after" and the path toward righteousness is much more difficult for those who had practiced evil. Satan is now bound and nothing evil is any longer made to appear good.

It is a secure world ruled by love and policed by spiritual forces so that none may hurt or destroy worldwide. The love of money, the root of evil, has ended and there is no money to be found. There are no poor or homeless—everyone is abundantly provided for. Pain, sickness, disease and dying have no place in earth's new society.

The only trouble spots are found in the ugly baggage returning with those made alive again. Lev finds an old enemy and is challenged to turn him into a friend. Old hatreds and prejudices still abound and must be overcome as society sheds its vices and struggles to regain the divine image.

Lev and Rebekah are called upon to mentor Hitler and Eva Braun respectively. That becomes their greatest challenge and a character builder.

Preface

The ashes of death will be turned into the beauty of the resurrection from the dead, and that resurrection truth of the Bible and of Christianity is central to Jesus' teaching. It is because Jesus died for Adam, and all mankind are Adam's descendants, that the resurrection hope shines brightly. If all men will return to life, the resurrection holds joyous prospects—but also some agony. When men shall live again, they will bring with them every virtue that they possessed—as well as the remembrance of every evil deed.

Fortunately, most people have lived reasonably good lives, which will play back beautifully in the resurrection. However, the murderers and the murdered will share the same stage again—as well as the severely exploited and those who did the exploiting.

Those who spoke truth and those who spoke error, though it may have been popular error, must stand together again. The whole truth and only the truth will be known clearly by all. None will find any hiding place from the evils committed in the past, nor will loving and courageous deeds fail to be recognized and remembered with gratitude.

The words from Isaiah 61:3 read, *"To appoint unto them that mourn in Zion, to give unto them beauty for ashes, the oil of joy for mourning, the garment of praise for the spirit of heaviness."* Jesus read Isaiah 61:1, 2 while in the synagogue, saying, *"The Spirit of the Lord is upon me, because he hath anointed me to preach the gospel to the poor; he hath sent me to heal the broken-hearted, to preach deliverance to the captives, and recovering of sight to the blind, to set at liberty them that are bruised, to preach the acceptable year of the Lord"* (Luke 4:18, 19).

That work began at Jesus' first advent, but the main fulfillment of Isaiah 61:3 awaits his second advent. The human race continues to die, turning into dust and ashes—but Christ will change this. From the ashes, the human family will be called forth in the resurrection. *"All that are in the graves shall hear his voice, and shall come forth"* (John 5:28, 29).

The resurrection Bible truth has been treated strictly on a theological level for many centuries. Few have thought about the emotional aspect and what it will really mean to have mankind returned to life again. *From Ashes to Beauty* attempts to envision the emotional impact on human relationships when our Lord Jesus undertakes to reconcile men to each other and then to God. The work of "regeneration" and "restitution" will be the most ambitious endeavor to ever occur on earth (Matthew 19:28; Acts 3:19-21). The billions that have died will be regenerated in an orderly and logical manner.

God does not do for men what they can do for themselves. Those who are regenerated will need to be clothed, housed and provided with sustenance. Those living who are eager to receive their loved ones back to life will gladly contribute these needs.

The stories that will unfold can only be imagined. The resurrection will provide an endless series of dramas—greater and more fulfilling than those of this present life. The resurrection has escaped the attention of mankind because the "regeneration" and "restitution" concepts have been forgotten due to inadequate Bible teaching.

When "heaven" and "hell" were the only alternatives offered by theologians, the "regeneration" and "restitution" were moot. However, when all the prophets of Holy Writ speak of "restitution," how long can the regeneration be hidden? The Day of Judgment has been locked into a twenty-four hour period scenario when all would be raised to stand before a literal "great white throne" and receive their final judgment.

The idea that death "ends all probation" makes the Day of Judgment redundant. If one were judged at death, why would any need another judgment? Why the Judgment Day should be confined to twenty-four hours is strange indeed, when "one day is with the Lord as a thousand years" (2 Pet. 3:8).

The "heaven" and grotesque "hell" theology have left out a massive amount of scriptures on the "regeneration" and "restitution." Fortunately, now that thorough Bible study has brought them to light, we are presented with a refreshing look at the seemingly never-ending drama about to unfold. When "restitution" was hidden from view and "heaven" and "hell" were the only options, there was no drama.

No one can intelligently grasp the realities of "heaven." On the other hand, "hell" was so wicked and monstrous that most were uncomfortable with the horrors concocted by ghoulish minds. We can, however, grasp the thought of life on earth in the beauty of a "regenerated" human race, coming forth with all the baggage accumulated in this present life while trying to start over again. Many have said, "If I had this life to live over again, I would do things differently." The fact is—they will have such an opportunity. It is wonderful to contemplate living again with all the advantages of experience gained in this present life.

Our first book, *Alive Again*, began with the regeneration of some who died in the Armageddon conflict, when an unbelievable number of people perished in an ill-fated endeavor to take Jerusalem from the children of Abraham, Isaac and Jacob.

Our present story moves backward in time to an earlier generation who returns to life in the resurrection. It is conceivable that only a little while will be required for each generation to return to life once preparations are established and operating at peak efficiency. The "regeneration" will be much more rapid than the original generation of mankind was. It took over four thousand years for eight people to multiply to the billions now living. It is not unreasonable to conjecture that a century is all that will be required to receive all mankind back to life.

As the regeneration continues, more and more people will be engaged in making preparations for fewer and fewer people returning. Finally, the whole world will stand at that monumental day when they shall receive our first parents, Adam and Eve. There will be joy and jubilation when all men shall receive our first parents back to life— that is when the "ashes" will be turned to "beauty."

From Ashes to Beauty follows the unfolding drama. Our human makeup does not allow us to grasp what is happening to everybody. We can only appreciate what happens on a personal basis. Ten thousand people dying in a foreign land does not have the same impact as one person dying in our arms.

We will share in the lives of individuals only because that is all we are able to fully appreciate. The drama of Christ's kingdom will reach every human being who has ever lived, but we can comprehend best what happens to individuals one at a time.

We open the scene with the generation of 1945, the time of World War II. The place is Hiroshima, Japan.

*"If a man die, shall he live again?
All the days of my appointed time will I wait, till my change come.
Thou shalt call, and I will answer thee,
Thou wilt have a desire to the work of thine hands"
(Job 14:14, 15).*

Chapter One

Strangely, I felt no pain. It was so quiet. No nurses or doctors were tending my horribly burned body. I felt clean sheets below and a light blanket covering me. My present position was comfortable—but I was terrified to move. Any movement might bring the intense agony. I determined to lie still as long as possible.

Was this the moment before I would die—when people said one gained a moment of peace? As I laid here, it became increasingly noticeable that I was experiencing no discomfort at all. I felt my chest and found my skin was fresh and supple.

Having successfully moved my hand, I decided to try to move my legs. I was shocked—there was no pain. Did I dare open my eyes? My left eye was seared and blinded, with wretched burning. Yet, for the moment, I felt no painful throbbing in either eye. I was tempted to open them. First I squinted, opening a small slit. To my amazement I could see through both eyes. I opened my eyes fully and saw a bright ceiling above. The sun was cheerfully shining through the window and a gentle warm breeze fluttered the curtains.

Was this a dream or was I hallucinating? Slowly I lifted the blanket. There were no scars or burns on my skin. My body was in beautiful form—not even the slightest evidence of having been seared. No one could ever describe the immense heat and force unleashed by that bomb. I clearly remembered the awful moment. I was in a room of my house furthest from the conflagration. Only this protected me from the full impact of the explosion. The house seemed to collapse and burn simultaneously. It wasn't a very sturdy structure, but there was enough framework to limit the intense heat from incinerating me instantly.

How often I wished I had died instantly like my dear wife Junko. She didn't have to endure the pain of burns over most of her body as I did. How I longed for death—my body was so racked with excruciating pain, I could barely endure it. No one arrived to help me for a long time. A few times I mercifully lost consciousness, but then I regained it to face the worst agony I had ever known.

Finally, someone found me lying in my small scorched garden. My clothes had burned or been blown away. It didn't matter. My body was barely recognizable. Burnt flesh hung from my seared frame. Those who tended me looked in horror. Mercifully, they injected me with something that eased the pain slightly. The hospital overflowed with burn victims in the hallways. The smell of burnt flesh and hair polluted the air. I faded in and out of consciousness only to hear the groaning and occasional screaming of victims being touched by nurses. The lucky ones expired quickly, but my torture seemed endless.

One of the nurses told me I had been there for a week. It felt like an eternity. I couldn't catch my breath—every fiber of my being convulsed with unrelenting pain. I heard someone whisper, "He'll never make it." That was good news—I wanted to die—it would end my torment. I was delirious, calling for Junko. I wanted someone who loved me nearby to help me.

Dying was lonely. I was amazed that with all my excruciating agony, the presence of my wife would mean so much. I was indifferent to the cries of others. Fading into unconsciousness was a blessed feeling. That's all I remembered, as darkness came over me.

Lying in bed, my mind was racing, trying to make some sense out of it. I could remember the sound of an airplane overhead. I knew it was an enemy plane. Why would one lone plane be coming toward us? Where were their attack planes? I heard the motors of the fateful bomber—and then, suddenly, a bright flash of light, an explosive roar, winds and fierce heat. We were being fried alive. In seconds my world was forever swept away, replaced by unbearable burning.

I remembered one nurse saying that the enemy had dropped an atomic bomb. I didn't understand what this meant, but sensed awesome power and destruction. No one should have to endure anything like this. War was brutal—why were we killing each other?

Even when we thought Japan was winning the war, I had hated reading about the carnage. When Germany and the Axis powers of

Europe fell, we knew Japan would surrender or be destroyed. It was false bravery to think we could take on the whole Allied world. I clearly saw the "land of the rising sun" sinking beneath the waves.

I couldn't explain my healthy body without any evidence of the damage I had sustained. I slowly stood up, excited to be whole again, feeling vibrant—eager to live. Then again, I didn't dare trust my feelings—this had to be a dream. I was so afraid of waking and finding myself back in that awful hospital with excruciating burns. Glancing around the room—everything looked real. I noticed clothing neatly folded at the foot of my bed and immediately dressed. To my amazement everything fit perfectly. The surroundings were orderly and beautiful. I could only hear birds chirping outside. There was nothing to alarm me, except my own fears that this would disappear and I'd find myself where I didn't want to be.

I cautiously opened the door, quietly stepping out of the room. A man sitting in the living room saw me.

Trying to Understand

"Good morning, Suno Ishakawa. My name is Lev, Lev Aron. I am here to help you. We have been waiting for your return."

"Excuse me, sir, do I know you? How do you know my name? Why would you wish to help me? You are not Japanese—you look like an American or European. Am I your prisoner? Did Japan surrender? Where am I—how did I get here?"

"Please, Mr. Ishakawa, please sit down—one question at a time. I am Jewish. You are not a prisoner. Japan did surrender to the Americans, but all nations have surrendered to Christ. Now, the hardest question to answer—how did you get here?

"As hard as it may be for you to believe, Mr. Ishakawa, you did die and now you have been brought back to life by Christ. He has given you a new, healthy body with the same genetic makeup you had before, but all the defects have been removed. Every electrical sensory impulse your mind ever had has been recorded into your new body.

"You died in 1945, Suno. Nearly a century has passed since then. You are now living in a new world without war, hatred, pain, falsehood, misinformation or deceit. No, Suno, you are not dreaming." Lev reacted to Suno's look of utter disbelief and shock. "You are very much alive in a new body that Christ has given you. Do not worry. What you are experiencing is not a dream—it will not go away if you blink."

Suno cautiously thanked Lev, but little he was saying made sense. Suno wished he could talk to someone he knew to give credibility to his present experience.

"Mr. Lev, do you know anything about my wife, Junko? I know that she died—at least the market where she had gone was very near the center of the bomb's impact. Most people in the area were vaporized instantly. Is it possible that Junko will live again, too?"

Lev beamed. "I have good news for you, Suno. Junko returned to life a day before you. As a matter of fact, she will be calling on you in about half an hour."

"Please, Mr. Lev, do not play games with me. I am somewhat disoriented. I believe you are a good person, but how do you know that Junko has returned to life and will call upon me? You could not possibly know this, Mr. Lev. You do not seem to understand—she was incinerated. How could she possibly return?"

"Suno, look at me. I, too, died—and I have returned to life. People are returning to life every day. Junko has already returned to life and she will soon be here. Perhaps when you see her you will be convinced that this isn't a dream. I know everything seems unreal to you right now. You probably noticed that you're about eight inches taller. All your teeth are gleaming white and straight. You have no missing teeth. You are better looking than ever before—but you're still the same Suno you always were."

"Forgive me, Mr. Lev, I didn't mean to be rude. It's just that I'm somewhat frustrated—I'm not sure why. You're right. My teeth are all there!" Suno took a moment to absorb this fact. "How could I be taller? I feel so very well! I can't believe I have no discomfort. Everything is so nice—your home is very beautiful. But I still feel disconnected from my old environment."

His Own Home

Lev smiled with the joy one feels when bestowing a gift. "Suno, this is your home, your very own home, now and forever. However, you are now living in another part of Japan, in an area formerly not very populated. Your property is indeed beautiful. Come, let me show you around."

Lev led the dazed Suno through the bright spacious house, showing him its many wonderful features. He turned on a switch. The whole wall lit up like a movie picture screen—in full color with every detail vivid and clear. Someone was speaking, but Lev turned it off before Suno could understand what was being said.

"This is a television set, Suno, something that didn't exist in your day. You will find all the information in the whole world here. Television is not used for entertainment as it was in the years after it was invented. You'll be much too busy and happy to need to be entertained anymore. You have much to learn, but learning will be easy. Every day you live you will become more keenly alert until you reach absolute perfection, and you will have a perfect memory. You will only require one good clear explanation—and you will be able to retain it. We call our teachers the Ancient Worthies, or Ancients, like Abraham, Isaac and Jacob of the Christian Bible. You will soon be educated in the history and truths it holds. These Ancient Ones are perfect instructors. When they finish a lesson on television, you will understand it very well."

The Japanese man was trying to grasp all he was being told as quickly as he could, but he was having difficulty believing his own senses. This stranger was telling him the Christians were running the world! What about his beloved Shinto? What happened to the brave kamikazes? And where was Junko?

Lev took Suno through a large patio door opening to a sculptured garden and a beautiful orchard with fruit trees. Never was there room for such a spacious garden in the city where he had lived. Everyone had their miniature gardens planted upwards, squeezing flowerpots on every square inch of window ledge and porch.

"These fruit trees will provide all the food you will ever need—and you will never have tasted such good fruit. They're from seeds of the trees in the Garden of Eden. Those eating this Eden fruit may live forever. The Eden fruit will satisfy your nutritional needs, as well as every eating pleasure. Well, Suno, we must return quickly—Junko should be here anytime now. We don't want to keep her waiting."

They had not returned to the parlor for long when the doorbell rang. Lev motioned for Suno to answer the door. He hesitated, fearing that his dream would suddenly burst, but finally forced himself to do as Lev had suggested.

Suno and Junko United Again

Suno gasped—there stood Junko—taller, more beautiful than he ever remembered. She saw him at the same instant. They bowed politely to each other. (These two Japanese were very reserved—as was their custom.) They stood speechless, staring at each other as though it were some apparition. Finally, Suno broke his reserve and embraced Junko tightly—he didn't want to ever let her go—he wanted to hold her forever.

"My dear, dear Junko," Suno whispered. "Tell me this isn't a dream. Don't disappear on me—don't go away, promise me you will stay with me always."

"Oh, Suno, you are back." Junko began crying. "I can't believe it! Suno, please—don't ever let me go."

Lev could see they both had the same fear—that this wonderful dream would suddenly end. They clung to each other desperately, fearing the spell would be broken. At last, he intruded and brought them back to reality.

"How about having breakfast and some tea?"

They both stood smiling, not quite willing to let go, but nodded, yes.

Holding each other, they followed Lev into a bright, cheerful kitchen. Large windows were opened to allow the scents of flowers and the songs of birds to waft in. The walls were painted a lovely shade of green, and the appliances and furnishings shone as the sunlight hit them. It seemed larger than the whole house where Junko and Suno had lived. Lev had prepared a fruit salad from the orchard. He poured a new and very aromatic tea and served them generously from the large bowl of fruit.

Just before they were about to eat, Lev said, "Please, let me pray. Thank you, dear Heavenly Father, for this wonderful provision, as well as for the gift of life so generously given to Junko and Suno. Thank you for Jesus Christ, who has made this all possible. In his name we pray and give thanks."

They were not Christians and his prayer sounded strange to them. In the days ahead they would learn that Christ was Lord of earth. For now, they were both in a state of semi-shock, but they bowed graciously, not wishing to offend him. They were too happy at the moment to be disagreeable.

Lev watched them sample the fruit with their chopsticks. Their faces lit up—it was like nothing they had ever eaten. It was not only delicious, but also totally satisfying. They felt strengthened and delighted—a diet perfectly suited to their taste and needs.

Junko had already been enjoying this menu from yesterday, but she couldn't get over how delicious the fruit was. Lev poured more tea and served them cookies he had made from dried fruit flour. He said he had learned the recipe from Rebekah, his best friend and one-time wife.

Lev knew that Junko and Suno needed to be alone to pick up the pieces from the past and weave them into the present. Suddenly they both had each other and the world was not so strange.

Lev told them he would be in the garden if they needed him—he would be planting vegetables and herbs.

Tragedy and Hope for Mori

Suno turned to Junko, holding her tenderly not wishing to lose her. They could hardly keep back their tears. He could tell Junko needed him, too, because she still felt disoriented.

"Have you heard anything about our son, Mori? Did he survive the war?"

"I inquired about Mori and was told he was among the last kamikaze torpedo pilots who gave their lives when it was clear that Japan would surrender. The captain insisted that Mori guide his manned torpedo to sink one last American vessel before the war ended."

Suno's face darkened. He loved his son very much. He had tried to dissuade him from his super patriotic desire to become a kamikaze volunteer. But Mori insisted that the honor of his country demanded his willingness to sacrifice. Why did it have to be Mori? Why did he have to die when the war was virtually over? What captain would command such an unnecessary sacrifice of their only son?

Suno's joy was turned to sorrow and anger. He was a quiet, reserved person; but news of his son's death cut his heart like a sword.

Junko saw his anguish. "Suno, he died almost at the same time you did. He shall be made alive in a few days. Mr. Lev and some other people have already built his house. Mori is due to return next week. We will both be there to greet him."

Suno was puzzled. "Is this possible? How can all these things be happening? If our son died, explain it—how can he return again?"

Junko softly spoke, "Suno, you and I were dead. We have been dead for nearly a century. We are here, alive and breathing. Look at me. I was dead. I was incinerated. There was nothing left of me but a shadow on the pavement. I am living, can you see? Are you not holding my hand, honorable husband? Why can't you believe that Mori will likewise return?"

"Oh, Junko, I want to believe, I really do! Why didn't I ever hear about the resurrection of the dead before? Were we not to have become a *kami* after we died? How could such a wonderful thing be hidden from us all of our lives? We were devout in our Shinto religion—we always honored our ancestors. How were we so deceived and mislead?"

"Suno, when we lived, there were thousands of different religions, all teaching different things. It stands to reason that if they all taught something different, they could not all be true. I have asked a thousand questions since yesterday. I cannot believe how much I can remember! There is a spirit being whose name is Satan, who had the power to blind men from the truth. He is the enemy of the one true God because he rebelled against Him. God let him try his tricks on mankind because God knew that men would learn from their experiences with evil. They wouldn't just listen and learn. But now that Satan is bound, the truth is clearly known. Religions were founded on traditions and what people wanted to hear—not the truth. There is only one religion now. Truth is the only thing being taught today. Truth is everywhere, all the time. There is no false religion anymore, anywhere in this whole wide world. They are all gone, thank God."

Suno recognized Junko's powerful logic and sat pensively trying to digest it. Finally, he said, "Junko, tell me about what happened that dreadful day the atomic bomb was dropped upon us."

Junko Recalls Her Last Day of Life

"I left you that morning very sad because I knew Japan had lost the war. It was only military stubbornness that was prolonging the misery for everyone, our own people and our enemies. As I walked down the street to the market, I heard a lone plane coming inland from the coast. I knew it had to be an enemy plane—but why only one plane? Usually the Americans would have a fleet of bombers to rain death and destruction on us.

"I could see the plane coming clearly. I saw it drop a bomb, but it was far away so I didn't run for cover. All I remember next was a bright, blinding light, hot wind, and a ferocious roar that swallowed me up. That is all I remember. I don't even remember any pain.

"I am told the only thing left of me was a shadow on the pavement. The next thing I remember was awakening a day ago in a house very much like yours. A very kind lady by the name of Ms. Rebekah was there to welcome me. She is the former wife of Mr. Lev who welcomed you this morning."

"Time for us has stood still nearly a century. The world seems so different. None of our old thinking has any relevance today. The war is over. I have no idea how much suffering occurred when we surrendered. I can only imagine the Americans treated us cruelly—we certainly treated American prisoners very badly."

"Ah, no, honorable Suno. Japan was given exceptionally good terms. Food and money were generously supplied. Perhaps the United States wanted to use Japan as a hedge against the spread of communism. Our country rose from the ashes of ruin to become a prosperous industrial nation. We produced the highest quality products and soon became a giant in world trade and technology. The Americans were actually very good to us. In a way, they returned good for evil. Our leaders looked like savages compared to the honorable treatment we received."

"But they dropped a savage bomb on us, didn't they?"

"Yes, Suno, but as awful as that was, it hastened the end of the war. If Japan had surrendered immediately, they could have avoided the second atomic bomb dropped on Nagasaki. Right after the second bomb, our country surrendered. Our economy was in ruins and the war brought great hardships to everyone. However, the United States treated us fairly, with more kindness than we deserved. We had treated China and Korea terribly, and they hated us for it. You and I paid the price for our country's cruelty."

Death Proved to Be Blessing

"Fortunately, we both died. I only suffered about a week—but no one should have suffered as I did."

"They told me what had happened to you, Suno—I feel so bad I wasn't there to comfort you. My death was easy, in comparison. I know that those who lived suffered greatly. Some died from burns, others from radiation. Some lasted for years before they died. You were spared prolonged agony. Thankfully, they tell me this will never happen again. We can see the historical documentation on the wonderful invention, the television. You know, Suno, the whole world is now under the rule of Jesus, who was also resurrected as Christ, and the laws come from Jerusalem."

"Well, one thing I know is the whole world has changed since I died. Yet you have not changed, Junko. You are a refreshing oasis in the desert. To have someone I can love and trust means everything to me. Mr. Lev has been very nice and very truthful, but I don't know him. I can't trust him like I would someone I have known for most of my life. Yet, Mr. Lev seems to know everything about this new world, and I really know nothing. I'm totally dependent on what he says. How do I know he's not leading us into some bitter pathway?"

"Suno, you must trust him. Mr. Lev is totally honest. You know he left us alone, and he arranged our meeting together. He worked several weeks building your house. It was Mr. Lev who called the Ancient Worthies in Jerusalem to arrange for your return to life, as well as Mori's and mine. He has been doing wonderful things helping people return to life. Mr. Lev is one of the leading scientists in the world today, but no service is too small for him to do for others.

"His wife, Ms. Rebekah, whom you shall meet tomorrow, is also a lovely person. She, too, has worked on your house and has helped you come back to life. They've been doing this for many years. The more you come to know Mr. Lev and Ms. Rebekah, the more you will like them and trust them, Suno. You won't find a kinder, more generous person than Mr. Lev."

"Well, Junko, you must be right. You always read people better than I did. I believed that Japanese propaganda when the war broke out. Later I realized they had misled us, causing untold suffering in the world. You always told me they were wicked leaders and would bring disaster to Japan."

Junko sighed. "Let's not discuss them—let's talk about us. We have to catch up on everything. We're in a new world now. There's no more war—no guns—no hospitals, doctors or nurses. No one is sick or getting old. Everybody is getting younger, more handsome and more beautiful. People are becoming more knowledgeable every day as they eat the Eden fruit that God has provided. There aren't any weeds or bad bugs to bite us—no one can hurt anyone in this wonderful new world. You'll notice, honorable Suno, there aren't any locks on the doors or screens on the windows. People don't need them anymore. There aren't any armies, navies or military establishments. It will take us months to get used to this different world. How beautiful it is! We've been given beauty for ashes. How blessed we are to be together again.

"Soon we shall work together to receive my mother and father back to life, as well as your parents, Suno. We have so much to learn. And we will be permitted to help prepare for the resurrection of our venerable ancestors as well. The hardest thing we'll have to learn is to be loving and kind to every human being we meet."

"And let the beauty of the LORD our God be upon us"
(Psalm 90:17).

Chapter Two

Suno was surprised by Junko's assessment of present conditions. She made the remarkable return of people sound like "Alice in Wonderland," the American story he had learned in his childhood. Junko had only returned to life shortly before he did, but already she knew so much. But Suno trusted Junko—he knew if anyone spoke the truth, she did. She was always more perceptive than he and could sense insincerity instantly. It was so good to have her near. Suno had died without his Junko, but no matter—she was here now when he needed her most.

Mori to Return

"What about our son, Mori? Did you say he was coming back to life again soon?"

"Yes, Suno, Mr. Lev has arranged for his return to life exactly one week from today. Mori will be with us again and we will be able to hear his story. How sad he must have been to go on that deadly mission, especially after knowing the war had been lost. Mori would not have hesitated to take the torpedo to destruction. He was like so many of our sailors who placed honor above reason."

"I tried to talk him out of joining that kamikaze force. But Mori and his friends decided this was the supreme sacrifice they'd make for Japan. I hoped the war would end before Mori was called to make his sacrifice. It did end, but not in time to save his life. I'm so sorry Mori's life ended that way. Our whole little family died. Yet we are here. I still can't believe it. I must hold your hand—don't leave me. I keep thinking this must be a dream."

"Forgive me, Junko, I'm so mixed up—I feel so insecure. Everything is too good to be true. One moment I remember being racked with terrible, unbearable pain. The next moment I find myself feeling healthy in strange but beautiful surroundings. Then, you appear from nowhere. Now, I learn of Mori's death and am told he will return. Tell me this isn't a dream, Junko."

"I know exactly how you feel, Suno—I feel the same way. The only difference is that this is my second day of living again, and I know it's real. Everything I hear turns out to be true. I watched the television and saw the Ancient Worthies, men and women of noble distinction. These are the people ruling the world—people who were proved worthy and faithful to God. They are changing the world under their righteous rule. You will see, but first we must live in this moment of happiness we have together. We are both alive and well. Let's rejoice in this moment! Christ is the true ruler on earth now. Only he has the power to raise the dead to life. If he has given us life—and he must have, or how else would we be alive again—we must be thankful to him."

Lev, the Enigma

They had spent nearly two hours together before Lev returned. He was very happy and outgoing. By nature Suno was extremely reserved and suspicious, especially of people he didn't know. But Lev disarmed him of all his suspicions and reservations. Lev was genuine and loving. Suno had never met anyone like him in his entire life. Lev was also striking in his appearance—very handsome, with his lustrous blond hair and brown eyes. The glow of health on his muscular body was unmistakable. He was so knowledgeable, yet very humble and gracious. Suno heard that Lev was a great scientist, but he never talked about it and didn't spend all his time in laboratories.

Lev loved people. One could feel the warmth of his love. He had taken time to help build Suno's home and plant his orchard and garden. Why would anyone do that for a complete stranger? In the world Suno remembered, no one was interested in helping anyone else unless they benefited their business or social circle.

Lev was certainly different. He loved Junko and Suno as their own brother would. Again, he wondered—was this a mask that would fall off? No one could be that selfless. Did Lev have a covert interest in them for his own benefit? He'd wait—in time his true motives would become apparent. His suspicious nature was taking over again. He went along with all that was happening, but kept reservations in the back of his mind.

Suno knew many nations loathed the Japanese. Their military had committed terrible atrocities to prisoners of war. He knew it would come back to haunt them. He hadn't realized that all those who suffered under their cruel authority would be returned to life. But if all he was learning were true, this time they'd have no power over them. They'd have to meet those they had abused and tortured face to face.

If this resurrection business was for real, and Suno was beginning to concede it was, it sure posed a multitude of problems for evildoers. It may have been easy to torture or kill people and walk away from it. Those victims were powerless. They could continue daily living, forgetting their merciless actions, and in time, people would forget what had happened. None would believe they had been so cruel, especially if they could block the press from referring to these events. Soon what they did became an idle tale.

Suno's son, Mori, had told them how the Japanese had used live Chinese people for bayonet practice—how they had buried some alive, beheaded others, and tortured many. It made him shudder, but the military was a killing business. A soldier's job was to be tough and heartless to enemies. War wasn't for the softhearted.

Suno was slowly realizing how sins would come back to haunt perpetrators. His mind began arguing again. The resurrection was a myth. But then, how could it be? They were here. His emotions were racing in all directions. Nothing that was happening was reasonable. His mind fought against the present reality. Yet his heart wanted to accept the present. He wanted to cling to Junko—she was real—or so he thought.

But for this Lev— Suno didn't know what to make of him. Why was he here? Why should he spend his time with them? He was only a dead man walking. Suno had absolutely no explanation for what he was doing here. Nothing, nothing, nothing made any sense.

Coming to Reality

Lev interrupted Suno's pensive quandary.

"Suno, you seem to be in another land. I know how you feel. It's strange to live again, isn't it? The length of time in the grave has no significance. There is no time for those asleep in death. Being dead one day or one hundred years is the same. There was no consciousness of time or anything else before we were born, and the same is true when we are in the grave. The Bible stated the truth when it said, 'the dead know not any thing' (Eccl. 9:5). Still you are aware of a time lapse because you are in a different world.

"It will take a few weeks before you feel secure about life, Suno. I understand the thoughts racing through your mind. On one hand, you are enjoying a world in which you are a stranger. On the other hand, you fear that, if you blink, the next moment you'll be back in the hospital groaning in pain. Take my word for it, Suno, you will never, ever find yourself back in that hospital. You will never know pain as you knew it then. No one will ever drop another bomb on you or hurt you in any way again. You can forget your worries, Suno—none of your fears will be realized. Life and happiness are here to stay."

Lev changed the pace. "It's time for lunch. Let's try some fresh fruit that I picked from your orchard this morning, Suno."

Junko arose eagerly. "I can help get it ready."

"All we need are plates and tea, Junko. There is nothing else to prepare. The food you are about to eat will make you mentally brighter, physically stronger and more beautiful each day, Suno. God himself planted these trees back in the Garden of Eden. The Eden trees are filling the whole earth giving abundant life to everyone."

When they sat down, Lev asked them to bow their heads as he prayed to thank God for making all these provisions.

Suno was annoyed with Lev's habit of forcing prayer on them. He certainly didn't worship Lev's God, nor did he believe in Christ. All he remembered was that Christians were always going to war and exploiting weaker nations. Though, Suno had to admit, if professedly Christian nations treated them fairly after the war, they had done better than the Japanese had.

Suno had worshiped at Shinto shrines all his life and so had his forefathers. He resented Lev's abrupt intrusion of his God and Christ. But he decided not to spoil the first day of his new life by being contentious. He'd let it pass for now. Lev sensed his disgust.

"Suno, I know you worshiped at the Shinto shrines all your life. I don't want to be rude. But it wasn't a Shinto god that brought you back to life. Christ alone has this power. He raised me, he raised Junko, he raised you. And soon he will raise your son, Mori. Christ will raise every human being that ever lived in the proper time and order. No matter what you believed before or how much you venerated the Shinto religion, no matter how strange all of this may seem, now is the time for truth. Christ and Christ alone has the power to raise the dead. The sooner you can accept this truth, the better it will be for you.

"At one time over five thousand religions controlled the world, but only one religion exists today. Christ is King of the whole earth. I know you have no way of understanding this yet. This is only your first day of being alive again. As you become aware of Christ's rule, it will be easier for you to believe. You will not find anyone who is living again who believes in the Shinto religion or any other religion anymore."

Junko added, "I have only been alive for two days and already I'm a believer in Christ. The evidence of his power in raising the dead and the righteous way that the world is being governed gives me unspeakable joy. There are no armies, navies, air force, or police—no slums, poor, or homeless—no sickness, suffering, sadness, or quarreling—no drunkenness, jails, hospitals, doctors, nurses, drugs, locks, taxes, or bills. No one is above the law, but law protects all. Honorable Suno, you haven't stepped out of your house. You don't know how wonderful the world has become."

Lev was very persuasive. But when Junko joined him, Suno quietly laid down his defenses. If the world had changed so much, it was certainly more than any human ruler could do. Suno knew in his heart it wasn't the Shinto god that brought him to life again. Who else but Christ could have done such a great thing? How could he resist Christ's power and love?

Gentle Persuasion

Suno turned to Lev. "You must have read my mind. Please forgive me for being ungrateful. I didn't mean to be contrary. Please understand, I was trained in the Shinto religion and knew of nothing else. Now, suddenly everything has changed, including me. I'm taller and more handsome than I ever dreamed. I can't deny the magnificent changes that I've already seen. Give me a little time, Mr. Lev. I don't know how to handle it all. In a few days, maybe I shall understand more. I do want to change for the better. Please be patient with me—I came from such a dark repressive world."

"That's okay, Suno, I do understand. I was a Jew in my former life. I knew of Christ, but always associated the Christian religion with their persecutions heaped upon Jews for being Christ killers. I felt exactly as you did, hearing Christ's name in prayer. Whatever your feelings, remember, they are because of your past religion and superstitions. You won't be able to shake them in a day. Give yourself a little space to learn of the new world."

Junko added, "Yes, Suno, Mr. Lev is speaking the truth. He has been alive again for several years longer than we have. In that time he has distinguished himself in accomplishing some remarkable feats in science, but he divides his time between science and helping people return to life. Mr. Lev and his family are known and loved by many nations. I'll tell you about this later. Let's eat this Eden fruit now—it's a gift from heaven."

As they ate, Suno asked, "Mr. Lev, you said our son Mori would live again next week. He must have died after Junko and me. How can you be sure of the date for his return to life?"

"Just as we knew you would be raised to life today, so we know the appointed day of Mori's return. We informed the Ancients that all preparations had been made and our prayers for his return could be granted. It will occur like clockwork. We know the day and hour of Mori's return. After lunch, we'll walk over to his house. It's less than a mile. With your new bodies, walking will be pleasure.

"As you can see, everything around us is vibrant. No factories spew out smoke or toxic chemicals. No trucks are speeding about delivering food from fields to stores. Everybody is self-sufficient in food and energy. Life is much simpler—but there's much to learn. We're being taught everything correctly. There are no mistakes being made anywhere. The world's resources are being used wisely to build, plant and sustain the millions of people returning to life. You, too, will soon join in the work preparing for your parents, brothers and sisters."

Suno's eyes grew large as he tried to hold back tears.

Junko said, "Suno, you're starting to believe what Mr. Lev is saying. Maybe you will be assailed with doubts from time to time, but soon you'll understand; only truth is spoken. You won't have your hopes dashed in this world. Not only will our health, strength and knowledge increase by leaps and bounds, but also those who obey Christ will live forever. We never heard that before, did we, Suno?"

Suno smiled, shaking his head. "I think I've gotten over my first round of suspicion and anxiety. Mr. Lev, will you be so kind as to take us to Mori's new home? I'm beginning to feel excited at the thought that we'll soon be seeing Mori. First Junko, next Mori! I don't deserve such kindness. I haven't been the noblest man. It's hard for me to understand this love."

They quickly cleaned up and Lev led the way to Mori's. As they walked briskly through picturesque orchards and gardens, they met a few Japanese people along the way. Suno greeted them with his usual Japanese.

"Good morning!"

They smiled and said, "You must be newly returned to life."

Hebrew Spoken

"How do you know that?"

"Because you are speaking Japanese. Those of us who have lived for many years speak Hebrew."

"Hebrew?"

"Yes—Hebrew is the universal language today. It is a beautiful language with an alphabet of twenty-two letters. Hebrew is nothing as complicated and limiting as the Japanese sign letter. You'll learn it easily in a few months. Today learning is easy."

They were learning as people along the way gave them information and encouragement. Most were warm and friendly—so different from the great reserve of their former life. It was an extraordinary day.

Junko said, "You know—I feel like doing a cartwheel. I used to be good at that."

Suno was embarrassed. "Junko! You'd better not—what will people think?"

Lev said, "Go ahead, Junko. People will know you're filled with the joy of living again."

Junko quickly did a perfect cartwheel, landing on her feet with the grace of a gazelle.

Suno laughed. "I didn't think you could do it, Junko! You haven't done anything like that for a hundred years!"

Before they knew it, they came to a new home with a charming courtyard and garden. "Who built this?" Suno asked.

"I helped. So did Rebekah. Many people joined, and in a couple months, the work was done. Building and planting are very efficient. That's the main work of the day. People returning to life need provisions, and the regeneration program is very orderly. Christ only does what men cannot do. He raises the dead, but we must provide for them. Some used to believe that the dead would be raised and judged in a literal twenty-four hour day. The good were supposed to return to heaven and the wicked were supposed to go back to eternal burning torture."

Suno responded, "I, for one, had enough burning torture. What kind of sick minds conceived of eternal burning torture? Even Shinto doesn't teach such wickedness. At least we worshipped nature, and we never had anything as lovely as I see all around me on this amazing day."

Lev explained, "People used religion as a form of coercion or intimidation to get control over others. If you didn't accept their beliefs, you were labeled heretics. One branch of the Christian religion assembled crusades to conquer the Holy Land. If anyone died while making the crusade, they were promised an immediate entrance to heaven. Some Muslims promised paradise to martyrs who blew themselves up with explosives tied to their bodies. They even crashed aircraft into skyscrapers, causing thousands to die. These terrorists were instilled with hatred and rejoiced in spreading death and destruction to infidels."

Suno could feel his face turn crimson as Lev spoke. He solemnly reflected, "Ah, Hirohito used the same tactics on our people. My own son was a victim of this distorted thinking. Mori died in the deployment of a kamikaze torpedo. The war was virtually over, but Mori's captain decided he should sink one more enemy vessel. I argued with my son repeatedly about his false ideas of honor. There was nothing honorable about blowing up a ship and its crew who thought the war was over. However, Mori had joined the kamikaze force under a patriotic craze. He felt compelled to complete his deadly mission. Mori was the last kamikaze member to die in the war. Junko and I would have had continual sorrow had we known of his suicidal death. Fortunately, we both died shortly before Mori. Our little family was wiped out in that war."

Mori to Return to Life

"Yes, Suno, but for the resurrection power of Christ, our little family would have perished forever. How wonderful to think Mori will be here in a few days. We have so much to be thankful for, don't we?"

"Yes, we do," Suno admitted. "Once I get rid of this walking-in-a-dream feeling, maybe I'll be able to respond in a truly thankful way."

Lev took them on a tour of Mori's new house. The home had comfortable furniture of the Western world. There were beds instead of sleeping mats. However, Suno was pleased to see the Oriental designs in the decor and bamboo shades in the sunny kitchen.

Lev loved to point out the self-sufficiency of each home. He demonstrated the new power unit that produced electricity out of water after breaking it into molecules of hydrogen and oxygen. You could feel the freshness of air from the oxygen being released into the rooms. The hydrogen fuel cell silently produced electric energy without the sound of a generator.

Hydrogen gas was also used to heat the hothouse during the colder months so that the orchard could produce fruit through every season. These features would bring an incredibly high standard of living to each individual.

The rooms were large, bright and airy—two sizeable bedrooms, the living room with a high ceiling and large skylights, floor-to-ceiling windows facing the garden, and an open loft study overlooking the orchard. The library had floor-to-ceiling bookshelves and a computer area. One wall was a full screen television and the other had windows facing a large solarium where luxuriant plants, herbs and vegetables grew year round.

Lev also showed them the bathroom. Nothing was wasted. The facilities were designed for emptying every six months into rich, dry nitrogen powder. This fertilizer was then used to replenish the plants so that the environmental cycle was never depleted. The scientific achievements were impressive.

Suno exclaimed, "Everything here is used to bless and sustain mankind. Nothing here is used to hurt or destroy, is it?"

The Law of Love

Lev nodded, "I am so glad you observed this without me calling it to your attention. In our new arrangement, nothing is permitted to hurt or to destroy another human being. Man's life today is more precious than gold or silver. All of mankind's efforts are expended in making provisions to receive the dead to life. But it doesn't stop there. Every human being has to learn to live by new laws that are summed up in the word, LOVE."

Trees and plants that were deciduous remained outside the hothouse enclosure. Food was in abundance. Never would anyone be hungry or homeless again. Junko was overwhelmed with the provisions that had been made for Mori. She said, "We should have been the ones to build this house for Mori."

Lev answered, "Usually it is the children who build for their parents. But when children die about the same time as the parents the procedure may be reversed. In Mori's case, everyone wanted him returned as soon as possible after your return, so they joined to make the preparations before you returned. Love is a wonderful thing, isn't it?"

Suno didn't understand selfless love, but he knew it was marvelous to be on the receiving end of it. Suno was cold and reserved by nature. If he had loved others as much as he loved his wife and son, he might have been more prepared to understand the willingness of people to give so freely in serving others. However, he was thankful to have time to engrave god-likeness in his heart.

The time passed quickly as Lev showed them the wonderful features in Mori's home. Both Junko and Suno were spellbound with the high standard of living that everyone enjoyed.

It was hard to believe the competitive world had changed so drastically. There's no competition in heaven. There never was—nor ever would be. On earth, competition had some value when it drove men to work hard. But too often the losers suffered greatly, while the victors accumulated all the rewards. Sometimes politics decided the winners.

An End of Competition

Yes, competition was an incentive influencing men to work hard for success. But it created a mixture of good and evil at the same time. Unfortunately, the negative elements of competition had not remained in the grave. Its selfish spirit returned with those who lived again. It would require much re-education to rid the world of its unwholesome effects.

The time had come to leave. They were invited to Junko's where Rebekah had remained to finish some gardening. As they walked toward Junko's home, they took another route and met others along the road. They were friendly and interested in knowing everyone in the area.

Junko and Suno spent extra time talking with people, inquiring about their return to life. Suno was surprised to meet his neighbor who had also perished in Hiroshima's atomic explosion. This broke his reserve—the neighbor was also excited to meet him. They promised to meet at the first opportunity and exchanged addresses.

Rebekah was at the door greeting them warmly. Junko introduced Suno to Rebekah with highest praises. He was taken aback at Rebekah's striking beauty. Even Lev remarked, "Rebekah, you're more good-looking every time I see you."

"That's true of everyone, Lev. As we grow toward perfection, how can it be otherwise? You must be hungry. I made extra treats to celebrate the occasion of Suno and Junko's return. Some Christians preached the resurrection, but nobody believed them. It was a difficult teaching to grasp, no matter what the scriptures said. Even now as we witness it before our eyes, we can hardly believe the reality of what is happening."

Suno nodded. "I can't believe what has happened to me this day. There is so much good news—I can scarcely believe it. Yet, I know everyone tells the truth and doesn't lie or even exaggerate. If Christ is responsible for this, I must thank him. When we eat, please let me offer my first prayer of thanksgiving to Christ."

Junko was stunned. While she believed in Jesus, she was not prepared to pray to him yet. But Suno knew his announcement warmed her heart.

"Suno, I would never have believed you would render allegiance to Christ so easily. But I'm glad you did. I have, too. Without him, where would we be?"

Suno Acknowledges Christ

As they sat down, Lev asked Suno to thank the Lord for the food and the blessings of the day.

Suno stood up, bowing his head, and prayed. "Dear Christ, with trembling lips and heart I stand before you to offer my gratitude and thankfulness for returning Junko and me to life. You have delivered me from all the pain and suffering of my last hours to health and happiness beyond my dreams. Most of all, I thank you for promising to raise my son Mori to life again. You have done more for us than we ever imagined. Now, we thank you for this festive table with all the bounties from your hand. Amen."

All joined with a hearty, "Amen."

After the prayer they were silent for about a minute. Rebekah had made their meal into an artistic masterpiece. Her fruit salad was served in a hollowed out watermelon. They had never bothered to serve food so attractively.

Suno marveled, "This is better than heaven. Of course, what do I know about heaven? I only know I have never ever enjoyed my meals more than now. Our former foods fed us, but also contributed to sickness and discomfort. Now we are not only gratified by what we eat, but we also taste what perfect food is like for the first time."

Junko laughed, tears streaming down her cheeks. "I'm crying because I am so happy. Thank you, Ms. Rebekah, for being a true friend and a servant of mankind. You have been a tireless worker ministering to my every need and a faithful instructor. To think that someone who never knew me would give of herself so freely in helping others is something that I wish to emulate. I want to be like you, Ms. Rebekah. Also, I must thank you, Mr. Lev, for your untiring labors on behalf of Suno and Mori. I've been told of all your scientific accomplishments, Mr. Lev, but it is most amazing to me that you would take time to help us common people. I heard that you even helped prepare for Hitler's return and that you personally guided him for a short time. Is that true?"

A Remembrance of Time Spent with Hitler

"Yes," Lev answered. "I was asked by the Ancients John the Baptist and Enoch to undertake this task. There were few people interested in helping Hitler's return. He was so hated for his cruel past that they felt they needed someone with my experience and knowledge to deal with him. Hitler tended to admire people who were skilled scientists, but his admiration for me ended quickly when he learned I was a Jew. However, he was totally dependent on me for all his information and education, so he had to put up with me."

"You actually helped that terrible monster?"

"I did it as a favor to the venerable Worthies, Suno. He was not so cruel and terrible in his new environment. He was more like a spoiled child. In the first place, all of the power Hitler held in the Third Reich was gone. He was alone in the new world. When he learned that everyone was going to return to life, he suddenly realized that those he had killed and tortured would confront him. That was a terrible fear for him. There was no place to hide and no one who would consider his former conduct as anything but bloody, cold murder. When people learned who Hitler was, they wanted to viciously attack him. However, when they tried to strike him, their hands became paralyzed. Hitler quickly observed this and relaxed, seeing that divine protection kept him from being beaten. But his relief was turned to confusion when he tried to shove an angry person who wanted to block his way. He found both of his hands became paralyzed. I told him what he must do to be healed.

"He refused for several hours to follow my advice. Finally, in desperation, he asked me to telephone the Ancients. I had to dial the phone for him and hold it to his ear. I told him to tell the whole truth of what he did and not to color it in his favor. He gave an accurate account to Sarah, who responded to our call. Hitler was healed within the hour, but this experience made him realize there was no going back to his old ways. The great Fuehrer was now little Adolf in a world that held him in contempt for his evil course. How deflating to his ego!

"I knew Hitler was hoping to find his old comrades—perhaps his SS men—to form a little band of friendship. He will probably find some who secretly long for the good old days when they had influence and power. When he finds them, and I'm sure he will, it will only increase their weaknesses. Hitler's only hope is to stay clear of those comrades who shared in the gross conduct of his former life.

"I found little repentance in Hitler's demeanor. His big worry was how to avoid the millions he had tortured and murdered. He was also worried that many Germans were turned against him for prolonging a war that everyone knew was lost. I had made it plain to Hitler that he was going to have to face these people sooner or later. There was no escape from his past conduct. God's ways are equal, I kept reminding him. There is still time for him to change his mindset, but the whole time I was with him, I found no repentance or sorrow in his heart for what he had done. Perhaps he will awaken to the fact that continuing in his old patterns will only bring death. Hitler took his life once not wanting to face his sins, and he will be destroying his chances for life the second time if he continues his old ways. Still, he has only been alive again for a short time, and the Scriptures promise he will have at least a century to make progress. It will be exciting to see what happens."

The conversation was intensely interesting to Junko and Suno, for they knew their son had drunk deeply of a similar fanatic fringe mentality. It was labeled patriotism and Japanese honor, but they perceived it to be brainwashing. Young people are full of idealism and this was often turned into kamikaze mindsets by demagogues. Lev identified this worry on their part.

Tuning in the Ancients

After an unusually long discussion at the supper table, Lev suggested it was time to listen to the Ancients in Jerusalem. Junko had heard them the previous night, but Suno had no experience with television.

Suno was astonished that people so far away could appear as if in their parlor. The screen was large enough to make the speakers life size, and they were so real in appearance that one could imagine they were in the room with them. The Patriarch Abraham, the first to receive the Promise that ultimately became this blessing for all mankind, was speaking. His message could be heard in any language by pressing the right button. Lev made sure it was in Japanese.

Abraham announced that those wishing to learn about any who returned to life that week could click their mouse on the country and city where they would find complete listings. For future awakenings up to one week in advance, they should indicate the date and country of origin and the names would be listed in alphabetical order.

Lev selected the day for Mori's return as well as the country and city. To their delight, the name of Mori Ishakawa appeared. Now they were absolutely convinced that this would happen. They asked Lev if they might be there on that occasion next week.

"Of course! This will be a great moment in your new life's experience. You shall have the privilege and honor of witnessing the power of Christ as he brings Mori back to life."

Suno and Junko were so excited that the rest of what Abraham was saying was lost to them. Lev explained the educational programs that were available by selecting the subjects they wished to pursue. He also told them that, as they ate the Eden fruit, the capabilities of their minds would experience a daily acceleration. Soon what would have taken years of college courses to learn, they could learn in only months.

Because the Ancients were physically and mentally perfect, they made learning interesting and stimulating. Seeing perfect people captivated Suno and Junko. They were continually startled by their beauty, dignity, and brilliance.

Suno's stiffness and resistance to this new life had collapsed. He was becoming a true believer because the evidence was so overwhelming. Lev and Rebekah knew this. For about a week Suno would have flashbacks to the old world, but it would quickly pass as he accepted the new reality.

"The sea gave up the dead which were in it"
(Rev. 20:13).

Chapter Three

A week had passed. Junko and Suno arrived at Mori's future home to receive their only son to life. They were earlier than planned. They had been too excited to sleep as they counted the hours to Mori's return.

Lev and Rebekah had promised to arrive an hour after Mori's awakening. They wanted to give them time alone, but not too much time lest any lack of wisdom mar the day's happiness. Suno had severely disagreed with Mori about his kamikaze commitment. It was difficult to anticipate how Mori would respond to his new environment.

Lev and Rebekah were familiar with the terrorists who had died on September 11, 2001, using aircraft to annihilate New York City's Twin Towers. Those terrorists had returned to life facing harsh reality. They had chosen to die on a hate mission, fully assured of a glorious entrance to paradise. Upon awakening to life again, the terrorists at first thought they had survived the plane crash. Then they thought they were in paradise, but they soon learned they were back on earth. Islam's paradise of virgins had been founded on falsehood and fantasy. The terrorists were upset to learn of their leaders' deceptions, but even more angered to find themselves living under Christ's rulership. They had developed a consuming hatred for Christianity, which proportionately affected their lack of capacity to love Christ and Christians. They found themselves misfits in the regeneration.

Some of the terrorists ultimately thawed from their hate-and-destroy mentality. Others were traveling on a dangerous road of bitterness. They were convinced they were victims struggling against Christian and Zionist aggressors. Hatred was preventing them from responding to love. For this reason, Lev and Rebekah had been asked to help the Ishakawa family adjust to their new life together.

The kamikaze mindset was permeated with brainwashing techniques that severely damaged character development. It created an elitist complex that focused on the death and destruction of the enemy. Commitment to the cause was idealized as superior to any personal commitments. The individual envisioned himself endowed with untouchable sainthood.

When awakened from the sleep of death, the terrorists not only found themselves robbed of sainthood and paradise, but their evil deeds were fully unveiled and despised. Instead of being glorified heroes, they were hate-filled murderers. It wasn't easy to adjust to a world where love reigned supreme and evil carried the label of evil. They needed to relearn the true values of life. It would take great humility and love for God and fellow men to turn their characters around.

Mori Screams

The hour for Mori's return to life arrived. Junko and Suno heard Mori screaming as he awakened. He apparently had been screaming as he guided his torpedo into the unfortunate vessel doomed for destruction. Then the screaming stopped.

Mori found himself physically well and whole, but terribly confused. This certainly wasn't heaven. How did he survive that crash and explosion? His awakening followed the normal pattern.

Mori first imagined that he had survived his ordeal. Then he was amazed—there wasn't even a scratch on his body. He felt great and jumped out of bed. He quickly found his clothes and was pleased they fit him perfectly. He glanced around the room and saw the peaceful setting outside his window. This certainly wasn't a prison hospital.

Why was he in a private room so beautifully furnished? Quite a change from that cramped torpedo hatch. If he was alive, it wasn't his fault. He had done his duty. Or did he fail on his mission? He surely had seen the vessel dead ahead. He knew he crashed into it. Did the torpedo fail to explode? How could anyone have rescued him anyway? There was a black void—something was missing. Nothing was making any sense. But one thing he did know—he was very happy to be alive. How would he explain this to his officers?

Mori paced around his room. He noticed the adjoining bathroom— more lavish than any he had ever seen. He looked out the window again to see gorgeous flowers and trees. Everything was tranquil and quiet. Where in the world was he? How did he get here?

Mori finally got the courage to open the door. What awaited him? Slowly he emerged. Where could he make a quick exit, if needed?

From Ashes to Beauty

He was about to dash toward a door when suddenly he heard a voice. "Mori, my son, welcome home."

It was Suno's familiar voice. At the same moment Mori saw his father standing next to his mother. He ran quickly to them and embraced them. Tears of joy filled his eyes. No one spoke a word. They stood there embracing and crying for happiness.

Finally, Mori broke the silence. "Father, where are we?"

"My son, you are home, safe at last."

"But how did I get here? I drove my torpedo into a ship. I thought I would surely die. How did they save me? How could I have no bodily injuries? How did you get such a beautiful home? Oh, Father—Mother—I'm so glad to see you! You look wonderful! You look better than ever! You even look younger. But you are without a doubt my parents. Forgive me—I'm so confused."

Junko softly answered, "Please, son, sit down here next to us. Now, only ask one question at a time. We don't know how to tell you this, but we must. You have been dead for nearly a hundred years. You came back to life this morning. This is your very own home, now and forever.

"The world is different now," Junko continued. "There is no war—no enemies. If you look out the window you will see beauty everywhere. The war has long been over. Yes, Mori, you did die, though needlessly. Japan had surrendered before your captain commanded your deadly torpedo attack."

Hearing of Surrender

Mori became agitated when he heard that Japan had surrendered. "I knew we were losing the war. But why would Japan surrender? The Japanese are brave. We would have fought for the honor of Japan."

Suno tried to calm Mori. "You know they dropped atomic bombs on us, don't you, Mori?"

"Yes," he said, nervously wishing to avoid the humiliating fact.

Junko said quietly, "Did you know your father and I both died in the atomic bomb explosion at Hiroshima? I was vaporized. Your father was so badly burned that he survived only one week."

Mori listened in disbelief. "What?" he shouted, pacing the floor. "Have you lost your mind, Mother? How can you be here if you died?"

"Son, listen to your mother. She is telling you the truth. The three of us died in 1945. Your mother and I returned to life last week. We both know how frustrating it is to be alive again without understanding the logical sequence of events. You are suddenly awakened into a new environment with new arrangements and so much to learn. Fortunately, Mori, we are here with you. Japan is not the nation we once knew. The world is now at peace."

"Why are you deceiving me, Father? Are you preparing me for some great disappointment? This talk about being dead is crazy. I know I'm alive. I know you are both alive. I can see you and hear you and touch you. But when you talk about returning from the dead—this is ridiculous! And you speak of being dead for a hundred years! Please! Don't do this to me! I remember what happened yesterday. Maybe I'm dreaming. I am thoroughly frustrated! What is going on? I demand an answer! Please, tell me the truth! The whole truth!"

"Son, we experienced the same feelings that you are now having. That's because there is a century's gap in your life. You fear this is a dream—if you blink, you'll wake up in the awful torpedo world you left behind. It will take you about a week to comprehend that you are really alive again."

Junko added, "Christ answered our prayers and returned you from the dead this very morning, Mori. The whole world is under his control and we are governed from Zion's Hill in Jerusalem. Mr. Lev and Ms. Rebekah Aron will be here soon. They are from Israel. They helped build your house for you and planted your orchard and garden. It is they who made arrangements for you to return to life. We knew the day and hour when you would be raised to life. Look, Mori, you are much taller. Your teeth are white and even. Even your skin is clear without a blemish. The little hump in your back is gone. You are more handsome than you ever were. Can you explain this, Mori?"

Afflicted with Inner Panic

"No, Mother. Maybe that accounts for my strange feelings," Mori sighed, calming down. "I guess my inner time clock is messed up. I do feel well. But nothing is logical. I begin to panic inside thinking I will wake up steering that horrible torpedo."

"Son, your commander should not have sent you on that mission. He knew the war was over and that two atomic bombs had been dropped on Japan. The unconditional surrender had not yet been signed, but it was agreed upon. I shall never forgive him for that."

When Mori heard his father say this, he turned red. "So that's why he half apologized when he said, 'Mori, I'm sorry to send you, but you must fulfill your commitment to Japan.'"

Junko agreed. "All he did was to send you to an unnecessary death. He caused needless death and destruction to the vessel you struck. Many men perished."

A long silence fell over everyone. Mori, for the first time, realized what his commander had done.

He confessed, "As much as I was willing to die for the honor of Japan, I must admit, when he asked me to mount that torpedo, I didn't want to. I felt the war was virtually over. We all knew it was. What good would come from my death? He just wanted to add one more little medal to his badge before stepping down as captain. My life meant nothing to him." Mori felt astonishment as this revelation came over him. "I said nothing as I turned to my assignment. He saluted me, but I didn't return the salute. When faced with certain death, I realized I didn't want to die—I wanted to live. But my commander had the power of death over me. I did what I had foolishly promised to do. I was cheated out of life for nothing."

Suno checked his watch. "Mr. Lev and Ms. Rebekah should be here soon. We'll be having breakfast together. We are eager for you to meet these wonderful people."

Mori wished otherwise. He wanted to escape to his bedroom and brood. He was quite upset with his captain and didn't want to meet anyone. However, he knew he must be polite, if only out of respect for his parents.

Meeting Loving Strangers

The doorbell rang. Junko jumped to open the door.

"Come in, please, come in! We are so glad you are here Mr. Lev and Ms. Rebekah! Our prayers have been answered! You must meet our son, Mori. He was raised to life at precisely the time the Ancient Worthies appointed! It is such a miracle! Suno and I can hardly believe it!"

Lev and Rebekah greeted Mori with the traditional Japanese bow. As upset as Mori was, he, too, bowed in respect. He could not deny that both Lev and Rebekah were unusually attractive—more beautiful than anyone he had ever seen. He found himself staring at them. He suddenly became conscious of his impolite gawking and forced his gaze elsewhere.

"Hi, Mori! Rebekah and I have been looking forward to this day for months. The Ancients assigned this plot of land to you. It will be your home forever. They told us a little of your history, so we knew of your life and death. Would you do the same thing if you could choose again?"

"Before you answer Lev's question, Mori, let's sit down to breakfast. You'll find eating a special pleasure now." Junko knew that Mori wasn't ready yet to answer such a question. He was still too overwhelmed and shaken to be able to reason clearly. A little Eden fruit would help that problem.

When they were seated, Suno asked Lev to thank the Lord for the food. Lev prayed with great earnestness, thanking the Lord for the provisions and for Mori's return to life. Junko explained to Mori that they would be eating Eden fruit from the trees of life. She had several freshly squeezed juices along with dates, nuts, figs, and a host of delicacies.

Junko encouraged Mori to try the Eden fruit first. He had never seen such fruit and surely never tasted anything from Eden. Enjoying the fruit, he tried not to think about Lev's prayer, which he had not liked. His Shinto faith found the Christian religion galling.

"This fruit is very delicious!" Mori exclaimed. "It isn't Japanese. I've never tasted such great food!"

Returning to Lev's question, Mori said, "No, Mr. Lev, I would not do it again, knowing what I do now. They thought I was expendable. I didn't want to die when the time came. My bravery was an act. I was weak and trembling when I climbed into that cramped torpedo chamber. I did what I had promised to do, but it wasn't what I'd imagined when I signed up for this supposedly honorable service."

Death—As an Enemy

"I felt the same way when I was dying," Lev agreed. "I felt it wasn't supposed to happen to me. I was mortally wounded and knew I was dying. Nothing could save me. I fought bravely, but it was a hopeless battle."

"Were you fighting Japan, Mr. Lev?" Mori inquired intensely.

"No, I was fighting in the last battle, the Battle of Armageddon, defending Jerusalem," Lev explained.

"Do you mean you died, too, Mr. Lev?"

"He most certainly did, Mori," Rebekah interjected. "He was so badly wounded I could scarcely recognize him. We buried him with heavy hearts. Lev was the love of my life. Our son, Allon, was devastated. Death is never easy. Everyone wants to live. You say you were weak and trembling? So is everyone who faces death."

Mori brightened when he heard Lev's story. "That means you were brought to life again, too, Mr. Lev?"

"Yes, just as you were, Mori. When I awakened I thought I was in some enemy hospital. I couldn't believe my body was whole without any wounds or pain. I dressed quietly wondering if I should crawl out the window or bolt out the front door."

"That's just what I did, Mr. Lev! I found myself screaming just as I had done when I saw I was going to hit the vessel. I awakened screaming, but stopped quickly hoping no one heard me. I was terribly confused, but feeling wonderful physically. I could not imagine how I could still be alive. I could only guess that my torpedo had somehow failed to explode and I had been rescued."

"That torpedo exploded, all right, Son. You were blown into a million pieces, just as that atomic explosion at Hiroshima vaporized your mother. At least you didn't suffer greatly, nor did your mother. Do you remember any pain at all, Mori?" Suno could hardly think about it without choking on tears.

"No, Father, I can't remember anything except seeing my torpedo speeding toward that vessel. That's the last thing I remember."

"I wasn't so fortunate. I was further away from the center of the atomic explosion and blown into our garden. I was burned from head to toe. Burnt flesh just hung on me. The pain was unbearable. Fortunately, I died within the week."

Finally, Mori asked the question that was plaguing his mind.

"Did Japan really surrender to the Americans? How were we treated? How terrible, to surrender! What has happened to Japanese honor?"

Mori remembered stories of cruelty that the Japanese had inflicted on the Chinese and Koreans who were taken prisoners.

"Maybe I was better off dead. At least they couldn't torture me."

Japan Was Treated Humanely

"Not so, my Son. The Americans were very generous with us. We were given food and they helped us rebuild our country from the ashes. They helped us become a great, industrial nation. We became much more prosperous after the war than we had ever been before. The United States provided money and technology to rebuild our shattered factories. They also purchased our products generously. They treated us much better than we had treated our prisoners."

When breakfast was finished Lev suggested that they show Mori his house and property. He seemed eager, especially when he learned it was his very own. Mori had never owned a home before—it was very special for him.

Lev led them on a grand tour of house and land. Mori had joined the military at an early age. He only knew the austerity of navy life. The old submarines were crowded and depressing, with little personal space. He thought his new home was magnificent with every necessity and comfort amply provided. Mori felt he was rich beyond his fondest dreams.

Mixed Emotions

Still Mori couldn't believe this was so lavishly provided for him out of love. His harsh military training had made him wary and apprehensive. He had learned hatred for Americans and Western culture. After the initial congeniality, his old nature began surfacing. He had mixed emotions. He was so excited to have such a grand estate. Yet he was suspicious that foreigners were here to deceive or use him.

"Thank you," he said after being shown the various features of his home. "I must tell you, Mr. Lev, this makes me very nervous. All of this must have a hidden price. Nobody is this generous without a motive. Is this supposed to buy my devotion to Christ and the Western World? I am a loyal Japanese sailor. I cannot betray my nation and leaders."

Of course, Lev had anticipated Mori's reaction. He listened intently, nodding. When the young man had finished his indignant insinuations, Lev said, "Mori, there is no Japanese nation, only historical tradition. There is no American or Western culture anymore, either. Christ is ruler over the world whether anyone likes it or not. I am a Jew, Mori. Christ was a name that I did not like either. Jews were accused of being Christ killers. Those who were supposed to be Christians persecuted us bitterly for centuries. Not that I didn't feel sorry for the way my people had treated Jesus. He may have been a good man from what I had read of his teachings. Certainly, he didn't deserve to be crucified. No one should have been crucified. That was very cruel punishment for even an evil person. Jesus was a good person. But I didn't like Jesus because of the way his followers had treated the Jews. Why should I accept Christ? I was a Jew, not a particularly good Jew, but a Jew nonetheless. I wanted no part of Christ."

From Ashes to Beauty   39

Mori agreed. "Yes, that's precisely my feeling, too. I want no part of Christ. I am a worshiper of the Shinto gods. I am loyal and will not betray my nation or people. I was in the imperial navy of the Land of the Rising Sun."

Suddenly a staggering thought struck him. Turning to his parents, Mori asked, "Why have you forsaken your heritage in Shinto religion? Why are you so accepting of Christ? Has Christianity bought you with its material wealth?"

Junko shook her head. "Mori, you must not speak to your Father and me in such a tone. We know you are under great emotional strain finding yourself in a different world. We all had the same feelings. You must understand one thing, Mori. Only the truth is spoken now and only the truth is allowed."

Mori was becoming increasingly disturbed.

"How do I know who is telling the truth? I still belong to the Japanese navy. It has to exist."

Seeing His Glorious Nation Surrender

Lev said, "Mori, come, let's sit down in your living room. We'll look at scenes from the war in which you fought. We will see how the war ended and how bombs destroyed Hiroshima and Nagasaki. We will show you scenes of the unconditional surrender of Japan."

As they sat before the huge screen, Lev selected the programs that covered these scenes. Mori saw the Japanese navy being destroyed, the bombing of Tokyo, and finally the two atomic bombs detonated at Hiroshima and Nagasaki. He couldn't believe his eyes. Mori realized that was where his Mother and Father died. He saw the Japanese surrender. He even spotted his old commander in the group signing an unconditional surrender, which greatly agitated him.

"How do I know this is true?"

"Son, I saw an airplane come in that morning to deliver that death bomb. It came from the coast, so I thought it was an enemy plane. The plane gleamed in the morning sunlight as I watched it drop the bomb. I thought it was far enough away, so without concern I turned toward my garden. Then I saw a flash of light and felt the wind and scorching heat. The whole landscape was laid bare. This is all true. Everything Mr. Lev tells you is true."

Junko continued, "Yes, Mori, everything you have heard and seen here is true. You cannot live in a past that no longer exists. Mr. Lev and Ms. Rebekah have helped make provisions to bring all three of us back to life. You may ask, 'What do they get for their labor?' I will tell you what—'Nothing.'"

Lev interrupted, "Really, we get joy out of helping others. We love people and we are especially glad to help those who suffered unjustly. The only thing I enjoy more than pure science is the joy of helping people."

Mori sensed a big difference in his own attitude. He was trained to hate and kill in the military. He would rejoice in the pain and injury inflicted on his enemies, but the idea of loving others was foreign to him. Yes, he loved and respected his parents, for this was an honorable tradition. Yet, he had always looked upon them as weaklings—good parents, but of little value to the rising Japanese empire.

Japan needed strong and courageous people who knew how to sacrifice—those willing to die for national honor. Mori still believed this, but that was all he knew. The things he heard today were quite disturbing. Japan and its national aspirations were being totally disregarded. From the news he had seen, Japan lost the war. Mori could believe that. But he believed Japan would rise from the ashes wiser, stronger, to greatness among the nations.

Once again Mori found himself between two emotions. His loyalty to Japan conflicted with his grudging admiration for Lev and Rebekah. He was drawn to their largess and warmth. They were open and genuine, not manipulative. Mori had never met anyone like them before. He also admired their superior knowledge. He was still living in a cramped submarine mentality. Lev and Rebekah were at home in a large world of human relationships and scientific accomplishments. Mori envied them, but felt secure only in his old world of hate and suspicion.

Mori Being Deprogrammed

Lev sensed Mori's withdrawal. He knew that part of his problem was misinformation from the old world. Mori's mindset had been drilled into him. He was a loyal cog in the wheel of a system where patriotism and duty had replaced individual responsibility and sharp thinking. He was more like a programmed robot than an independent thinker.

Mori was a victim of mass psychology—similar to the order of Hitler, who kept his soldiers constantly marching. What does a soldier think while marching? Nothing! That's why Hitler kept them marching. Lev knew Mori was clinging to his past too tightly to change. However, Lev could start at the other end and bring the knowledge and understanding more quickly to Mori.

After dining on the Eden fruit, Mori was more relaxed. It wasn't like eating his submarine rations that only kept him half alive. Mori knew his life was being enlarged in a very enjoyable way. He was living in the lap of luxury, dining better than the wealthiest of men.

Lev asked Mori to return with him to the television information center. He wanted to show Mori how to use this wonderful tool to learn what he needed to know in this new society. This interested Mori. He had a thirst for learning. He had done well in school, but his education was on hold waiting for the war to end.

An Age of Knowledge Opening

Lev showed Mori how to select any subject he wanted. By selecting the correct window, it was instantly available. This was thrilling to Mori. Like Lev, he loved electronics and was swept away with all the advances. Lev told him if he engaged in the courses provided by the Ancient Worthies in Israel, he could learn more in six months in his spare time than he would have learned in four years of college. That excited Mori.

Lev told him he needed to learn many things before he could be useful in society. He also reminded Mori that every day his new diet would increase his learning capacity.

As the days passed, Mori found himself being pulled into the world of knowledge from the moment the door opened to him. He saw knowledge as a new guiding star; and this attached him to Lev, who soon became his mentor in his newly found field of knowledge.

Mori knew that Lev was brilliant and had accumulated a broad base of knowledge. He had the ability to unravel the answers to the most complicated problems. This world of knowledge was better than the misguided and distorted ideals Mori had previously held. Unfortunately, Mori did not yet see the greater side of Lev, his capacity for selfless love. However, from the moment that Lev opened the door of learning and knowledge to Mori, he succeeded in changing the direction of his life.

That afternoon they spoke about undertaking the preparations to receive Suno's parents. They had died later than Junko's parents, so they would be next in order to return to life. This would require a lot of work by family and friends, but both Junko and Suno were eager to undertake the building and planting preparations. Mori would also interrupt his studies to help.

Lev announced that his next assignment would be in the research and development of anti-matter for new applications. Because his office would be near the former city of Hiroshima, Lev invited them to pay him a visit. Mori was all smiles at the invitation. He immediately wanted to know what Lev's research was about so he could prepare himself.

"Mori, this field is so new, there are only general bits of information on it available. You will need studies in physics, electronics and chemistry as a beginning. Maybe in a few years you will be ready to help us at the laboratory.

"Remember, Mori," Lev went on, "Man does not live by bread alone, but by every word that proceeds from the mouth of God. I study God's Word, the Bible, as well as scientific matters. Actually, studying God's Word inspired my thinking in the sciences. You see, in studying about God, you have to reach higher. That is what you have to do in science as well. By the way, there is a chapel meeting in your neighborhood. Rebekah and I will stop by in the morning. We will go to the chapel and then return to your house for breakfast together. What do you say to that?"

Worship at a New Altar

Junko and Suno agreed instantly. Mori, hesitating but wanting to please Lev, said, "All right."

Lev had plans for Mori's education. "Tomorrow, after breakfast, I'll line up some studies I would like you to take, Mori. You have to catch up on many years of science. You'll find it easy. You will surprise yourself on how quickly you can learn. Every day your mind will become brighter and sharper from eating Eden fruit. I've got a head start of many years, Mori, but in a few years you'll catch up. Don't try too hard to learn everything at once. Take the courses I assign to you.

"You will find for the first time what a difference a perfect teacher makes. Don't forget to read through the New Testament Gospels to learn from the greatest teacher of all. The man named Jesus Christ. As a Jew I was taught to avoid his teachings. What a mistake! The first night when I read the Gospels of Matthew, Mark, Luke and John, I found what I had been looking for all my life."

Mori was softened a little by his exchange with Lev. He tended to be a hero worshiper. Lev was a living model, not like the lifeless Shinto gods. However, Mori still felt a measure of loyalty to his past.

For the time, he was torn between two worlds. He knew he couldn't belong to both, but he would ride the fence until his mind cleared.

Mori had absolutely no interest in the chapel meetings, but he couldn't get out of going. Anyway, Lev had become his new friend. If Lev were there, it wouldn't be too bad. After all, Lev was a very intelligent man. He wouldn't be involved in a strange religion.

The next morning the Ishakawa family made their way toward a small chapel in the neighborhood. They were greeted at first in a strange language, but when they spoke in Japanese, people understood and spoke Japanese to them. Lev spoke to the pastor, asking him to speak in Japanese for their benefit.

The music started and it was majestic. Mori had never heard such beautiful music. Most of the music he had heard was from old radio sets that transmitted poor quality sound. He didn't join in the singing, but sat through it all somewhat pleased. Mori secretly enjoyed the music, but he didn't want anyone to know it.

The pastor started speaking after the opening prayer. As much as he tried to tune him out, Mori found him so informative that soon he forgot his resistance campaign and took in everything he said. This was the first time Mori heard someone speaking so intelligently and with such conviction on religious subjects. It was hard not to believe what he was saying, but Mori was determined to remain the loyal opposition. He had no way to refute the speaker, but he could be stubborn and resistant when all else failed.

After the service the pastor came to greet Mori and welcomed him back to life again. He knew of Mori's former life and death, and he expressed appreciation for Mori's high idealism that had led him to make such a supreme sacrifice. Then he said something that stayed in Mori's mind.

"Mori, we have better things to devote our life to now. We are all learning to build and to plant. There is nothing left to destroy but death itself. We are all involved in the great regeneration program underway. Your friend Lev has had a long head start in this field; he's been doing it for many years. You will find him your finest teacher, outside of the Ancient Worthies in Jerusalem. How fortunate you are to have him as your friend. Lev is a man sought after everywhere."

This made Mori very pleased, because he liked Lev, and more so now that he realized that people were clamoring for his services. He had thought that Lev and Rebekah were celebrities the moment he saw them. They were nothing like his military officers who were often rude and demanding. The military men always made you aware of their status and authority. Lev and Rebekah were interested in him and treated him like royalty. They were easy to like, except for their religious bent. Anyway, he knew his emotions were still playing tricks with him and, therefore, he was not stable enough to make any decision, good or bad. He was still having torpedo panic attacks. Every flashback caused him to shudder, though the memories became less frequent as the hours passed.

They walked back to Mori's house after the service, admiring the gardening designs in all the homes they passed. There was no evidence of poverty. All the homes and orchards were warm and inviting. There were no slums or shanties. The Japanese were gifted in horticulture and the splendid arrays reflected their breathtaking ingenuity. It was invigorating. In contrast, Mori was used to sharing cramped submarine quarters with a lot of nervous, edgy men.

The Old Shrines Disappeared

Suno was never very religious. Stepping out of his Shinto religion became increasingly easy. It had been a tradition of his family and ancestors. He could find no one who believed in the Shinto religion anymore. It had vanished. The old temples were gone. Nor was he interested in looking for them.

As they sat at the breakfast table, Suno wished to offer the blessing on the meal. This seemed strange to Mori. Even his mother was respectful, but not fervent about Shinto beliefs. However, if Christ did raise them from the dead, how could anyone not be grateful? Suno didn't feel his early resentment about praying and had joyful acceptance.

Lev announced that he and Rebekah would be leaving in the morning. They were engaged in specialized fields of research and development—Rebekah, in the field of horticulture, and Lev in the forefront of science. They'd both be working in the former Hiroshima area.

Lev mentioned that his brother Jake and a team of scientists from Israel had succeeded in harnessing anti-matter in minor applications. Hopefully, they would soon be building aircraft as small as automobiles to fly over local areas. These vehicles would be able to stop in the air and hover for indefinite periods. This type of craft was vital to stopping the endless building of roads that took up valuable space and produced nothing but needed maintenance.

"With modern electronic systems, these aircraft would avoid air collisions without control centers. The speeds will not be as the giant aircraft of today. They would stop automatically if contact with another craft were imminent. Safety was the main concern. Most of the problems had been resolved, but the solutions needed fine-tuning. We'll have a plant here for making these craft. Soon they'll replace automobiles. We have to cut down on roads. They're not friendly to the environment."

Mori listened in utter amazement. While he knew nothing of the sciences that could make such things possible, he always wanted to fly but had not been accepted by the air force. Now he could see flying with a personal aircraft parked in one's driveway.

Mori said, "Mankind has always envied the birds that need no pathways and could fly easily wherever they willed. They can look down on the earth and see it as God sees it from above."

He paused immediately after saying, "as God sees it from above." He knew that he had caught this thinking from the Christian religion. Everyone noticed his observation with considerable delight.

Lev teased, "Mori, I must warn you to be careful. You may unwittingly become a Christian."

Mori smiled with a sheepish grin. "Well, I guess I'm half converted to Christ. What else is there to believe? I know it's not a Shinto deity who raised me to life."

Lev then said, "It didn't take me long to accept Christ's power."

Suno added, "Nor me. To tell you the truth, I never had much faith in Shinto teachings. It was more of a tradition than serious belief. It was an honorable tradition that I kept out of respect for our ancestors."

Junko agreed, "Yes, that expresses my sentiments exactly. Shinto religion never taught the resurrection of the dead. The only religion to do that was Christianity. All of us are a living testimony to Christ's power. We can't stick our heads in the sand like a foolish bird. The one who raised us to life deserves our worship and veneration."

An Invitation

Rebekah added, "We do hope to see each of you as soon as you get oriented to your new life. I'll be at the horticulture center in Hiroshima. Lev will be in the new research and production center. These are both off the main road into the city, very close to each other. You may tour both facilities in one day. Because the two facilities are so close together, we could even have lunch together. You will see firsthand both technical advances and horticulture in its most advanced form."

"We'll look forward to your visit," Lev added. "Maybe all of you will be donating some of your time to working at these facilities. I must admit, Rebekah's work is more important than mine. Our abundant life has been made possible by a whole new way of living off small plots of ground. Each person may dwell under his or her own vine and fig tree, as it were. No one will ever be hungry again."

Mori could not understand why Lev would dismiss his work so lightly. To him, Lev's work was awesome. Just the thought of small aircraft that could fly and hover was a dream come true. However, Mori also realized how abundantly the earth now provided food with seemingly little effort. He could remember the war years when rations were a handful of rice a day. He knew what it was to be hungry. The world of yesterday and today contrasted like night and day.

Lev made one more comment before leaving. "Mori, did you know that the commander of your submarine is coming back in about three months? You may wish to help in bringing him back. You will meet soon. Don't forget to be kind to him."

Mori growled, "I ought to wring his neck."

"Careful," Lev said. "If you try to use any form of violence, you will be paralyzed on the spot. We're living in a nonviolent world now. Remember that I tried to flatten an old adversary of mine. My arm was immediately paralyzed until I confessed what I had done to an Ancient Worthy. I was healed quickly because my adversary had incited the violent behavior. By the way, Mori, we are now the best of friends and I hear from him from time to time."

*"Let my mouth be filled with thy praise
And with thy honor all the day"
(Psalm 71:8).*

Chapter Four

Lev arrived at the research and production lab in Hiroshima relaxed and refreshed. He had enjoyed helping the Ishakawa family; watching people return to life never lost its magic. Although each rebirth was thrilling, almost incomprehensible, people coming back with their old habits and vices brought immense challenges. Housing, feeding and clothing them were systematically accomplished, but dealing with human weaknesses and animosities utilized every talent he possessed. He loved it!

The staff in Hiroshima eagerly awaited Lev, showing him great respect. His name had become a legend and they were honored by his visit. It was different from the earlier days when few were bright and knowledgeable. The regeneration had been ongoing for many years now. Large numbers of people were nearing perfection. Lev's staff was particularly responsive and armed with information. The old competitive system had dissolved. Everyone was dedicated to success.

The Japanese people had always been oriented toward quality, so the most intricate designs posed no threats. Lev found this refreshing from earlier experiences when change was repulsed. Yet, some old scars lodged in human hearts still needed healing. While some had made positive strides forward through life's experiences, others hadn't changed their old habits and evil tendencies.

Lev called a meeting of his staff so he could get acquainted with them. Finding no prejudices or rivalries was a very good start. While they seemed extremely intelligent and knowledgeable, he knew the processes he was introducing were even further advanced. Since they would be almost totally dependent on him, he would have no rivalry in the early stages. Pride stalking the hearts of men could cause trouble down the road. The spirit that drove men to seek power and distinction had not died in the grave, but returned with those coming back to life.

Mr. Kumada was Lev's immediate assistant. He was a very knowledgeable man and soft spoken. He had lived through the anarchy that erupted in Japan after the Lord destroyed the armies that had been sent to take the Holy Land from the Jews. When the forces that went against Israel were annihilated, the people rioted against their leaders and institutions. The leaders had perpetuated the lie that Israel was to blame for all the trouble in the Middle East, but fortunately the anarchy was short lived, though severe. When the nations soon learned that God and Christ had taken charge of human affairs, false religion suffered the most. For countless centuries there had been no way of knowing who was telling the truth. Suddenly, under Christ's rule there was no place for falsehood to hide. Truth was made apparent to all.

Miniaturizing from Large Aircraft to Small

Lev began to explain that research and development would be minimal because most of the anti-matter techniques had already been developed in Israel.

"That is a science we understand and can control. Our task here is to miniaturize it from its present application in larger aircraft to small utility aircraft that will operate as the old helicopters did, but without a rotating blade. We will use the power of anti-matter to create aircraft that can land on a dime, stop in midair and fly without any possibility of crashing. We have the necessary technology to do this—all we have to do is get it done." Everyone clapped enthusiastically.

Lev continued, "We will need machinists to make various components and assembly stations. We'll engage various levels of skills. Those nearer to perfection will deal with the concepts and supervise. Those with less knowledge will work in operations. Those most recently returned to life will serve in production until their level of knowledge base expands enough for greater responsibility. This is temporary work. In time, the Ancients will call many of you to greater challenges.

"Knowledge will not stop here. As mankind nears perfection, products will improve. Perfection won't stop greater accomplishments. As the human mind expands, so will knowledge. Once all have returned to life and are amply provided for, we can take time to enjoy life. Until then, we must be diligent and resourceful. We owe our ancestors every blessing we can bestow upon them. We must not relax until the great work of regeneration is completed."

Again, their enthusiasm broke into spontaneous applause. They understood their responsibility and took it seriously, and the opportunity to bless their ancestors particularly resounded in their Japanese hearts. Lev concluded saying that he would meet privately with each one to review what talents they brought to this operation, reminding them that they were a team.

"Every suggestion will be considered. No grievance or complaint will be deemed unimportant. We're all volunteers. Our only reward will be in getting the job done correctly and on schedule. All the praise belongs to Christ."

"And There Was a Great Earthquake"—Revelation 16:18

The morning session went smoothly. Lev could sense the commitment of his staff. He asked Mr. Kumada to join him for lunch. His former wife Anna also joined them. She had a Christian name because her Christian parents had lived in Japan.

Anna was a charming lady. She assisted her former husband and was his backup in his absence. Mr. Kumada had lived through the anarchy, but Anna died in the violence that ensued. Her regeneration followed eight years later. It was always enlightening to speak to someone who had died and come to life again.

It was because her father was a Christian minister that Anna had died. When the armies, encouraged by the churches, were destroyed in Israel, the people angrily turned upon them and those who had promoted the ill-fated invasion.

"Anna," Lev wanted to know, "tell me about the circumstances of your death."

"I happened to visit my parents the day an angry crowd stormed the church." Anna was calm, but her soft hazel eyes reflected remembered sorrow. "My father and mother lived in the rear of the building. I had just arrived. I hadn't heard the news reports and was unaware of the destruction of armies in Israel. Even after I heard about it from the angry mob, I was sure there must be some mistake. My parents had seen scenes of the destruction on television, so they knew it was the truth. When I tried to dismiss any fault on the part of my family, it only made the mob angrier. I had inadvertently made my parents' situation worse."

Anna continued, "Without any warning, one of the men ran up to my father and struck him with a pipe. I tried to help my father who had fallen with a broken skull. Everything turned black. Someone had struck me. Apparently, I died without regaining consciousness.

"When I awakened to life again, it was quiet and peaceful. I feared the angry crowds would attack as soon as I stirred, but all I heard were the happy birds singing. I wanted to tend to my father. You know the story from there. It took awhile to realize I had awakened from the dead and was living in a very different world."

Anna's Return to Life

Mr. Kumada then added, "It was such a joy to have Anna back! I could scarcely believe it! It was a dream! Perhaps her death had spared Anna all the ugliness that I saw in that terrible rage of mankind. It was bad enough that we had lost our precious dead in Israel, but the churches and temple shrines were desecrated and destroyed by angry mobs. Looting and lawlessness were rampant. I survived by keeping out of sight and changing my hiding places. Finding food was the hardest thing. When our infrastructure and industry were under siege, the organized movement of food stopped. Food was stolen. Law and order disappeared for weeks.

"Luckily, I found food in places the looters had overlooked. Law and order became gradually restored. We started building from the ruins. But it wasn't until we asked for help from the Ancients that things started to turn around. An unseen spiritual force ended all violence and oppression and soon things improved noticeably."

Anna said, "I was mercifully hidden from all of this. I hate violence—I always did. I'm glad I died rather than to have contributed to it."

Armageddon Recalled

Lev took all this in with great interest. "Well, Anna," he said, "You were nobler than I. My machine gun was firing at full capacity when I was hit and died. I was among those Jews defending Jerusalem on the first day of the invasion. The invaders were so successful that they thought the next day would be a mopping up operation. That next day the Lord fought for Israel causing the biggest massacre of all time. I wasn't there to witness the Lord's victory, but when I returned to life again, it sure made me happy."

"Ah, yes," Mr. Kumada said, "That day the world changed forever. It was a day of truth. The misinformation and lies we had been fed fell to the ground. We began to realize we had been fighting against God. What a very foolish thing to do!"

Lev told them that he would begin instructing them on the new technology, and how it would be miniaturized so that it could be used to build safe small aircraft. The major nations would be starting this project at the same time. This was the next phase of transportation to bring earth's inhabitants closer to one another.

Instructing the Brightest

Lev began his afternoon lecture by showing how the use of anti-matter had been harnessed in building the large aircraft. Not only had it reduced traveling time, but they were able to continue to travel for months before needing refueling or servicing. This brought a level of safety never before enjoyed.

Now these advances would be brought to smaller aircraft for personal air flight. He demonstrated how many thousands of square miles of land were needlessly covered with concrete roads, parking lots, and related structures, which would become decreasingly important.

When Lev explained the technical data on anti-matter and the capability of using it safely on small aircraft, his nearly perfected audience was awed.

Lev began to relax, thinking that everything was going to flow without any hitches. He would soon learn that gifted minds are not always dedicated to helping and prospering the task at hand.

Dealing with Animosity

Aida, one of the staff at the Hiroshima facility, began questioning Lev's assertions. She was so brilliant that at first Lev thought she might have a valid point. However, after checking his presentation, he found it was absolutely correct. Lev tried to explain this to Aida, but nothing he said deterred her from discrediting his conclusions.

Lev finally declared, "Aida, whatever may be your doubts and misgivings, you must trust me. I know my facts and figures are correct. We're not just talking about theoretical hypotheses. We have built both large and small aircraft successfully using these schematics. If you have personal doubts, I can understand that. However, if you are challenging the validity of what we are presenting, whatever may be your reason, you are incorrect. I welcome valid criticism, but not derogatory cynicism."

Aida's anger boiled. Lev knew this confrontation wasn't beneficial. Yet when presenting proven formulas, he couldn't afford Aida's constant antagonism negating his statements. Aida's belligerence could disrupt the whole operation. Finally, Lev said, "Aida, may I please see you in my office after this discussion? Perhaps we can come to a meeting of the minds."

At the end of the session, however, Aida stormed out without even looking at Lev. He knew it was best to calm the situation as quickly as possible, but when she left in anger it was clear she would only become more antagonistic if she allowed her anger to fester.

Lev was frustrated, and the whole afternoon felt tainted with an unwholesome atmosphere in what had started out as a very positive day. Many approached him to express appreciation for his informative session. Some even apologized for Aida's attitude.

"Honor is not as important as being correct." Lev said, "When something is correct and it is assailed without a clear explanation, we have a serious problem."

Someone said, "Maybe Aida will be more reasonable tomorrow. Perhaps she will realize how badly she behaved today and will do better tomorrow."

Lev countered, "Usually anger does not get better with time. I don't know what I said that upset her, but I will try to find out. We can't have angry people working here. It isn't good for Aida, and it will affect everyone's ability to function efficiently. This matter must be resolved very soon."

Lev called Rebekah that evening to ask how her first day had gone. She gave a glowing report. "It couldn't have gone better, Lev. Everyone has been great! They're all gifted in horticulture. What a joy to work with so many dedicated people!"

"How did your day go, Lev?"

Lev sighed. "In the morning it was fantastic. The people have been on an Eden fruit diet nearly as long as we have. You can tell they're very near mental perfection.

"But the afternoon was a disaster! When I started presenting the concepts of harnessing anti-matter for small aircraft, one lady was absolutely certain that I was mistaken. She was determined to battle with me. I've been wrong before, but I know I wasn't here. I finally had to ask her to meet with me after the session, but she stormed out of the room. How should I deal with that, Rebekah?"

"Patiently and lovingly, Lev, as you always do."

The next morning Lev decided to go to Aida's office and get to the bottom of the problem. She was there on time and was startled to see him enter her office.

"Shalom, Aida. I'm sorry to have had to affirm the correctness of my assertions yesterday. However, my task is to present proven facts. When you continued assailing my formulas, I was forced to either turn the class over to you or assume authority over it myself."

A Belated Admission

Aida stared at Lev grudgingly. "Mr. Aron, I have since concluded that you were correct. As much as I hate to admit it, I was wrong."

"Then we can shake and get on with our project, right?"

"No, you have humiliated me before everyone. I cannot forgive you for that."

"If you admit that my assertions were correct, how could I be guilty of humiliating you? That certainly wasn't my intention. I simply had to state the facts clearly for everyone to understand. I wasn't trying to embarrass you. It was critical for me to explain my facts in a logical way for everyone in order to be sure the work is understood." He made sure his tone of voice was gentle, with no hint of accusation. "Why would you take it as a personal assault?"

Aida was carrying some deep anger or frustration. Lev knew she hadn't known him long enough to build up such resentment toward him personally, so he realized he would need to look deeper to find why. Obviously, Aida wanted to make an impact by refuting his conclusions. Instead of distinguishing herself in the eyes of the staff, she had made herself look foolish. When she rehearsed the facts, Aida was bright enough to know they were correct. However, since she would not acknowledge her mistake publicly, she felt it appeared that Lev was being rude to her. She seemed determined to play the victim, holding, at the end of the session, others responsible for her poor judgment.

Lev knew there was some deeper resentment eating away at Aida. He finally said, "Why don't we have lunch together? Perhaps we can become better acquainted." He smiled tenderly. "If you get to know me, Aida, you'll find I'm no ugly ogre. How about it, lunch at noon?"

Aida was reticent, but Lev's appeal was so genuine she finally consented. "Well, if you insist. I don't know what good it will do. You'll probably try to convince me into believing that *I'm* the ugly ogre."

"Forget the ugly ogre bit. There's no reason why we shouldn't get along. I'm too new to have trampled on anyone's toes. I'm only going to be here a short while before I move on to another frontier. Since I became alive again, I've been on the move from one assignment to another. Why would I want to waste my time here hurting anyone? I have a job to do, and I need your help to get it done. You are very talented, Aida, and I want to use that to help get this job done correctly and on time. Lunch at noon, okay?"

"You have an appointment," Aida affirmed.

The rest of the morning's presentations went smoothly. The students needed few notes. They not only retained what they saw and heard, but they were able to understand it fully. Aida seemed attentive. Her deep-rooted resentment had been temporarily pacified. Lev noticed, though, that when Mr. Kumada spoke Aida became withdrawn and pensive.

At lunch Aida seemed more friendly and approachable. Lev asked some of the usual questions to see if he could uncover the cause of her unrest. Whenever Lev mentioned either Mr. Kumada or his former wife Anna, he noticed Aida would retreat from the conversation. He sensed that she had some deep-rooted resentment toward them.

However, a competitive and belligerent attitude could not be allowed to fester for Aida's own character development, as well as for the project. It needed to be addressed and diffused. Lev wasn't able to find why there should be nervousness on her part, but at least he knew the source. He could probe a little further, but it had to be done as delicately as possible. He asked Aida if she attended the chapel services.

No, to Public Worship

Aida was very direct on this point. "No, Lev, I do not. I am grateful to Christ for the abundant life I now enjoy. In my prayers I never cease to express my appreciation. I know our country went through some very difficult times, especially after our army and armies of the world perished trying to wrest Jerusalem away from its rightful owners.

"After that debacle we knew hunger and desperation. That's all gone and past forever. I have many of my family members living again, for which I am thankful. However, I do not need to go anywhere to express my thanks."

Lev challenged Aida. "I felt a little that way for a short while, too. Now I look forward to daily devotionals. We learn so many beautiful

Bible truths and it's wonderful to express our praise in hymns. Music makes our praise to God richer. Come and join us tomorrow. I'll walk to your place and we can go together."

"Please, Lev, you are very forceful, but I have my reasons for not wanting to go to the chapel. Thank you, anyway."

When lunch ended, Aida did say, "Thank you, Lev, for having lunch with me. You are a most kind person. I wish I could be like you. You don't have a mean streak in you."

"Are you saying that others do have mean streaks?" Lev teased.

"No, I won't actually say that," Aida replied, "but some of us are still carrying feelings that we can't drop easily. Thank you for the lunch time that we shared."

The afternoon meetings went well. Lev was thinking how scientific facts did not have emotions or virtue. If one worked with correct information, the results automatically followed. However, this was definitely not true of human relationships. But human relations were infinitely more rewarding. Love was the most rewarding part of life. When you reached out to love and it was returned, it was priceless. It was only when love was unfulfilled that hurt remained. Until all men reached perfect love, hearts were still vulnerable.

That evening Lev called Rebekah. He leaned on his dear friend for comfort and advice. Rebekah asked, "Well, how was your lunch with Aida today?"

"Well, Rebekah, she was much more pleasant. She actually conceded to having made a misjudgment yesterday. She's very gracious, but I couldn't get to the bottom of her problem. She admitted harboring some ill feeling but locked me out of her confidence. I invited her to our chapel meeting tomorrow and received a firm, 'No.' I wish you would have been there to talk to her."

"I know you, Lev. You won't let go until you help her find peace."

Locating the Problem Area

"Well, I think I know the source of her problem. Every time I mentioned Mr. Kumada or Anna, she froze. There must be something between them that brings unpleasant memories. I haven't figured it out, but I have my antenna raised. I don't want to pry into her personal life, but I would like to lance the festering wound. If she can't control her emotional hurt, she'll have to be reassigned. She's very bright and gifted, but in dealing with anti-matter there's no room for emotions."

"The Ancients assigned you not just for your technical expertise, Lev. There are a lot of people with that. It's your ability to work with people's problems that sets you apart. They must have known there would be people problems, otherwise you wouldn't have been assigned here. You'll get to the bottom of it. Remedying it will be the hard part. I'll pray for you, Lev."

"I know you're right, Rebekah. We've learned time and again, haven't we? Love changes things. Old hurts must be replaced with love. Good night, Rebekah. I love you, dear friend."

A Need to Have Forgiveness

Lev arose early. He was living in a new house that was ready for someone returning to life. Although he'd be there only a short while, he enjoyed the abundant orchard and garden. He picked some fruit and hurried off to the chapel a half-mile down the road. It had rained during the night, leaving everything showered and bright.

Lev met a man on the way who had died in World War II and returned to life several months ago. He had been a general in the Japanese army. He told Lev he had been very ruthless in the war with China and also against the United States. He confessed, "My heart now hurts remembering my past. If there were no protection from violence, I'm sure there are people who would gladly die for the privilege of killing me. They remember what I did and have every right to hate me. What can I do? That was the day of my pride. I was drunk with power. I didn't like the things that I did. They were terrible, and I would awaken during the nights tormented as I recalled the faces of those I murdered. The Japanese military praised me for my ruthlessness. I would be granted greater promotions for being so cruel. I allowed my love of power and prestige to make me into a monster. At times I hated myself."

Lev responded, "There is forgiveness with God. If he can forgive, then all those you tormented and killed may one day find it in their hearts to do likewise."

Believing in Forgiveness

"Sir, if I could only believe that. I hate what I did. I had children whom I loved dearly. If someone injured them I could not forgive them, yet I injured people who were the children of parents who loved them as I did my children. How could I have been so despicable? Why did the world praise me for my ruthlessness? Standing here in this perfect world, I feel so vile."

From Ashes to Beauty

Lev answered, "Seeing you have such godly sorrow is a good thing. I was there to receive Hitler back to life, and I could not find an ounce of godly sorrow in him. It was not that he was so mean by nature, but he didn't feel any responsibility for what he had done. He just wanted to close the doors on his past and go on without any remorse. Perhaps by now he has improved. I don't know whether he has or not. I only wish I had seen such godly sorrow in his heart, but I didn't see any."

Lev and his new friend arrived at the chapel before the singing started. He greeted a few of the friendly faces he had recently met. He saw Rebekah at a distance enjoying fellowship with a circle of people. As the singing was about to begin, he found a seat in the middle of the chapel. He looked about quickly hoping that Aida had changed her mind, but she wasn't there. The songs of praise ascended—it was a joy to worship a God of love, who could forgive iniquity, transgression and sin, and yet not clear the guilty. The chapel leader was a gifted speaker and well versed in the Scriptures. His subject was, "Love, Lost and Found." It was such an inspiration that Lev went up to him. "I just have to tell you how thoroughly I enjoyed your message."

"Thank you," he said. "The praise belongs to Him."

Returning to work that morning, Lev couldn't help wondering if perhaps Aida had been hurt in love somehow. Those wounds were the hardest to heal.

Everything went well that morning. People were grasping the concepts and were preparing to make the machinery that would be needed. Some of the basic machines were already available, but others would require precision with next to zero tolerance. Assemblies were being set in motion.

Lev needed to talk to Anna about a matter in her department and went to her office immediately after lunch. She was a very pleasant lady whose experiences had matured her character. Lev's business only took about five minutes. As he was about to leave she inquired, "Were you able to help Aida the other day?"

A Broken Heart Found

Lev responded, "Oh, we had a pleasant lunch together. But she seems to be carrying some old wounds. I found out that it wasn't me who was responsible for her present irritability. I haven't known her long enough to have offended her. But I still don't know what experiences contributed to her burden."

With a sad expression Anna twisted her long hair as she quietly replied, "I may be the culprit."

"What makes you say that, Anna?"

"Well, Mr. Kumada and Aida were once engaged to be married. A week before their wedding, they had a serious argument – over what I still don't know. The wedding was canceled. Perhaps they might have reconciled in time; but, in the meantime, Mr. Kumada and I met by chance in a rainstorm. I was waiting for a bus and my umbrella had collapsed. He drove by in his car and saw me getting soaked. He offered to take me home. At first I refused. He said to me, 'I am an honorable man. I just don't like to see a lovely lady like you getting drenched. Trust me, I shall drive you home. You will be perfectly safe with me.'"

She explained that after hesitating a moment, she accepted his kind offer because the rain became more intense and her bus was nowhere in sight. There seemed to be almost magic between them from the first moment. She thought he was extremely handsome with a very gentle manner.

"Mr. Kumada must have found something he liked about me because he paid extravagant attention to me, even though I was uncomfortably wet and self-conscious. I lived only a couple of miles from my office, but this gave him time to find out more about me. He asked my name and about my family. He even asked me about my work. He was a perfect gentleman and solicitous for my well-being. As he arrived at my residence he said, 'I had no intention of asking for your phone number when I stopped to help you, but after spending this brief time with you, may I have your phone number? Would you accept a dinner invitation? You do not have to answer now; but, if you give me your phone number, I will call you. I would like to know you better.'

"I was happy to provide my number because I was overwhelmed with his charm. I wrote my number on a piece of paper, hoping that he would call me. This dark rainy day turned into one of the brightest days of my life. As I left the automobile, I thanked him for his kindness. I then said, 'I have never gotten into a stranger's car before, but I am glad I did. I enjoyed the ride home. Thank you, again.'"

Lev then said, "I guess he did call you, and you did get together again."

"That must be obvious to you now," she said demurely. "He called that very same evening. As you can imagine, one thing led to another and within a year we were married. Now perhaps you can see why Aida may feel some antagonism toward me and Mr. Kumada."

"Yes, now I begin to understand. A certain feeling of rivalry and hurt is still there."

Love That Was Lost

"Even after my death," Anna continued, "Mr. Kumada never showed any interest in renewing his relationship with Aida. She had tried on several occasions to rekindle the old flame, but it wasn't there on his part. Aida never married. I am sure she had many opportunities because she was a bright and beautiful woman. Sometimes it happens that people are unlucky in love. That had to be a heartbreaking experience."

"This explains things. Aida is one among millions who suffered like that. No matter how successful one might have been in business or science, it would not heal a heart broken in love. How do you fix that, Anna?"

"I am afraid I'm not the one ideally suited for the job in this case, Lev. Aida stiffens whenever I'm around. I think you are better qualified than I am. You are nearer to perfection than most people. If you can't do it, who can?"

"That's what Jesus and his disciples were commissioned to do. 'He hath sent me to bind up the brokenhearted' (Isaiah 61:1). Perhaps we have to work harder at it. We can't restore the lost love that caused the breaking, but we can lift a heart up to a higher plane. When we view things from God's viewpoint we can love as He loves, with an *Agape* love, the kind of love that God and Christ have for the world. *Agape* love is an unselfish love that is not fulfilled by receiving love in return. *Agape* love will 'never fail.' We have to help Aida know that she is loved!"

Healing a Broken Heart Takes Time

Anna agreed, "I suppose I am to blame for always staying clear of Aida, knowing that I had taken the man she had really loved. If there was some way to make everything right, I'd be glad to do it. But I always feel so uncomfortable around her. I don't want to make matters even worse."

"Yes, but love is always kind. That is the secret of touching wounded hearts," Lev asserted. "We must show kindness in all our actions. In our former lives we could live with hearts of stone, but not anymore. Love is the principle thing. Love for God and Christ, love for God's truth and love for our fellow man. Without such love we will never have our names written in the 'Lamb's book of life.'"

Lev continued, "We are not here to eat, breathe, and take up space. The great work has always been within us. We must be as our Father in heaven 'who maketh his sun to rise on the evil and on the good, and sendeth rain on the just and on the unjust' (Matt. 5:45)."

"Well," Anna sighed. "That was a better sermon than I have heard before, but I certainly welcome those wholesome words. It gives me a perspective of what our new life is all about. I'm afraid I was guilty of just being here, functioning on a very low level—of only being tolerant and forbearing. I'll have to put in a better performance than that if I want to get my name in the Lamb's Book of Life. This has been quite an inspiration, Lev. Maybe I can do more just to simply put Aida at ease – extend more of a hand of friendship, or something. I can see that you have learned weightier matters than science and human relations."

"Anna," he said, "I must tell you that I have met with some of the noblest people on earth, our beloved leaders, the Ancient Worthies. They all lived and died in faithful devotion to God. If you want to get some real inspiration, be sure to meet with the delegation of them when they come here next month. Now that most of their critical work is done, and things are following in a more automatic fashion, they are free to travel the earth as ambassadors of goodwill. These men and women are completely perfect, the most beautiful people you have ever seen, but even more beautiful on the inside than on the outside. Every time I have met with them, it has been inspiring. Anyone who is absolutely sincere and honest will be greatly blessed in meeting them. However, those who are not sincere and honest will meet with their stern rebuke. No one can deceive them. The Christ makes known to them everything that human perfection is not capable of knowing, so nothing is hidden from them. People who have tried to fool them or who are less than forthright with them soon get into trouble."

Anna replied excitedly, "I will make a note of that. Perhaps we can arrange for everyone in this operation to meet with them. Could we extend an invitation for them to meet with us here? They must surely be interested in the work being done here because they made everything possible. Would that be bold or presumptuous for us to invite them?"

Lev answered, "That's a great idea! Not only will this be a thrilling experience for everyone to meet some of them personally, but also it will have a stimulating effect on all of us. When you come before such great people, it makes us all look into our hearts a little deeper."

A Missing Signature

Lev had spent more time with Anna than he intended, but now he knew the basis of Aida's problem. As soon as he returned to his

From Ashes to Beauty

office, he dictated a letter to the Ancients regarding visiting Japan next month. He invited them to visit the Science Center if they could spare a day. He sent the letter around the whole facility requesting the personal signature of each to extend a warm invitation. He noticed he had every signature except Aida's on the letter. He went to her office to see if she had somehow been missed.

When Lev entered, she said, "I thought you'd be here. I didn't sign the letter because I'm not a gregarious person. I don't know why they'd want to meet me."

"Oh, come on now, Aida. Actually, there are six of them coming, three men and three women. They are all persons of extraordinary distinction. The three men are: Father Abraham, the Prophet Isaiah and King David. The three women are: Sarah, Abraham's former wife, Huldah the Prophetess, and the Prophetess Deborah. I was intending for you to be the one who will entertain Sarah overnight. How about it, Aida? This is your last chance to have the greatest experience of your new life!"

"Well," Aida hesitated. "Oh, okay, Lev. You are definitely the most persistent person I have ever met. I'll sign the invitation. If they accept, I'll entertain Sarah. You win again."

Lev was thrilled. "Thank you, Aida! Thank you! Thank you! You have a soft heart. You're a little hard-shelled on the outside. But inside you are a jewel! You won't regret this decision—I guarantee it! I've met these wonderful people dozens of times,—they never cease to thrill me! They are the greatest!"

For the first time Aida smiled and laughed. This was a rare event! Lev teased, "Be careful, Aida, you may find yourself happy again, and falling in love with love itself."

Aida felt a surge of warmth in her heart. It felt good. The smile and laughter on her part were surprisingly coming from within. She felt more lighthearted than she could remember for a long time. She felt Lev cared for her as an individual. There was nothing artificial in his approach. He was simple and sincere. And from his humility, one would never have guessed that he was a brilliant scientist.

Aida wondered what made Lev so effective. She knew he wasn't trying to take advantage of anyone. Lev was concerned with the well-being of others. No wonder his projects were so successful. He managed to turn even more hostile and aggressive opponents into friends. Aida regretted having been so cold with Lev. And she began to wonder what kind of woman Sarah would be. What was total perfection like? Would Sarah look with disdain upon someone as imperfect as she?

"Having obtained a good report through faith"
(Hebrews 11:39).

Chapter Five

The Ancients' visit to the Science Center was indefinite until a week before their arrival. Lev was excited to learn they would be spending one day and night at the facilities and be hosted in private homes.

When Lev announced the news to his staff, everyone clapped enthusiastically—except Aida. She still had reservations. She didn't know why Lev had assigned Sarah as her guest. If she had read her Bible, Aida would have known Sarah had suffered much anguish of heart and that Aida could learn much from Sarah if she were open to it.

Operations on manufacturing the new mini-aircraft had gone smoothly, and the staff was amply qualified to perform the entire process. Because it was intensely complicated, the staff became stymied at times and had to consult Lev. If he hadn't taken the time to completely absorb the information, he, too, might have been confused. Jake drilled Lev backwards and forwards covering every angle until it became crystal clear.

Lev realized that Jake was more technically astute than he, which was why the Ancients kept Jake based in Israel developing the most advanced scientific technology, while Lev was sent into the field as their expediter. Jake and Lev worked effortlessly as a team, seeming to be able to read each other's minds. Jake's division discovered the scientific breakthroughs. Lev took the new concepts from theory into production, adding his unique talents in relationships with personnel.

When the Ancients' arrival date came, excitement electrified the atmosphere. Lev arranged to pick them up at the airport with Mr. Kumada, Anna, and Aida. Lev knew it would be awkward for Aida. She stiffened at the thought, but since there was no gracious way out, she silently submitted.

Our Guests Arrive

The arrival time was six a.m. and while Mr. Kumada, Anna and Lev waited breathlessly for their guests to disembark, Aida sat like a stone. The three women exited first, Sarah, Huldah, and Deborah—then Abraham, Isaiah and David. Each greeted Lev with a hug because they knew him as a valuable friend. Lev, in turn, was overjoyed to introduce his distinguished guests to their hosts.

Lev watched Anna's and Aida's eyes widen, and they were almost speechless in awe. Fortunately, Sarah seized the moment while graciously putting them at ease. The word "Ancient" was misleading, Lev thought. These men and women were youthful in appearance, handsome beyond imagination, and very vivacious.

Sarah looked at Aida. "Shalom, Aida! I understand I am to be in your home tonight, is that right?"

Aida managed to find her tongue. "Yes, it will be my privilege if you accept, Ma'am. I have been looking forward to meeting you. Lev has tried to describe you to us, but I feel as though the half was never told. What makes you all so different?"

Abraham was tall and noble with a face that reflected the profound faith that formed the basis of his character. "There are only a few things that set us apart from others. We were promised a 'better resurrection' (Heb. 11:35), because we proved our faith in God under difficult circumstances in our previous life. God did not forget his promise to us. We were rewarded for our faith when we were raised to life with perfect minds and bodies. All the disciplines we had learned in our former life were tailor-made, preparing us for our present role. We have proved our devotion to God and righteousness, and we cannot be tempted away from our commitment to serve our King and Lord, Christ."

Then Mr. Kumada, Anna and Aida listened to the remarkable man, hardly breathing in out of their deep respect. "We are privileged to have communication with Christ and his body members daily. This is the most moving and provocative experience anyone could have. We have physical perfection, but Christ and his body members have divine wisdom and glory. Without them to guide us, we wouldn't be nearly as effective. We are not left to our own judgments, but we are directed to the best decisions by divine counsel. Nothing is left to chance. All the glory belongs to Christ." Abraham almost seemed to glow as he spoke.

Lev suggested they stop at the park for breakfast and then go to the chapel for morning devotions. The chaplain would turn the meeting over to the Ancients, after which there would be a question period followed by lunch. Aida was definitely not happy about going to the chapel, but she knew she had no choice this time. She tried to control her troubled emotions.

They found a convenient pavilion with a table. Lev asked David to thank the Lord, which he did. Huldah turned to Anna, "I heard how you and your father died. Do you have any bitterness in your heart from that experience?"

Still Retaining Vivid Memories

Huldah's sincerity removed any self-consciousness Anna might have been tempted to feel as she answered. "I can still hear the cries of the mob as they attacked my father. I understand their anger. My father was deceived by church leaders into thinking they could settle Israel's affairs as easily as the United States cut down the Taliban in Afghanistan in the early part of the 21st century. The religious and national leaders believed it was their responsibility to correct Israel's problems. My father supported the nations invading the Holy Land. I even remember him praying for their success. Oh, but he couldn't have been more misinformed. He listened to church leaders instead of reading the Bible. I pointed out scriptures to him indicating the destruction of the invading forces, but he dismissed my observations. He was convinced the ruling hierarchy knew better."

Isaiah, as dynamic as ever, entered the conversation. "We're sorry about his tragic death—but now he has his life again. With Christ reigning, there won't be any deceptions or misinformation."

"Yes, since my father's return to life," Anna continued, "he's been humbled to realize how misled he'd been. He can't believe he actually ignored God's Word to side with the mass deceptions blinding the nations. The church leaders always knew their claim to the kingdom of God was hollow without their control of Jerusalem. Everyone knew the word of the Lord was prophesied to come from Jerusalem. Remember how for centuries Christians had led crusading armies to rescue the Holy Land from infidels and had failed. Armageddon was their last attempt—and greatest failure. My father believes his death was a just punishment for sending thousands of young people to their death. He wishes he had been a better student of the Bible instead of parroting leaders who often contradicted it."

Russet-haired David asked gently, "How do you feel about your death, Anna? You died simply because you loved your father."

"I knew the crowd was outraged. I would've been, too. But because my father had been active in supporting this mission, I felt I should remain loyal to him. The Japanese are possessed by a sense of honor. I honored my father and mother. I can understand why the crowd took their anger out on me—I was a victim of circumstances.

"At least I can be glad I died without engaging in their violence. When I saw a man strike my father, I chose not to attack him—though I could have easily. I had a small, hard briefcase. I was tempted to hit him with it as he bent over my father. But it wouldn't have saved my father from the bloodthirsty mob. I could have saved myself by pretending to be a part of the mob—but I would not disown my father. He was a good man even though he was deceived."

David acknowledged, "You have an excellent attitude, Anna. You lost your life, but now you have it back. Unfortunately, many others are having problems meeting all the people they injured face to face. It's very painful to ask forgiveness from those they wronged."

Hearing David's Confession

David went on to share some of his own experiences from the life he had led in ancient Israel. This information had double impact upon those who had not grown up with knowledge of biblical history and had only come to learn it since their resurrection.

"I myself committed grievous sins against one of my soldiers, Uriah. He was in my honor guard and daily put his life on the line in defense of my throne. I didn't reward his loyalty to me. Instead, I coveted his wife, committed adultery with her, and then had Uriah killed in an attempt to cover my sins."

David shook his curly head at the memory. "I repented with deep sorrow, and God forgave me, but Uriah will learn the whole truth when he returns to life. He was a mighty man of valor and will undoubtedly have difficulty controlling his anger when he learns the truth. How painful it will be for both of us when we meet face to face! I passionately hate what I did to him. Even though God forgave me, I suffered severe punishments for my sins. I would have chosen death for myself rather than the tragedies that followed my life thereafter. Fortunately, we have a spiritual police force on duty all the time to keep violence out of human relations, but it was not so before."

Everyone listened to David's confession in deep silence. He spoke so openly about his past and made no effort to sidestep the issue in his favor. David was guilty of great transgressions, but equally determined to correct the wrongs he had committed. David had always been known for his physical beauty, and they found themselves staring at him as he spoke. But as handsome as he was, everyone could see how the punishments he endured for his sins had developed an even more crystalline and lovely character. David had learned his lessons in a most exemplary way.

The spell was broken—time was running out. They had to leave for the chapel. They arrived just before services began. After the prayer, the chaplain asked Lev to introduce the Ancients.

Lev approached the podium. "This will be a day never to be forgotten. I am thrilled to introduce you to six of the greatest heroes who have ever walked this earth, the Ancients! These men and women have been rewarded for their faithfulness to God with a better resurrection—as perfect leaders responsible for executing the great regeneration of the human race under the authority of Christ.

"Most of you have either been brought back to life like I was, or have had your loved ones returned to you from death. In this session, the past will meet the present. How did these Ancients perceive in their former lives the great regeneration we are now experiencing? How does this great work appear to them today? After we hear their testimonies, be prepared—you will have an opportunity to ask them questions. Now, we will begin with Abraham and Sarah."

Sarah

They walked to the podium together. Abraham signaled Sarah to begin. Sarah's regal beauty had once captured the hearts of kings. There was no question in any mind that she was the most exquisite woman they had ever laid eyes on, her long glistening hair framing a face renowned for its grace.

She began, "Thank you, Lev. Good afternoon! I want you all to know, Lev is one of our favorites. Can you guess why? No one has worked harder helping people in the regeneration. We thank Lev and the rest of you who are giving yourselves tirelessly to this monumental task. We were the first of the human race to return to life after Armageddon—can you imagine how that shocked the world? And who would have ever imagined the second surprise? We returned with a priceless treasure—seeds from the trees of life in Eden. Our first task was to plant these seeds for fruit-bearing trees. Now you are well acquainted with the life regenerating powers of Eden fruit. The

Eden trees are filling the face of the earth, supplying perfect nutrients to all those returning to life."

Seeing Rebekah, Sarah motioned, "Have you all met Rebekah Aron? She is working on your horticultural developments. Rebekah's parents are Benjamin and Deborah Obadiah, two great horticulturists in the forefront of research. The Obadiahs have overseen programs developing the Eden trees from seedlings and have succeeded in filling the earth with these precious trees. Untiring devotion of people like the Obadiahs makes the regeneration process successful.

"We never tire from receiving our beloved dead back to life, do we? Did you know I would have had to wait longer than most of you? How long ago do you think my family lived? A thousand years? No— my family lived in Ur of Mesopotamia some four thousand years ago. What did the people of Ur believe? They were worshipers of the moon god, Nannar. When Abraham was called by God to leave the heathen city of Ur, I was honored to leave with him as his wife. Abraham and I both hated the temple worship, which demanded human sacrifices for Nannar. When my family is scheduled to return, I will leave the offices at Jerusalem to build their homes and plant their orchards, as many of you are doing for your families today. As your families are disturbed at first to learn the Shinto religion no longer exists, my family will be shocked to learn Nannar the moon god who demanded human sacrifices and orgies through the temple priests of Ur was really a pagan religion of Satan. One day, by the grace of Christ, all shall return to life—those who worshiped in pagan temples and those who lost their lives as human pagan sacrifices. And one day we will all be there when at last our first parents, Adam and Eve, return. What a triumph of God's grace and power that will be!"

Sarah turned to Abraham, who stood tall at her side. "And now, may I introduce you to my best friend and life-long companion, Abraham."

Abraham

Abraham's majestic appearance commanded respect the moment they saw him. His eyes reflected a man of wisdom and experience beyond any they had ever seen. Abraham was the first of the three Patriarchs who received God's immutable covenant.

"Shalom, my dear children! I am your father Abraham. How can I be your father, you may ask?

"God promised me two families of children for my faithfulness—a spiritual seed as the stars of heaven, which referred to my children of faith, Christ Jesus and his church. God also promised an earthly seed, as the sand of the sea.

"When God called me from Ur to go to a land that He would show me, God promised me He would make of me a great nation. I believed God then, and Sarah and I took our journey of some eight hundred miles to the land of Canaan. And I believe God now, as the multitudes of my children return to life.

"God promised the land of Israel to me and my seed after me. But how do you think this could be? I died without owning even one square foot of land! I even had to buy land to bury my beloved wife Sarah in the Cave of Machpelah.

"God promised me 'in thee shall all the families of the earth be blessed' (Gen. 12:3). How could that be? '*All* the families' — when so many had already died? How could I bless them? What would you think if you had been me? Little did I know back then that one day, through one of my heirs, would be born the promised seed — Christ, the Messiah. But I didn't know anything about that. I was ninety years old with no children. Finally, Ishmael was born. Was he the promised seed and heir? No, he was the son of a bondwoman. Both Ishmael and his mother Hagar will be resurrected some years from now. We will rejoice to see them again. Then Isaac was born, son of my wife Sarah. We thought he was the seed God had promised. But no. Who was the real heir of God's promises to me? Whom do you say?

"Yes, Christ — one of my grandsons. I waited all my life without realizing the full promise of God. Yet, I still believed God. How glad I am that I did. Now I have received all the land God promised me for an everlasting inheritance. I have returned to life to see the most dramatic of God's promises to bless all the families of the earth, only possible through the resurrection of the dead!"

No one in the audience even moved as they paid rapt attention to the Patriarch.

"I lived all my life in a tent. What does a man dream about while living in a tent? I dreamed of a city! A city whose builder and maker is God — a city with foundations. And God has built such a city for me! I see God's promises unfolding on such a grander scale than I could ever have anticipated. I knew God had something magnificent in mind. But God tested my faith by making promises I could never have imagined would be fulfilled in such an overwhelming way.

"When Christ delivers the Kingdom to God at the end of the Millennium, earth will be paradise restored and mankind will enter into full harmony with God in the joys of his glorious eternal Kingdom re-established on earth.

"What shall I say, my beloved children? Have faith in God. I never dreamed when I left Ur of the Chaldees what a glorious future would be mine. Each one of you was in my future—and I did not know it. I am so glad that I had faith in God."

A thunderous applause followed. Lev looked at Aida—she, too, was clapping. She had lost herself under the spell of Abraham's story. It was her first conception of how the past and present were intricately intertwined.

Huldah, the Prophetess

Lev then presented Huldah, the prophetess. "With great pleasure, I introduce to you Huldah, the prophetess, one of the very few women of the Bible to earn that title. God directed Huldah to speak to good King Josiah (2 Kings 22:13-20). When the nation of Israel had strayed from the Lord, under Huldah's encouragement, King Josiah returned to the Lord with his whole heart. Huldah lived in a monumental period of history. Now she lives again in a still greater moment. Huldah was eminent in the past and is still more prominent in the present. Please give her your undivided attention."

After another round of enthusiastic applause, Huldah stood. She, too, had the indescribable beauty of perfection. Almond-shaped eyes shaded by gracefully arched brows looked out over the gathering. While she looked poised and elegant, her greatest attraction was not apparent to the eye—only the mind could begin to perceive it.

"Shalom! Thank you, Lev, and all of you for this privilege of sharing with you. How many prophets were men? Yes—that's correct—only three major and twelve minor prophets are recorded in Holy Writ, with some individuals who prophesied without a book in their name. Now—how many prophets were women? Not many, but two of us are here. So you see, by God's grace, I was used in a moment of Judah's history and had the privilege of seeing reforms made by good King Josiah. Josiah was a young king and God used me to teach him righteousness from the law. From those small beginnings of faith, I have lived to see the majesty of Christ's glorious Kingdom here on earth. I dreamed that someday God would intervene and start the world back in the right direction.

"The righteousness and justice of God's laws and precepts have been so important to me. However, my fondest dreams could not compare with the wonderful rule of righteousness now taking place under Christ. You are witnessing the power of Christ on a scale I never dreamed. Never did I envision how such a staggering process of bringing everyone back to life could take place. Never did I think how 'righteousness would cover the earth as the waters cover the sea.' It is being fulfilled before your very eyes, and lost loved ones are now coming back into your arms. It only gets better every day. I am waiting, like Sarah, for my beloved dead to return. I trust you will all join in ceaseless and untiring effort to hasten that day. Thank you."

Isaiah

Huldah, too, received heartfelt applause. Isaiah, the legendary prophet of the Bible, was next. Lev said, "It gives me joy to present one of the grandest writers of the Old Testament—the most quoted author in the New Testament. He is one of the most illustrious writers, one that spoke of our day in prophecy. He was rewarded for his beautiful writings and faithfulness by being 'sawn asunder' by enemies of God's Word. He died a martyr, but now lives a prince of men among us. I introduce you to Isaiah."

Isaiah stood in overpowering grandeur. He was a man mighty in word, and mightier in his devotion to Christ. One could easily imagine his dynamic delivery of pronouncements to men of old. He was vigorous and handsome and commanded the people's unwavering attention.

"Shalom! I saw our day in prophecy—a day of blessings such as earth has never known. I saw a world without war, without pain (except for the last vestiges of pain caused by sin in the human heart). The words I was told to prophecy have found fulfillment as I witness this wondrous power. Surely, 'sorrow and sighing' are fleeing away.

"I longed for the day when the 'blind' would see, the 'deaf' would hear, the 'lame man would leap as an hart' and 'the tongue' of the mute would 'sing.' That day has dawned—and it is more beautiful than I ever imagined. Think of the long years when sin and death relentlessly pursued men to their graves. There was no way of escape for anyone.

"Only the burning hope that God lit in our hearts kept our feet firm on the pathway to Christ's Kingdom. That day of Christ has now dawned and nations are coming to his light and kings to the brightness of his rising—the day when all nations will flow to the mountain of the Lord's house in Jerusalem. We saw this day dimly, but we embraced it. That day promised something greater than our personal life.

"Here I am, today, standing in the land I had seen afar off. The reality of the blessings Christ is pouring out upon the nations will only swell in sweetness and grandeur." Isaiah's grand gesture embraced the crowd. "The day has come when we can all say, 'Lo, this is our God; we have waited for Him, and He will save us: this is the Lord; we have waited for Him, we will be glad and rejoice in His salvation'" (Isaiah 25:9).

There was a quiet pause when Isaiah finished. The audience tried to grasp the full meaning of his message. Soon he received a standing ovation. This vision that Isaiah proclaimed was embraced by all those heroes of faith. Neither life nor death could cause their faith to waiver. They stood as servants of the Living God, a strong testimony of the triumph of faith.

Deborah

Lev arose to present Deborah. "Especially inspiring for the women among us, I present a courageous and faithful judge and prophetess of Israel—Ms. Deborah. In a dark hour of Israel's oppression, because of the delinquency of men in neglecting the Divine Law, God used a woman as His channel to judge and admonish His chosen people. In her new life, Deborah continues to be a counselor of wisdom, dedicated to fulfilling the righteousness of Christ. I present to you, Deborah."

Deborah arose almost instantly to address the packed chapel.

"Thank you, Lev. He's truly beloved by all of us!" Her dark eyes sparkled vivaciously with enthusiasm. "Shalom! I am so happy to be in your midst! I'd like to talk to you about something very personal today. Each of you has it, man or woman, young or old! I'm referring to individual responsibility!

"I'll tell you a little story. I was a wife and mother in Israel, living in the northern highlands of Ephraim during a time when the people had become very idolatrous. The Lord punished them under Jabin, a powerful Canaanite king that oppressed them for twenty years. Our leaders had no courage to fight Jabin—he had nine hundred iron chariots and fierce warriors.

"Our people were so depressed and discouraged. I knew they were being punished for neglecting God's laws. I sent letters to the leaders of the tribes to encourage them to turn back to the Lord. My home was under palm trees and I invited everyone to come and study the laws of the Lord. In this way, I tried to uphold the standard of the Lord among the people. The Lord blessed these efforts. Many of the leaders and people came to visit me to discuss the ways of the Lord. We prayed to the Lord for deliverance. I had faith; the Lord had delivered us in the past and He could do it again, if we repented.

"And what do you think the Lord answered? He told us to go and fight Jabin and He would give us the victory! So heed the lesson, the Lord can use each of you to accomplish a service for Him if you have a willing heart and trust Him.

"I relayed God's message of victory to Barak, a mighty Israeli general. What do you think Barak's reply was?" Deborah paused a moment for effect. "Barak said he would go only if I went with him. Now, that put me on the spot! What could I say? Well, I didn't hesitate a moment. I said, immediately, 'Let's go and fight Jabin!' When the Lord tells you to do something, do not procrastinate.

"However, I had to tell Barak that because of his lack of faith, the honor of victory over the enemy would belong to a woman. And it was, in fact. And that woman was not me. She was Jael, a Kenite, who took the life of the opposing General Sisera.

"Do you know what happened? Those nine hundred chariots met us at the River Kishon. I told Barak that God would deliver each one into his hand if he went forward. Barak did pursue the chariots—and not one of the enemies was left alive.

"The lesson is—we're each responsible for our righteous living! Today, the war is against the sin within. Just when one generation learns the lessons of righteous living, another generation returns with the old propensities for evil, and the cleansing process must begin again."

It was easy to see how Deborah had given enthusiasm to the people of Israel.

"Don't give up! Never give up! Soon every knee shall bow and every tongue will confess to the Lordship of Christ. Since the Garden of Eden, we have never had a better environment for every human being who loves righteousness to gain eternal life. Everyone can achieve this goal if they desire to overcome the old vices of sin and degradation. Only you can overcome—no one can do it for you. Arise and shine, for the glory of the Lord is risen upon you!"

As Deborah stepped down the applause was deafening. It was clear that she had laid the responsibility for success at each individual's doorstep. Eternal life was in reach for every human being that made the effort to overcome the sin and misery they had inherited.

David

Lev was all smiles as he presented David. "I have a man of many hats to present to you. Our last speaker is a poet, warrior, king, prophet, sinner, penitent, harpist, shepherd, sharpshooter, a great grandfather to the man Christ Jesus and, most of all, a man after God's own heart. That is about as good an introduction as any man may have. I give you King David."

David arose with stately majesty. He was, perhaps, the most handsome man reflecting glorious perfection, but also a man who knew God.

"Shalom! Thank you, Lev. That was a very kind presentation for a very bad sinner. Mercifully, whatever mistakes I have made, the Lord has forgiven and restored me to His favor. And by grace, my life wasn't all mistakes.

"The greatest moments of my previous life were when my heart was in tune with God. When I wandered from Him, I would lose my way temporarily. The dark days of sin are now gone. There is only joy and blessing before me and before each of you.

"The Ancients were returned to life when society was in anarchy. The world leaders had goaded the civil leaders to take Jerusalem. That invasion became the Waterloo of the world, precipitating Armageddon."

"God raised us from the dead when the world's hope was gone. The world was being sucked into a dark hole, and there was no way of escape. But, 'for the elect's sake' those days were shortened. We arrived in time to save the world from total disaster. At first few believed that we had returned to life. We did not come back without power, however. Nor did we come back to be stoned and 'sawn asunder' again."

The former king warmed to his subject.

"Never have leaders had such powers as we were given. We had the power to do everything that was needed. Those who accepted our leadership were immediately blessed and prospered. Those who stubbornly refused to accept the new King received no rain. How long will any people last without water? Strong nations languished as they stubbornly refused to accept the leadership of Christ in Israel. The people soon demanded to come under the new King. The leadership of earth could not repress the will of the people who saw how blessed those nations were who accepted Christ. Eventually every nation surrendered to the sovereignty of Christ.

"I'm happy to say that Japan was among the earliest of the nations to request help. Did you know that some so-called Christian nations held out against Christ the longest? Isn't that strange?

"I'm giving the overview that we had from the top. Even on an individual basis, the greatest problem people have to overcome is pride and prejudice against Jerusalem being the center of the world. Today, the greatest difficulty continues to be the evil encased in hearts of men returning to life. Some lives were not far from the kingdom of Christ. Others were so steeped in evil that they are seriously handicapped in a world of righteousness. When they are unable to dominate and abuse others and find themselves completely powerless and discredited, they still struggle against the iron rule of righteousness. The harder they fight, the more pain they inflict upon themselves."

David paused for a moment as he noticed one individual.

"I see Mori Ishakawa here. Stand up, please, Mori. You died driving a kamikaze torpedo. Did you really want to die?"

"No, your honor—I wanted to live. But I did what I had promised to do, causing my own death and hundreds of other deaths. I am sorry now. I died in vain, a deceived agent of unrighteousness, but I had been trained by leaders in a world of darkness and hatred."

Teaching Your Commander

David continued. "Mori, your commander will be returning in a few months. You must meet him again. At first he will think he has command over you. Mori, you must now be his teacher. He taught you unrighteousness. You must teach him righteousness. The world is turned upside down. Parents used to receive and nurture children. Now children must receive and nurture parents in a very righteous world.

"I am taking more time than the others, but I wanted you to see this new world as it appears from the government in Jerusalem. We are here to strengthen your allegiance to Christ's glorious kingdom. Your work is cut out for you. As you labor to receive your loved ones, remember, it is not only trees from paradise and shelter that they need. 'Man shall not live by bread alone, but by every Word that proceeds out of the mouth of God' (Matt. 4:4).

"And it is not only righteousness that all must learn, but love, *Agape* love, must confront savage hearts as they return to life. We must teach them a new way of unselfish love. The best way to do this is by example. If you truly love people, they will know it. Love is very contagious." His eyes twinkled.

"Another thing to remember is that the first century will find us concentrating on the task of regenerating mankind. When that is accomplished, we will turn all of our energies toward subduing the earth and exercising mankind's dominion over the animals and all living creatures. We will be able to turn the minds of all men and women toward this ambitious goal. This is Christ's wisdom for this age.

"Before you are life, honor, and glory. Before you also are misery, frustration and death. Choose life that you may live. Yield to the King and you shall have all the desires of your heart. Resist the King, and death, the second death from which there is no awakening, will be your end.

"Remember, we must all appear before the judgment seat of God when Christ's reign as Mediator will end. 'The Lord bless thee, and keep thee: the Lord make his face shine upon thee, and be gracious unto thee: The Lord lift up his countenance upon thee, and give thee peace'" (Numbers 6:24-26).

David concluded with the whole assembly giving him a standing ovation. His message was direct and simple. He spoke with the authority of a king and no one could misunderstand his message. He had clearly expressed both the love and severity of God.

Lev then opened the meeting to questions from the audience. They were not to ask routine questions, such as when loved ones would be returned to life.

Questions on the Regeneration

How the hearts of the people burned with appreciation of all they had! Yet, their newly alert minds hungered for even more information. The wisdom of the Ancients had anticipated this by providing a brief question-and-answer session. The first question asked was, "How long will the regeneration of mankind take before our first parents are raised to life?"

Abraham answered, "We do not have a definite date for Adam and Eve's return as yet. However, it has taken us less than twenty years to awaken the first century of life that contained the largest population of the world. We accomplished this starting with a world in ruins. As we reach backward, not only do populations diminish dramatically each century, but we will also have more living people making provisions for loved ones returning to life.

"Remember, we don't have sick, aged or infirm people. No blind, deaf or dumb—no mental illnesses or human deformities. We have eliminated hospitals, medical services, accidents, wars, and every hurtful circumstance. We have no prisons, no armies, no armaments and no police force, at least not a human one. Every mature person is engaged in building, planting and nurturing life.

"We have weaned the world from being constantly entertained, to constantly learning and growing mentally. The world's wealth used to be measured in material riches, but today's wealth is measured by people growing toward perfection.

"If you see the constant acceleration and overview of this whole regeneration program, my educated guess is that Adam and Eve should be restored to life in less than one hundred years. It took over six thousand years to generate all the people in this world—my guess is that they will all be regenerated within one hundred years. What do you say to that?" A smile brightened his wonderful face.

Again, there was enthusiastic applause. The questions kept coming and so did the answers. Before long the morning was spent, and this marvelous time with the noble guests had to end. When the service ended, the Worthies mingled with the entire congregation. Everyone surrounded the guests, asking endless questions to which they graciously responded.

After lunch, Lev took the Ancient Worthies to the Science Center. The venerable guests asked to meet the staff, engaging them in friendly personal discussions.

They were able to perceive the entire project readily and were obviously pleased with how wisely and speedily it was being executed. Each retained all the information given them instantly. In turn, they offered several constructive suggestions. It became immediately obvious that the corrections would be totally advantageous. Everyone marveled at his or her discerning analysis.

"Love never fails"
(1 Corinthians 13:8).

Chapter Six

Aida enjoyed her first visit to the chapel. Although she had only gone out of courtesy to Sarah, her guest for the evening, while there, her pain from spurned love was momentarily forgotten. Aida failed to realize she wasn't the only person to have been disappointed in love. Many had lived and died with broken hearts.

Love was so gloriously beautiful when fulfilled. But more often, love was intensely painful when denied. Friend or physician could not heal the grief and sorrow of a broken heart. It was said that time alone could heal the wounds—but not always. Aida's heartbreak had been carried over from her former life, but she had to learn to put it in perspective in her current life.

As Aida and Sarah walked home, Aida mentioned how much she enjoyed the chapel meeting that morning. She confided to Sarah that it was her first visit to the chapel.

"Why Are You the Last to Welcome Back the King?"

"Are you going to be the last to welcome back the King, Aida?"

"Well, I never looked at it exactly that way. I must seem like a disloyal subject. I do love the righteous world Christ has brought us. It's been the answer to my hopes and prayers. However, I carry pain from my former life that spoils my happiness daily. I feel helpless to remedy the matter, Sarah. The passing of time only makes my heart sick and bitter."

Sarah asked knowingly, "Is it about a love that failed to blossom?"

"Yes, how did you know? Has Christ told you about me?"

"No, but those of us who have experienced broken hearts and bitterness are very sensitive to this aching condition in others."

"Why? Have you ever had such an experience, Sarah? You were married to Abraham, such an incredibly wonderful man. You both seem so happy and in love with each other—how could you understand the pain of rejected love? Were either of you forced to marry against your will?" Aida asked as they turned into the garden entrance to her home.

"No—but we'll talk about this after we get settled, all right?"

Aida thought Sarah was the most gracious guest one could entertain. She admired all the beautiful features and the adornments that Aida had so attractively created in her home.

"Your home is charming, Aida. Did you know that I lived in a tent all of my previous life? We had pillows for chairs and mats for beds. A dwelling like this with all its conveniences was far beyond my greatest dreams. I do hope you enjoy it."

"Oh, I do very much, Sarah! I shared a little matchbox-sized, two-room home with my parents and six brothers and sisters, plus a few of our livestock. Our homes today are not only beautiful and spacious, but every human need and desire is more than amply provided for."

"I'm sure you do appreciate your new life style, Aida! I live in Jerusalem with the other Ancients in a less lavish home than you have. Because of our intense operations, we live near each other in condominiums. With our worldwide transactions, we must be on call around the clock to assist all needs and emergencies. But, as the number of people returning to life lessens, our burdens will lighten.

"Someday we'll have our own homes and gardens, just like you have. Don't misunderstand me—Jerusalem is a beautiful place to live. I, *we,* love it as it is the city of 'the Great King,' 'beautiful for situation, the joy of the whole earth' (Psalm 48:2). Our facilities are comfortable, just not extravagant."

Aida was surprised to hear this. She said, "I thought you would be surrounded with luxury and a life of leisure. You definitely deserve it! You've done so much for the world—you should have the very best!"

"Aida, they tried to surround us with extravagance, but we are used to living with hardship and great discipline. We have deliberately refused luxuries. Our operations require constant attention. We receive hourly instructions from Christ and his members. Sometimes we can operate through normal national channels, but we receive tens of thousands of personal emergency calls. People who have been punished for attempting acts of violence must call us to be healed. We hear each individual case and decide the correct action to be taken. We get absolute information from The Christ members. They tell us if the one calling has told us the whole truth. It's hard for people to believe that we have access to absolute information. They often try to color their situation in their favor. Then, they are shocked to find we know everything about the case!"

"That's fascinating, Sarah! Shall we eat our dinner while continuing our discussion? This is like a dream—having you in my home. Thank you so much for being willing to stay here for the night. Dinner is ready—I'll just take it out of the refrigerator and we can sit down and eat."

Aida asked Sarah to offer the blessing on the food. She appreciated hearing Sarah's prayer. Sarah was like a breath of fresh air to Aida. Never had she received such warmth and love from anyone. Aida felt she could open her heart to Sarah and receive healing balm. And this is exactly what Sarah had come to do.

Abraham and Sarah in a Life of Faith

"Have you read about the story of my life with Abraham?"

"No, I've never read the Bible. I believed in the Shinto religion, which is now non-existent. Religions could teach anything if they had a following. It didn't have to be true, just popular. Now, I know only truth can be taught. The five thousand religions of the old world have failed the credibility test. I'm sorry I haven't read the Bible to learn of your past. Please forgive me, Sarah."

"Oh, Aida, you don't need forgiveness—you haven't done anything wrong. However, I think if you knew a little of my former life, you would find we have some things in common. There are no experiences we have had that have not been experienced by someone else."

"I would never have imagined you and I shared anything in common, Sarah! You have had a wonderful husband, a son in the lineage of Christ, and you were given some of the greatest promises of the Bible! I have learned that much about you through others. How could you possibly understand the heartbreak I have experienced from losing the man I loved? We were to be married and had a lovers' quarrel one week before the wedding. Our relationship shattered. I always hoped and dreamed he would come back to me, but he never did. I never married. I have never known the joy of motherhood and children—the joy of a family. I was a wrinkled, withered prune that had little purpose in life."

"Just because you didn't share the ideal experiences that many women have, does not diminish your value as a person, Aida. True, some women did not have your type of experience—but be assured, there have been no perfectly happy lives. Many marriages have been without love—with great afflictions. Many marriages have been without children. And many mothers with children have been severely disappointed because of terrible relationships with their children. Whatever you may have experienced, be assured, others have had similar sorrows and some have had deeper grief. None of us is unique.

"God tried my faith very sorely, Aida. I was a beautiful woman. I married into a wealthy family. Abraham was successful and became even more wealthy with over three hundred servants. Everything was wonderful. My girlfriends envied my marriage. Ours seemed the perfect marriage. But then a dark cloud arose. I was barren and could not conceive. Abraham would have been free to take other wives to fulfill his desire for a family. Other sheiks added many wives to their harems for multiple children. And make no mistake about it; many women had cast their eyes Abraham's way, hoping for this honor. However, Abraham was very loyal to me and never reproached me for my inability to bear children.

"God appeared to Abraham and promised him a 'seed' that would result in blessing all the families of the earth. We both thought this meant that God would surely bless our marriage with children. Abraham was seventy-five years old when we left Ur of the Chaldees and I was sixty-five. I was still able to bear a child. However, twenty-five years passed and I remained childless. I was past the age of having children when I was ninety years old. What a burden this was on my heart, especially since I was quite aware of the fact that while God had promised Abraham a seed, God did not say that I should be the one to bear Abraham a son. I felt left out of God's purposes, which only added to my frustration. However, my feelings were unjustified. Never at any time was it God's purpose to exclude me from the promise he made to Abraham. I was in God's purpose, but I was not told that.

"I could barely watch other mothers with their children. I had failed Abraham. My heart was heavy with pain, even becoming bitter. His loyalty and love for me left him without an heir. I allowed my barren womb to cause a rift between us. How could Abraham possibly love a wife who couldn't fulfill his fondest desire for a child? I then decided, according to the customs of our day, that I should give my personal maid, a young, beautiful Egyptian girl, to my husband. Perhaps God would give us a child through her. Maybe in this way my reproach would be taken away.

"Abraham was reluctant to do this, but because God had not told him that I was to be the mother of his children, I encouraged him to try it. Of course, this was agonizing for me—to see my husband share the tent of my beautiful young slave, Hagar. And even more piercing to my broken heart was the reality when Hagar did conceive and had a child by my husband. My life became *unbearable*. She, a slave, was able to give the great Abraham his fondest dream. Hagar knew she had won Abraham's affections by her son. It seemingly raised her status from being merely a slave above mine, his wife. Hagar looked down on me and despised me. The only son of Abraham was hers—not mine. Hagar began to usurp my role as Abraham's wife. I was totally driven beyond jealousy. I felt I had lost my position as wife and the affections of my husband forever."

Learning of Sarah's Burden

Aida listened in total absorption. Under her pain, her heart was tender and tears blurred her vision as Sarah continued.

"Abraham grew much attached to Ishmael, his son by Hagar. Abraham fully believed that this child was the seed God had promised him. I would have accepted this, but Ishmael was a rather wild type of child, not having the dignity and carriage of his father. He didn't seem to be a child through whom all the families of the earth would be blessed.

"I was sorry that I had ever suggested this union between Hagar and my husband. I felt locked out of God's promises. I was a barren, worthless old woman. An 'old prune,' I think you called it? Only Abraham's loyalty to me kept me alive. I began to wither and languish, feeling I was nothing more than a liability to Abraham."

Aida forgot her own disappointment and entered into Sarah's anguish and grief. "Why did God leave you out of His promises? Surely, He knew you were to have a son. Why didn't He tell you that you must be the mother of Abraham's son?"

"God finally did include me in the promise He had made to Abraham, but not before my faith was tested to the breaking point. After I had finally given up all hope of being a mother, the angel told me I would bear a son. I was ninety years old by then! How could this be? I laughed within my heart and the angel asked why I laughed. I denied it, but angels can't be fooled.

"He reminded us, 'Is any thing too hard for the Lord?' While I was reproved, my heart was made glad. Why, I could have danced for joy! This was the first time that I knew I was to be a partner in the promises God had made to Abraham. It was going to be our son! And I would once again be the chief wife to my beloved husband. What an overwhelming thought that was!"

"If God knew you were going to give birth to the child of promise, why didn't He tell you sooner so you could have peace of mind?" Aida wondered.

"Ah, dear Aida, we were asked to trust God where we could not trace Him. I should have realized this from the extravagant care God showed in watching over me. On two different occasions men of power saw my beauty and wanted to marry me. God intervened mightily on my behalf. These two men were visited by God in a dream and were terrified. It was evident to me that God would not let these men touch me. Abraham would have been powerless to protect me. Yet these two incidents demonstrated that I was being preserved for some place in God's purpose."

The Seed of Promise

"Finally," Sarah added, "I was with child. I felt I was living a dream. Here I was ninety years old, and growing great with child. Abraham and I were both ecstatic. We could hardly wait for our son, Isaac, to be born. Here was another lesson. While Abraham and I were brought together again closely in our marriage, this made Hagar, my maid who had borne Abraham a son, very unhappy. She perceived that the advantage she had gained over me was soon to be lost."

"Oh, my!" Aida exclaimed. "I never dreamed that you had such a dramatic life with so many trials and disappointments. How could you be so sweet and accepting of these experiences? Why didn't it make you bitter?"

"You must know, Aida, that God had given us great promises. He repeated these promises seven times, adding enlarged understanding along the way. Abraham and I knew that God had something very big in mind. As long as hope burned in our hearts it was easy to accept the hardships and disappointments. It was when God deferred our hopes that our light almost went out. The promises were very clear to us.

"Over the passage of time, when God seemed to have forgotten us, we didn't know what to think. We began to blame ourselves, thinking we had offended God in some way, or that God didn't deem us worthy of His blessings. We didn't understand the truth of the matter. God was testing our faith. If God had fulfilled His promises to us all at once, our faith would not have grown. God was teaching us to trust Him even when we had reached the realm of impossibility. I felt that God had left me out of the Abrahamic promises. It made my heart heavy; but, even so, if God did not choose for me to share in these promises, I thought that I must bow to the Almighty.

"Now I am happy every day of my life. God is no longer testing me as He once did. Abraham and I are now being rewarded for our faith with the most wonderful blessings. That is what He will do for all mankind when they prove that they love the Lord with all their heart, with all their mind, and with all their being."

"How far must God go in testing His people? It seems your tests were unbearable."

"No, Aida, God's grace is always provided in the trials if we are ready to receive it. I was overjoyed when our son Isaac was born. At last I knew I was included in the promises of God and that our son also was included. Isaac was a very dear child. Perhaps we spoiled him a little with our love and affection.

"However, when our son Isaac was weaned, I found Ishmael mocking him. I realized that the rivalry that had existed between Hagar and me was now apparent between Isaac and Ishmael. The old bitterness had not gone away. Two jealous mothers had planted their envy in their children. This broke my heart. As long as we lived so closely, this rivalry would grow and become oppressive. I didn't want it for myself. But even more so, I didn't want it for my son, Isaac."

Hagar Driven Out with Her Son Ishmael

"How did you resolve that conflict?"

"I went to Abraham and demanded that he drive out Hagar and Ishmael from our household. He thought this was just a little quarrel I had with Hagar, and he was quite unwilling to send them both away. I realized then that he loved Ishmael dearly. After all, Ishmael was his son, too. But I was distraught. I didn't want Isaac growing up in competition with Ishmael for Abraham's favor and blessing. I knew Abraham loved Isaac most, yet he also loved Ishmael and wanted to be fair to him. This brought an impossible situation. I expected that Abraham would ignore my request."

"What happened then?"

"God intervened and appeared to Abraham telling him to drive out the bondwoman and her son, because he would not be the heir. This was a very painful thing for Abraham to do. He loved Ishmael and probably still had some affection for Hagar. But when the Lord gave him instructions on this matter, Abraham immediately complied.

He sent Hagar and Ishmael away, with specific directions of where to go and how to find sustenance. However, when Hagar arrived at the destination, she could not find the well of water. Their water supply was exhausted and they were in danger of death. But God intervened and revealed the water source to her. Both Hagar and Ishmael were saved and managed to prosper in the area where they then lived."

"That was wonderful that you were able to rid yourself of vexation just by sending it away. I wish I could have done the same or at least that I could have moved myself away from my heartache."

"Let me finish my story, and then we will share your burden. Life comes in seasons of blessing and moments of crushing trials. Sometimes we are astonished at our happiness. I know it was so when Abraham asked me to marry him and finally again when the angel told me I would have Isaac. We need moments such as these to carry us through those times when our hearts are being broken, and we lack strength to go on."

Abraham Asked to Offer Isaac in Sacrifice

"The day came when God was going to ask us to do the unthinkable. Yet, I was spared from doing what Abraham was asked to do. When our beloved son Isaac had reached his teen years, God said to Abraham, 'Take now thy son, thine only son Isaac, whom thou lovest, and get thee into the land of Moriah; and offer him there for a burnt offering upon one of the mountains which I will tell thee of' (Genesis 22:2). Abraham didn't tell me of this until after he had complied with the Lord's instructions, or more correctly, when he had nearly complied with those instructions. He knew I would have rebelled."

"How could God ask anyone to do such a dreadful thing? I know I couldn't have done such a thing—to offer my own flesh and blood in sacrifice."

"God was testing Abraham to see if he loved Him with all his heart, soul, strength and being. Abraham was asked to play the role that God himself was to play three thousand years later."

Aida gasped. "You mean that God was going to offer up His own son Jesus in sacrifice?"

"Yes, however, at that time Abraham didn't know that God was casting that picture. Abraham had left Ur with its human sacrificing religion to follow the one true God. Now God was asking for his only son as a human sacrifice, a thing Abraham knew God had always abhorred. With heavy heart and footsteps, Abraham took Isaac, our only son, three days' journey to Mt. Moriah. When they arrived, Isaac asked, 'My father,' and he said, 'Here am I, my son.' Isaac said, 'Behold, the fire and the wood: but where is the lamb for a burnt offering?' (Genesis 22:7). I am sure this broke Abraham's heart. What do you say to your only beloved son whom you are about to offer up in sacrifice?

"My poor dear husband felt as if his very being was being wrenched from inside him, but he only said, 'My son, God will provide himself a lamb for a burnt offering.' They at last arrived at the place God had designated to build an altar. Isaac and Abraham both collected stones to build the altar. Still, Isaac didn't expect what was about to happen. Abraham hid what God had requested from Isaac as long as he could. But finally the time came to tell him the truth. Isaac was young and fleet of foot and could have easily fled, and Abraham could never have caught him. However, to Abraham's surprise, Isaac consented to his own death on that altar, because it was God who had made this request. Abraham bound him and placed him on the altar. His son's acquiescence made it even harder for Abraham to continue."

"You mean that he really went ahead with it?"

"Yes. When God is making the request, what choice is there? With utter anguish, Abraham stretched forth his hand, and took a knife to slay Isaac. And then, the angel of the Lord called to Abraham. The angel said, 'Lay not thine hand upon the lad, neither do thou any thing unto him: for now I know that thou fearest God, seeing thou hast not withheld thy son, thine only son from Me.'"

Sarah Admits She Could Not Have Done It

"You know, Aida, I don't think I could have done what Abraham did. Maybe God knew I was too weak in faith to share that experience. Mercifully, Abraham bore this test alone. It was only after they returned that I was told. When I learned what had transpired, I almost fainted. I was quite upset with Abraham for almost killing our only son. I was even upset with God for demanding it. It almost caused another rift between us."

Aida could almost feel the stress of the experience, she was so involved. "Why, oh why, would God ask Abraham to do this and then stop him short of doing it? I had no idea why God held Abraham in such high esteem. Now I can see that he was of such great character that he could go against every fiber of his being to do what surely must have broken his heart."

"Exactly, Aida; but, when God asked him to do this tremendous thing, He was only asking him to do what He, Himself was going to do in sending His only begotten son to die for us. Only there was no angel to stay God's hand. He had to do what Abraham was prevented from doing. Yes, God offered His son. But even Christ was not forced to die against his will. Just as Isaac willingly placed himself on that altar, so Christ willingly placed himself on that cross."

Aida found herself in tears. "I always procrastinated reading the Bible. Never in my furthest imagination could I have thought of what you just told me. But you lived through that experience and I am learning it from a heart that shared in that anguish. How great must be God's love! To give us His only begotten son!"

After a moment, Sarah prompted, "Now I have told you my story. Please tell me yours. There is little that has happened to you that has not happened to others. We are living in a beautiful time in human history. We once lived in a sinful world for over six thousand years. Now, in less than one thousand years, all of human experience will be played out in memory, while gradually healing the entire pain and heartache. We used to desire only happiness for our loved ones and ourselves. But our will was ignored. Sometimes life became so painful and filled with sorrow, we even despaired of life itself. Some even took their lives."

Aida Tells Her Story

Aida replied, "Well, you have exactly described my life. I grew up in a strong family environment. My father and mother were good to us children. Although we were poor, I was provided a good education. Like any young girl, I imagined I would have everything a woman could desire—a happy marriage with children, a comfortable life and fulfilling career.

"I was engaged to be married, but after my fiancé and I had a lovers' quarrel my marriage plans abruptly ended. I thought he would call and we would be reconciled. I never dreamed that he would end our beautiful relationship forever.

"When I tried to phone him, he wouldn't answer. I couldn't believe what was happening to me. I kept thinking that he would soon call, and we would make up and go on with our plans together. It never happened. Soon I learned he had married another woman."

Sarah smiled and gently held Aida's hand. "Love can be both wonderful and cruel. For every beautiful love story, there is a love tragedy. Sometimes it even seems that the tragedies far outweigh the glories of love. But today is the time for healing all the wounds of love. We cannot change the past and replay it as we would like. What can we do about it? We can rise above our past. How? That is the question. We must see things as God views them. We must love as God loves, with *Agape* love. 'God is love' (1 John 4:8).

"You know, Aida, God has never had a marriage partner—and He never will. He was alone until He created His only begotten son. He did not create because He was unhappy being alone. He 'created all things,' and for His 'pleasure they are and were created' (Rev. 4:11). He is a God who has pleasure in giving and blessing others. No one can give Him anything He does not already have. We can only give Him our love and obedience."

Aida responded, "Sarah, Mr. Kumada was my fiancé. That is what makes it so difficult for me to be working on the same project with him and his wife, Anna, who has returned to life. She was killed by some who supported the forces who went to take Jerusalem away from the Jews. She was visiting her father, a Christian minister, and an angry mob stormed his residence. They were angry because the Christian church had encouraged the Japanese to join that ill-fated mission. They were told that God would bless that mission, and that it would save the world from Armageddon.

"But the reverse happened. The crowds knew they had been deceived, and they started destroying the Christian churches. Someone struck her father with a metal object; I think it was a pipe. She screamed and rushed to her father's side, only to be struck with the same instrument that killed her father. Anna never recovered and died there with her father."

"Yes, I know of her case. I was the one who arranged for her return to life. Her marriage to Mr. Kumada did not last long. Sorrow and tragedy have never been far away. In a moment everything can change."

"Yes," Aida confided. "When I heard of Anna's passing, I thought that in time Mr. Kumada would surely remember me and return to me. I even tried to reach him, but he never would return my calls. This hurt me even more. I finally painfully realized that my hopes were all withered and gone. I can't believe how disappointing my life turned out. All of my dreams were cruelly swept away. Why is love so cruel, Sarah? Others had beautiful marriages and relationships, like my father and mother. I wanted so desperately to have a similar marriage, but instead, my life has been painful and lonely. I had material comforts and a good job, but it meant little. I was consumed with my loss, loneliness and pain."

Another Dimension of Love

Sarah comfortingly said, "My dear Aida, you conceived of love only in a happy marriage and family relationship. True love has no family borders. You have been free to love others as you loved yourself, but it was too difficult with your pain. You have been free to love God with all your heart, but you did not know Him. Even now it is hard to love a God you do not know.

"Marriage is not everything! Solomon had seven hundred wives and concluded that 'all was vanity and vexation of spirit.' (Ecclesiastes 1:14). How many a marriage has been a matrimonial furnace of affliction. Men and women have kept their marriage commitments under excruciating, heartbreaking grief. Marriage has not always meant happiness—in fact, often it has brought anguish.

"Aida, you must find happiness not in a personal love affair, but through giving yourself to help others. That is the only way to rise above the heartbreak of love lost. The more we give of our love to others, the stronger our love grows. When we learn to love others, we are learning how God loves."

A little frown clouded Aida's pretty face. "I don't know that I fully understand what you're saying, Sarah. But I see that principle of loving others in your example," Aida observed. "I've never been so conscious of how small my world was until talking to you. You live in a world that knows no bounds. If I could be like that, I believe I would be happy."

"Well, Aida, you certainly can have this kind of love. Jesus said, 'He that findeth his life shall lose it; and he that loseth his life for my sake shall find it' (Matthew 10:39). When we seek too much for ourselves, it can hurt us. When we learn how to give of ourselves for others, we are following the example Christ has given us. The heart will always return to those places touched by love.

"Love is the most beautiful emotion. You only focused on one object for love in your former life. Today there are no limits to it. You have friends and family to whom you may give your love. Countless individuals have been cut off in death with no children to care for them. These people must all be returned to life and they will need someone to love them and demonstrate selfless *Agape* love to them. You can no longer box your love in a self-serving romantic dream. Once the unselfish love of God possesses you, you will live a life filled with both loving and being loved."

"You make it sound so easy and desirable. Can I really attain such love?"

"In Him It Is Always Yes"

Sarah smiled. "Yes! Through Christ all things are possible. 'In Him it is always yes' (2 Corinthians 1:18-20). When you learn to love in a selfless way, with purity, not expecting love in return, you will have opened the door to boundless happiness and joy.

"Marriage, as we once knew it, is no longer functioning. If marriage in the previous life was built on mutual love and respect, it will continue as deep friendship in this present time. Many of those unhappily married will need to mend their love for one another on a higher plane—it will be quite a challenge. Those who do not learn to love God supremely and to love their fellow men as themselves will not be prepared for the tests unleashed upon them when Satan is let out of the 'bottomless pit.'"

The evening had ended with such intense discussion that Aida was shocked to realize how quickly time had passed. She said, "I have intruded unmercifully upon your time. You must be very tired from your travels and being in a different time zone."

"Yes, I'm tired, Aida, but our fellowship was very meaningful to me. It was important to discuss the burden on your heart and point you to the real remedy. In God's unlimited mercy and grace, love is never lost when it is not returned. When properly extended, it will grow and increase. The more love we express, the more love will bubble up in our hearts. Sometimes those who refuse our love will remember it later with comfort. Should our love never be accepted, it still would not whither. 'Love never fails' (1 Corinthians 13:8). Only those who refuse love will in the end be the worse for it."

"Thank you from the bottom of my heart, Sarah, for the joy and comfort you have given me. I will forever remember the evening we have spent together. You have opened up a new world to me. I realize I've been living in a dark hole of my own making. You are so right in pointing out that there is a whole new world of love now. Loving those who love you is not God's kind of love. God loved us while we were enemies of His righteousness."

Aida added, "I am so sorry to have deprived you of rest. Please forgive me."

"We'll have forever to catch up on sleep. Who has not had sleepless nights? Even these are not wasted if, in the lone hours of the night, we were able to meditate on God and His holiness."

Aida showed Sarah her room as they retired for the night. She said, "Lev will be here early in the morning to take you and all your noble associates to the airport. Anna and Mr. Kumada will not be here, as they must remain to oversee the day's activities at the Science Center. Will five a.m. give you enough time to be ready?"

"Yes, Aida, that will be plenty of time. I don't need to be awakened. I automatically wake up at the correct time. Being perfect is wonderful! When I contrast myself now with my former days, I'm still amazed. I was so often weary and frustrated. Sometimes my unhappiness showed. I had everything a woman could hope for, but for years I languished because God did not give us a child. Having this child of promise was a burning passion in Abraham's life—he looked to me in vain to give him that son. Yes, I am so glad those days of heaviness are gone forever now! And, Aida, have faith! Your days of heaviness will also be gone forever! God bless you, dear Aida! I love you very much, and so do God and Christ!"

"For a day in thy courts is better than a thousand"
(Psalm 84:10).

Chapter Seven

Aida slept little that night. She had just experienced a spiritual awakening that profoundly affected her outlook on life. Aida had been living in her own little world, hedged in by her own likes and dislikes, eager to take more than she gave.

Aida was an honest and good person, but short on love for her fellow man—even shorter on her love for God. The religion with which she had been formerly acquainted was ritualistic. Shintoism did not challenge Aida to transform and enlarge her heart. So when Aida was confronted with a loving God who wished His children to emulate His love, it opened new horizons for her. Never had Aida been challenged to such high and lofty goals as in those moments spent with Sarah.

Aida heard Sarah stirring early. She soon emerged bright and cheerful and gave Aida a big hug. She told Aida how she had enjoyed their discussion. Aida was a very reserved person, but she loved Sarah's warm and genuine affection. It was love that had begotten love within her. Aida had been trapped for years like a person in solitary confinement, thinking of love existing only between a man and a woman. Now the first rays of an expanded understanding were beginning to shine in her heart.

"Did you sleep well, Sarah?"

"Yes, I did, after reflecting on the day's events, and especially thinking about you, Aida. Thank you for our lovely time together. I shall take your phone number—perhaps I can keep in contact with you from time to time. After you finish the project you're working on and finish providing homes for your immediate family, you must come visit me in Jerusalem. When you finish your current duties, please give me a call. We can spend a day together—there is so much I would like to show you! Do I have your promise?"

"Oh, yes! I'd love to visit Jerusalem! I must tell you, Sarah, that the time spent with you has been like visiting heaven for a day. As beautiful as you are on the outside, you are even more beautiful on the inside. I want to be just like you, Sarah."

"No, Aida!" Sarah's smile showed her understanding. "I'm but a reflection of Christ. You must try to be like him! Christ is the pattern we all try to copy. He is the only one who truly knows God. We may begin to know God only as He is revealed to us through His son. It will take eternity to know God—He is so great! His power, wisdom, love and justice are without limit. For the first time since our first parents lived in Eden, we have the privilege of knowing God without any misrepresentation by the devil or his agents. We had been deceived so long that it was hard to accept truth."

"Oh, dear, honorable Sarah. You have been such a blessing to me. By the way, I have fruit ready for your trip home. You may wish to eat something while we wait for Lev. He should be here in about five minutes."

"Good, I'll have the fruit of the month to start. We never tire of this food. It's so fulfilling. I often think of how Adam and Eve must have longed to eat it, but weren't allowed back in the Garden of Eden. None of their children had ever tasted Eden fruit before, so they wouldn't miss it the way our first parents did. We had no idea what perfect food was like! However, once you have eaten it, there's nothing like it. God knew what He was doing when He planted the Garden eastward in Eden!"

Sarah scarcely finished her fruit when Lev arrived. Sarah and Aida were the last of the passengers. Aida was so excited. Abraham had a mystique about him that commanded everyone's respect. He jumped out of the van to open the doors for Sarah and Aida and greeted them with genuine affection, as did the others.

A Private Plane Rejected

They were soon at the airport. There was no security at the airport, no ticket agents. Everyone boarded as though it were their own personal vehicle. The Ancients had been offered a private plane if they wished, but they wanted to mingle with the people on the plane. They asked to be spread among the passengers so they could make their ambassadorship for Christ's kingdom felt.

As Lev and Aida bid farewell to the Ancients, she could not hold back her tears. Sarah hugged her as they parted. "Remember your promise to me!"

"I will never forget it! 'Next year, in Jerusalem!' when my duties have been met here."

Soon the plane was boarded. The aircraft lifted vertically, using the same technology being prepared for smaller flying vehicles. Aida found this exciting. How marvelously the needs of mankind were being met! Man's desire to fly was inspired by watching birds fly wherever they wished. At last, private flight would terminate the need for more roads that were environmentally intrusive.

Lev noticed the change in Aida. Yesterday she was polite, but very reserved. But today, Aida was smiling and more pleasant than he had ever remembered her. He finally asked, "How was your visit with Sarah?"

An Afterglow of Sarah's Visit

"Wonderful! Never in my life have I met a more beautiful person within and without. When she shared with me some of her experiences, I was spellbound! She reminded me that these things were all in the Bible. I was so embarrassed I had never taken the time to read them. I can hardly wait to read my Bible now!

Now that her reserve had been broken, Aida bubbled with enthusiasm like an artesian well. "Without chiding me for my inattention to God's Word, she told me of her past and how God had dealt with her. Everything she told me was awesome! What great faith she and Abraham had. No wonder God placed them in supervision of the world's affairs. Truthfully, at times in the past I wondered why God didn't take some of the best people to lead the nations. Now I see He has chosen the noblest, wisest, kindest, and most loving leaders. No one compares with them!

"Lev, do we have time to stop at the chapel this morning before work? Yesterday, when I heard those beautiful people speaking, I was lifted into a world beyond myself. For the first time I realized I had been living in my own little one. I received so much from the messages given yesterday. It was as though each one was speaking directly to me! I caught the vision of this glorious kingdom and the work before us."

Lev was thrilled! "I was hoping you'd say that, Aida! Welcome aboard! You were a pretty tough little nut to crack, but it looks like Sarah not only cracked the shell, but also removed it! It's wonderful to see you excited! Now you know why those of us who love the Ancients cannot praise them highly enough. I came away walking on air when I first met them. Every time I meet them, I am inspired by their dedication and vision of the work before us. It is their responsibility to make sure this world reaches the full potential of the opportunities Christ is extending to all.

"Aida, don't expect the chapel service to be as high powered today as it was yesterday. Still, you will have the Word of God clearly presented to you. And God's Word is powerful! It is not like religion used to be, with preachers giving different messages. They said what the people wanted to hear, whether it was true or not. Now everything has to be true. If the speaker fails to speak accurately, someone in the audience will stand up to clarify his point.

"We all are studying our Bibles. You'll find there is no end to learning and applying God's Word to your personal life. We have near perfect retention. Many former authors stand embarrassed by what they had written. They were once proudly acclaimed professionals—now perceived as badly misinformed at best, or as deceivers. They were, in fact, deceived, but no one knew it. Everything appeared right because a little truth was mixed with so much error—it was difficult to distinguish between the two."

They entered the chapel just as the music started. The room was filled. Apparently yesterday's inspiring service wasn't forgotten. After the singing and prayer the chaplain said with a humble grin, "I am sorry that our services today will not measure up to yesterday's. We were honored and blessed by having the most distinguished servants of God in our midst. Did you all notice true perfection as we saw it yesterday?"

Everyone had seen it and had been exhilarated. The congregation exclaimed, "Yes!"

The chaplain then said he would read about the lives of our visitors from the Bible in the next series of meetings to remind us of their faithfulness. When he said his first lesson would be about Abraham and Sarah, Lev saw Aida smile and nod joyfully.

After the morning service, Lev took Aida around to introduce her to many of the regular attendees. They welcomed her warmly. When the chaplain came to greet her, she was so pleased. She thanked him for his readings and then said, "Last night Sarah opened up her past to me, and having you read some of the accounts she referred to was a great help to me today."

"I hope we will see you tomorrow and often, Aida."

"As long as I am physically able to attend, you will definitely see me! I have missed so many blessings by not coming. I could have learned so many things. I am going to try to make up for lost time," she declared with great determination.

Aida's Transformation

Lev went over to Rebekah. "I've never seen someone transformed so quickly. It's as though Aida has been electrified. Obviously, she and Sarah must have bonded perfectly. I don't think this is just an emotional high, either. I really think Aida has seen a great light and is responding to it. She'll be twice as effective at work now. She operated a technically correct desk, but never generated warmth. Look at her now! She is bubbling over! No one will recognize she is the same person!"

When Lev and Aida arrived at the Science Center that morning, some knotty problems had emerged. Mr. Kumada, with all his managing abilities, seemed unable to resolve matters. He was relieved to see Lev. "I'm so glad to see you, Lev. Did you get our honorable guests on their way this morning?"

"Yes, we certainly did, in fine order."

A Communication Problem

"Well, Lev, I don't wish to burden you with this problem, but we haven't been able to make much progress with it. Unfortunately, it stems from Aida's department where communications are not the best. Do you mind taking charge of this matter, Lev? You seem to be better at this than I am."

"Let me look at it carefully and see what I come up with. If we have a communication breakdown, we must address it quickly. Our work is extraordinarily complex. If we're not clearly focused at all times, it could be dangerous, especially when we start dealing with anti-matter."

Lev then took the paperwork from Mr. Kumada. "Give me an hour to review this."

After analyzing the material, it was plain to Lev that there had been a serious communication breakdown. To his dismay, all indications pointed to Aida's department. She was just starting to come out of her shell, and he hesitated about speaking to her regarding this matter. At the same time, it wasn't possible to let the situation slide. Too much was at stake. Lev decided to take the information to Aida for her opinion.

When he entered Aida's office, she was still bubbling. Lev tried to be as diplomatic as possible. He knew she had not anticipated any problems. It was done by default and certainly not done deliberately on her part.

"Aida, we are running into a little bit of a problem. I need you to look over these papers. Tell me what you think. How can we remedy this situation? Let me know by tomorrow morning how we can resolve it, okay?"

"Hope to see you at the chapel tomorrow."

"I plan to be there, the Lord willing."

Aida Confronts Her Past

When Aida studied the material Lev left with her, she was almost moved to tears. Suddenly she realized that her reserved way of dealing with other members of the staff had made them reluctant to speak with her about important matters. They chose to leave matters unresolved rather than approach her for the necessary information. Although she had not been rude or abusive to anyone, Aida realized people were avoiding her to the point that they were missing necessary information. Why was the staff leaving her out of the circle? Yesterday she had been on the mountaintop. Suddenly, she dropped down into the pits with a thud. Just when she was ready to be the new Aida, she felt like quitting.

Aida decided to seek Lev's counsel. As she entered his office, she felt tears running down her cheeks.

"Lev, you knew what the problem was when you gave me these papers. Do you want me to quit? If I'm part of the problem, perhaps I better step out and let someone else take over. Have I been some kind of monster that everyone is avoiding me?"

"Aida! Don't you dare consider quitting! You are as important as anyone else in this operation, and I depend on you a great deal." He put a brotherly arm around her shoulder. "This is what we'll do. I'm going to send everybody that has avoided you into your office. I will tell them to get the information they need from you and to do this without delay. I'm going to tell them that, by avoiding getting this information, they are not only hurting our operation, but they are hurting their character.

"When they come to you, apply what you learned from Sarah about love. Remember how warm and loving she was. This will be your golden opportunity. Don't only tell them the scientific data they come seeking, but make them feel loved and appreciated. If you do this, by the end of the day our problem shall have been solved. You will have gained a great victory. You can do it—I know you can, Aida. It takes strong character to override the hurt that you feel, but you have that kind of greatness, Aida. I have every confidence in you."

Sweet Reconciliation

The woman visibly relaxed. "Lev, I came to your office to resign. But if I did that, you know I would be crawling back into my old shell and I'd not only let myself down, but Sarah would be very disappointed in me. You're right, Lev. I'll try to be not only a well-informed scientist, but also, more importantly, a loving human being. I'll do it! Pray for me, Lev. I'm not very good at this. I can't change as fast as I'd like, but by God's grace I'm going to give it my best. If I fail, I fail. But, I'm going to try harder than I have ever tried anything before."

"That's the spirit, Aida—I know you'll succeed beyond your best expectations. The staff doesn't know you as a person. Communications work best with those we know. I took the trouble right away of getting to know you, and I've found you a delightful person. This trial has come up to test your mettle. It's going to be love under the test. If you try, I guarantee you won't fail. Our staff members will come away feeling sorry that they misjudged you."

"If I had left, I would've failed myself first, the Science Center second, and my Lord most importantly. I'm going to try a little love in my relationships. If I hadn't spent the day with Sarah and at the chapel, I know I would've walked out the door today."

"And we would've lost a valuable member of our team while you'd feel you were a failure when you aren't. Now go and show your sweet side that they haven't noticed yet. Remember to forgive those who are being distant toward you. The best thing to do with enemies is to make friends of them."

As soon as Aida returned to her office, Lev picked up the phone, instructed the staff members that information was available in Aida's office and to check with her immediately. He also chided them for the communication breakdown that was seriously hindering their progress.

Anna Kumada was the first to respond to Lev's urgent message. She appeared in Aida's office a little embarrassed and hesitant.

"I'm sorry, Aida, that I didn't check with you earlier. I know that we've had at best a stiff relationship—I can understand why. We should have been able to override our feelings for the good of this project and the blessings it will bring to mankind."

Aida stood up and, walking to the front of her desk, put her arms around Anna.

"It's I who have been stiff and unapproachable to you, Anna. As of yesterday, I am determined to be a more loving and tender person. You have never been unkind to me, and there was no reason for me to be less than loving and kind to you. Yes, I lost to you, but you weren't responsible. I drove Mr. Kumada into your arms. I have learned from Sarah what a loving person should be like. My heart was scarred and I was bitter and insensitive. I know that now." With sincere tears of remorse in her eyes, Aida implored, "Forgive me, Anna. I've been my own worst enemy all these years. No more—I learned of a higher love from Sarah. I'm going to be in love with love itself from now on. Can you forgive me, Anna?"

Anna's eyes filled with tears. "My dear Aida, what a blessing to hear you try to break down all the barriers between us. I'm as much to blame as anyone. I never tried being loving toward you. Not that I ever spoke ill of you, nor did my husband. We just kept you at arm's length. Often I felt sad that I was the one who was the cause of your sorrow. I knew nothing of you until after we were married. Our marriage was wonderful, but short. We had no children, but perhaps it was too troublous a time for children to have a decent life. The world fell into anarchy and lawlessness for a time after the nations were defeated in trying to take Jerusalem. I'm glad I died in the early stages and didn't have to endure that awful unleashing of human passions. You weren't spared as I was."

Survival

Aida replied, "I don't know how I survived those awful times. I lived in constant fear, often freezing and hungry. It wasn't until our people voted to come under the authority of the Ancients at Jerusalem that law and order were restored. Food was shipped to our country; and soon life not only became livable, but it started to become beautiful. What a difference perfect government makes. Suddenly all our resources were being used to uplift and sustain our people.

"When our loved ones started returning to earth and we had the trees of life, everything became delightful and peaceful. The only savagery left in the world was in the hearts of those returning to life. That is the only sorrow of the regeneration—it's a fact that those returning to life are bringing all their evil and hatred with them. While the beauties of this earth tend to mellow people, it's not easy for us to undo the evil of the past. It's a dramatic change for mankind to awaken and suddenly find they're under an iron rule that prohibits sin and evil. Whether they choose to or not, we all have to learn righteousness."

"You have been blessed in a way, Aida, by living through those awful times. Not that it was pleasant—but you learned a lot about human behavior under stress," Anna affirmed. "It's amazing how people who are good and perfectly normal can become crazed in times of great distress. The people that killed my father were regular people from our neighborhood, some who even greeted us on occasion. But when they thought my father had deceived them by telling them that God would bless the mission to take control of Jerusalem and that this assembly of nations could prevent Armageddon, they became absolutely rabid.

"And I understand," she went on, "it was not only here, but it was like this all over the world. The collapse of religious organizations was almost a replay of the French Revolution on a larger scale. The world knew that a small group of non-orthodox Christians had warned against the nations invading Jerusalem. That group predicted exactly what would happen. For the first time the world knew who told the truth and who didn't. It was plain that God had a faithful few who spoke the truth and that's what made it so difficult for those who deceived the nations into this terrible tragedy."

Aida listened intently. "Yes, now that you mention it, I do remember hearing about those Christians who stood up, warning against the invasion of Israel. They were ignored until after the total disaster that followed, when God destroyed our forces. I must admit my experience with religion was more ritualistic. There never was anything intellectual about it. My whole family went through a ceremonial observance of tradition. That's all we wanted and that's all we got.

"When the majority of Christian churches urged the nations to attack Israel, only that odd little group stood up and said, 'No, don't go. God will surely destroy this invading force.' We dismissed them without a second thought. Looking back, I realize that God never left Himself without someone as a witness to His truth. Now that truth is everywhere, it's hard to imagine the confusion we formerly had in religion."

"My father was a good man," Anna affirmed. "He wasn't a good student of the Bible, but he read sermons that others had prepared and even offered prepared prayers. They were high-sounding prayers, but seemed superficial even to me. Being a minister was his job— that's how he made his living. It's not like the presentations we have at the chapel today. Now we have such meaningful explanations of Scripture.

"Most people know what's in the Bible, so they're a more perceptive audience. Before, religion was a series of ceremonies and methods that you followed in order to get into heaven. The only reason anyone wanted to go to heaven was because the only alternative to heaven was a terrible place of burning hell-fire. Now we know what death was like. We didn't go floating around anywhere. Why intelligent people believed in a mythical soul seems strange now. We should have known that the Bible nowhere speaks of man having an immortal soul. I was dead. When I awakened years later, I had no consciousness of the time that had passed. As the Bible says, 'The dead know not any thing' (Ecclesiastes 9:5) and I knew nothing! I was simply dead. We were deceived by mythology carried over from the heathen false gods. It took a while to blend my past and present together with the time lapse between."

Communication Returns

After considerable further discussion, Aida and Anna became better acquainted. Aida finally began to outline the technical details that were being omitted because of a communication breakdown, and Anna readily noted what needed to be incorporated into the project.

"I'm happy I spent this time with you! Aida, you've totally disarmed me of my resentment against you. I know we're going to be close friends! I hope we can get together more often in the days to come. Thanks again, Aida."

There was warmth and love in their little meeting. As Anna left, she returned Aida's gentle embrace. With tears in her eyes she said, "May this be the beginning of a love like that of Ruth and Naomi." Aida made a mental note to look up that story in her Bible!

As Anna left, she saw others were waiting to see Aida. They had watched the love expressed in tears and an embrace between Aida and Anna and were very much impressed.

By the end of the day, Aida had met with all those who had avoided her, and left them feeling much better about her. They couldn't help but wonder about the change in her.

Aida popped her head in Lev's office just before leaving. With a big smile, she said, "I did it. I came out of my shell and showed my love for them, and they all responded. It's been such a beautiful experience. I've been living below my privileges for so long. Lev, thanks for helping make this a beautiful day of victory. If I had yielded to my old impulses, I'd be going home miserable and most unhappy. Today is the first day I'm actually leaving very happy. You've been a good friend."

Lev smiled. "Aida, I knew you could do it. This experience was timed perfectly. You still had all the momentum of Sarah's influence in your heart. That's why you were inspired to rise above your old inhibitions."

"Will I see you at the chapel tomorrow?"

Lev grinned. "Remember when I asked you to attend the chapel meeting earlier, and you didn't want to come? I hope to be there, Lord willing. I'm glad you're starting to encourage everyone to attend worship in the morning."

The following morning the chapel room was almost filled. The visit of the Ancients had left a new resolution in everyone. It is one thing to find yourself growing toward perfection, but it is quite another to witness someone already there.

Lev thought he was early, only to find that most people arrived ahead of him this morning. He found Aida sitting and anxiously waiting for the opening hymns to begin. Everyone seemed buoyant and enthusiastic. "A day in thy courts is better than a thousand." Lev remembered that beautiful text and saw that it was indeed true. Written in the heart of man was the innate desire to worship God. Mankind desired to worship in times past, even when they only dimly perceived God's truth and His purposes.

Now that so many had returned to life and absolute truth was known regarding God's purposes, worship was so much better. "The Lord, the Lord God, merciful and gracious, longsuffering, and abundant in goodness and truth, keeping mercy for thousands, forgiving iniquity and sin, and that will by no means clear the guilty" (Exodus 34:6).

Lev thought how wonderful it was to see so many hearts seeking the face of the Lord in hymns and prayer. Yet, only God could look down and see who among the worshipers were seeking to love Him with "all thy heart, and with all thy soul, and with all thy mind" (Matthew 22:37).

God would one day put all those who professed to love Him supremely to the test, even as He did Adam and Eve. Only He could recognize those who secretly held a penchant for sin, who remembered fondly the forbidden pleasures of wickedness, wishing secretly they were not forbidden.

When the services ended, Lev spent time fellowshipping with various members, trying to become acquainted with as many as possible. He worked his way over to Aida who was aglow, reaching out to various ones. Lev asked her, "Has it been good to have been here, Aida?"

"Oh, yes," she exclaimed. "I wouldn't miss these services for the world now. I feel alive to myself, alive to God and to other people. No wonder I was so heavy of heart before. I had just made up my mind to be miserable, I guess, and now I hardly remember why!"

A Call to Return to Help Fix Some New Problems

"I have news for you, Aida. I will soon be leaving Japan. I received a call from Jerusalem last night to move within the week. I told you I was here only for a short time. I came to serve and was, as I always try to be, a servant."

"Oh, we're going to miss you – you've been an angel among us. Thank you for helping me crawl out of my shell. I will never forget what you did for me."

She continued, "May we call you if we find problems we cannot resolve?"

"Of course, technical problems are usually the easiest to remedy. I've had a lot of experience with technical things. However, I love people and the challenge of working with them tops the technical challenges one hundred to one! One day everyone will be perfect, and the problems we are experiencing in human relations will fade away. But for now, our problems, as well as our joys, are in those returning to life. For many, their new life will be the first time they experience the love of God. It will also be the first time when the knowledge of God fills the earth as the waters cover the sea (Isaiah 11:9)."

Rebekah came up to greet Lev and Aida. "Rebekah, I will be leaving Japan soon. I received a call last night, and our leaders in Jerusalem think things are proceeding well enough for me to move on. Actually, it was John the Baptist that called me requesting I return to Austria. It seems Hitler has found some of his old Nazi officers who have returned to life. They have been spending a lot of time reminiscing about the 'good old days' when they were in power and world conquest was in sight. He didn't mention Eva Braun. Did John possibly ask you to return to visit her?"

"No, not yet. Maybe Eva has had her fill of the 'good old days.' I hope so, anyway. Some people loved being in power. You'd think that with the light now shining, they'd want to renounce the past with all its evil. This news is certainly not a good turn of events. I don't know how you'll handle it, Lev; but if anyone can, it's you."

"I can't say that I exactly look forward to this," Lev admitted. "I found dealing with Hitler a bit trying before. I sensed no remorse in anything that he did. He disconnected himself from all the horrendous crimes for which he was responsible. He felt since the Germans had suffered and died in that war, and he also had died, nothing more needed to be done. Everyone was coming back to life—why should he be singled out in some special way?

"John the Baptist told me I had been originally assigned here for another month, but with events developing in Austria, I'd better go now. I'll be leaving next week. I know the project we're working on is in good hands. It will prosper until it is accomplished."

"Ye worship ye know not what: we know what we worship: For salvation is of the Jews"
(John 4:22).

Chapter Eight

Lev arranged a flight back to Austria for the following week. After a tearful departure from Hiroshima and those he had learned to love, he knew he would be facing a more serious challenge. He would enjoy the beauty of Braunau, Austria, but Hitler was well-adjusted to his new environment and had grown more clever, if not wiser, than when Lev first received him back to life.

Landing in Austria, Lev obtained a small automobile to drive to Braunau, where Hitler lived. He had arranged for lodging at a new home built for someone who hadn't yet returned to life. It was within a few miles of Braunau. The drive was through a picturesque countryside dotted with new homes and thriving orchards. Everything had been beautifully landscaped. Flowers and homes looked as though they had been sculpted by artists. It was a veritable paradise. Arriving by evening, Lev decided to phone Hitler. Lev dialed the number he still remembered. Hitler answered, "Hello, Adolf speaking."

"Can you guess whose calling?"

"Yes, Lev. Am I right? Why are you calling me, Lev? What did I do wrong now?"

"You can't get away with doing anything wrong." Lev laughed disarmingly. "We both know that!"

"Well, I got violent when I was surrounded by that nasty mob, if you remember. But having my arms paralyzed was something I wish not to repeat. Thank you for helping me out of that one, Lev. But, seriously, why are you calling?"

"I'm in Braunau for a brief stay. I'd like to visit you tomorrow. Will you be available?"

"Well, I'm having a few friends over. It might interrupt the purpose of your visit. But if not, you're welcome to join us, Lev."

Lev Invites Himself

"I'd be glad to meet your visitors. As a matter of fact, it's part of my purpose to meet them. So this is very fortunate for me. What time will they be calling?"

A long silence followed. Obviously, Hitler didn't wish to answer and wondered how he might discourage Lev from visiting. He didn't want to lie—he knew he'd be punished immediately for that. Hitler finally realized he had no choice but to follow through with the meeting. "They'll be here around ten in the morning. Is that convenient for you, Lev?"

"Yes, I'll be there. How have you been, Adolf? And what are you doing with your time these days?"

"Well, I did help build a home for each of my parents and planted those wonderful Eden trees. Since then I've rested. It was harder work than I'm used to. Anyway, I avoid being out in public. People are quite ugly about confronting me. They think I can undo the past—they forget that I, too, died and paid for whatever harm I may have done anyone."

"Hmmm. We'll talk tomorrow."

"Very well. I hope my visitors will be respectful of you, Lev. I'll look for you tomorrow."

Lev knew his call had distressed Adolf, but Lev was a very important person in the new government. Hitler dared not treat him rudely. Such a meeting with a couple of Hitler's old operatives might be very timely. Lev suspected that Hitler had been spending his time trying to contact his old cronies in the Nazi movement. Perhaps he was lining up a support group for the Nazis. They were clearly a hated group now, having committed such terrible atrocities. Perhaps Hitler was trying to form a "good old boys" club who would try to glamorize the "old glory days." Trying to live in that murky past was extremely detrimental for anyone wishing to return to human perfection. The crimes of the Third Reich would leave a morally healthy person feeling terrible remorse and anguish at what had been done.

Lev arose early the next morning to attend the chapel meeting and meet some of his friends. He received a warm reception. He inquired whether Hitler had attended any of their meetings. The answer was a polite, "No." After the services Lev returned to his house for breakfast. He prayed and meditated about how he might be helpful in the forthcoming meeting. Lev knew that these former Nazis would be uncomfortable with him being a Jew. If they were to be helped, they needed to own up to what they had done and try to learn how they might repay in some small way the debt they owed humanity.

Lev drove to the residence he had helped build for Hitler. It looked well kept and tidy. Adolf's artistic skills were displayed in his floral gardens. He had an eye for physical beauty and had shown remarkable aptitude in landscaping. There were two automobiles in front of the residence. Lev's car would be the third. The comrades had probably arrived earlier to map out a strategy to explain their meeting to Lev.

Lev knocked on the door. It opened slowly, which might indicate the lack of enthusiasm about his visit, yet Hitler's greeting was proper enough.

"Welcome, Lev, my valuable mentor when I first returned to life!"

Lev greeted him with a friendly smile and shook his hand. The two gentlemen in the living room rose to meet Lev. Hitler presented the first as Mr. Eichmann and the second as Mr. Goebbels. They already knew his name and greeted him with cool reserve. This was no longer the day of their power—of which they were painfully aware. They also recognized that Lev was a Jew. They were definitely uncomfortable about that, but tried to be congenial under the circumstances.

Hitler looked well physically. None of his old infirmities afflicted him. He could not have been happier with his new diet. He had been on a careful diet in former years, trying to remedy his infirmities, so the fruit of paradise was much appreciated by him. He had grown mentally much sharper than when Lev had first been with him. He groomed himself differently so that he wouldn't be easily recognized. However, people were too perceptive for his disguise to do much good.

An Explanation Required

Lev immediately asked about the purpose of their meeting.

Hitler had anticipated his question and replied, "We are just old friends. It's true we made some mistakes in the past, but we're not so well received by the general public, so we find some solace among ourselves. It gets lonely—so we find some acceptance with those who share some friendship instead of hostility. Is that wrong, Lev?"

"I'm not your judge. But do you think you're going to pay your debt to society for all the evil you did by avoiding that same society you treated so badly?"

"Lev, you don't understand. Society loathes us. We can't mix with them."

"Well, they might not loathe you as much if they found you engaged in constructive contributions and works of love toward your fellow men."

"We've done all that has been expected of us," Mr. Eichmann added somewhat stiffly. "We risk harassment when we travel around. Why should we have to endure this while we would engage in some good work? You know I endured terrible punishment at the hands of the Jews in Israel. They weren't satisfied until I was executed. So I paid my debt. Why should I be humiliated further?"

"What makes you refer to the people who confront you as insensitive? Perhaps they are trying to remind you of your own insensitivity in times past. You certainly don't think of your former deeds as sensitive, do you? You sinned greatly against humanity and above all against God. How do you address God for your past?"

Mr. Goebbels replied, "Do you always go about preaching at people, Lev? Why have you singled us out on your list of those you wish to reprove? Have you no sins or have you not made mistakes in the past?"

Adolf interceded. He saw his comrades were running short on patience, and he knew that Lev was not one to be trifled with.

"Lev, please be patient with my friends. They don't know you as well as I do. My guess is that the Ancients have sent you here. Am I right?"

"Yes, otherwise I wouldn't be here. When they find people going in the wrong direction, they usually send someone to them as a wake-up call. Obviously, they don't see you overcoming your weaknesses. You and your friends will only harm one another unless you begin to show some remorse for your heinous crimes of the past and try to demonstrate your change of heart with devotion to righteousness."

Hitler's two visitors held their peace, although Lev could see they were seething in anger. Adolf tried to change the direction of the discussion.

"Surely you must understand we aren't trying to recreate the Third Reich here."

"I know and you know Christ is the ruler now. Even if you could manage to get all the loyal people of the Third Reich behind you, you would have zero possibility of restoring it. If you don't stop reveling in the past, you'll soon be dead, as well. Once you were on top of the world and were powerful. Now you're about as welcome as skunks at a picnic. This doesn't feel good and you don't like it, right?"

Adolf turned red. Lev could see he was shaken by this tough talk.

"Lev, you were never that harsh before. Why have you come to demean me in front of my good friends? We don't mean any harm to anyone. Let's find a more agreeable subject for the moment."

Mr. Eichmann tried to keep his composure. Hitler had probably warned him of the consequences of losing it. However, he said, "Mr. Aron, perhaps your Jewishness is showing. Even God spoke of your kind as a 'stiff-necked people' (Deuteronomy 9:6). You must know that Jews were a problem in our former society. What we did was probably wrong; but then the Jews were the cause of many problems."

"I'm not here to defend my Jewishness nor the deeds of any Jew that may have transgressed the laws of justice and decency. However, your assertion that Jews were a problem is the same rationalization that caused you to sin against humanity and God. The Third Reich spoke of the extermination of the Jewish people to address the so-called 'Jewish problem.' There is nothing that can describe your former ruthless mass murder as anything but diabolical. The sooner you acknowledge your gross sins against humanity and God, the better it will be for you."

We Paid for Our Mistakes

Eichmann replied, "You seem to forget that we have paid for our sins by our own deaths."

Lev answered sharply, "How can you pay for all the pain, suffering, humiliation, broken families, torture of innocent human beings, the ghoulish death chambers, the lies, the deceit, the cattle car death trains, the arrogance and brutal exercise of power? You ran the most ruthless killing machine in history. There was not a shred of mercy or human kindness in your atrocities." Lev was intense in his recounting of the dark history associated with these three men.

"How can you say you've paid for your sins? Can your one miserable life atone for millions of lives you willfully destroyed? Stop fooling yourself, Eichmann. As painful as it is to me to do it, I've been sent to tell you there is a way to find reconciliation with God and your fellow man, but it won't come by keeping fellowship with a sick past."

They all sat stunned by Lev's relentless portrayal of their past and their attempt to find fellowship in it. A long silence ensued. They knew Lev was a powerful figure in the ruling powers of earth, so they gnawed their tongues to keep from saying anything that would bring immediate consequences upon themselves.

Hitler, sensing that they were not capable of a good defense, decided to play wounded and hurt.

"Lev, I'm sorry that you have such a low opinion of us. If we were so bad, why did Christ bring us back to life? We didn't ask to return. We could have remained in the grave. We felt no pain there. No one censored us there. No one could heap insults and ridicule upon us there. Why have we been returned to life to face such abuse and criticism?"

The Need for Change

"If you don't change your ways, you'll have to go back into the grave. God is love, and only those who learn to love as He loves are going to be rewarded with eternal life. You must understand that the time you have left is for the purpose of developing a character that will meet with God's approval. Without all living beings in harmony with righteousness and with each other, none could be happy. Surely you have seen that you haven't achieved happiness yet in this new order. And you aren't going to develop a god-like character associating with people who still look upon their evil past without true remorse and reformation of heart. You all must seek the fellowship of men and women who know and love God and their fellow men. That is the only hope you have of keeping away from eternal death."

Again, a stunned silence followed. No one knew what to say. Lev was speaking as a prophet among them. They dared not challenge him, but sat glumly, not able to respond. They knew life was pretty great now, if not exactly as they'd like it to be. The dark grave offered nothing to really commend it.

"Why is it that not one of you attends chapel meetings to worship God? Could it possibly be that you've succeeded in alienating yourself from God to such an extent that you feel like hypocrites at worship? Can you receive all the benefits God has so graciously given without even lifting your hearts to thank him? Ingratitude is a terrible sin. Why can't you thank God for his mercies?"

Hitler answered, "We aren't welcome at these chapel meetings."

"When did you go to a chapel meeting to learn that?"

They paused in a long silence. Mr. Goebbels finally cleared his throat. "We just knew we weren't welcome there. We have to be careful meeting people on the streets—people hate us."

"No one hates you. They hate what you did. It's time you should hate what you did also and try to pay the great debt you owe humanity."

Lev's voice conveyed a new gentleness. "Everyone knows you can't undo the past. It's only the present that can be changed. But you'll never change unless you are determined to work at it. Otherwise it's not going to happen."

"Well, then," Adolf asked, "what should we do? Walk around carrying a sign saying we repent? As it is, as soon as we are recognized, people start pointing and telling everybody 'There is Hitler.' That's the best-case scenario. In some instances they gather around to show their displeasure. We don't want to be objects of scorn and derision. We aren't among those who have so much to be thankful for. We just want to be left alone. We are hurting no one, nor can we. However, we do everything that is required of us. We even keep the laws that these Jews in Jerusalem have made."

A Slur against Jews

The last comment Lev interpreted to be a slander against the Jews. He held his peace, not wishing to defend his heritage. He knew that it was Christ who ruled supreme and God Himself selected his representatives. However, this statement indicated that Hitler and his cronies still harbored animosity toward the Jews.

Even in the light now shining, they were not able to accept responsibility for the unparalleled evil they had precipitated. They, who had victimized millions, were now playing the victims. He knew that unless they first saw themselves from God's perspective they would not last beyond the century. They had practiced unrighteousness for so long in the previous life that it had become ingrained in their hearts. They were unable to discern between righteousness and unrighteousness, good and evil.

Lev knew this meeting had reached an uncomfortable level, so he decided to leave, but only until the next day when feelings had a chance to settle and the hostility would mollify.

"Well, gentlemen, I must be going. I am sorry to have dampened your day, but a little rain may cause you to appreciate the sunshine even more. May I return tomorrow, Adolf? I would welcome seeing your guests as well. I find them very interesting. I specialize in understanding human behavior. That is my first area of accomplishment—my second area is in science. Right now I'm learning a lot about the human heart—it 'is deceitful above all things, and desperately wicked' (Jeremiah 17:9). May we meet again tomorrow, Adolf?"

Adolf turned pale, but he knew Lev was determined to have another visit. He felt compelled to respond, "Lev, you will be welcome. I do not know if my friends will be here. We shall see what their plans are. Thank you, please come again."

As he left, Lev wondered what these three devious men had in mind. Perhaps he need not wonder. It might be well to call John the Baptist and find out more about their plans. His call went directly through.

"Shalom, Lev." John had been waiting to hear from him.

Lev Struck Out

"Shalom, shalom, John. My first day here didn't go very well. Mr. Eichmann and Mr. Goebbels were there. They feel what was done is behind them. They claimed they had died for their mistakes, so why should they bear any more responsibility? They still have resentment against the Jews. They aren't engaged in any constructive activities.

"They said they've worked to receive their relatives back to life, but after that they've contributed nothing to society. They don't volunteer for any services and simply live a comfortable life, enjoying the fruit of paradise and all the good things abundantly provided. I think they're trying to relive the glory days of their power. All three of these men love that power and are hurting badly because they have none."

"This is exactly our assessment, Lev. They loved the days of their power, even though it was in a swamp of wickedness. They have hardened their minds to the millions of lives they destroyed, the families they crushed, the pain and despair they caused. They enjoyed serving Satan even in their grotesque business. Lev, keep trying to awaken Adolf and his friends to the perilous course they are taking. We have observed no movement indicating true repentance or reform of any kind."

"That's my observation, too. I tried to awaken them to their lack of love for their fellow man. They have only done what was expected of them in building and planting for their immediate family. Since then they have gone into early retirement. Goebbels and Eichmann were both there—I wonder if you can shed any light on the reason for these untimely meetings?"

"We know they have been endeavoring to find some of their old Nazi party people. They have no plans for a revolution or anything like that, but they want to build an exclusive country club where they will be shown respect and be received warmly. They feel isolated and rejected by society; so, instead of trying to reform and engage in good works to pay back for some of the evil they did, they are trying to comfort themselves with Nazi sympathizers. They talk about their old building plans for the chancellery that was never built—the one with a dome three-hundred and fifty meters high and one hundred thousand seats for their followers and a sports stadium for five hundred thousand spectators and a marching ground for one million people. It was to have an apartment for Hitler one hundred and fifty times larger than Bismarck's. It's just talk, but it shows where their dreams are centered."

"I thought that might be the case. I worried that possibly they were up to some form of mischief. However, they know full well that they're on a tight leash, and that spiritual powers know everything they are up to. I tried speaking directly with them, but they won't accept that they have any problem. It seems everybody else is to blame for their unhappy lot."

"Well, Lev, don't feel you are responsible if you can't change their heart condition," John the Baptist explained. "They know they're guilty of sin, but they think they can fool the world into believing that what they did wasn't all that bad. They are playing the role of victims of intolerance. They're only deceiving themselves—that's the problem. Unless they fully acknowledge the horrible things they did and desire to change, they won't survive beyond this century. Lev, just try to awaken them to their peril. That's all you can do. Not everybody is going to escape the second death, you know."

"Thank you for the privileges of service that are mine. I shall do my best. I won't take any more of your time, John. Shalom."

"Shalom, Lev. Be steadfast and unmovable in the service of the King."

A Surprise at the Chapel

The next morning Lev arrived early at the chapel for more fellowship. There were many old and new friends he wished to meet. It was a joy to have such warm fellowship. When the music started he sat down toward the rear, for most of the seats were filled. To Lev's surprise, in walked Adolf. He sat quietly in one of the few seats left in the rear, hoping no one would notice him.

Immediately, someone did notice and a whisper spread through the audience. When the first hymn ended, the chaplain asked the audience to be gracious and not let anything disturb the worship. After that, everyone settled down. Lev noticed that Adolf sat nervously, but was relieved that calm prevailed. He had apparently taken Lev's reproof for not attending chapel services. He liked music and perhaps he would remember some of the hymns from childhood. He always claimed to be a Catholic, though he never had a good relationship with the church.

After the services, Lev went up to Hitler to greet him, but additionally to make sure no one created a scene. He was pleased that everyone behaved in a normal manner, though perhaps a bit uncomfortably. The chaplain hurried to the rear with the same thought Lev had in mind. Lev introduced the chaplain to Adolf.

"I encouraged Adolf to attend, so I'm very pleased he is here this morning."

The chaplain replied, "Well, Adolf, you are welcome to worship with us. I hope this will be the happy beginning of many such meetings to come."

Adolf could be charming when he wanted to be. "Thank you, Chaplain, for your kind remarks. I must tell you the music is superb. And you are a very gifted speaker. Thank you for your kind invitation."

Adolf did not wish to visit, fearing that the crowd would gather outside and confront him. He said goodbye to Lev and the chaplain and headed out the door. Lev reminded him as he left, "I will see you shortly."

Adolf just smiled and waved.

Hitler's visit did create a stir. The chaplain reminded everyone that Adolf should be encouraged to be here.

"Being kind to him is not sanctioning his evil past. Please do not create a stir of any kind. We all know his past and so does he. We must remember we meet here daily to strengthen our resolve in walking in the way appointed for us. We all have much to overcome, so let's encourage Adolf to work at overcoming as well."

Upon leaving, Lev wondered whether Adolf had come just to prove him wrong. Perhaps he was hoping for a nasty scene to emerge so he could justify his absence. Whatever the reason, it did take a lot of courage for Hitler to attend a public place of worship. Perhaps, Lev contemplated, he had scored some points in that discussion yesterday after all.

Adolf Greets Him Warmly

After breakfast Lev studied the Scriptures awhile to gain added direction. Then he departed for Adolf's house, wondering if the guests had stayed over. When he arrived he found both automobiles gone; apparently they had left.

Adolf greeted him cordially. "Welcome, Lev! You know you are always welcome. I have not forgotten all the kindness you have shown me. I'm sorry that our visit yesterday turned out a little confrontational. We shall try to do better today."

Lev knew that Adolf could change his demeanor quickly. He was here to encourage Adolf, if possible, to improve himself and join the human family as a respectable, God-fearing human being.

"Thank you, Adolf. I truly want to be a blessing and a help to you. Your lack of progress has been of concern to our leaders in Jerusalem. You know what death is like, but you still do not know what real life is like—I mean perfect life. Death is painless once the dying process is ended. Everyone, by his or her daily life, is tending toward life or death. God has no pleasure in anyone's death. He places life or death before all who return to life and urges them to choose life that they may live."

Adolf asked him to be seated and asked if he could serve him some juice or fruit.

"No thanks, Adolf. I just ate breakfast. I was admiring your artistic skills in your garden. It's much improved over our original layout. I'm glad you find pleasure in gardening."

"Oh, very much! It is different having to do all the work yourself. It was easier when I had gardeners do the work, but I enjoy working in nature. I never cease to be amazed at how efficient and satisfying life is now. Everyone is safe and secure, free from want, illness or hardship of any kind. This present government has powers we never had. I want you to know, Lev, that my friends and I aren't planning any revolt against the present arrangement. We realize we are being governed better than ever before."

"Adolf, are you spending time in the great learning programs available now? Learning is so easy and the whole teaching process is perfect. Added to this, as we eat Eden fruit, all learning disabilities disappear. We can learn so easily that by taking a course you cannot fail to understand and retain it."

"Well, Lev, I had never been a good student in my former years, so I haven't taken advantage of the learning sessions. I have tuned in a few programs and found them informative, but I was never motivated to become a committed student. You know, I love music; and, between gardening and music, I find my present pleasure."

Lev Seizes the Moment

"The music today is extraordinarily beautiful, far better than the best in former years. Music satisfies the mind, and I like it too.

However, we have to learn to be able to contribute to society. This is an age of knowledge, growth, and utility. To meet the goals we have, we need to work intelligently.

"We are learning on a scale unparalleled in history. In the first place, mistakes are not being made in our instructions. In our previous institutions of learning, you learned the prevailing opinions of that time and place. Being popular and accepted was all that mattered. Most things did not have to be right, as long as they were accepted by the prevailing opinion. That kind of education was terribly flawed."

"Can we help it if we were not perfect?" Adolf responded somewhat defensively. "I know everyone is exceptionally bright today. If we were that bright before, we could have accomplished much more. We did take good care of our bright people."

"Well, I'm sure you took care of your bright people, hoping you could use their brains to improve your military machine. I can't praise you for that. Selfishness motivated much of what the nations did."

"Yes, but we were in competition then. Germans felt the heel of oppression on their necks. We knew what it was to have world markets closed to our industry. We were forced to print 'MADE IN GERMANY' on all our products. At first the label denoted inferior quality, but soon Germans turned it into a mark of excellence. We soon wanted to bury our competition instead of just outsell them."

"Ah, my friend," Lev continued. "There was a lot of injustice and exploitation practiced. We can only learn from past mistakes. Competition isn't of God. God has never been in competition with anyone. If He were, we'd be crushed. Jesus never was in competition with anyone. Everything he received came from being obedient to his Heavenly Father. He was given 'all power in heaven and earth.' He never wrested it from anyone.

How Lev wanted to help turn this man's heart to his beloved Father! "Eternal life can only be gained by obeying God. We are in competition with no one. Each of us individually stands or falls before our Creator. All we have to do is reach the mark of perfect love for God and man. Now we have the benefit of Christ as our Mediator. When the thousand years end, we must appear before the bar of God's perfect justice. 'It is a fearful thing to fall into the hands of the living God'" (Hebrews 10:31).

Adolf listened very carefully. Lev could not tell if he was making any impact.

"Thou hast set our iniquities before thee"
(Psalm 90:8).

Chapter Nine

Adolf Begins to Confide in Lev

"Did you enjoy the services at the chapel today, Adolf?"

"Yes, the singing and music were wonderful, and the chaplain seemed very knowledgeable about the Bible. I have never heard such rational teaching. My memories of religious services were a repetition of liturgies no one understood. I must say the chaplain was extraordinarily informative. However, I am still a problem there. I know the main reason I am not attacked is because spiritual forces prevent it. I'm grateful for that.

"I can't say I'll continue visiting the chapel." Adolf was thoughtful. "Perhaps I will, unless I sense my presence is a discomfort to many. Lev, you can go anywhere and everyone loves you. But I'm an object of hatred. Perhaps I deserve it. I realize now more than I did before what havoc I caused to so many for so long. None of that accomplished anything.

"The Jews are in charge of the world despite all that we killed. You know, Lev, part of my problem was that I was possessed of an evil spirit. I felt as though I had cotton in my head all the time. I never felt good. I could be mean or sweet without any explanation. This evil spirit obsessed me—I wasn't my own person. Some say I was possessed by the devil, just as Judas was. I think this may have been true. There was an aura about me that my generals told me they could sense. This evil influence possessed my mind and drove me to do much of what I did. I must tell you, when I was taken to see Jews shot down in large groups, my stomach became upset and I had to turn away. I knew this was brutal, and it was dehumanizing to our troops. I asked our foremost scientists to make our killing process more humane. And they did."

"Well, now you're speaking like a human being." Did Lev dare to be hopeful that Adolf was beginning to think more clearly? "You obviously felt some guilt or shame in what you were doing."

"I didn't feel good about it, I can tell you that much. I would get reports of the thousands that died in our camps each week. Sometimes I wished I could be in Austria in a little cottage—painting—away from all of this. But, there I was sitting in the seat of power. Oh, I enjoyed the power, but not everything that went with it. I was a victim of my own fiery preaching. I got into power by blaming the Jews for everything that was wrong with the world. People loved it, so that is what I kept doing.

"I didn't start out killing all the Jews. But once I started this hate machine, it just kept rolling along. Somehow, my mind was locked in on killing the Jews. I knew that what we were doing was wrong. I am not an insensitive man, and yet here I find myself known as one of the world's greatest murderers. I'm mixed up, Lev. I feel full of contradictions. I've never told anyone this before."

A Faint Call for Help

Lev listened intently. For the first time he was hearing a faint call for help. Here was Adolf, admitting he needed to be saved from himself. The once great leader admitted he had lost his way as he led a nation over the precipice, taking millions with him.

Lev asked, "Where do we go from here? I came to tell you that you must change your ways. You must not find fellowship with those who surrounded you unless and until they begin to walk up the "highway of holiness." They weren't good wholesome people then and they still aren't. You didn't allow good people into your circle. You surrounded yourself with 'yes' men who strengthened your weaknesses. Who among your officers dared look you in the eye and say, 'You are wrong to do what you are doing'? No one could dissuade you from your madness because you did away with every sane person. You were under the thumb of an evil spirit. That explains both your success and your failure. You know the devil is the greatest failure of all time, don't you?"

The morning passed and Adolf served lunch. This was extraordinary. When Lev lived with him previously, it was Lev that did the meal preparations. Here Adolf was actually serving and seemingly enjoying offering hospitality to Lev.

He even asked Lev to offer a prayer before they partook. Lev spoke as they ate.

"You know, Adolf, this is the first time you have come down from your lofty pinnacle to the level of a common human being. I must say it is good to see this. Keep it up and you will have a happier future."

"I killed myself once, and sometimes I think I was planning to do it all over again by being contrary. Maybe that's just the way I am. I hurt everybody that I loved or befriended. Even Eva has cooled toward me."

"I have been sent here to remind you that you may still choose life or death. It's your decision, Adolf. I have always tried to encourage you to choose life. I want to love you as my friend, but so far you have a heavy burden to carry. You must live down the evil you have done. You will never do it by rationalizing that this was something of the past that you couldn't help. You must take responsibility for it. You must not only admit your sins—but you must also give yourself to humanity in good works to show that you love your fellow man. You must change or nothing will happen. If nothing happens, you are doomed to failure. It's that simple."

"Lev, you make it sound so easy."

"I know it's not easy. I was a Jew who didn't need Christ. That change wasn't easy, but I did change and now I serve the Lord Christ. We all have the ability to exercise our will. You are just as capable as I was to will in accordance with righteousness. There is nothing to stop you from overcoming except yourself. Your love for mankind must be demonstrated in decisive action."

"Lev, I wish I could be like that. Thank you for reaching out to me. I knew I was going in the wrong direction. At times, death does seem to be my destiny and I think, why fight it? I have confided my problems to you, a Jew, of all people."

Lev smiled. "You know that 'salvation is of the Jews.' Here we are, you, the greatest Jew killer of all times, confiding in a Jew, trying to find a ray of hope."

They both smiled at the irony of the situation. "I will be leaving soon. Here is my phone number. If you need me, call any hour of the day or night. I have a personal interest in seeing you turn around and head up the "highway of holiness."

"Well, thanks, Lev, but I wouldn't think of intruding upon you."

An Unexpected Visitor

The conversation was interrupted by a loud knock. Adolf hesitated, so Lev rose to answer. There stood one of the men he had recognized at the chapel meeting.

"Come in Mr. Smultz. What is the purpose of your visit?"

He looked very upset. "I'm here to see Hitler. I'm a German who was tortured to death by Adolf's men in a concentration camp. I was accused of criticizing the Fuehrer. While I didn't like what was happening in Germany, I did nothing to betray our country. I spoke out on occasion, wishing to return to the rule of law that we had under the Weimar Republic. The Gestapo seized me and without a trial took me away to be tortured to death. Do you want to know how I died, Adolf?"

"Well, I can assure you that I did not order your death," Hitler exclaimed. "However, our country was at war, and we needed the support of every German. If my men abused you, I apologize."

"No, they did not abuse me. They tortured me to death. If you don't want to know how I died, I'll tell you anyway. I had a wire tied around my body, and I was hung up that way until I died. I was gagged, bound and hung until gangrene set in and I died. The pain was unbearable and constant until I lost consciousness and died."

Adolf Confronts His Past

Adolf turned pale and was visibly shaken. "I didn't know what went on there. I regret my men did such awful things."

Mr. Smultz sat there trembling with uncontrolled emotions. Finally, he said, "Adolf, you've caused so much pain that it is excruciating to even look you in the eye and know that you are breathing. You not only killed millions of Jews, but Gypsies, Poles, Russians, Germans and God only really knows who else! There are probably not many men in history that are greater murderers than you. No, you didn't kill us with your bare hands, but you engaged a massive killing machine — one that was cruel and relentless and without a shred of compassion or decency. How can you live with yourself? You are a monster, inhuman and ruthless."

Then turning to Lev, he continued. "Why in God's name do you, a decent upright man, stay with this notorious murderer? Why did you bring him to the chapel meetings? Hitler deserves to die a million deaths. That wouldn't even begin to pay for his crimes against humanity. Not one day since I returned to life have I forgotten what was done to me. The pain lives like a sword in my body. Then I hear others tell me stories of what was done to them. It's too gruesome to even talk about."

Lev found himself almost speechless. He could feel the mental anguish and agony of this poor tortured soul reliving the horrors he had endured. Finally, he said, "No one should have endured what you experienced. The hearing of it makes me sick. Mr. Smultz, if killing Adolf could undo the past, perhaps the Ancients would consent to it. Remember, Christ has given you your life again. It is a life surrounded with peace and beauty. No one can hurt you anymore. Yes, you have nightmares remembering the savages who took pleasure in your pain and humiliation. Yes, Adolf is guilty in all that transpired then. I do not lift one finger in his defense. That is what he was—an evil murderer that would stop at nothing. He engaged his underlings to do his dirty work, so he thought the blood was not on his hands. It was, nonetheless. I am very glad you stopped by to confront Adolf. He has been using his home like a fortress wishing to hide from his past. What do you have to say to your fellow Aryan German, Adolf?"

Adolf was trembling as he faced just one moment of his heinous past.

"What can I say to justify myself and my former actions? It was wrong, very, very wrong. If God had left me in the grave, it would be just. I don't deserve to live again. I freely confess this. Yet, I am here. I have no magic wand to undo what I did. In that time and place I was drunk with power. Anyone who criticized me was to be killed and tortured. Once evil comes into power, it becomes brutal and ruthless. Did I know I was causing pain and suffering everywhere? Yes. Did I care? No. I was drunk with power. I thought I would be emperor of a great Third Reich with the world at my feet. I would allow nothing to deter me from attaining that dream of mine. People were just pawns to be used to reach my goal. You, sir, were just a thorn in my side that I needed to be rid of. Can you understand that my men needed to be ruthless to suppress everyone that stood in my way?"

The End Justified the Means

Adolf continued, "The end justified the means. That has been the justification for every evil in the world. I was no exception. I dreamed of a glorious Third Reich that would last a thousand years with the glory and honor of the nations pouring into it. The good would always come later. However, this was a good that never came. It was an illusion that masked the evil being done. There is no way I can justify what my henchmen and I did. How often I wish I had become a successful painter. I would have lived a common life and the temptations that possessed me would never have been there. I would just be a little man in a big world and not the mystical Fuehrer that I had become."

Lev interjected, "Mr. Smultz, nothing that anyone can say is going to satisfy your heart. You were unjustly condemned and cruelly destroyed by an evil force. The power behind Adolf was Satan himself. Just as Satan entered Judas, so he entered Adolf. Just as Judas opened his heart to Satan, so Adolf made his deal with the devil. Did he not know that evil would result? Of course, he did. However, when the devil shows you all the kingdoms of this world and their glory, and offers them to you with only little strings attached, few take the strings seriously. Adolf did not get all the kingdoms of this world as he had gambled. However, he did perform very well for Satan by killing off millions of Jews. Satan knew that the Kingdom of God would be established with the Jews in Israel and that Zion would be the ruling seat of authority. He tried to prevent this from happening, but it failed. Neither Adolf nor the devil succeeded in getting what they wanted. They did succeed in leaving a trail of death and blood. All Adolf got was miserable defeat and the need to take a poison pill along with putting a bullet in his head. He could not face the world then, and he is having a hard time facing it now."

Lev continued, "But according to God's divine plan, the devil did not succeed in destroying the Jews! No. Did he prevent the birth of the nation of Israel? No. Did he try again to do the same thing, when he gathered all the nations of the world to Jerusalem, to take the Holy City and to offer his second final solution of the Jews? Yes, but that is when the devil overplayed his hand. Oh, he succeeded in deceiving the nations using both church and state to gather the nations to Armageddon. But that is where the devil and his deceived followers met their Waterloo. His forces were destroyed completely. The Jews now possess the Holy City, and the Kingdom of God is set up in Jerusalem. The law of Christ comes from Mt. Zion in Jerusalem. 'Salvation is of the Jew.' Not one word of God can fail without fulfillment. Where is the devil now? He is in the abyss, unable to function anywhere in the universe until the thousand years are ended.

"Look at me, Mr. Smultz," Lev asserted. "I died fighting the forces sent by the churches and the nations combined. We were a handful of soldiers trying to fend off the combined armies of the world. It seemed hopeless, but we fought anyway. The first day our enemies were successful. I was prepared to die that day in battle, but when

I was fatally wounded I couldn't believe it had happened to me. I thought that with my death our cause would go down in defeat. Little did I know that on the following day the Lord would destroy the devil's forces that were assembled. They were the most deceived people—deceived no less by the churches and governments in their nefarious mission."

Mr. Smultz nodded, "I know the armies of the world were destroyed in Israel. I have been told that literally the whole assemblies of forces were miraculously destroyed. However, I didn't understand that Satan met his limit along with the churches. I was told that the people turned on the churches, and it was a terrible time of anarchy in the world. Yes, I know that Satan was taken in chains and cast into the abyss. That is where he is now, thank God."

Truth Required

Lev continued, "Now there is no more deception. Even Adolf is not permitted to lie."

"How does it feel now, Adolf, to be not only out of power but to be unwanted in this world?" Mr. Smultz asked.

Poor Adolf spoke quietly. "Mr. Smultz, I have never been a happy man. I was disappointed in love. I was a failure in my early life. And even when I came to power, it was fleeting and I was obsessed with staying at the top. I knew that the men who surrounded me would not hesitate to take my place if they could. They were all seeking power wherever and however they could find it. I could not acknowledge my mistakes. I left five hundred thousand of my best troops to die at Stalingrad. My generals all told me to withdraw them, but I was convinced the city would fall to us. I condemned these soldiers to death by not allowing them to retreat. They died in a cold and terrible winter surrounded by Russians. They almost all suffered cold, hunger, despair and finally death. Yes, I think of these men. Now they are all back again and they all probably hate me as you do, Mr. Smultz."

Lev added, "Let's not forget that Christ is going to mete out justice. All the evil that men have done that they did not pay for in their former life will become a source of pain and sorrow to them now. Adolf would like a magic wand to erase his past and take up life like other people who lived sane and honest lives. However, just as Adolf must try to live down his past and show the world he is seeking a new heart of flesh, so all those who suffered under his evil rule must learn to forgive his unspeakable brutality."

"How can I forgive this man and his assassins for what they did to me, much less all the pain and suffering he inflicted on millions of people?" Mr. Smultz shouted.

Lev spoke firmly. "Mr. Smultz, do you think Hitler could have done all this by himself? He was surrounded with war-crazed supporters who would stop at nothing. They were as demented as Hitler. All of them were deceived and tangled in a web of evil that no one could believe possible. How could a whole nation believe they could conquer the world? Did anyone think of the price that would have to be paid in human sacrifice? When the allies had one thousand bombers over Germany every day, there was gloom over the nation. The thousand pound bombs by day and the blockbusters by night brought death to thousands; maiming, blinding and tormenting those who cheered when war was declared. The German people paid a price, as did the top brass of Germany. That war brought a nightmare on earth to millions of people."

Mr. Smultz was not to be sidetracked from his singular experience.

"Lev, I know that war is brutal and millions suffered and died because of it. I am not talking about war in my case. I would have been willing to fight on the battlefield and even die there—millions of men have done so. Those are the fortunes of war. If they had killed me with a gun, I would not be here confronting Hitler. It was the cruelty of my death; the searing pain of hanging from a wire, not for an hour or a day, but until death finally came. Oh, blessed death. Hitler tells me of his unhappiness. What does he know of real pain such as I endured? What does he care? He looked the other way when I died. In that same room in which I hung, his Gestapo had other men in similar positions. What does he know of such pain? They knew what they were doing was wrong, however, no one showed us any mercy."

Adolf shuddered in horror. "Mr. Smultz, how can I make up to you for what my evil followers did to you? When I heard reports of torture, I didn't like it. However, once an evil piece of machinery began to function, I could not stop it. Supposedly, these men were doing all of these evil things for the glory of Germany. I could not show myself ungrateful. In my heart of hearts I regretted it, but I was not strong enough to do the right thing. I myself am amazed how evil flourished without any encouragement on my part. Please understand me."

The once-tortured man could not seem to let go of his bitterness. "I could not wish on any human being what happened to me. I could not even wish it upon you, Hitler. If anyone deserves it, you surely would. However, I could not have pleasure in seeing even you tortured as I was," replied Mr. Smultz. "It is too cruel for any man to endure. I confess, I am amazed how cruel human beings can really be. I could not believe such cruelty was possible, except that it happened to me. Dear God, why me?"

Hitler sat there with his head bent low. From this personal exchange, he could feel the pain he caused as never before. He could not dismiss it with a shrug of his shoulders. He was facing the man who endured unspeakable pain and humiliation. Death was a kindness compared to this man's suffering. Hitler had both hands on his face while his sins were paraded before him. He was obviously very uncomfortable and found no defense for himself and nowhere to hide. He struggled to keep tears from overflowing those well-known brown eyes.

Finally, he choked, "Mr. Smultz, what do you want me to do? I cannot undo the pain I caused you. I am in a very troubled place. My sins have all come back to haunt me, and I have no excuse and no way out of my dilemma. What do you want from me? Saying 'I'm sorry' is meaningless in the face of such pain I brought on you. A thousand apologies wouldn't ease your pain. Yet, you are too kind to want me hung as you were on a wire. What can I do for you, Mr. Smultz?"

Adolf Grapples With His Crimes

Lev found this discussion somewhat of a breakthrough. For the first time Adolf was faced with his crime. Talking of millions of deaths did not work. The mind glazes over when one speaks in terms of millions. Mobs reviling him had little effect. However, hearing one man telling of his suffering and excruciating pain was something to which Hitler could relate. He felt this man's suffering, and it penetrated all his defenses. He found himself helpless in excusing himself. Clearly, now he was having afterthoughts that were uncomfortable.

Mr. Smultz answered, "You cannot undo the past. What was done is done. I know that. Thanks to Christ, I am alive and well and happy. It is just that I shudder every time I think of my past. I cannot forget it. I awaken with cold sweat at night reliving that awful time. The calloused faces looking at me suffering, some laughing at my pain—the heartless cursing I endured along with the unbearable pain that seemingly never ended—leaves me weak and trembling. I cried out to God in vain, but there was no one to help anywhere, no pity and no relief. Only death, sweet death, finally, at last, ended my agony."

Lev again tried to bring some understanding to this discussion.

"What happened to you seems to have come from an evil spirit world. Evil spirits and Satan are much more cruel than men. They have no regard whatever for such human suffering. All the demon religions were unbelievably cruel. They required human sacrifices, and human torture was common. Satan had our Lord Jesus crucified, a most painful death. Do you think Satan cared one bit about your pain, Mr. Smultz? Certainly he did not. Once men enlist under his banner they cease to be human beings. This is the only way I can understand the cruelty you were subjected to."

Finally, Mr. Smultz replied to Adolf, "Yes, there is something you can do. I know you cannot undo the past. You have had a clear connection with evil and evil forces that you must renounce. You must join the human race and Christ. I do not know how you can change from a snake like Satan into a noble human being. That seems an impossible transformation to accomplish, but if Christ brought you to life again he must also provide some way of escape from your evil past. I could forgive you if indeed you were transformed into a caring human being."

With that he stood up, "I have told you my story and hope that I was able to burn into your mind the evil of what just one man suffered under your reign of terror. If every human that suffered under your rule could do the same, perhaps you could grasp the enormity of your crimes against humanity. I am afraid that you will insulate yourself from your past. If so, that will be your downfall. Good day."

He arose quickly, moving toward the door. He turned to Lev and said, "I know you have been assigned here by the Ancients, so I apologize for impugning your association with Adolf. Never have such noble and good people ruled before in human history. I dare not question their wisdom or fairness in sending you here. Please forgive me, Lev."

"Mr. Smultz, no apology is necessary. You are a man who has dreadful memories. No one should have suffered as you did, and I could feel your pain even now. Thank you for coming. Maybe this will help Hitler realize the enormity of his crimes. If he does not start facing up to them now, it might be too late."

Adolf Trembles

Lev had never seen Hitler tremble so. His face was ashen. He arose slowly from his seat and entered his room, closing the door behind him. He did not even appear for supper. Lev decided to head home. If this day did not get Adolf to see himself as the monster he had been, he probably would be less likely to accept another moment of truth. Lev could see that Hitler was in a crisis. Hitler did not know whether to reach upward or to harden his heart and refuse any true reformation.

If he could find some explanation to justify his former actions and make people believe that he was not so evil after all, he might find the courage to go on. It was extremely difficult to be a marked man. He had made the Jews carry a mark of their Jewishness, but now he was the one marked—not with an armband, but with an evil past that hovered over him relentlessly. Truly this was an age when men's sins followed them, and justice was the standard for which men needed to strive.

Lev left Adolf's home and returned to his residence. He called John the Baptist who answered with exuberance. "Shalom, Lev. How is it going with you and Hitler?"

Lev explained what happened that day and how he felt this was a moment of crisis for Hitler.

"John, I know he was deeply moved. Mr. Smultz broke through his every barrier. Adolf could dismiss hearing about thousands or millions of people, but here was one man with one powerful story that he could not deny or fail to understand. He was powerless to defend himself and never have I seen anyone so uncomfortable. For the first time he faced his evil past squarely. This was a moment of truth in a life full of lies and denial. He went to his room, so I left for the evening. I just wanted you to know that this is the first time I can say he came to grips with his evil past. I will see if he comes to the chapel tomorrow. It will take a lot of courage for him to come out, because there are people who were hurt by him waiting to confront him. If he doesn't come out tomorrow morning, then I think he may be using his home as a hiding place."

"Lev, we will have another assignment for you tomorrow if he does not show up at the chapel. You are absolutely right. If that experience does not make him want to change his heart condition, I fear there is little more that can be done. He may prefer death to life by his actions. However, we will not write him off yet. We do need you for another assignment. We cannot have you wasting time on Hitler if he will not accept all the pain and suffering he must endure in the process of regaining a noble human heart. Call me in the morning. If he does not show at the chapel, I will have you return to Israel for a week's vacation and then we can talk about your new assignment. Shalom, and God bless you."

The following day Lev rose early to take care of household chores. He was anxious to visit the chapel, because he truly needed to worship and praise the Lord. Working with some people took a lot out of him. He wanted to help, but it was so hard sometimes. Hitler would almost get to the point of facing the truth, and then suddenly he slammed the door on communication. Lev knew he would be very disappointed if Hitler didn't appear this morning. It would mean he couldn't face another person whom he had destroyed.

The room at the chapel was full and the worship services were beautiful. Every voice sang from the heart. Lev saw Mr. Smultz there and he nodded when he saw Lev. Lev looked about, sitting in the back purposely, so he would not be conspicuous in turning about. Alas, Hitler did not appear. He hoped that Hitler might slip in a little late; but, no, he wasn't there. It saddened Lev's heart, because Hitler was at a point were he could turn his life around if he willed to. Yes, it would be difficult, but it was not impossible. It was with a heavy heart that Lev realized Hitler lacked the will to change, at least at this time. Lev feared Hitler would sink into a victim complex and spend his days brooding over his past without the will to change from the inside out.

Lev had planned to visit Hitler before leaving, but now felt he had best leave Hitler to himself. Lev arranged for the earliest flight available to Israel. He could hardly wait to return home to his family and friends.

"Shall the throne of iniquity have fellowship with Thee?"
(Psalm 94:20)

Chapter Ten

Lev arrived in Israel with great anticipation of meeting family and friends whom he loved dearly. Stepping off the plane he was pleased to see his son, Allon, and his parents. Allon ran to embrace his dad. Lev's parents hugged him.

"You look fantastic! I could hardly wait to get off the plane to be with you. I can't tell who looks younger or better."

Ariel, Lev's father, said, "It's mutual, Son. What a joy to see you again! We've all been looking forward to your return. We've been so busy with wonderful projects—the world looks a lot different after these years of progress."

Hannah Aron looked so young and beautiful now; no one would have guessed she was Lev's mother. "You must tell us how things went in Japan and about your second visit with Hitler. All I can say is, none of us envied that assignment. We're going to my home to celebrate our reunion. Jacob, Rachel and Annie are there now. There will also be another surprise visitor."

"Wonderful!" Lev exclaimed.

Lev rode with Allon, delighted to see his son. He was still young looking, but he had matured greatly in character. His operations in Ghana had been completed, and the factory was in full production with its own research and development departments. The prosperity it brought to Ghana was unbelievable.

Allon said, "The people in Ghana are so eager to learn and advance. With all the educational opportunities, nothing is holding them back. No more superstition or ignorance. No more exploitation by large corporations or corrupt politicians or military wastefulness. No sick to tend to, no diseases or ailments of any kind. Everyone, outside of little children, is productive in a nation that had been poor and struggling. The wealth of Ghana has magnified a thousandfold. Everyone has his private home and orchard—it's a little paradise now."

"I thought when our factory had reached full production that the Ancients would reassign me. But when the people learned that, they begged the Ancients to keep me on. So I stayed and headed the research and development. Uncle Jake has given me ample leads on projects needing to be developed, so we picked some he wanted to push forward. We've made phenomenal progress. Our research and development has come up with some exciting breakthroughs. Even Uncle Jake was amazed at how well we had done."

A Society without Liabilities

"Yes, Allon," his father beamed with approval. "That's exactly what we need. Never before have so many advances been made and the benefits equally distributed to society. There are no massive failures caused by overproduction and endless competition. This is the kind of world people have dreamed of. With human selfishness and evil so prevalent, it could never be realized before."

They arrived at Hannah's home before long. There to greet them was Jacob, Lev's brother; Rachel, Jacob's former wife; and their daughter Annie. Some time had passed since they had last seen each other and everyone was excited. Soon Ariel and Hannah arrived. There to Lev's surprise and delight he found Rebekah, his former wife and now best friend and favorite person in the world. They embraced each other with a long hug.

With the whole immediate family there for the reunion, they sat down to a delightful meal to celebrate the occasion.

Annie was shining like a star. Lev asked her to report on her work in Brazil with Indian tribes. After supper they retired to the living room, all eyes on Annie.

She seemed so young and innocent when she left on her assignment. Now she had grown into a graceful lady. Her words were wise beyond her years. She was eager to share her experiences.

Annie's Story

"When I arrived in Brazil, the people felt I was a novelty. They knew I came from a powerful nation and that I was more educated than they. They had lived in abject poverty, at least from my viewpoint. However, that is all they had ever known.

"In many ways the Indians were good people, but they were steeped in superstition and ignorance. Some had accepted Christ through missionaries, but they were really ignorant of Christ and his plan for regenerating the whole human race. They had been told that if they accepted Christ they would go to heaven, but if they did not, they would burn in hell's tormenting fires forever. They felt that Christ must be some powerful ruler, but even they could see that something was very wrong here. Christ seemed to them the same as the rulers of the Western world. If you did what they wanted, they would give you some benefits, but if you didn't, you would be driven from your land or killed. While the missionaries were kind and did bring them some schooling and medicine, they knew that after the missionaries, there would be companies seeking to take their land and destroy their way of life."

Annie continued, "As a result, they were a little suspicious of me; and, although I certainly understood, I couldn't easily convince them. But because I was a young woman and seemingly no threat to them, they were finally willing to have me in their company.

"I taught at a little school the missionaries had once used. You know how much I love to teach children. However, they were so poor and undernourished that it broke my heart. The Ancients had arranged to have the trees of Eden planted there to bear fruit in six months to a year. These were now mature trees. They started bearing fruit about the time I arrived. So I gave this fruit to the old and infirmed and those with physical ailments and deformities first.

"Most people were curious about the Eden trees. They feared that there was some kind of magic potion that would dull their senses and make them slaves. However, once they saw the effects of the fruit on their own sick people, they were amazed. They couldn't believe how quickly people began to recover from their illnesses and return to vital health. Soon everyone wanted to eat the Eden fruit. However, I pleaded with them to make it available first to those who needed it most. I promised that soon everyone would have their own orchard of trees and a private dwelling. I even showed them layouts of what their territory would look like once we received their full cooperation."

Mistrust of the White Man

"They were impressed, but didn't have much faith in the white man's promises. I tried to explain that the Ancients and Christ were running the world now. Not one word that they spoke would fail fulfillment. Fortunately, about that time surveyors arrived and began measuring the land for building and planting orchards. They even placed little signs with the names of those to whom the property would belong. This convinced the people that it was no idle promise.

When Eden trees began arriving and they began to plant them in their strategic locations, the people were fully satisfied. I then had no trouble dispensing the fruit of life to those who needed it.

Annie positively glowed with enthusiasm over the whole project. "When the time came to start digging the foundations for private homes, they were like children in Wonderland. A factory had been set up about forty miles away to build housing components. When trucks and planes began delivering materials, I became the job foreman for a while. After we had built four or five homes, they quickly learned how to build the houses with little assistance from me. They had a little trouble understanding electrical components, but they were very eager to learn and willing to take instructions even from their white female instructor. They loved planting the Eden trees and could hardly wait for them to mature.

"We made marvelous progress. Soon everyone had his or her own home with the modern facilities like we have here. They were very happy. I began teaching them how to learn on their modern television screens. Some had to learn to read and write, but many could start learning the sciences on an elementary level. That's when friction began. Some of the younger people were far advanced on the learning scale and some of the old tribal chiefs and witch doctors were the last to learn anything. The witch doctors especially were becoming angry and frustrated. People were no longer sick, and these powerful people found they were no longer needed or wanted in their former roles.

The chiefs also had trouble because they wanted to rule over the community and their rulership was no longer needed or welcome. They understood least what was happening in this transition. They found their positions being threatened, and they didn't like it one bit. They used to exercise authority and if anyone failed to obey them they were punished, sometimes even put to death. Here is where my trouble really started."

Jealousy at Work

"What happened?" Allon could hardly contain his interest.

"The witch doctors perceived me as the source of their troubles. They tried using their voodoo curses on me. In my home I would find dolls picturing me with nails driven through the heart. I wasn't afraid because I knew they were powerless to do the evil that was in their hearts, but at first I felt a mixture of amusement and sadness for their lack of understanding. I tried to talk to them, but they wouldn't look me in the eye, nor did they even smile at me. I knew I was an object of their hatred, and they engaged the old chiefs to support their opposition toward me. Instead of trying to learn and enlarge their understanding of the world, they retreated into their dark superstitions.

"Witchcraft was dead, and try as they would they couldn't revive it. They found themselves being dismissed as old ignorant men by their own people. I was so naïve about these things. I was used to intelligent respect for true virtue and knowledge. Here was a class craving the days where they could use black magic and physical force to dominate others. I tried to explain that this was a thing of the past. Now Christ ruled with justice and love. That's *not* what they wanted to hear.

"Fortunately, most people were overjoyed with the progress they were making. No one really wanted to go back to little huts and impoverished ways of life. Soon no one was sick. The Eden trees started producing enough fruit for everyone before long. This helped greatly, because even the chiefs and witch doctors felt the genuine affects of Eden fruit. They were amazed at how easy it was to learn. However, as they grew a little smarter, they began plotting against me. They believed that I somehow had taken away their respect and power among the people."

Annie held them fascinated as she continued. "I sensed that they were planning something against me. They knew they could not hurt me physically. Some of them had tried to strike their fellows when angry and found an arm or two paralyzed. When the witch doctors couldn't heal them, I called the Ancients. This made them furious. I could talk on the phone and soon they would be healed. They couldn't accept being demoted in this way.

"They said they wanted me to go with them to help one of their members who had been injured. I would have to go down the river in a boat with them to reach this person who was back in the jungles. I said I could call in an airplane if the river was wide enough to land on, but they claimed it was too narrow and dangerous for an airplane to land. They wanted me to go there and heal the man. I told them I didn't have healing powers. Only the Ancients could arrange for his healing. They were so insistent that I go with them as a white doctor that I finally listened to them."

Annie had everyone at the edge of his seat. "I begrudgingly went with them in their small canoe. The river was full of snakes and crocodiles and all kinds of the old predatory creatures. Almost instinctively, I was afraid of them, but I knew that 'nothing could hurt or destroy in all his holy kingdom,' so I ignored my fears.

"At the end of the day we stopped to make camp for the night. I thought this was strange, because they said it was a day's journey. However, I had taken some fruit along and had my supper while they ate fish they had caught. I made myself a bed of leaves and went to sleep for the night. The fire soon burned low; and, when I awakened, I felt strangely alone. These men had all left during the night in the canoe, leaving me alone in the jungle. At first I was terrified. I waited quietly till daybreak. I had entered a baited trap. They were determined to lose me in the jungle. However, I had taken a knife and ax along in case I needed to make splints. I still had a few pieces of fruit. I decided to eat one fruit for breakfast and save the other until supper."

The entire family cried, "How brilliant, Annie!"

"I thought at first I could follow the river bank, but it was too marshy to walk along. Fortunately, Christ had given me a keen sense of direction. While I was not familiar with the territory, I decided to go inland about a mile, and see if I could then parallel the river in its general direction. I prayed fervently before starting my journey. I didn't know if all the wild animals were changed from being carnivores yet, and I still feared snakes and most cold-blooded creatures. I knew enough not to drink the water and my canteen was almost empty. I remembered hearing how the natives would chop down a certain plant and drink its water. I remembered having this plant shown to me once, so I kept an eye out for it. Sure enough, I saw the plant. I took my little hatchet and cut it quickly and lifted it to my mouth to catch the water. It didn't taste particularly good, but it was water and wouldn't make me sick. I not only secured a good drink, but also was able to add about a half cup to my canteen. I saw some large snakes, but none bothered me. I managed to keep on course, and from a little rise I saw the river to my left."

Nightfall in the Jungles

Whenever Annie paused, everyone urged her to continue.

"I knew I would have to spend another night in the jungle, because you can't make good time walking through all the trees and plants. I found a place where I decided to bed down. I cut a lot of large leaves and leaned against a huge tree. I had my last piece of fruit, but that satisfied me for the night. It was hot and sticky, and I heard all the night animals and birds everywhere around me. I prayed more earnestly than ever that night. Soon I fell asleep, awakening at night to see the eyes of some large animal in the moonlight looking at me. But it just walked away. I was so tired from walking all day that I fell asleep again not waking till first light. I figured I had about another day's journey, perhaps less, to make it back home. I remembered that the riverbank was less swampy further up river, so I decided to move back toward the river. After my morning prayer, I started out again, singing hymns to comfort myself. I got to the river when the sun rose, and I found I could move a little faster. However, I remembered the crocodiles and decided to stay about fifty yards from its banks.

"Thankfully, I found another plant from which I was able to get another drink. This time I was able to get about a cup of water into my canteen. At noon I sensed I was getting nearer home. I didn't want to spend another night in the jungle, so I didn't pause to rest. I kept moving closer to the river. Suddenly I saw a big crocodile not more than twenty feet from me. He looked at me and opened his jaws. I froze. I knew I couldn't outrun him in the open. I found a branch above my head and was prepared to lift myself up in the event that he would charge. However, the crocodile decided to slither back toward the river. Apparently, the animals are beginning to come under human dominion as the Lord had promised. I then proceeded more confidently on my journey. Soon I came to a riverside clearing I recognized as one I had seen on our journey downstream the previous day. I knew now that I was within an hour from home.

"From there I pressed on. About four o'clock in the afternoon I saw my home site and all the lovely houses and orchards. It was so beautiful that I shouted for joy. Soon a crowd of people gathered around me. They hugged me and offered me fruit juice to drink and food to eat. It all tasted so good. I then inquired about the men that had left me in the jungles. They had all returned; but, as soon as they arrived, each one lost the use of both arms. These were the two witch doctors and one chief who had deceived me. Apparently they were allowed to do this so they would learn a lesson. I asked if I could see them. I was told they didn't wish to see me if I returned, but I told my friends to relay the message to them that they would not be healed unless I saw them. However, I would wait until they wanted to be healed before I would see them.

"About two days passed before I received a call to visit my abductors. When I came to the home of the first witch doctor he was ashamed to see me. He begged me to forgive him. I said to him, 'You intended evil to come to me, but it has instead come to you. The guardian angels permitted this to teach you a lesson. I was protected on my journey home. You were all punished for your wicked plot. However, there is forgiveness from Christ. You will have to speak to the Ancients. You must tell the whole truth of your wicked plot to them. They will know whether you tell the truth or not. Nothing is hidden from them. They will heal you quickly if you tell the truth, but if you try to deceive them you will continue without the use of your arms.'

"Once he understood matters clearly, I phoned the offices of the Ancients, and then turned the phone over to the former witch doctor. He told the truth from what I could hear, and he was promised the use of his arms by nightfall. I followed through with all the men who had conspired against me. They all were ashamed of themselves and each begged my forgiveness.

"That evening when they were all healed, they came to my home to again beg my forgiveness and to thank me for their healing. They had thought that this plan of theirs would restore them to power, but instead the people were very angry with them and they lost the respect of their fellows. I knew that the Lord had overruled in this matter to end a festering problem. This experience made them realize they must amend their ways, and they actually became my best friends and supporters after this. I spent extra time teaching them how to use the instructional courses on their television screens. As they were able to eat from the Eden trees, they began to grow mentally. Soon they realized the witchcraft they had practiced was of the demons and were ashamed of their past. Even the chief began to act like a normal human being, and stopped looking for respect and power that he didn't deserve."

Annie Concludes Her Story

Everyone breathed a sigh of relief as Annie finished her story. It was plain to all of them that the struggle of the great regeneration process was going to be fought against entrenched evil in the human heart. It was inescapable that, as people returned to life, they would be bringing with them all their prejudices, hatreds, meanness and wicked propensities. They would also bring with them all the beauties of character that they had attained in their former life. God's ways were equal. It was going to take much effort to regain ground that was lost in sin and evil practices. There was no magic wand to give them beautiful characters. Such character was dearly won by effort and discipline under the mighty hand of Christ.

It was getting late so they decided to return to their homes. Lev asked Rebekah if he could walk her home and she gladly accepted. It was a beautiful evening—the moon was shining brightly and the stars were in their glory. They were so happy for the day's experiences.

Lev said, "That little Annie had us spellbound. I can see why they love her in Brazil. She is such a brave girl. I guess I still thought of her as the child I used to know. She has grown so mature and wise for her years."

"I understand she's going back to open a factory, to build a manufacturing site for the production of clothing. The people are crazy about her! Soon they'll have plenty of clothing to receive all their lost ones to life again. The further back they go, they'll be bringing back some pretty savage people. It will sure be interesting!"

When they arrived at Rebekah's, she invited him in for tea and cookies. Lev wanted the extra time with his best friend, so he stayed to chat with her awhile. He loved every moment with Rebekah, the one with whom he freely shared his innermost feelings. Rebekah told him of her work in horticulture and how the Lord had staggered the maturing season for the Eden trees into twelve seasons.

"This is what gives us trees bearing luscious fruit all year around. We don't have to store, freeze or dry these fruits to have them out of season. There are always some trees in season full of luscious fruit. Only God could make such benevolent plans."

Lev hated the thought of being separated from her, but it was way past midnight and they had a full day ahead. After a good night hug, Lev said goodbye. He walked home looking up at the beautiful starlit heavens, thanking the Lord for the many blessings of the day.

The family had agreed to meet at the chapel the next morning for worship and fellowship. Everyone welcomed them with open arms, and each member of the Aron family was asked to give a testimony of their service activities. The audience listened intensely to their reports. They rejoiced to hear of the world gradually becoming like the Garden of Eden. Gradually the cleansing arrangements would wash the human race of its sinful propensities and return them to the image of God.

Relaxing at the Dead Sea

After the morning services, the family returned to Hannah's home for breakfast. They planned to visit some friends and neighbors and have a picnic day at the Dead Sea, which was no longer dead.

Ezekiel 47:8, 9 was now fulfilled where it had been prophesied that the waters from Ezekiel's Temple would issue "out toward the east country, and go down into the desert, and go into the sea: which being brought forth into the sea, the waters shall be healed. And it shall come to pass, that every thing that liveth, which moveth, whithersoever the rivers shall come, shall live: and there shall be a very great multitude of fish, because these waters shall come thither: for they shall be healed; and everything shall live whither the river cometh."

They had wanted to spend a day at the Dead Sea (its old name having been retained as a memorial to the amazing changes that had come about on earth) but were always too busy to visit it as a family. Driving toward Jerusalem, they first went to the Temple's Golden Gate to witness the stream of water issuing forth from it. The water was as clear as crystal and gushed from under the gate toward the east, descending through the dry valley, dropping hundreds of feet until finally reaching the Dead Sea. From the Temple Mount they could see the flowing of sparkling water gushing downward. Trees grew on either side of the stream. The view was spectacular!

They then drove down to the sea, arriving in time for a picnic lunch. They thought they would taste the water, remembering when it was so salty that a person could literally sit upon the water without sinking. Nothing had been able to survive in all that salt. But now it was clear as crystal and everyone said it was fresh and sparkling and delicious. As they sat enjoying their meal, they watched the waters swarming with all kinds of fish. Because the water was so pure and clean, the fish were clearly visible. Having known what the Dead Sea had been like before, they couldn't contain their excitement. It seemed the fish enjoyed the water from the Temple as much or more than they did.

The family decided to cool off with a swim, as it was very hot so far below sea level. The fish scattered as anyone neared them; but because they were so abundant, they were easily touched if the swimmer stood still long enough.

Rebekah and Lev decided to swim out far from shore—they were both excellent swimmers. The panoramic view was even more breathtaking from a distance. Jake and Rachel decided to swim out to them, and soon everyone joined. Everyone was so relaxed and refreshed. It was a day of much needed pleasure without problem solving or confrontations of human relationships.

Vacation Cut Short

Soon it was time to head back home. They arrived later in the evening and had supper together at Hannah's. Everyone then headed home to rest for the next day.

However, when Lev arrived home he found a message waiting for him from John the Baptist. He wished to see Lev at Jerusalem the following morning. Although time with his family was precious, he had pledged his unconditional support to those in authority and would fulfill his pledge at any cost. Actually, Lev thoroughly enjoyed his opportunities of service.

Allon said he could walk everywhere he needed to go the next day so Lev could use his car. Lev arose extra early, wondering what lay ahead. After the morning devotions and breakfast at Hannah's, Lev bade his family farewell and left for Jerusalem.

Lev arrived with about twenty minutes to spare for his appointment with John the Baptist and whoever else might be at the meeting. Everyone at the offices knew him already and welcomed him as an old friend. Soon Lev was called into a room with three Ancients— John the Baptist, Moses and Abraham. This was Lev's first visit with Moses, who had lived such a legendary life in Bible times. All the men were like the salt of the earth, seasoning it with wisdom and healing properties, some of the greatest men that had ever lived. Lev thought it must be an important assignment to command such an impressive body of Ancients.

A Man of the Cloth

This time Moses spoke to Lev first.

"Lev, you have never met me, but I have learned of your faithful service to our King. We commend you and thank you. Now we are asking you to take a most difficult assignment. Having Hitler to deal with was hard enough, but now you will have to deal with a former man of the cloth, thought to be holy by many, who still commands respect in certain circles. This man is similar to the religious leaders of Jesus' day. They appeared holy and righteous, but they were hypocrites and lacked the true virtues. They played religious politics and corrupted themselves in the process. You know, Lev, religion was the cause of much brutality and war. These men could appear to represent God; but, in fact, they served Satan very well.

"We do not need you to build his home or anything like that. This man came from a stable family, and he has his own home and is living very graciously—probably not as graciously as in the day when he was in office, but still very comfortably. He has strong family ties and many of his family members wish to see him retain the prestige he once enjoyed. On the other hand, many people remember all the evil that happened under his supervision. They would like to send him to Siberia, or some place less comfortable, if possible! This is creating quite a stir and we need you to pour oil on the troubled waters.

"This man did not perform evil in the same way officers in the Third Reich did, with blood all over their hands. His fault was that he remained silent while others murdered millions of people. Yet, he could be quite forthright in defending the interests of his church. He did not have the personal power to directly do evil or good, but because he had countless millions of devout followers, the political rulers could not ignore him or mistreat him without facing the anger of his loyal subjects."

John the Baptist added, "Make no mistake; this man bore greater responsibility than officers responsible for World War II. He was supposed to represent Christ, but by his actions he was in league with sinister forces. Yet, he succeeded in making the people believe he was a saint. If he had been a saint he would not now be in Italy. He would be in heaven. However, no door in heaven was open to him. He was earthbound and was not entitled to any special privileges or to be recognized as a representative of Christ. There is tremendous pressure being exerted to make this man a chaplain because of his former prestige and the fact that he had been rather talented in the past. At the same time, this man needs help if he is going to change into a true man of God. He does have God-fearing qualities, but needs to step down from the lofty positions he once commanded to be a man of low estate. He might be able to make it if he gets over his love for prominence and power. He should spend time building homes and planting orchards—that might clear his mind."

"Here Am I, Send Me"

When a lull occurred, Lev responded just as the faithful men of old had, "'Here I am, send me.' However, you know because I am a Jew, I'm not on the most-loved list. He will probably suspect that you sent me and will deal with me as a necessary evil to be endured, but not loved. I must tell you that I can't stand hypocrisy. I might find myself being a little short with him."

Moses said, "He needs someone to stand eyeball to eyeball with him, and not flinch. He respects power and brilliance, even though he cannot be accused of being sympathetic toward Jews. We know you are wise and kind in your dealings. Even Hitler came to respect you, if not even to like you a little bit. Your Jewishness was hard to swallow, but he managed to do it. We have discussed this among ourselves and we agree, you are the man for the job, Lev. If you are willing, you will leave for Italy tomorrow morning. Are you prepared to accept this assignment?"

"I'll be ready for what comes."

With that said, the three legendary men stood up and shook Lev's hand. "May God bless you on this mission. Pray for wisdom from above, Lev, for you will need it dearly. Shalom, friend." Lev felt a little shaky inside.

When he entered his vehicle for the return home, he took their advice and prayed for wisdom and strength for his new mission. He didn't feel sufficient for the task. Christ could strengthen him and give the help and succor he would need. These men of the cloth would know that he had been assigned to Hitler, so they might suspect that he was there for a special purpose. However, he didn't wish to disappoint the Ancients and Christ.

The Ancients knew that some men of the cloth were trying to recreate the past by taking control of the present. They needed to renounce their past and turn their attention to helping their fellow man in a self-forgetting way. Once people got a taste of power it was hard to wean them from the love of it.

Lev spent the remaining hours of the evening studying the Book of Acts. He was interested in following the experiences of the Apostle Paul as he bore witness to the truth and how badly the religious leaders treated him at that time. Lev knew that his own experiences wouldn't be nearly as difficult as Paul's had been.

*"God looked down from heaven upon the children of men,
To see if there were any that did understand, that did seek God"
(Psalm 53:2).*

Chapter Eleven

Arriving in Rome

The next day, Lev arrived in Rome and secured a loaner car to go to a new home that was waiting for its occupant to return to life. His visit had not been announced, but those who had built the house were most gracious about having him live there for awhile. They could not do enough to make Lev feel comfortable. Old Mediterranean hospitality was still in their hearts, and it was precious.

Lev had not been given any introduction, so his visit was unannounced and his purpose in being there was even more closely guarded. He was given the names and addresses of several former prominent prelates established in the religious community. These men had lived before Jerusalem was attacked at Armageddon. When the armies of the world were destroyed, the recent religious leaders faced the wrath of angry mobs, and most of them had died. When these men returned to life, they eagerly remained out of sight, keeping a low profile.

However, the prelates Lev was to see had lived in Europe before and after World War II. They had not fallen from power, but maintained their high offices throughout that Great War and after it. When they returned to life, they had strong family ties and friends who still held them in high esteem. Being out of power was almost a form of persecution to them, and they used their cunning to invent some excuse for religious prominence.

The afternoon of Lev's arrival, after he had settled in his temporary home, he decided to take a walk. He knew he lived in the vicinity of several of the prelates of the church, so he memorized their addresses. Actually, he was only about a quarter mile from one, and it was right on the way to several small manufacturing sites. As Lev passed this home, he saw the prelate doing a little work on his front lawn. As Lev passed he waved and asked if this was the road to a certain site. The smiling prelate stood up and came over to Lev.

Lev Meets Eustus

"You must be a stranger here."

"Well, yes, I am. I just arrived today and I'm here for a visit. I happened to be looking for a site that manufactures electronic components. I was told it was just down the road."

"Yes, you're going the right way. My name is Eustus and I'm always glad to welcome visitors. What might be the purpose of your visit?"

"My name is Lev. I'm sorry I didn't introduce myself. I was going to check in with that electronics site and see if I could be of any help. Do you, by chance, work there?"

Eustus picked up on Lev's name. "You aren't Lev Aron, by chance, are you?"

"Well, yes. How did you know my name?"

"I have heard of the great work you did in Germany and other parts of the world. You are highly regarded."

Lev repeated his question. "Do you work at the site down the road by any chance?"

"No, I had been a religious man in my previous life, so when I awakened to life again, I didn't think I had any training for such things. I prefer to deal in spiritual matters. However, I know we all need some of these temporal things."

"Perhaps we will meet at the chapel in the morning. I plan to attend there as I enjoy spiritual things and especially clear biblical teachings. The nearest chapel is down the road in the opposite way I have been going, I understand. Is that where you go?"

Lacking Credentials

He was taken back by Lev's question. Clearing his throat, he said, "Well, I do not attend that service. I went there a few times and I was totally ignored. I wasn't even asked to offer prayer. The chaplain is a fine person, but lacks some of the credentials that a man of the cloth should have."

"What kind of credentials should he have? If he teaches the truth of God's Word, what more credentials does one need?"

"My dear Mr. Aron, I do not mean any disrespect of this gentleman. I am sure he is a good man. However, some members of that congregation have wanted some variations in the services, but he seems unwilling to use any local talent. Perhaps he is a little insecure, but he is a good man, mind you."

Lev sensed that perhaps some discontent had been sown at those services. He said, "Perhaps I will see you there tomorrow morning. If there is any way I can alleviate whatever differences there are, I would be glad to do so."

The prelate thought that Lev might be taking his side, so he warmed up to him. "Well, perhaps I should go there again. Perhaps you could put in a good word for me. I know you are a person of significant influence in this new arrangement of things."

"No, no, I do not even know who is in charge of this chapel. I would not think of suggesting changes as soon as I walked in the door. That would be arrogant, I'm sure. However, in that we all love the Lord, let us sing his praises together tomorrow. We can't be too thankful, can we?"

"Well, Lev, you almost sound like a preacher," the prelate intoned. "Still, you are right, we do need to worship. Perhaps I will take your suggestion. I shall hope to see you there in the morning. In the meanwhile, just go down the road a bit and you can't miss the place you are looking for. Have a good day."

Lev knew that Eustus knew who he was and that he was also very much concerned about his presence in the area. He was an extremely intelligent man, even more so now since eating the fruit of life. He would not have survived in the political and religious rivalry of his day without great cunning. Lev needed some pretext to engage this prelate to help him accept the present without trying to recreate his glorious past of power and control over people. Lev would visit the plant not to manage it or to become heavily involved. His presence there would be to suggest some improvements in technology that were steadily being made. This plant was not having any problems and it was turning out good products. However, there were always new ideas and improvements needed.

Lev arrived to speak to the management. When it was learned that Lev Aron was there to see them, they gave him a warm welcome because his name had become a legend both in management and technical expertise. Lev explained that his visit was unannounced because he had no official assignment here, but being in the area it was an occasion to learn of the progress being made here. He also wondered if they had come up with some advances that should be shared by others since everyone would be interested in promoting the common good. He explained that today he only wished to make contact and get acquainted with a few people, but that he would be spending time to learn and observe their operation. All seemed delighted to have the honor of his presence.

After a short visit, Lev returned on the same road passing Eustus' home. He saw him talking on the phone as he passed. Lev was certain he hadn't noticed him. He wondered whether other prelates and former church dignitaries might be learning of his visit. He knew they had developed a close-knit community. They had lived a life avoiding physical labor of any kind and seemed content not to learn to do any even now.

Lev returned home to settle in. He picked some fruit for supper and decided to do a little pruning. Fortunately, all the basic tools needed were supplied with each house. He thoroughly enjoyed working with nature.

Lev Is Joined by Eustus

He arose early the next day for chapel services. Whom should he meet on the road to the chapel the next morning, but Eustus? They shook hands and greeted each other cheerily. Eustus stood tall and erect with the typical Italian olive skin and Roman nose and was a handsome figure now, but he did not exude any warmth. He hadn't been known for his congeniality before, but he seemed to have developed some since he returned to life. He did not want to appear like a religious dictator, so he worked at making good appearances. Lev thought Eustus seemed to have an inordinate amount of self-concern and self esteem.

"I am very pleased to see you, Eustus. I hope you are as eager as I am to get acquainted with the people of this chapel. I don't believe I've ever met any of them, but I hear the chaplain is a deep student of the Word of God. I always enjoy it when I learn something. Most of the chaplains today are so well studied. They always open a window on biblical insights. When I used to go to the Jewish synagogues, I learned very little about God's Word. Now only the truth of God's Word is taught—it's very edifying."

Lack of Training Implied

Eustus frowned at Lev's observations. "Lev, I don't know how it was in the Jewish synagogues, but our churches had gifted and educated priests to lead the people. Today's leaders seem content to work in factories by day and then play preacher in the mornings. They don't have much training to be preachers."

Lev thought, Eustus is dissatisfied with the type of leadership provided in this chapel. He spoke aloud, "Well, perhaps laymen have poor judgment in choosing a leader. Would that be your thought, Eustus?"

"That's being rather direct, but you must agree, Lev, that the long years of training church leaders had made them eminently more qualified for the task than the lay leadership now in vogue."

"Yes, church leaders were trained for long years, but they weren't taught the truth of God's Word, were they?"

"If you mean how they encouraged that disastrous assault on Israel to wrest Jerusalem from them, we all know that was a mistake. The church in my time didn't make that mistake," he asserted. "That was done later by leaders who apparently had been carried away with worldly philosophy."

"Didn't the church have that philosophy originally, in the great Crusades to take the Holy Land?"

By the time they had arrived at the chapel, Lev could see that his comments had made Eustus uncomfortable and rather annoyed. As they arrived, many of those assembled recognized the former church prelate and came rushing over to him with almost an adoring attitude. He apparently had many family members at this chapel that still remembered fondly what a great and powerful church leader he had been.

They had tried earlier to secure Eustus as the chaplain, but too many people angrily remembered the millions who had been destroyed because of misguided church and civil leaders. No one here seemed to recognize Lev, so he gladly faded into the background. Because Eustus was surrounded with his admirers, Lev quickly took a seat on the other side of the room.

As the music started, Lev could see some chapel members asking the chaplain to somehow work Eustus into the services that morning, suggesting what a nice gesture that would be. Even though the chaplain was not too keen on the idea, he yielded to the pressure and, after the general singing and the opening prayer, he asked Eustus if he would like to say a few words.

Eustus arose, making a rather impressive figure; but, without the robes he once wore, he did not appear so overwhelming. However, he was a gifted man and knew how to speak. At the podium he stared at the audience in quiet contemplation.

"Thank you, my dear Chaplain Panucci. It is with humble heart that I stand before you. Yes, I know I was overlooked as a candidate for heaven as some more faithful Christians have attained to, but that doesn't make me less desirous of serving our great God. I know the great church I represented erred in sending so many of our people to their death by trying to take the Holy Land away from the Jews. Thankfully, I was not involved in that mistake. As the renowned Shakespeare once penned, to err is human, but to forgive is divine. We all need forgiveness, and I'm no exception. None of us can fix the past, but before us is a great future."

Eustus was just warming up. "Ah, yes, we do have gifted leaders in Jerusalem, but they need all the help we can provide them. And I, for one, will be happy to serve in spiritual leadership in the present. Some of us are not gifted with bricks and mortar, not dexterous in industrial complexes and not even very capable in planting and gardening. Our training is in spiritual leadership and that's where we may indeed best serve. We leave our small abilities to serve in your hands. If we may help to relieve our dear Chaplain Panucci of the very heavy load he is under, we would gladly proffer our assistance. Thank you and God bless you."

Having finished he sat down. Poor Chaplain Panucci was stunned. This former prelate was offering to replace him in part or in full. Even more, the chaplain was dismayed with the content of the prelate's self-serving presentation. Not one edifying word did he hear and not one verse of scripture. He managed only to place himself as a candidate for chaplain. Under a pretext of humility, he reached for leadership in this house of prayer and praise. It was so carefully presented, that a refusal to grant him his desire might even appear as a lack of appreciation of the leadership in Jerusalem.

Eustus Seeks Office

Lev realized that if a motion was made from the floor to have Eustus assist Chaplain Panucci, it might just pass. He immediately asked that the normal services for the morning continue and, if business of any kind were to be considered, that it be put off until a properly announced business meeting could be arranged. Someone quickly seconded his suggestion and enough votes prevented the prelate from getting the immediate action he desired. Lev knew that Eustus was annoyed with him for stalling his bid for a position, but being a diplomat he carried himself very well.

After the services, the prelate found himself surrounded with his avid supporters, mostly relatives and friends who wanted to relaunch a past legend into a rising star again. It was this type of emotional thinking that created the kind of religious structures the prelates liked, but were not pleasing to God.

Lev wanted to get acquainted with the chaplain, because he seemed well versed in the Scriptures and very talented in his presentations.

"Chaplain Panucci, I must tell you how much I enjoyed your service this morning. I hope you will not on your own decide to share your services with Eustus. I witnessed a chapel with a similar situation where a renowned minister wanted to take over the chapel and he succeeded, but before long most of the congregation left. The self-proclaimed minister tried to blame others for the membership loss, but in the end he found that his old way of preaching would not work anymore. Spiritually, he was not really qualified for the task, and the old honors he wanted weren't possible when truth and righteousness were top priorities."

"Thank you, Lev. I appreciate your advice. I know you have accomplished great things for the good of mankind and have excelled in your ability to deal in human relations. I wasn't planning on resigning. I know the history of this prelate and several others, and if they had been true servants of God they would be reigning with Christ. Heaven's gates were closed to them, so we may conclude they were never acceptable servants of God. We worship Christ here and not personalities. Truth is more important than eloquence."

The chapel soon emptied and after many greetings, Lev decided to leave. Eustus left at the same time, so they walked back together toward his home. Lev could feel a little tension, but he tried to be cordial.

Eustus said, "That was wise of you to defer any business until another time. We needed the worship and services we had this morning. Business meetings often lead to divisiveness. My only concern this morning was to address the burden that falls on our chaplain. He is a good man, but I am sure he would appreciate a little help on occasion."

Sincerity Questioned

Lev would have been pleased with his remarks if he thought they were sincere. However, here was a man not engaged in any way to help the common good. He sat around all day looking for an opportunity to live as he once lived, a powerful religious figure. Not only so, never did he admit that his former teaching and ministry were fatally flawed. Here was the man that assumed the right to send people to heaven while he was now earthbound himself. Through his church organization he had blessed the armies of the warring nations and had a history of treacherous dealings and unspeakable evil in perpetuating the "Holy" Inquisition. There was no remorse ever shown for such failure to practice the ideals of Christianity. Yet the desire for prominence and power was still present. To feed this uninhibited ambition would be a serious mistake.

Lev decided to be very frank about this matter. "I know you have a large family and a few friends backing you, but I'm afraid they are savoring the past glory when they could say they were related to such a high prelate. Those were the days when pride and ambition ruled the world and also, unfortunately, ruled the church. In that time nearly all religious groups could make extravagant claims of being representatives of God. Those days are gone forever, Eustus." Despite the obvious irritation his companion showed, Lev continued.

"You and I both know that God had them overthrown with violence. They were unfit rulers on earth and certainly not fit to reign with Christ in heaven. Not a single church building or organization remains, nor a single religion of the thousands of religions that once existed. Only the Ancients are worthy of the honor of serving Christ now. If you are thinking that serving as chaplain will give you a base to operate a renewed religious base of some kind, I'm afraid it won't work."

The prelate turned red. He was aghast at Lev's boldness. How dare Lev question his sincerity! However, being the diplomat that he was, Eustus said, "Well, Lev, I'm sorry you hold me in such low esteem. Perhaps your Jewishness is showing here. I know your people suffered greatly in the World War II years, but it was not the church that operated the gas chambers."

"I know they didn't overtly operate the gas chambers, but neither did they do much to protest this genocide. The days when people can rationalize what was done are past. The truth is everywhere known today. Unfortunately, you bear a heavier burden than you are willing to acknowledge. There are millions of people who look at your hands as covered with blood. You could have easily defeated the Nazi movement in the early years of its existence, but you were willing to look the other way as the rule of law was stolen from Germany. You wanted a strong leader to defeat communism and nothing else mattered. I should think you would be out there trying to help mankind in building and planting and in receiving the millions of earth back to life. Maybe then people would believe that you loved someone besides yourself."

The Prelate Stunned

This strong language stunned the arrogant man. No one ever dared speak to him that way before. In the day of his power he could have very easily punished someone who spoke so frankly. However, Lev was now aligned with the ruling power of Christ, and there was nothing the prelate could do with Lev but endure his directness. Eustus wanted to say something, but he didn't know how to defend himself. He remained silent as they walked for a while and then said, "Lev, you seem to be my judge and jury."

"No, I'm not your judge and jury. Christ is. You know that as well as I. Instead of renouncing your past you are trying to relive it in another world. It isn't working. What if you gain the whole world and lose your own life—what will it profit you? There will never again be false religion in this world. There will never be rulers that aren't qualified to rule. Christ is reigning from shore to shore and from the river to the ends of the earth. You are living a fantasy if you think you can create a religious seat of authority, even a small one. You may get yourself a role as chaplain, but that won't last if you don't use it to glorify Christ. Eternity is too long for anyone to be self-seeking."

"Well, Lev, I'm glad to reach my home. You apparently have decided to be my adversary. Good day to you."

Lev simply said, "Faithful are the wounds of a friend."

Frankness Not Appreciated

Lev had seldom been so frank in his life. He realized that for someone once so high and exalted, it must have been painful to face such brutal criticism. Sooner or later those countless victims, whether from the "Holy" Inquisition or the gas chambers, would confront the chain of men of the cloth who ruled without Christian charity. Eustus had the advantage of having family and friends surrounding him. He also was one step removed from some of the atrocities. He could plead innocent, when, in fact, he bore considerable guilt. However, the prelate's main ploy was to secure a role of trust and religious leadership so that no one could bring up his past.

Lev was somewhat discouraged. Eustus would probably despise him for his efforts to awaken him from the peril of his course. If it was only Lev's observation, he might have doubted it. However, the Ancient Worthies also saw that this man was not responding in a normal way to blessings of this time.

Lev ate his late breakfast with a troubled heart. Dealing with people could be both rewarding and painful. Once the heart had learned hypocrisy, it was difficult to undo the damage. Lev wondered what Hitler was doing. Was he still hiding in his house, seeking to avoid the scorn of so many in society? He knew Hitler had faced reality for a brief moment when Mr. Smultz confronted him. Unfortunately, he didn't like it—it had been too painful.

After finishing his meal, Lev found the need to find comfort in the Scriptures. It was a breath of fresh air to read in Psalm 19:7-9: "The law of the Lord is perfect, converting the soul: the testimony of the Lord is sure, making wise the simple. The statutes of the Lord are right, rejoicing the heart: the commandment of the Lord is pure, enlightening the eyes. The fear of the Lord is clean, enduring for ever: the judgments of the Lord are true and righteous altogether." It was the purity of the Word that was so refreshing.

After a while Lev thought he would check on some technical matters pertaining to the plant he had visited yesterday. Knowledge was so neatly packaged now that one could check on just about anything very quickly. Lev decided he would have his lunch at home and then walk over to the plant in the afternoon. As he passed the prelate's house, Lev again observed him on the phone. The prelate did not see him, or if he did, he pretended not to.

The staff at the plant was eager to meet Lev and glad to spend time with him. He was shown the operation in considerable detail. They had a splendid facility and a staff eager to turn out quality material. After several hours of observation, Lev only found a few suggestions for improvement. When called to their attention, they gladly acknowledged the improvements. Lev thought, if only human relations could be that easy. He asked if the prelate had ever offered his services here. The answer was, "Never!"

The manager of the company said, "Besides, I am not exactly eager for him to come. I know he lives just down the road and this would be an excellent place for him to try to pay back his debt to society. Yet, he uses his home as his castle. He keeps in constant contact with all his old church allies. He seems to feel that any type of work is beneath his dignity. He has asked former nuns to come and clean his home, and a few are quite regular in doing that. He seems to like being lord of the manor."

Lev Encourages the Manager to Engage Eustus

"Well, if he does show any interest in working here, please go out of your way to use him. He needs to mix with those who are carrying on this great work of regeneration. I know it was easy for preachers to send all their old parishioners to heaven, but finding themselves and their parishioners here on earth again is little humiliating, to say the least. If God received everybody that was supposed to go to heaven, it wouldn't be heaven anymore. It's easy to see that the burden of sin and selfishness that people carried could never have allowed them into heaven. Even on earth, there's a lot of work to be done in the human hearts of men before they will be washed and cleansed of their contamination with sin."

The afternoon passed in an uneventful way. Lev returned home enjoying the walk through the old Italian communities. It wasn't like the old days when one could smell garlic being cooked in the various little homes. Now everyone craved the Eden fruit, and life had become simple, having it already grown and at hand everywhere.

Lev passed Eustus' home and was glad to see him in his orchard picking ripe fruit for his supper meal. Lev waved as he walked by and asked, "Will we see you at the chapel tomorrow?"

"I hope to be there, thank you."

Lev noticed that some of his trees needed pruning, so he said, "Do you know how to prune trees?"

"No, I just know how to pick ripe fruit. How do you prune trees?"

"If you will get me your pruning shears that are standard equipment in all homes, I will show you what needs to be done."

The prelate loved Eden fruit for he, too, had a sensitive stomach before. So he thanked Lev. "If you have a minute, I will get the shears, and you can show me what to do."

He returned with the shears and Lev took them and showed the prelate how to prevent trees from going into wood-making instead of fruit-bearing. Lev pointed out to him branches that needed pruning. Lev began snipping away here and there and had most of the trees trimmed just as they should have been.

"I'm glad you enjoy your orchard and garden. There's something purifying about working with nature."

"Yes, I think you're right," responded the prelate. "By the way, I understand you were there when Hitler returned to life. How did you manage with him?"

"Not too well. I've been with him twice already, and I'm afraid he lacks the courage or strength to live down his past."

Lev then told Eustus about Mr. Smultz's visit with Adolf and how this man recounted the terrible torture he endured before he died. "I thought this would be a great revelation to Hitler, because he was hidden from some of the murder and torture that prevailed under his rule. I understand that he's still hiding in his house, still meeting with some of his former officers. I'm sorry to report that he doesn't have the will to change."

Eustus Volunteers for Work

To Lev's surprise, Eustus asked, "Do you think they could use my services at the plant you visited?"

"Certainly, they would be glad for your help. You might need to take some courses to come up to speed. However, they teach everything so clearly that in a short while you could become a helpful contributor. They'll tell you the exact programs you should take. In a few days you could learn enough to work intelligently there."

Lev couldn't understand this change of posture by the prelate. Perhaps he really wanted to help after all—or was it that former church leaders encouraged him to act like a normal member of the community and contribute to the common good? Whatever the reason, his attitude changed toward doing manual labor. From pruning trees to working in the factory down the road, Eustus seemed to have changed his attitude about work.

As Lev got ready to leave, he said, "I'll see you in the morning at the chapel."

"Yes, the Lord willing I'll be there."

"Shalom," Lev said as he left.

Lev rose early the following morning to do some chores around the house and collect fruit for the day. Soon he was on his way to the chapel. Lev left for the chapel earlier than he had yesterday, so he didn't meet the prelate on the way. He arrived early to get better acquainted with the members there. He was well received except for some of the prelate's relatives who were cordial, but cool toward him.

*"Who shall ascend into the hill of the LORD?
Or who shall stand in his holy place?"
(Psalm 24:3).*

Chapter Twelve

Lev Meets Chaplain Panucci

Lev found the chaplain deep in thought assessing his upcoming services. However, he was eager to talk to Lev. "Will you be in the area very long?"

"I'm really not sure. I should be around a couple of weeks at least."

"We appreciate having you with us. We've heard wonderful things about you, and I can understand why. Would you like to serve us some morning?"

"I'd enjoy that, but I think it is more important that you continue your excellent presentations from the Bible. Nothing does more good to the human heart than hearing the Word of the Lord. What is your background?" Lev asked.

"I lived through World War II under Mussolini. That war was painful for many people in Italy. However, Mussolini found a steadfast friend in Hitler. You know, the Italians were strong family people for the most part and never really liked the way Hitler operated. When his officers killed several hundred Italians in cold blood, it left people bitter toward him. The Allies knew that Italy was the weak underbelly of Europe, so that was one of the fronts they opened up. I was in the army and we were pitted against the Allies, but our hearts weren't in it. Most of us knew the men leading Italy and Germany had ambitions much greater than their capabilities. We liked the Americans who acted more like human beings. The Germans were desperate people, and desperate people will do desperate things. They were either driven by their own propaganda or by fear, but they didn't endear themselves to the Italian people.

"I managed to live through the war and was actually happy the Allies saved us from Hitler and his goons. The Marshall Plan helped Europe get back on its feet and we were grateful to be in touch with our American relatives again. War seems so insane now, but it was a part of life then. I knew that the Papacy was operating the ratlines, getting many of the Nazi war criminals out of Europe, mostly into South America. I got a job in the government agency that provided visas and passports out of the country after the war. I knew these war criminals were being provided phony identifications, but we were told to close our eyes and help these criminals get out of the country. Our bread was buttered by the agency, so we did what we were told and were silent about it.

"So, Lev, I know the complicity the church had in relocating war criminals to South America. One of the priests that had been my boyhood friend also told me during the war about the death camps of Europe, but he said those Jews were going to hell to burn forever anyway, so what did it matter if they were hurried toward their destiny. I never liked that, but I knew nothing different at the time. I know firsthand, Lev, how corrupt and evil religion could become. What was once just a euphemism, the 'Jewish problem,' was the most sinister and evil practice ever visited upon mankind. Only Satan could have masterminded this."

Panucci Tells His Personal Knowledge

The chaplain continued with his story. "I lived to marry and have a lovely family. I died before the final battle against Jerusalem. However, I know two of my sons died there. I know that 'salvation is of the Jews.' Lev, you know why I'm not eager to have the prelate on this platform. Church leaders were cunning about playing holy men while being involved in some very wicked activities. Consequently, I'm not about to turn over leadership to someone I know had a slippery past. Especially, when I realize they aren't repenting of anything. They leave the impression that they were pure in heart, but I happen to know better, and so do many of the members of this chapel. I would be happier to hear the prelate say, 'Lord, be merciful to me a sinner.'"

Lev was relieved to know Chaplain Panucci was so well informed. The chapel was filling up and Lev saw Eustus enter, surrounded by his relatives. As everyone was seated, the music started and the morning worship began. Lev noticed some of the people from the plant in this neighborhood were also at this congregation. Lev knew they didn't think well of the prelate and were hoping he wouldn't seek employment there.

After the prayer, one of the relatives of Eustus asked that a business meeting be appointed when convenient. "Would tomorrow be acceptable to everyone?" the chaplain asked. Most hands went up. "Tomorrow will be set aside for business. Does anyone have a specific matter to place on the agenda?"

One of Eustus' relatives said, "I wish to place Eustus in nomination to share the chaplain's role here."

The chaplain asked, "Is there a second to this nomination?"

Immediately another relative stood up to second the nomination as a motion.

"Very well. Tomorrow we shall consider this proposition. You all know the rules. There may not be any pressure put on anyone in this vote. Any activity that tends toward a party spirit will be punished. This vote may be taken based only on Eustus' present performance in society, and he must not be considered for his former role as a church prelate. Everyone should pray sincerely for the Lord's will to be done before you come tomorrow to vote."

His statement drew some scowls. He then began the service for the day with a sermon on 2 Corinthians 7:10: "For godly sorrow worketh repentance to salvation not to be repented of: but the sorrow of the world worketh death." He showed how true godly sorrow brings a clearing of oneself from past sins, but worldly sorrow brings death.

His sermon spoke to the heart of the congregation. No one could fail to be impressed with his clear logic. Everyone knew their personal need for godly sorrow over past sins and mistakes – that this kind of sorrow would bring repentance and reform and a desire to make a clear separation from past sins. Worldly sorrow that only admitted mistakes, but made no effort to repent and reform, would only bring death. His message was brilliant.

History Was Being Replayed

After the service Lev spent time getting acquainted with many new faces. Most of them had recently returned to life, and that was exciting. People were returning to life at an accelerated rate. Each one was bringing back a part of history. One day the whole fabric of history would be replayed in living testimonials of those who lived in a certain time and place. The rationalizations, platitudes, and unfounded arguments of the past would be seen for what they were — an endeavor to cloak evil in white garments. The good would stand as a monument to godlikeness in the human heart. The evil would remind all of us of the poison of Satan and the evil spirit world, as well as wickedness in the human heart. History was so exciting when you learned it from those who lived it!

The prelate left before Lev, not wishing to have another painful confrontation. However, he didn't even seem phased by yesterday's ordeal with Lev.

After breakfast and some spiritual reading time, Lev visited operations again at the same plant. When he arrived, he was surprised to find the prelate inquiring if he might find employment. Because Lev had asked them to, they decided to engage him. However, they gave him things he must learn, the very simplest taking a week of intense study to make him competent.

They knew he was an extremely intelligent man, so he would have no trouble learning what he needed to function in the operation. Eustus seemed surprised to find that he didn't qualify for any function despite his impressive degrees. However, he thanked everyone for giving him the list of courses and promised he would take them. He said he would return as soon as he finished them.

Lev greeted him as he was leaving. "I'm so glad you decided to join the real world. We need everyone's help in accelerating the process of regeneration. It used to be that two parents raised five or six children. It will be a lot easier for five or six children to prepare for two parents. When the grandchildren and great grandchildren join in the work, it will accelerate in an amazing way. If we love our ancestors, we won't rest until all have returned to life."

"Lev, you should have been a preacher. Maybe I have been in the wrong profession. Anyway, I want you to know I am reaching out to help my fellow man as I always did. I took my responsibilities over the flock of God very seriously."

Lev smiled. "One thing is certain, you didn't tell them the truth. Everybody returning to life is asking how come he or she was never told about the regeneration? What do you tell them when they ask this question?"

"Oh, Lev, give me a break. It just so happens that the religious leaders of that time drew a blank on the regeneration. I wasn't properly informed, obviously. I certainly believe it now.

More Truth Was Known Back There Than Is Admitted

Lev replied, "I have books back home of people whom the church persecuted who taught very clearly about this Millennial Kingdom and the great work of regeneration that would take place. This information was certainly known, and it was preached rather extensively. Why was it suppressed?"

"I heard of some people who held these views, but they were small groups and we just ignored them, hoping they would go away. Maybe we should have listened, but we didn't. We still believed we could set up God's Kingdom on earth by our own strength and resources. We just happened to have been ill informed. If I knew that these small groups were preaching the truth, I would've owned it. In that time and place it didn't seem right. Lev, we were serving God with some shortcomings—I admit that."

"Well, my friend, the past is not nearly as important as the present. Now we're in the light and no one may teach or preach any errors of any kind. Anyone serving merely for personal pride or ambition will be rejected. Only what is done in love for God and mankind will meet with divine approval. That's how it is now."

"Thank you for your second sermon, Lev. I must get home and start my studies. Maybe you should put your name up for chaplain."

Lev felt the sting of rebuke, but said, "Thank you, but I move about on different projects and don't stay in any place very long. Anyway, I'm not sure you meant that sincerely."

"There you go again, being my judge and jury. I'm afraid I'd be in trouble if I stood in judgment before your throne. I hope I shall receive more mercy from Christ."

With that he said, "Good day, Lev. I hope to see you at the chapel tomorrow."

Lev saw that nothing he had said found any place in the prelate's heart. He remained focused on his personal goals and was determined to carry through with his game plan. Lev wondered if the prelate might receive a majority vote the next day. He had a rather large family who seemed very supportive of him, plus he had some friends who were eager to forgive his past, even though it wasn't they who had suffered under his authority. Only those who suffered injustice or pain of any kind because of his rule could grant forgiveness. One must first recognize his sin before one may seek forgiveness for it.

Lev spent the rest of the day analyzing the whole operation and found it very good. Only a few changes seemed necessary and most of the staff was eager to make the operation prosper for the good of mankind. They seemed to have a good spirit and genuine love for their fellow man. All workers were voluntary and as the number of volunteers grew, the hours that each individual needed to donate decreased.

Prelate Causes Some Anxiety

No one said much about the prelate's visit, although Lev knew that many of them were very nervous about his being there. Fortunately, they all knew a whole lot more about this operation than he did, so he was in no position to direct anything. While he was an intelligent man, no one really expected him to stay long.

At the end of the shift, Lev walked home. Passing the prelate's home, he didn't see him anywhere. Lev arrived home to have supper and relax. He was surprised to hear the phone ring. It was the welcome voice of Moses.

"Shalom. We have been informed by spiritual forces what has transpired. On the morrow, do not take an active role in trying to defeat the prelate. Every man's work is being tested and the only one he can hurt in the long run is himself. If Eustus succeeds in being assistant chaplain, tell Chaplain Panucci not to retire from continued service. He is an excellent person of noble character. He will not fail as a true leader. This is a request by the whole body of Ancients who serve Christ. Thank you, Lev, keep up the good work. Shalom and God be with you."

Lev realized from this message that more was at stake than just another person joining in the service of chaplain. He realized it must be a part of a design for certain elements to establish some kind of bridgehead. It was apparently a part of the whole apparatus for Eustus and others to get into religion again.

It was clear to Lev that Christ himself was being very permissive to the community of prelates to let them work out their little schemes to reveal what was in their hearts. Christ could have prevented this, but apparently was allowing these men to try to retrieve some of their former glory. Even though that glory was sodden with corruption and pride, it was this spirit that initially had caused the church to lose its way.

An Assistant Chaplain Elected

The next morning Lev arose a little earlier than usual to get to the chapel and convey the message he received from the Ancients.

Chaplain Panucci was surprised to receive a personal message with instructions to stay on as chaplain. He thanked Lev for the message because he had actually planned to resign rather than share the service. However, if the Ancients wanted him to stay on, he would do so. He would not refuse those who represented Christ.

As the members gathered, the prelate arrived smiling and cordial to one and all. His family members and friends surrounded him. This morning, however, he arrived early enough to go around greeting all the individual members in a most gracious and conciliatory manner. He even came to Lev with outstretched arms as though he had found a long lost friend. Before he got to the chaplain, the music started and the chaplain began the morning worship with songs of praise.

After the morning's prayer, the chaplain opened the floor for business as requested. A motion was soon made to have Eustus, the former prelate, serve as assistant chaplain with the thought that they could alternate days or weeks of service according to how they personally wished. The motion was seconded without a pause. Lev restrained himself from commenting, according to the instructions from Moses. A few people commented that the services of Chaplain Panucci had been beautiful and fulfilling and this addition might be an unnecessary intrusion to his gifted contributions at the chapel.

After a short discussion the vote was called for. A mere fifty-one percent majority passed the motion.

Eustus stood up to thank the members. "I hope I can be worthy of your trust for those who voted for me; and for those who did not, I hope to gain your trust and support by being a good and faithful servant. Thank you."

After Chaplain Panucci finished his morning service, the prelate came up to him seeking to be congratulated on his new role. However, the chaplain simply asked how he wanted to share in the services. "Do you wish to alternate days, weeks or months?"

The prelate thought a moment and said, "Perhaps it would be best, and less confusing, to alternate months. If you finish out this month I will begin services next month. Is that acceptable to you, my dear Chaplain Panucci?"

There were only a few days left in the present month, but the chaplain acquiesced to his new partner's wishes.

"That will be fine with me. You may have the next month, and I will take a little vacation. I was going to ask Lev to take my place for a month. I am sure you know he is a foremost scholar of the Bible. He has served in several chapels for short periods of time. However, since the congregation voted for your services, I do not need to seek help during my absence. May the Lord bless your services. I hope you will be a very careful exponent of the Scriptures, because present audiences will not sit through anything except clear biblical teachings."

Eustus seemed a little indignant to have this lowly chaplain giving him advice. After all, he had a sterling education and had graduated with high honors. He was known to have filled churches with happy parishioners. This small body of people should respond to his outstanding abilities with acclaim. Being as gracious as he could be, the prelate said, "Well, thank you chaplain, your humble servant will try his best."

Soon family and friends crowded about the prelate to congratulate him for this small step back into religious world leadership. Lev didn't congratulate him, but stood aside while Chaplain Panucci addressed him. He could see this was the beginning of trouble in this little chapel, as well as other chapels where former prelates were bidding for acceptance as religious instructors. Lev knew the Ancient Worthies were aware of this ploy and would wait and see how it worked.

When the new month arrived, Lev wondered how the former prelate would make out. He arrived at the chapel early to see what changes might be in store. Sure enough, Lev learned they would have a special choir singing instead of the usual congregation singing. While it was very good singing, it was not better than the whole congregation singing. However, no one could fault this for it was devotional in nature. He had a Bible reading of the Beatitudes, which was nice. His service however, was full of platitudes and little stories, which were interesting to follow, but lacked substance.

It was clear by the end of the service that the prelate was not familiar with the Bible. He made several mistakes in his sermon that some perhaps did not catch, but many did and were quite surprised that anyone so educated could be so lacking in biblical details. After his service, the prelate's loyal family and friends praised him for an excellent meeting.

The Prelate Reports for Secular Work

True to his promise, Eustus showed up at work saying that he had taken the courses given him and was now familiar enough with the operation to begin work. He was assigned to assist one of the workers and learn firsthand how the procedure was done. He did indeed have a good working knowledge of the project, but found he lacked the manual dexterity for the task. Try as he would, he could not insert the parts together in the time allowed.

The lady who served as his instructor was very patient. She finally gave him two parts to practice putting together and then quickly take apart. This seemed to have finally worked, and he learned the secret of putting the two parts together rather clumsily, but he was able to do it finally in the time allotted. It was clear the prelate had never been involved in physical work, but he had the discipline to succeed at it, as hard as it was for him.

Lev happened to be there that day and congratulated the prelate for deciding to do his share in the world that needed eager hands to move the great regeneration project along. He said, "Thank you, Lev, that is kind of you. I don't have the skills that I hear everyone proclaiming to me that you have. I do the best I can, and perhaps my motor skills will develop as I try to use my hands to help my fellows."

Eustus then asked Lev if he had been discouraging people from attending chapel services. He observed that about fifteen people had stopped coming.

"I hope no one is behind this. I know that there is a steady stream of those returning to life, and we should be seeing most of these people at the chapel meetings. However, none of them have shown up this last week. Can you shed any light on this, Lev?"

Lev replied, "I can tell you that I have never discouraged anyone from attending worship services. I know why those returning to life are not showing up, however. I have heard that when they heard you were the chaplain, they declined to come. One of them I met the other day said to me, 'I had enough of that hollow and empty teaching of the church.' So it's your past that is coming back to haunt you. You're going to have to convince people you are no longer playing politics."

This disturbed the prelate very much. It was hard for him to accept that he was no longer a respected figure and crowds no longer looked upon him with respect and veneration. He was now viewed sometimes as an object of scorn.

This was not only true in his chapel, but the same problem was being experienced in the other chapels about Italy that had elected former church prelates. He thought the devotion that his family members had showered upon him was what most people thought of him, so it was an unexpected disappointment. Eustus had really believed that he would have the chapel full of happy followers, only to discover the ranks steadily thinning.

By the end of the month Eustus had lost nearly one-third of the chapel membership. When Chaplain Panucci returned, everyone was surprised to find the chapel full again. The prelate could not help but notice about ten new people at worship the morning of Chaplain Panucci's return. These were people who had returned to life within the month. The newly raised were always exciting people to have at worship, because they had new stories and pieces of history.

Chaplain Panucci had used his month's vacation preparing dissertations on the Scriptures. At the end of his service, even the family of the prelate came up to express their appreciation of his inspiring insights.

"He that hath clean hands, and a pure heart:
Who hath not lifted up his soul unto vanity, nor sworn deceitfully"
(Psalm 24:4).

Chapter Thirteen

A Mysterious Visitor

There was, however, a visitor from former Yugoslavia sitting quietly in the rear. Lev decided to greet and welcome him. He said he was here to speak to Eustus.

"You mean you came all the way from the former Yugoslavia just to speak to him? Wouldn't a telephone conversation accomplish that without making such a long trip?" Lev was amazed.

"Sir, I am a former bishop of the once great Greek Orthodox Church. I must speak to the prelate personally. If you know who he is, point him out to me." The tone of his voice led Lev to believe he had a score to settle with the prelate.

Lev decided to avoid a confrontation at the chapel, so he said, "Yes, I can show you where he lives. It's on my way home, why don't you come to breakfast at my house and then I will take you to the prelate's house. That way you can refresh yourself and we can get better acquainted. By the way, my name is Lev."

"Well, thank you, Lev—you are not the Lev that I have heard so much about, are you?"

"Well, I don't know what you've heard, but yes, I have visited many countries in serving the new King."

"Pleased to meet you, Lev. My name is Papadopolis. I'm so glad to meet you. It is providential, I feel. I needed to talk to someone who knows a whole lot more than I do. Yes, I'll be glad to come to your house. Thank you for your kind offer."

As they walked toward Lev's temporary home, the new visitor seemed to be a man of influence and stature.

"What, may I ask, brings you here?" Lev inquired.

"I shall tell my purpose to Eustus when I see him. I would like you to be there as well. Then I will tell you both my story. It is very brief. However, I must have an answer from the prelate. I, too, was a man of the cloth. I don't deserve to be one again. I admit that we misrepresented God's plan to the people. We promised heaven to our constituents and hell to all others. That was wrong. Here I was a prelate of the great Orthodox Church; but I, even though martyred, did not find myself in heaven. I admit that I was not a true follower of the Lamb. I have to admit it, because I am not in heaven with the Lamb now. Some things can no longer be hidden. The truth is now known. I am no longer interested in pretense." Using the visitor's car, they soon arrived at Lev's home. His guest was tired from his journey and very glad to relax in a private home. Lev served him breakfast. He had asked for tea as his beverage, so Lev made a very aromatic brew. As they sat down, Lev asked Mr. Papadopolis to offer thanks. His was a beautiful prayer of thanksgiving. Comparisons are always difficult, but Lev sensed a great deal of sincerity in this man. He sounded like a man who had known pain and hardship, a man who was grateful for small mercies and sensitive to others about him. Most of all he did not want to use people to get to the place he wanted to go. He seemed to reverence God and had a sense of love for his fellow man. It was very refreshing.

After breakfast Lev asked if he wished to rest awhile. Mr. Papadopolis said he was tired and would welcome a few hours of sleep. He had driven most of the night, which few people did anymore. But Mr. Papadopolis felt an urgent need to make this trip and to get back, as he was working on preparations to receive both his parents back to life. While he went to his bedroom to rest, Lev called the prelate.

"Hello, this is Chaplain Eustus, how may I help you?"

Lev Wishes to Bring a Visitor to See Eustus

"Shalom, this is Lev. I am calling because I have a visitor who wishes to see you. He has traveled a long distance and is very anxious to meet with you. If you are free this afternoon or evening, I will bring him to your place."

"Who might this be?"

"He does not wish to make his name known as he wishes this to be a surprise visit."

"Well, may I ask if he is friend or foe?"

"I didn't know you had any foes."

"Why didn't he come to my house directly?"

Lev told him what had transpired earlier. "He had come to the chapel this morning looking for you. He was new to the chapel and I thought he might be someone recently returned to life. I went over to introduce myself. He just said he had come a distance to be here today and asked me to point you out to him."

"Since he had traveled much of the night and was very tired, I invited him to my home for breakfast and to allow him to rest. I promised to make this contact with you for him."

Lev could tell the prelate was very guarded.

"Well, I should think this gentleman would at least reveal his name to you."

"Oh, yes, he has done that."

The prelate then demanded, "Why, then, don't you tell me who it is?"

"All I can tell you is that he is a man of the cloth. He wants his visit to be a surprise. Why are you having such a hard time opening your door to someone who wishes to speak with you, especially when he is another former man of the cloth?"

The prelate seemed exasperated. "All I'm trying to get is a simple answer to my question. Whom am I to see?"

"You will be seeing one of God's children, what more do you need to know?"

"All right, all right," the prelate responded. "Bring him over this afternoon. I'll be back from working at the plant by two o'clock. Anytime after that I will receive him. I hope this isn't something you've conjured up to embarrass me."

"I'm only serving a fellow human being who has asked my help and who's presently sleeping. He is a Christian gentleman and I know of nothing that should embarrass you. He hasn't told me his purpose, so how can I tell you?"

"Very well, anytime after two," the prelate affirmed. "Mind you, I'm a busy man, and I am only doing this, thinking I may be of some help to this man."

"I'll have him to your place after two. Thank you. I can't believe how difficult it is to see one of our chaplains. Shalom."

Lev decided to skip operations at the plant today to take care of his guest. He somehow had the feeling that this visitor was an important part of a troubled past. Eustus was less than enthusiastic about receiving him without some identification. Of course, in his former office nobody had an audience with him without a thorough screening. The church kept its high prelates out of reach from most people. In the old world, the more difficult it was to have an audience with someone indicated the higher his office was. However, the great God of the universe could be approached anytime by anyone who earnestly sought Him.

Lev was grateful that this meeting would be private. It might have been embarrassing if these two men had faced each other directly in public. Obviously, Mr. Papadopolis didn't know the prelate personally. If he had, he would have recognized him even though he appeared much younger.

Mr. Papadopolis Meets the Prelate

Lev awakened his guest around noon, so he would have time to shower and eat before leaving. The few hours of sleep did help revive him. They had a leisurely lunch, and Lev learned of this man's return to life within this year.

"I was murdered in a church-incited attack upon the Orthodox Church in Yugoslavia. The Roman Church had incited the Nazi forces to attack these poor Christians. The Roman prelate of the area led a force, as well, and joined in this terrible siege against all the Orthodox members they could lay their hands on. The carnage was very great. It was a senseless, murderous siege to cleanse the area of a competing religion. Church history is full of the same—endless persecutions, killings, crusades or what have you. In the light now shining, none of this makes any sense."

Lev could see why this man might like some explanations about such barbaric attacks. However, this must not have been the point of his visit, because he wouldn't reveal the specific point on his mind. Talking about the past awakened a lot of horrible memories apparently, because at points his voice broke and his hands trembled.

As the time came to leave, Mr. Papadopolis said, "I am requesting that you stay with me at this meeting, Lev. I will tell the prelate of my desire to have you present. Even if he is reluctant, I am going to insist upon it. I was going to approach him in public. I think your idea of a more private meeting is proper. I need you to confirm everything that takes place. Not that anyone can get away with lying anymore, but sometimes things can get confused and a third party can keep the record straight because they are not as emotionally involved."

"Very well," Lev replied, "I will honor your request. I sense that your visit is one in which you are looking for some answers and that you have great emotional concern in these answers." They arrived soon after two o'clock and the prelate was nervously pacing up and down his foyer.

Mr. Papadopolis stepped out of the car and quickly walked toward the entrance. Lev followed dutifully behind. As soon as the door opened he said, "My name is Alexander Papadopolis of the former Yugoslavia."

Apparently the name was instantly recognizable for the prelate turned pale.

"Ah, so that's why you withheld your name. Sir, I really don't wish to speak to you. Some things are best left in the past. You are intruding on my privacy, and nothing I say will satisfy you anyway. Thank you. Good day."

Mr. Papadopolis was quick to step in as soon as the door opened, and he was not about to leave.

"Sir," he said, "I have come a long way to see you face to face. You owe me some explanation of what happened to me. Every crime is perpetrated by a criminal or by criminals. You knew who I was as soon as you heard my name. If you are pure in this matter, I will be satisfied. However, if blood is on your hands, you have some tall explaining to do to your chapel members. No one is going to tiptoe around his responsibility. You could have done that in the past. Now is the day of truth, everywhere, all the time. If you lie and deny the truth, you know what will happen to you, don't you?"

"You are both not welcome here. Please leave immediately," the prelate angrily shouted.

"I am not leaving. You and I are going to talk here and now. You are a chaplain of the chapel Lev is attending. You owe him the courtesy of inviting him in, and you owe me some explanation. I am not a man of violence, so I will not act upon my impulse to strangle you. Have no fear. I cannot attempt to kill you without being punished on the spot, and you cannot lie to me without being punished immediately. This is the moment of truth for you, and I must know the truth. That is all I want. You know the Roman Church was heavily involved in that ethnic cleansing purge."

Eustus Agrees to Be Confronted

Eustus sighed heavily. "All right. Come into the parlor and have a seat. I guess a man has to face the mistakes of the past. That purge was a sad chapter in our history. In that time and place the Roman Church was not as secure as it wished to be. The Nazis were, at best, tolerant of our church. We supported them for they served as a hedge against godless communism. The church gambled that the Nazis would win. They thought Russia would fall before the German blitzkrieg, but it didn't. If the Americans had not entered the war, perhaps the Germans would have prevailed. However, with the industrial might of that great nation, we knew the Germans would lose back in 1942. No nation could survive a thousand planes roaring overhead dropping bombs on our cities. We feared that with the Germans losing power, the surrounding satellite nations would create a backlash against the church. They knew we were supporting the Third Reich, and the best defense is an offense. That may account for what you called an ethnic purge. It was survival politics from our vantage point. There you have it, pure and simple."

Mr. Papadopolis fixed his gaze upon Eustus, and then he slowly spoke. "There is nothing pure about what happened. Yes, all the churches played politics more or less. We were not much better, maybe even worse, than some of the forces that were unleashed on the world at that time. However, you know how I died, don't you? You know who was present to direct this crime against me? Please tell Lev how I died."

"Oh for goodness sake, what can I do about the past? I know it was wrong. The whole thing was wrong, as I look backward. You did not get to be the biggest and most powerful church by practicing Christianity. You know every large church played politics. That was how the church existed. It was a part of the world and because it had millions of adherents, it had power that no ruler could ignore."

Mr. Papadopolis repeated, "Please tell Lev how I died."

"You played politics, too, didn't you, Mr. Papadopolis?"

"Of course, I did," he answered. "Please tell Lev how I died."

Poor Eustus sunk in his seat. He became pale and his eyes turned glassy. "Our church members poked out your eyes and skinned you alive."

Suddenly the room fell silent. Eustus had no place to go, no place to hide. He knew the truth and he told it. Telling the truth did not make him free. It was like an albatross around his neck. Lev sat there stunned and speechless.

Finally Lev broke the silence. "I read of the savage Assyrians practicing that kind of barbarism, but how anyone professing to follow Christ could do this is incomprehensible."

Mr. Papadopolis said, "It makes you sick to your stomach doesn't it, Eustus? I can never forget that experience. The pain of being blinded was excruciating. Then to be cut open and have your skin peeled away cannot be understood by you. You could never imagine the pain. And, unfortunately, one does not die immediately from it. How precious death was at last. The pain subsided and finally peace came."

Mr. Papadopolis continued, "I awakened early this year. They heard me moaning as soon as I awakened to life. I thought that I was in the same place that I died. I felt my skin back and my eyes did not pain me. I had eyelids again. I thought that maybe I had had a bad dream. I was all in one piece, and there was no pain anymore. Yet I knew that what happened to me was not a dream; my mind remembered every moment of torture. Then I thought that I must be hallucinating and that I was still without skin. I soon found that I was whole again and feeling wonderful. What happened to me? I could see clearly. I almost felt that I must be mad. How could I be living in two worlds? The awakening again to life would normally have been less traumatic. But for me, dying was an unendurable experience with pain that no man should ever have to suffer. Then the next moment I was alive and whole without an explanation. At any rate, the regeneration was a wonderful experience once I understood it."

How Am I Responsible?

The prelate quickly injected, "I did not order what happened to you. The mob spirit took over. I knew that there would be some bloodletting, but I did not think such savagery would occur until I learned of it later. Even when we knew the Nazis would lose the war, we were willing to use their resources in this purge, which would strengthen the Roman church in the area. This was expedient thinking and certainly not Christian. The church was in a barbarous world and to survive and thrive in such a world it, too, practiced its own barbarism. It is unfortunate. In the present time it all seems so awful and unexplainable, but at that time it was business, as usual."

Mr. Papadopolis turned red as he sat trying to control himself. He then blurted out, "Business as usual! Is that your explanation for this diabolical act? Dear God, how can what happened to me be explained by such words as these? Jesus taught, 'By this shall all men know that ye are my disciples, if ye have love one to another' (John 13:35). Whose disciples did such heinous crimes? You must surely have known in your heart of hearts that this was vile and evil beyond description. How could you play act Christianity on the one hand, and then support such evil on the other hand?" Poor Alexander seemed almost unable to control his emotions.

"You know the Scribes and Pharisees acted the role of holy men in pretense, but they murdered our Lord in the cruelest manner of that day. How can such black and evil deeds be done while professing holiness? Did you have no conscience at all? Did you not know that the church together with the civil powers were murdering and torturing innocent people?"

The prelate sat very uncomfortably, lost for an answer. He was not prepared to admit to hypocrisy, but he could not dodge the responsibility for much of this savage massacre. He finally gave a very weak response.

"I cannot justify what happened in the light of today. The world was bleeding at that time and death and dying were everywhere. Fifty million people may have perished in that war and the church did not have armies of their own. The blood somehow never managed to be directly on our hands. Like King David of old, we murdered with white gloves on. Did we have responsibility for our part? Yes, indeed. However, everything in that time and place was blurred and muddled. I must confess that I accepted the power and glory of office, but neglected my responsibilities on occasion. How can I make it right now?"

Lev broke into the discussion. "That is the best question you have raised yet. This is the all-important question here today. 'How can I make it right now?' Remember how the church used to make people who broke under the "Holy" Inquisition wear special garments of the penitents? They were forced to admit before the world that they had denied the church dogma. They were forced against their wills to admit to apostasy even when in their heart they may not still have believed what they were being forced to believe. If you are forced to admit your guilt, but in your heart do not own up to it, it will do no good. However, if you are truly repentant and admit the vile role you played, and from the heart show godly repentance—that is what is needed."

Mr. Papadopolis said, "How can you parade as a man of God, while serving Satan? He is in the abyss now. You are free from his authority today. What prevents you from being a true penitent by wearing some sackcloth and ashes? By admitting before the world whose servant you were?"

"Do You Want Me Skinned Alive?"

At this the prelate stiffened. "I am beginning to think that you want me skinned alive. That would not put your skin back on. Why are you bent on revenge? I admit that what happened to you was wrong. It should not have happened."

Mr. Papadopolis exploded, "What do you mean by saying you admit that what was done to me was wrong? No person in this whole world could dare suggest it was right. Everyone knows it was not only wrong, but also evil beyond description. You are virtually admitting nothing. Even the vilest and meanest person in this whole world should not have been treated to the torture and pain I endured. Of course it was wrong, *wrong,* <u>wrong</u>. The question is how do I even begin to explain this barbaric conduct being done under the umbrella of the church? What kind of monsters were people who did such things?"

The prelate was very distressed, torn between embarrassment and anger. No one would have dared speak to him in this manner in the day of his power. Now there were no layers of agents to protect him. Even the press dared not lay such charges at his feet in the day of his power. He was shielded in every way from adverse public opinion. Now, alas, this man was able to park on his doorstep and demand explanations that he could not comfortably give. How wonderful it would be to call his guards to thrust this man into the street and be rid of him. But here he sat, grilling him and demanding a true apology. The prelate was thoroughly exasperated with this menacing visitor.

For a moment no one said anything. The air had become very charged. Mr. Papadopolis had lived for this moment. He had waited and held his peace until now. This, however, was his moment of truth, the one he had thought about and worked to make possible. He had this prelate in a face-to-face confrontation, the last thing on earth the prelate wanted.

The prelate just wished this man would go away instead of demanding answers and explanations that, if he gave, would only indict him. He was protected from this before, but now he feared that not only this man, but also every person who had previously suffered wrong at the hands of the church, could confront him. He found it maddening. Never once in the days of his power did he ever imagine having to give an account for what had happened under his watch. He had nowhere to turn and no adequate defense. He finally just threw up his hands.

"I have nothing more to say to you, Mr. Papadopolis, or to you either, Lev. As far as I am concerned, I am ready to retire into my room. Good day, gentlemen."

Lev said, as the prelate arose from his seat, "You really haven't answered this man's questions, have you? Everyone knows what happened was wrong. Admitting it to be wrong took no virtue on your part. You should really think long and hard about this matter and give a humble, honest answer. If that answer should require an admission that you were guilty, that is the answer you should give. Failing to do so means you are not truly repentant and not prepared to reform and to seek to give back to society your full devotion to good works now."

"Who made you a judge over me?" the prelate angrily demanded. "I did not ask to come back to life. I am here not by my choice."

Mr. Papadopolis then said, "You never thought for one moment that I would be coming back to life either, did you? If you knew that one day you would have to sit down face-to-face with me, you might have had more sleepless nights. The evil that occurred under your watch will not go away. There will be others, countless others that I know, who would gladly kill you if there were not spiritual forces to prevent this. You are now a pathetic figure." Alexander's face was twisted in disgust.

"You are not willing to admit the great evils that directly or indirectly occurred under your watch. Until you do, you will be haunted by tens of thousands of people who, like me, want some explanation of why you allowed these crimes to happen. Obviously, you did not love righteousness and you did not hate iniquity."

The Prelate Decides to Leave

The prelate stalked into his bedroom and slammed the door. Unfortunately, he would find no more peace of mind in the bedroom than while confronting his angry victim in the parlor. Peace had to come from the inside. Peace with God had to precede peace with others.

Lev invited Mr. Papadopolis to come home with him. He could have supper and stay over until morning and then take his journey home.

"This has been a very hard day for you. You need some quiet time. You must find the strength to lay this whole matter at the foot of the cross. Once you do, it will no longer be your burden. Then you will have peace."

"Thank you, thank you so very much, Lev," Mr. Papadopolis quietly replied. "I am truly grateful for your kind offer. I am in no frame of mind to start driving home now. I would certainly appreciate spending the evening with you at your home. I can see that you have a lot more wisdom than I do in dealing with these difficult matters. I know I was so emotionally involved at the time that I cannot think clearly about it even though it occurred many years ago. Just to hear about what happened would make most people sick to their stomachs, and much more so if they were to watch it before their very own eyes. No words can even come close to describing the pain I felt. I have relived it a thousand times as clearly as though it happened yesterday. Nothing can relieve me of the horror of that cruel torture. Nothing the Prelate or anybody else can say or do will erase the torment from my mind. I just do not want to have this crime committed against me and similar crimes perpetrated against my countrymen to go unrequited."

"I understand your pain and it makes me sick to my stomach. Not that I haven't heard equally barbaric accounts, but the cruelty that men have forced upon others is incomprehensible. It sounds inhuman, and possibly demon spirit forces inspired much of it. Maybe part of the answer lies there. How men could find pleasure in maiming and torturing others is not conceivable to a normal, healthy person. Although some find sadistic pleasure in such detestable acts, you will notice most of the perpetrators of such evils do not own up to them now. They are all wishing it would go away. To a certain extent sin brings its own retribution to the sinner. I am certain that the bishop who led that nefarious mob is wondering, now that he is alive again, how he can avoid you, just as the prelate wanted to."

They returned to Lev's residence and had a sober supper together. Mr. Papadopolis was grateful for Lev's understanding and insights.

"I really didn't expect this visit to rectify the past. It is only the present that we have and must use to remake ourselves into the image of God. However, I thought if I could break through the denial of responsibility and start the process of remaking ourselves into the image of God with some who pretended to be God's agents, it would help me in the recovery process."

Did Mr. Papadopolis Score Any Points with Eustus?

"We will not know whether your visit touched his heart or pricked his conscience. Sometimes these things have to sink in for days and weeks to begin internal healing. What did you really expect to see happen?"

"I believed, perhaps, that he would hedge and play act complete ignorance initially, but when he was confronted with the wickedness that occurred, he would break his stoic endeavor to distance himself from any responsibility. I thought he might break down and embrace me, asking my forgiveness. I am a man of compassion. I can forgive what happened to me if I found a heart broken and contrite. However, I don't think I found that. He admitted that what happened was wrong; but, then, who could argue that it was right? He was shaken by the brutality I had to endure, but not enough to have his defense collapse."

Lev responded, "That was my impression, too. You know, I have observed in my many dealings with people that it is hard for those who once had power and prestige to accept this new situation in the regeneration process. It is a lot harder to step down than to step up. People love power and especially power over other people. It is strange that men who professed to represent God and Christ did not follow the example of Christ. He divested himself of riches, power and glory. He surrounded himself with men of low estate and was accused of being the friend of publicans and sinners. What he had that the other leaders of his day did not have was love for mankind and a meek and lowly heart. How could religious leaders have failed to see what even a blind man could see? How could those who professed to serve Christ have been consumed by a desire for power and control over men and even the politics of this world?"

"I can answer that," Mr. Papadopolis retorted. "A man starts out trying to serve God. He becomes oppressed with himself and his sinful ways. He accepts Christ and seeks to be renewed. Having closed the door to his original worldly goals, he accepts instead another mission in holding up Christ before the world. However, Satan reached people who had religious purposes. They were still very vulnerable to pride and the desire for power and recognition. The same weaknesses that they once had when in the world, and which they perceived to be vices, were not as visible when they took place in religion.

"Somehow they had religious goodness to bestow and that made personal pride and ambition less recognizable. I know now what happened to me. I loved the Lord, but I loved myself more. I loved power more. I loved public recognition more. Corruption of virtue came very easily, especially in religion. This may explain why so few really attained a place with Christ in glory. They may have started out with good intentions, but assumed corruption would not occur in religious pursuits. Under the mantle of religion, people committed worse crimes than even men of the world, but when they were conceived to have furthered religious goals, it was okay."

Lev replied, "That helps me understand it better. Religious teachers started out to help others worship God, but somehow in the process they felt justified in accepting honor, power and glory in pointing others to God. They learned nothing from their Master."

*"Am I a God at hand, saith the Lord, and not a God far off?
Can any hide himself in secret places
That I shall not see him? saith the Lord.
Do not I fill heaven and earth? saith the Lord"
(Jeremiah 23:23, 24).*

Chapter Fourteen

The following morning, Lev asked Mr. Papadopolis if he wished to attend the chapel services before returning home.

"Yes, I need to lift my voice in praise to God. I enjoyed Chaplain Panucci very much yesterday. Oh, how I wish that I had learned to preach the Word of God clearly and selflessly. His treatise yesterday was absolutely brilliant. I look forward to hearing him again today."

"Great! We'll take in the services this morning and then return for a breakfast—and then you will be free to take your journey."

They drove to the chapel to save time, arriving just before the organist started playing. They sat down together. They tried to see if Eustus was there, but they couldn't see him. Congregational singing was back instead of the choir, and it was heartfelt praise to God. Chaplain Panucci asked Mr. Papadopolis to offer prayer, which he did in a very humble and sincere way. The services were exceptionally enlightening, opening windows of understanding God's Word.

After the service, Mr. Papadopolis rushed up to the chaplain to express his sincere appreciation for the insights received. They soon were engaged in a conversation with many of the chapel members listening in. When they learned of what had happened to him, they were aghast. How could anyone do such things, they asked? When they learned that this inhuman treatment was inspired by religious hatred, they were doubly upset.

One of the chapel members remembered reading about the incident and had been horrified by it even back then. However, now to hear it from the very same victim made it exceptionally dramatic. A sense of righteous indignation swept over of them.

"How could people that did such things or supported such things live with themselves?"

"The people responsible for such things should be placed on some deserted island by themselves until they learn to live and love as normal human beings."

Suddenly someone else remembered. "Wasn't this done when our newly elected chaplain was in great religious prominence? Did he bear some responsibility for this?"

A few of the prelate's relatives' faces reddened. They knew what had happened but chose to forget how this wicked purge against Orthodox believers had taken place.

"Should we remove our new chaplain from office? This is an embarrassment to us. Why didn't he tell us what happened under his watch? We might expect this kind of evil from savages and barbarians, but for this to happen by a religious group that professed to follow Christ is unthinkable."

"Where is Eustus this morning? I didn't see him at services today. When he appears, I suggest we call him into account. Unless he has a good explanation, and I can't see how anyone can explain such vile conduct, he should be dismissed. He should also be censored for not telling us the whole truth about such activities."

Even his relatives were very quiet and embarrassed about what was unfolding. If Mr. Papadopolis started confronting the prelate about the past when he arrived, it would likely lead to demands for greater revelation of his past. Lev felt a little embarrassed that the truth was proving to be so very painful in this little chapel. Somehow, they assumed that everyone was a kind and caring human being. And most of the time they were, but sometimes when placed in certain positions it brought out the hidden secret brutality.

Soon Lev left with his guest to return home for breakfast. Mr. Papadopolis seemed comforted that his visit had not been in vain. He had been able to confront the prelate and make his case known. After a pleasant breakfast and fellowship, Mr. Papadopolis parted. They had become steadfast friends in this short visit. Mr. Papadopolis embraced him as he left.

"Thank you from the bottom of my heart, Lev. All the good things I have heard about you are true. You are truly a selfless servant of the King. May God bless you in the days to come!"

A Man under Siege

As soon as his car disappeared down the road, Lev decided to check in at the plant where he had tried to implement some minor changes. To Lev's surprise, the prelate was there.

"We missed you at the services today. Have you been well?"

"I'm about as well as a man under siege might be."

This statement left Lev a little uncomfortable. He had no personal axe to grind with the prelate. His only purpose had been to help him repair what needed repairing. However, Lev knew it was difficult for the prelate to look within. The power to rationalize and minimize made true repentance seem unnecessary. The fact that he could do all these things without impunity back in the days of his power made the prelate feel like he was being singled out for criticism.

"We looked for you today at the chapel and noticed you weren't there. That's why I wondered if you might be emotionally upset. I know people do not get physically ill anymore, but I know you faced a lot of unpleasant confrontation yesterday. I'm sorry for the distress this caused you, but this man had a just grievance and needed answers. I felt his pain and am at a loss to understand such savagery from anyone claiming to be a Christian."

"Enough all ready," the prelate retorted. "I'm not about to talk about it anymore. I didn't want to speak about it yesterday, but I was shanghaied into it. I suppose Mr. Papadopolis told his tale of woe to the chapel members today. They are probably looking to skin me alive now. He's using his sad story to make trouble. That's all I make of it."

"God's priesthood is supposed to be merciful and compassionate. There's a big credibility gap between what is required and the reality of what was. Please don't dismiss this man as nothing more than a troublemaker. You do owe him something. The least would be a heartfelt apology. You cannot close the book on his anguish. Either directly or indirectly, it lies at your feet. The first step toward resolving a problem is admitting there is one. If you share some guilt, you should not leave a stone unturned to remove the guilt and be reconciled to your brother. If you are pure in heart in this matter, then you should offer such evidence."

The prelate was thoroughly exasperated. He said with disgust, "Here you are a Jew, among those who for centuries never owned up to their guilt in crucifying our Lord, lecturing me on my guilt. I never thought I would see the day when those who tried to serve the

Lord were set aside and those who rejected him were in positions of power."

Lev could see his conversation was going nowhere. With one last comment he said, "Those who served the Lord are with him in glory, every last one. Obviously, you were not one of them, for you would be in glory, living and reigning with Christ in his glorious reign."

The prelate flushed with resentment. Lev could see that not one word of this exchange was sinking in. Lev walked away, not wishing to provoke the man further.

The Next Chapel Meeting

On the following day, Lev arrived at the chapel earlier than usual. It was a bright sunny day, and Lev wished to get in some extra fellowship for he knew his time in this location was coming to an end. There was no purpose in staying here as long as no progress was being made. Lev met Chaplain Panucci, who was always the first one there. Lev greeted him and learned that Mr. Papadopolis' testimony yesterday had raised serious concern among the members. They wanted an explanation from the prelate of how the church could have been involved in such heinous crimes against humanity. They were going to have a meeting to allow the prelate to make his case. The Chaplain had called him with the request of the chapel members to have him answer these charges, and he said he would be present today.

Chaplain Panucci said to Lev, "If you were expecting a blessed day, I hope you won't be disappointed. The prelate didn't sound very happy about this meeting, but as a fellow chaplain I insisted that he owed the members here an explanation."

"I shall be very glad to hear him out. I'm glad you will conduct the inquiry and not me. I'm afraid he is thoroughly exasperated with me. He finds it galling that I, a Jew, should be involved in this inquiry. I was there when Mr. Papadopolis demanded an explanation from him. All he received from the prelate was that what had befallen him was wrong, but he was not prepared to admit any responsibility whatever, only regret. This should not have happened to a dog, much less a human being. There is no justification for such cruelty and barbarism. I didn't hear any godly sorrow in his explanation. I truly hope he'll find a better explanation now that he has had time to think about it."

The members began to assemble with the usual warm greetings and exchanges. The prelate didn't arrive early, but at last he did arrive just before the devotions. His family members and friends did not surround him as usual. He sat a pensive and lone figure this morning.

Lev hoped that he would admit to any responsibility he may have had and show true godly sorrow.

Chaplain Panucci Asks Eustus to Give an Accounting

The time came for Chaplain Panucci to address the purpose of the meeting.

"Dear ones in the Lord, because of Mr. Papadopolis' revelation yesterday of the things that befell him, many members want to hear Chaplain Eustus' own explanation of those events. We know Mr. Papadopolis told us the truth of his personal experience. We are not here to determine whether it was true or not. How such savagery could occur under the shadow of the church is what we are asking to have explained. This whole period is set aside to hear your testimony, Chaplain Eustus."

The prelate stood in his full stature with a steady gaze.

"I, too, am sorry for what happened to Mr. Papadopolis. It was cruel and inhuman and certainly nothing that I ordered or had even imagined would take place. We knew of the Nazi purge that was going to take place in Yugoslavia, but did not intervene in any way. The Nazis were at war with the communists, and they simply equated that the people they planned to purge were nothing more than communist sympathizers or outright communists. Such are the fortunes of war. Yes, some of our church members did join in that awful purge and terrible things happened. I learned of some of the details after the fact. Naturally, our church stood up against the communists; and, therefore, we could not be expected to hinder the logic of this purge. Do I regret what happened to Mr. Papadopolis? Yes, I was appalled by it; but, again, the mob psychology seems to have taken over and these awful things happened."

There was a pause, and someone in the audience said, "We are all appalled at what happened. No one can defend the sadistic things that occurred. No one suspects that you were overjoyed at hearing of this brutality. The question that we must know is what did you do to discipline those guilty of these crimes? What actions did you take to censor the participants in this brutality? How did you seek before God to manifest godly sorrow?"

Eustus assumed a ministerial stance. "We lived in dread of the communists. They were the avowed enemies of the church, so it was the belief that communism was being swept back that kept us from speaking out against this whole episode. Millions had died in this terrible war. A few more hundred thousand deaths did not raise many eyebrows in those days. Death and destruction was a daily occurrence. This incident, while it was very sad, did prevent the communists from being a threat to the church in that region. So there were mixed feelings. In these uprisings one never knew who would win or lose. So our people took some risk in the carnage of that time. If the events turned out badly for our church instead of the enemy, you would not be questioning me regarding the matter. Can I help it if our side was victorious?" Surely, he thought, his position and demeanor would minimize the congregation's reactions to Papadopolis' testimony of yesterday.

But another person asked, "Are you saying that you had no responsibility of any kind in this matter? Did you censor and punish those guilty of such heinous crimes? Please answer that directly without any rationalization."

"I spoke to the bishop subsequently and expressed my chagrin at what had happened. He also regretted that it had gone so far. But the mob psychology had turned evil and he could not stop what was happening once it was aroused." What was wrong with these people, Eustus wondered, that they couldn't see reason?

A man angrily shouted. "Are you saying no one is responsible? This is just one of those unfortunate things that happened, and that you were a victim, too?"

His face red with exasperation, the prelate responded, "I feel in a way that I am a victim. I did not order what happened to Mr. Papadopolis. I could not have known how this purge was going to eventuate. I was not even sure if our own church members would have fared any better than Mr. Papadopolis. Such are the fortunes of war."

Lev then stood up. "The days are past when evils that have been perpetrated can go faceless with no one responsible. If there was a crime committed, there were criminals that must be called into account. This did not just happen. This was a crime that had faces and bloody hands. Even people with white gloves on may have to confess some part in this. These people who were massacred were not just generic communists. They were human beings that had a right to live and someone stole that right from them. This was not like the general war being waged at that time. This was a deliberate ethnic purge. The Nazis say they were 'just following orders,' so they plead innocence. You say the Nazis were the perpetrators and some zealous church people joined the fray, but no one was really guilty. I do not believe this for a moment. Where there was a crime, there was a responsible criminal or criminals. How else can it be?"

Eustus Refuses to Accept Any Responsibility

In exasperated tones the prelate tried to defend himself. "I am being held in contempt because I did not stand up against those who did these things. I was not in command of the Nazi forces. However, they were protecting the church from the communist horde in the north. Were we sympathetic to seeing Germany victorious? Yes, in that time and place we were. All of Europe was within the fold of the church and the Germans took care not to hurt our members, with minor exceptions. We wanted to do nothing that would turn the Nazis against the church.

"Those were dark and dismal days. The light was not shining like now. The world was on fire and death and dying was rampant. We made the choice of supporting the Nazis against the communists. Had the communists been victorious, the church would have been assaulted. It turned out that it was the Allied Armies that saved the church from being overrun by the communists. It was only when the United States entered the war that the Nazis were certain to lose it."

It was apparent that the prelate was not prepared to accept any responsibility for what had happened. He could not see things from any other window but his own. He was unable to identify right from wrong. He only saw things from the church's perspective even now. Of course, it was obvious to him that Mr. Papadopolis suffered a great evil, but who could not see that? He did not reproach those who perpetrated this crime. The killing business had been very much a part of church history, so what had happened under his watch seemed something very common.

However, the chapel members were becoming agitated with his constant rationalization. Another person stood up.

"We were used to these rationalizations before, because that's the way the world was. We just groaned and went along with it. We weren't real followers of Christ. We were 'Sunday Christians,' and the other days of the week we were free to do what we wanted. However, it was the Lord who finally brought about the downfall of the church. When the churches blessed the invading armies against Israel, it ended their charade of being God's agents. What we have heard from you is that you still profess to be a Christian who was involved in a lot of bloody politics. I for one cannot accept your rationalization about what happened. You did not seem to have loved righteousness and you certainly did not hate iniquity. What is even more painfully obvious to me is that you have not changed."

The prelate stood stunned. He was not accustomed to such outrageous boldness. Those in power were shielded from such confrontations with common people. He seemed unable to recover his composure for this was the height of indignity. He felt himself being pulled from his lofty perch into the lowest class of people. How could they be so insensitive to his dignity? However, he was forgetting what happened to those prelates following the destruction of the invading armies against Jerusalem. They were not just criticized, but assailed by the angry mobs.

Another member spoke up. "What did you do to punish those who blinded and skinned Mr. Papadopolis alive? All I heard was that you lamented what happened. How did you punish those responsible?"

The prelate was still trying to recover from the barrage of criticism leveled at him. Finally, he pulled himself up to his full height and he replied, "I feel that nothing I say will vindicate me or my former actions. My angry brethren whose blood lust is running high condemn me. So I humbly withdraw from being a chaplain in this chapel. I am sorry. Now you have two victims. Mr. Papadopolis and me."

No One Comes to Eustus' Defense

No one stood up to request he reconsider his withdrawal. Perhaps he thought his loyal relatives would come to his defense. However, even they were shaken and outraged at what had happened to Mr. Papadopolis. Had he shown some godly sorrow, perhaps they might have stood up for him. Clearly, his defense may have been satisfactory in an evil world, but in a world now filled with light it was not.

Soon someone said, "I move that we accept the prelate's resignation." The motion was seconded and without a dissenting voice, it was carried unanimously. There followed a very pronounced silence.

The poor prelate did not wait for the services to end, but with an ashen face he simply stood up and walked toward the door. From his own perspective, he was indeed a victim. His main concern, unfortunately, was not for the true victim or the many others that suffered and died without anyone lifting a finger in their defense.

The following day the prelate did not show up for work or even call in to say he would not report for duty. Lev hoped to see him there, but he realized that he would have to have a final personal call at his home after finishing his work for the day. Lev knew his assignment was over. He had done everything he could to help the prelate adjust to the new conditions of light and truth.

After Lev concluded his services that day, he told those in charge that he would not be there much longer. He had accomplished most of the improvements to the operation that he could and they gratefully accepted the fact that he would be moving on.

Lev paused in front of the prelate's house. It took courage to ring the bell. He knew he would be as welcome as a plague. The prelate dutifully opened the door. He tried to be as civil as possible.

"What brings you here, Lev?" he asked in a flat tone.

"Well, I've come to say farewell. I'm sorry that our relationship has not been a very happy one. We seem to come from two different worlds and are not having a good meeting of minds or hearts. I am at a loss to know how to the build a bridge between our two worlds. I've had many successes in overcoming differences with people in the past, but I confess I struck out with you. I hate to leave as such a failure. What could I have done to deal better with our differences?"

"Perhaps the best thing you could have done was to leave me alone. I suspect those higher up sent you here to get me to change or amend my ways. I was quite alone in the office I once held, and I am even lonelier now. I once could do no wrong, and now I find I can do no right. I have lost my reputation as a holy man, and I have lost my following of adherents to the faith. Even my friends and family no longer respect me. I have been driven from being chaplain—what further loss can I sustain?"

"It's not what you lose that counts, it is what you gain that matters today. If you learn to love your fellow man more than your former power and glory, that will bring joy to your heart and steal your loneliness away. You cannot justify a failed past that brought so much pain to so many. You can learn, like Scrooge finally did, to have a loving heart and give yourself and your resources to helping others. Forget the make-believe world you once enjoyed but did not use to glorify God or to bless your fellow man.

"Today is all that you have. Before you are life and death. You must choose between them. Overcoming is not easy, but it is the pathway of blessing and life. Choose life that you may live. I didn't come to condemn you, but to help you step up higher. If you live trying to recreate the past, you will find it is wasted effort. The past is gone forever. Christ is in power and you are not with him. Some of those that the church persecuted are also with him in glory. If he did not choose you to be with him, you must not be worthy of such honor. Accept that and go on to become as worthy as you possibly can be in the present."

"I Would Be Happier in the Lonely Grave"

"That's easy for you to say. You have friends great and small and a throng of people who admire you. I am the prince turned into a frog and I hate it. I didn't ask to be in this world and perhaps I would be happier in the lonely grave from which I was so rudely awakened. I didn't feel pain or rejection there. I have a host of people who look askance at me now as a failed spiritual leader. Many blame me for their former pain or loss of life. I see other people happy and rejoicing—so many are experiencing joy and blessedness. I'm not in that happy throng. Many times I wish I hadn't been awakened, but left to sleep quietly in my grave. I felt no pain or grief there. I was not loved nor hated, accepted nor rejected. It was beautifully peaceful."

"There you go again, instead of facing the present and making the most of life's opportunities, you want to give up on life and its opportunities and find a place like the grave where you have no struggles.

"Anyway," Lev continued, "I will be leaving soon. There will be other people like Mr. Papadopolis arriving to seek answers from you concerning the past. You may dismiss them or embrace them. However, you will not be able to hide from the past. People who suffered because of what you did or did not do will want to know how you will answer them. Your answer must be better than your explanation to Mr. Papadopolis. He didn't accept your explanation and neither did the chapel members. The answer that will satisfy them is one which reveals to them that you made hideous mistakes in office, but now you are renewed and eager to seek their forgiveness and eager to give yourself to society to show your love for them."

The prelate stood there pensively. For the first time his defenses were gone. Perhaps he saw a ray of light shining in a dark corner of his life.

He finally said, "Lev, you are a decent fellow, I have to admit that. It is just that I have lost the will to face life with my entire past coming back to haunt me. Why do so many people find life so beautiful now while I am languishing?"

"What can I say? Life is what you make it. It can be unbelievably beautiful or full of heartache and sadness. However, now there is nothing physical to cause pain. We have wonderful health. We are secure with an abundance of good things. Most people have some unpleasant things of the past to live down. We all made mistakes, but it happened not because of malice, but because of poor judgment or just bad timing. Many times we started out to do the right thing and it turned out wrong. These were some of the hazards of our imperfections. Now an open door is before every person. We can enter it and go upward or stay cringing at the portal. We all have some things of our past to live down and to correct. We may use our past experiences as stepping-stones or allow them to be stumbling stones. However, choose we must. Maybe you could even seek out those you owe amends to and hasten the process back to harmony with your fellow men? May the Lord help you to make the right choices."

Lev extended his hand, as he was about to leave. The prelate accepted it with a genuine handclasp. Lev was grateful to leave knowing that he was not considered an enemy any longer.

Lev Calls Moses

That evening Lev called Moses to tell him his mission had gone about as far as it could. Lev told him that he had brought the prelate to the point where he must confront his past and go on to repentance and reform. The other choice would be to live in denial in the present and keep trying to recreate the past. Whether the prelate would have the courage to move forward was the question. The way before him was a hard one. He had multitudes of people who would be seeking him out to know how or why he did certain things in the past. Many suffered and died because of the poor choices the prelate had made. He had kept a lot of bad company. He played in the politics of the world and had done poorly. Yet there was forgiveness and renewal that could make his life beautiful again.

"You have done as well as could be expected, Lev. Isn't it remarkable to see that the blessings and opportunities of life are equally before every person? It is only the weight of the past that holds people down and creates its own type of unhappiness. For most people the blessings of this time are so overwhelmingly beautiful, but for a few people their past sins still cling to them and are oppressive. God's ways are equal.

"However, Lev, with your permission, you will not be going home but to a little community in the area of what used to be Hamburg, Germany. There is a man who has returned to life who has a grotesque past. He was a doctor who performed all kinds of experiments on living people. He personally supervised the hideous experiments on hapless victims watching them die without a shred of compassion. The prelate helped him escape to Argentina after the war where he lived without having to face his past. His name is Dr. Raschor, and he, like others who did evil things, will have an extremely difficult time facing those he experimented on in the cruelest of experiments. Likewise, because of the pain people suffered, they have a vivid personal hatred of this man. He did enormous evil, the kind of evil that should have awakened his conscience at some point, but he seemed to be a man without a shred of conscience or compassion. If you will agree to go there, we would greatly appreciate it. This man needs all the help he can get to unravel his twisted mind. Are you willing?"

"Yes, I will go. I don't especially like dealing with such warped personalities, but usually you find some traces of decency that have been suppressed. I will be ready to leave tomorrow."

"Good. We appreciate your willingness. Remember that this is a double-edged sword. You will not only have to deal with this demented criminal mind, but also people overcome with passions as they remember what he did to them. They have every emotional right to be angry with him. He was a monster that never should have been left to perform his evil experiments. However, the powers of darkness were ruling the world then. And so, no evil was too great at the time. Shalom, Lev."

"Love your enemies"
(Matthew 5:44).

Chapter Fifteen

Lev decided to drive from Italy to his next destination in Germany. He secured a car to take a leisurely trip, enjoying the beautiful scenery en route and collecting his thoughts. He knew of many of the hideous experiments that had been carried out during the Nazi regime. How could anyone perform such abominable acts? How did their consciences become so badly seared? Was there any hope that such people could change from monsters into loving and caring human beings?

Lev arrived in the area formerly known as Hamburg and found the new home he was to occupy. It had just been completed and no one was living in it yet. Since the person whose home Lev was using would be returning to life in about three weeks, that was all the time he had. Lev inquired about the doctor to learn all he could about Dr. Raschor. Apparently he was very withdrawn, consistently avoiding public contact, not attending chapel services and not engaged in any community or factory projects. It was said he was polite, had a professional bearing, but was not interested in talking to anyone more than necessary. Dr. Raschor liked to work in his garden and kept everything very neat. Many people whom he had tortured had come looking for him, but he wouldn't talk to them or open his door to anyone.

Lev realized that he also might have a difficult time contacting Dr. Raschor. How could he reach the doctor, since he was apparently determined not to face any of his victims? It would be difficult to face anyone on whom he had performed such monstrous experiments. In the day of his power, he didn't have to think about the victims. People were non-entities whose cries and screams could be managed by simply taping the mouth shut. But here they had returned to life, something Dr. Raschor never expected, and it was most unpleasant to contemplate meeting them.

Lev made plans to contact Dr. Raschor the next day. He had an unpleasant task to do, and he thought it would be best to get it done as quickly as possible. In his evening studies of God's Word, it occurred to him that the doctor might be interested in knowing about some of his former partners in crime.

After the morning services at the chapel Lev decided to call the doctor for an appointment. A very abrupt message on an answering service said, "State your business and leave your phone number. Don't expect an answer. Good day."

That was about as cold and uninviting as it could be. However, Lev left his message. "This is Mr. Aron. I have recently met with Hitler and the prelate of Rome. Would you be interested in learning about them?" Lev then left his number.

As Lev ate his breakfast the phone rang. He answered, "Good morning. This is Mr. Aron."

"Yes, this is Dr. Raschor. I do not answer calls generally, but I would be interested in hearing about your visits with both the prelate and Hitler. When may we meet?"

"In about an hour at your home if that is satisfactory. I know your address and am very nearby."

"Yes, that would be satisfactory. I shall expect you in one hour."

Lev sensed some tension in the call, but Dr. Raschor's curiosity was stronger than his inhibitions. It is strange how bedfellows longed to keep alive the comradeship of the past. It was lonely to live in a world of righteousness where past evil deeds were as black as sin. It was easy to kill and torture people and then incinerate their remains without much thought. A few hours or days of pain, and the victims disappeared, forever – or so they thought. Had they known these same people would be made alive again along with themselves, it might have given some pause to their evil works.

In their wildest dreams they never thought they would have to confront their hapless victims again, but nothing was under their control anymore. They found their past deeds condemning them with no one to sympathize with them and no lawyers to defend them.

A Tense Meeting

Lev arrived at the doctor's residence at the appointed time. After confirming that his guest was Mr. Aron, he let him in. Lev reached for the doctor's extended hand and gave him a normal handshake.

The doctor was still very nervous and apprehensive.

"Did Adolf or the prelate send you here?"

"No, not really."

"Then why did you come to visit me?"

"Because you invited me is the most logical answer I can give."

"Yes, yes, indeed I did. Perhaps I am putting this visit in a difficult light. You do know of and have visited both Adolf and the prelate, is that correct?"

"Yes, indeed, I have visited Adolf, Geli and Eva Braun, as well as the prelate. As a matter of fact, I was with the prelate just a day or two ago. They didn't know I would be coming here and, for that matter, I didn't know either. However, I found myself in your neighborhood and thought I would give you a call to see if you might be interested in how these people were doing."

"Well, yes. So what have you to tell me?"

"I was with Hitler when he returned to life. He was very nervous. Like all of us who return to life, it was difficult to reconcile the past with the present. He demanded to call the Reichstag. When he found the number no longer existed, he became very confused. He thought he was the Fuehrer and could give orders, but everyone ignored him. He was worried that the Russians might find him or even the Allied Armies. It took a while for him to get adjusted. He did love the menu of fruits that he ate and the good health he now had. However, he was afraid to leave his home for fear that he would be recognized. He shaved his mustache and changed his hairstyle so that his appearance was not as easily discerned. He looked much younger and more vibrant and a few inches taller than in his previous life." Lev carefully watched Dr. Raschor's reactions.

"When he learned I was a Jew, it made him uncomfortable; but, since I was his only connection to the real world, he needed me. He did learn to respect me after a while. His first love was a woman named Geli and he wanted to see her. When he met her, he found she not only never loved him, but now that she knew what a monster he turned out to be, she was glad that she had taken her life so she did not in any way become involved in the terrible things that happened. He was devastated that she rejected him.

"Next, he wanted to see Eva Braun. At first she was eager to meet him again and they did enjoy being together for a while, but gradually, she, too, distanced herself from him. Soon he found himself alone in a big world without a shred of power and loathed for his past. He just had too much evil baggage that kept clinging to him."

A Past That Haunts Him

The doctor listened very carefully. In his former life, he had escaped to South America and lived comfortably there. No one seemed to know or care about his past, so he was hoping to do the same thing since he returned to life. However, there was a big difference now. In South America, few really knew who he was or what he had done. The church had helped him escape and also helped cover his past. However, now there was no cover from his evil deeds anywhere. People whom he had tortured and killed were looking for him and there was no Gestapo to cover for him. The days of his power were over, and the things that he had done clung to him like a stench. So far, what he was hearing brought him little comfort or cheer.

The doctor, wishing to hear something more encouraging, asked, "Well, then, how did your visit with the prelate go? Surely, here was a man you could respect and that the people could look upon with favor. You know, this man thought well enough of me to get me papers to live in South America." His flaxen hair and blue-eyed boyish good looks were in stark contrast with the character that was within.

"Yes, I am familiar with that. The prelate has been accused of operating the 'ratlines' in getting many criminals into safe havens. This and other things that happened under his watch are a tremendous burden to him. A man named Papadopolis came to call on the prelate. He happened to be the poor Orthodox Church bishop whom the Nazis and the ruling bishop of Yugoslavia had blinded and skinned alive. He confronted the prelate, leaving him quite shaken. So I have to tell you that those who did evil things or looked the other way when grossly evil things were done face a heavy load in this present time. None of the old rationalizations are working for them."

This was all very distressing to the doctor. He was wishing he had not opened his door to Lev. He was ready to dismiss him, but Lev was not ready to be dismissed.

Lev continued, "You know, countless millions have read of your experiments on so many hapless people. How do you close out all those tortured faces of horror from your mind? How could you do such things? Have you no heart, no compassion? How could you go home to your children and not realize that you were doing such terrible things to other people's children?"

Invited to Leave

The doctor was fuming. "You have used your knowledge of Adolf and the prelate to gain an entrance so that you might lecture me on my evil deeds. You are a slick operator, I must say. Well, Mr. Aron, there is the door, and I invite you to leave immediately."

"We Jews are still here to confront you. I didn't come of my own accord. Moses, who serves the Lord Christ, has sent me here. Make no mistake. Your very life is at stake and you better listen to me very carefully. Millions of other people have returned to life and are making wonderful progress. They have received life and all its blessings with thankful hearts, rejoicing to help their fellows return to life. They're eager to love and forgive other people, to be happy and equally eager to serve the new King. Dr. Raschor, are you the last to welcome back the King?"

The doctor was speechless. He did respect authority, and suddenly he realized that a representative of the King was sitting in his living room. He changed his hostile demeanor. This was a moment of truth for him. He knew that Lev had outsmarted him and out maneuvered him. What the doctor had hoped to hear was never spoken. He had wanted to know how these men with bloody hands were making out, and he found that they were having the same trouble that he was having. He had thought long and hard on how to justify his deeds, and that was basically all that he had done since returning to life. Now the moment had come for him to defend himself.

He cleared his throat, choosing his words very carefully. "Mr. Aron, I'm sure what I did was wrong. I cannot defend what I did given today's environment. However, then I wanted to make a name for myself. We had puzzled in medical school about what effect different things would have on human beings. I was given the opportunity to perform experiments on people who were slated to die anyway. I rationalized that my experiments might have been a bit more painful, but that they would die before too long. What difference would a little suffering make? We learned many things from my experiments. Did you know the entire medical world sought to get all the data on my experiments? We doctors are curious about where the limits of life and death are, so I created all kinds of experiments to answer those questions. Once I started, I became inured to the suffering and pain of my victims. Sometimes we just stuffed their mouths with cotton and taped their mouths so we didn't have to listen to their screams. I was so carried away with my experiments that I scarcely thought of them as human beings." A few beads of sweat had popped up on his brow.

"That's all very interesting, Doctor, but how is it that now you realize they *were* human beings, precious human beings that parents had raised and cared for? You were not raised a savage. Your medical oath included the caring for and preserving of human life. How could you turn into a hideous monster of torture and death? Have you no fear of God? Because the Nazis had become a people without law or decency, were you carried away with their madness?"

"You ask many questions, Mr. Aron. I wish that I could give you a clear and precise answer." Something flickered in his intense eyes. "In a way I am glad to start talking about what happened with someone. I have been living in this home as my fortress. I can present a host of rationalizations, but I cannot answer in my heart why I did such things. I still think of myself as a sensitive caring human being. Yet now I am known as 'Doctor Bluebeard.' That is really what I was. I admit it. I cannot defend it in any moral way. It was depraved wickedness that the dark power of the Nazi party gave me the opportunity to exercise. Now I look back with anguish. How am I going to face these people? What can I say to them to get them to receive me as a human being? I don't expect them to love me. How could anyone love me? I fear I am Satan's child." He sat with his head in his hands.

His Children You Are, Whose Works You Do

Lev knew he had to be gentle as well as clear about what was necessary to do. "There is little doubt that you were a child of Satan in that time and place, but now is the day of opportunity to confess your crimes against humanity and then move on to good works in helping build homes for those returning in the regeneration and to plant gardens. Now is the time to show who you really are. You must place the past at the foot of the cross and show mankind that you are truly repentant and reformed. You must love the Lord your God with all your heart, with all your strength and with your entire mind and your neighbor as yourself. You can do it. That is what I have come here to tell you. YOU CAN DO IT." Lev laid a comforting hand on the distraught man's shoulder.

"I wish I could undo the past. I cannot explain how I was so numb to the pain and suffering of my victims. Nothing I can do will ever take away the memory. The only way we could do such things was by dehumanizing these victims in our minds. They were just raw meat living in my butcher shop. Yes, we gained knowledge, but in the process we lost our humanity. Sometimes I look longingly back at death. I didn't feel guilt or shame there. I didn't feel pain. I didn't feel anything.

"Mr. Aron, can you understand my state of mind? Here I live in a beautiful paradise, with every joy to the human senses before me. I should be happy. Life is beautiful. People are beautiful. There are no sick people, no deformed people and no mentally ill people. I see so many happy faces passing by my house, but here I sit in the prison that I have made for myself. I don't know why I am telling you this, you of all people, a Jew. We treated Jews as subhuman. As you know, Jews were my victims and now, of all things! Salvation is of the Jews. The Jews are running this world and doing a great job of it. I was so terribly wrong. What can I do?"

Lev listened to his cry for help. This monster did indeed have a heart somewhere within. This was the first person involved heavily in crime that seemed to be willing to admit guilt and shame for his past. Whether it was a genuine plea for help or just the emotion of the moment remained to be seen. Undoubtedly this man needed help, and he needed to find some way to change his life around instead of trying to dodge responsibility of living down his sins in a just and noble way.

Other men were successful in doing so. Even King David sinned greatly, but with a humble and contrite heart he gained the approval of God and the respect of men.

Finally Lev said, "Do you think Christ brought you back to life again in this beautiful world just to show everyone what a mean person and a scoundrel you were? Let me help you know the King Jesus. The arrangement now is that every willful sin must receive a just punishment. You sinned against God first, when you tortured and killed human beings in your mad experiments. You must repent and reform and go on to works of love and compassion. True repentance will lead to godly sorrow, and godly sorrow to a vehement clearing of yourself from your past sins. You can do it if you will to do it.

"Your past will not go away until people see you are not the mean and ruthless person you once were. They know you cannot remove the memories that torment their minds even now, but at least if they could see that you have allowed Christ to take away your heart of stone and replace it with a heart of flesh, they will find healing and refreshment in that. You owe society ten times more devotion and self-sacrifice than most other men. You need to give of yourself unreservedly to prove your love for God and mankind."

Change Sounding Possible

"You make it sound possible, Mr. Aron. But how can I face the countless people that I mutilated, experimented with and then incinerated to make believe nothing happened? Satan could not have conceived of a more monstrous operation than I had. My justification that I was contributing to science sounds empty now. I had a license from the Nazi party to sin, and sin grievously I did."

"You can go out and show the world you are not the same person you were, that you are renewed, repentant and reformed. They will believe you have a heart of flesh when you begin demonstrating it.

"Only you can make the choice. That is why I was sent here. The Ancients know what is taking place because Christ is omnipotent and he knows at what level every human being is performing. You happen to be at a very low level, and you will be dropped from the Lamb's Book of Life if you don't have an attitude adjustment. This is the sober message I bring to you, Dr. Raschor. However, the mere fact that Christ has taken note of your lack of development is a sign that he does wish to help you change."

Lev then stood up, ready to leave.

"Wait! Don't leave just yet. You have brought a ray of hope to me in my darkness. Do you really think that I can change from the monster that I was into a man with a heart of flesh? Even if I do, people will still hate me, and I confess they have every reason to hate me. I would hate anyone who did such evil to me or my loved ones." There was great longing in the doctor's voice.

"Christ would have no purpose in bringing you to life again if there were no possibility of your overcoming your evil past and going on to perfection." Lev replied comfortingly. "Yes, it is possible, very possible. Yes, it is even probable if you will to change sincerely and faithfully. You can be an overcomer. You have a lot more to overcome than most people, but with Christ all things are possible."

Lev invited the doctor to come to the chapel meeting in the morning. He asked the doctor if he knew where it was.

"Yes, I know where it is, but I am afraid if I go there and if someone recognizes me there will be a riot."

"Well, I am personally inviting you to come, and I will be there to stand by you. I can't tell you that no one will recognize you; but, if they do, they cannot hurt you. You have to start facing your past with a sincere and genuine acknowledgment of the wrong. Then you must ask how you can make it up to those you hurt. You have to be willing to confess what you confessed to me. You might be surprised to find that people can forgive the sins committed against them. Remember, they, too, need forgiveness. We all have had need of forgiveness, because we all were sinners. Will you be at the chapel tomorrow morning?"

"Yes, I will try to be there. I will go forth with fear and trembling, but I have to start somewhere. By the way, your first name isn't Lev, is it?"

"Yes, I am Lev Aron. I didn't want to use the name most people recognize me by because I didn't want you to know who I was. Forgive me for that, but I wanted to see you and I thought the name 'Lev' might be waving a red flag."

"Well, it would have had I known who you were. However, now that I know you as a person, I must confess that for the first time I see a little ray of hope in my troubled life. I'm sorry I was so brusque with you at first. You have opened my eyes for the first time since I returned to life. Thank you. I never dreamed that a Jew would return good for all the evil that I did against his race."

"Shalom." With that, Lev shook the doctor's hand and strode out. "See you tomorrow at the chapel, don't forget."

"I will be there."

A Corner Turned by the Doctor

For the first time in dealing with those with a very dark past, Lev felt that here was a person who wanted to reach out to escape the darkness of his past. Would he have the courage to follow through? Lev wondered, since the doctor had had such an evil past, would he have the courage to change his mind and heart?

Lev felt a little encouraged after his experiences in those other cases. Here seemed to be a person who wanted to make good. He thought about it while walking home and decided to call Moses and tell him about it.

When Lev reached Moses, he said, "My first contact with the doctor turned out better than I hoped. He wants to undo his past and go on to higher ground. Whether he will have the courage to follow through, I do not know. He does see that he can change and that he must change. I feel like my visit here may have turned on a light in his mind."

"Excellent. Sometimes people who have done hideous things can change into beautiful human beings. We will give him all the help he needs. Keep up the good work, Lev. You must encourage him to take in the chapel meetings so he can get out and face the people. Shalom, Lev."

The following morning Lev spoke to the chaplain to prepare him for the possibility of Dr. Raschor's visit. He was a notorious figure and it was possible someone would recognize him, especially if he had the courage to give his name to those who asked. There were deep feelings in the hearts of many people, and the members of the chapel needed to be on their best behavior. Christ would mete out justice, so no one had to take matters into their own hands. While no one could control the fact that feelings of resentment would arise, everyone was responsible for behaving civilly.

The chaplain was an understanding person and shared the same sentiments. To Lev's pleasant surprise, the doctor did arrive in time for the morning devotions. No one seemed to recognize him when he entered, for nearly every day some new face appeared. However, he kept a low profile and seemed to enjoy the singing and services. Immediately after the services he quickly left without anyone recognizing him or showing any special interest in him. He was able to go without special notice for about a week. Meanwhile, he called Lev every day and talked to him about his concerns. He confessed that he enjoyed getting out and he enjoyed the services. It seemed these services were clean and holy—it was a different world for him when he was there.

The doctor confessed to Lev, "You know, I have felt so mean and unclean most of my life. In the professional world I could talk about knowledge gained by my hideous experiments and close out all the unpleasant memories associated with those awful moments. Nobody asked about the victims. Wasn't that strange for doctors who were supposed to be caring people? They seemed extravagantly interested in the data I had accumulated, though. Oddly, Lev, you are the only one who cared nothing for the data and only about the victims. If doctors had called my experiments into account and challenged my evil deeds, I probably would have modified my experiments to a humane level. Even the Allies after the war were more interested in my data without one word of reproach being raised about the poor people who'd been used."

Lev knew that this was good for Dr. Raschor to open up and see himself in a true light. This was a catharsis for him, and it seemed like he was wishing to shed his heart of stone and gain a heart of flesh.

As the week had passed and Lev seemed to be making progress in getting the doctor to acknowledge his evil past and start making positive changes, he encouraged the doctor to help in building homes for those returning to life and to seek employment in some of the facilities in the neighborhood to serve his fellow humans. He responded positively and followed through with both suggestions.

Two Russians Pay Dr. Raschor a Visit

The following week two Russian men appeared at the chapel meeting. They spoke Hebrew and German fluently as they greeted members of the chapel. Lev surmised they had been returned to life already for several years, for they were extremely intelligent as well as handsome specimens of humanity. They sat as far back as they could upon entering. While they joined in the singing, Lev, who also sat in the back to observe, noticed they kept looking around.

Then one of them spotted the doctor and pointed to him. He was sitting in a seat where they could see his profile. They stayed after the meeting, talking to various ones in a charming manner. However, they kept taking glances toward the doctor to keep him in view.

Lev decided to go over to the doctor and asked if he could walk home with him. He seemed pleased with Lev's request and invited him to have breakfast with him. Lev's reason for walking with him was to be with him just in case these two men chose to follow the doctor to his home. His suspicions were correct, for they walked just far enough behind so as not to be noticed, but still close enough to keep an eye on the doctor.

Lev and the doctor turned in at the doctor's home and Lev could see the two men nonchalantly observing where the doctor lived. Upon entering, Lev told the doctor, who turned pale and very nervous upon hearing that he would probably have visitors. Lev told the doctor to let him do the initial talking. He was sure these men would not try to do anything violent. They had lived long enough in the new arrangement of things to be careful of their conduct. Sure enough, the two Russian gentlemen knocked on the door. Lev opened it wide and gave them a broad smile inviting them in. He also asked if they might have breakfast in the doctor's home.

"We have not come to be entertained. We have traveled here from Russia to see Dr. Raschor. Perhaps he will remember us."

The poor doctor stood almost paralyzed, staring at the two men. He finally said, "Are you the two Russian officers that I had placed in a tank of icy water?"

"Yes, Doctor we are. You managed to keep us alive for five hours. Normally death would come within one hour, but you placed heat at the back of our skulls. My friend asked the officer to shoot us. I said, 'I expect no mercy from this Fascist dog.' We then waved hands with a 'Farewell, Comrade.' Do you remember that, Doctor?"

Dr. Raschor was miserable, but remained calmly composed. "Yes, now I remember your faces. You are so handsome now, not the gaunt prisoners I had placed in that tank. I left the room for a few minutes. When I returned a Pole who served there tried to chloroform you to end your pain, and I threatened to have him put in the tank if he ever tried that again. You were coherent for three hours, but shortly after became incoherent. You were exceptionally brave and strong men.

"However, you were two of many victims. Some of our experiments had people tied to a cot outside. Others were naked, covered with a sheet; and some were without a sheet. We did this in the dead of winter with freezing temperatures outside. Every hour a pail of cold water was thrown on them. They were outside so we barely heard their screams; however, we managed to hear them when the cold water was thrown on them. You were not the only ones to die slow and painful deaths. Now you have come to remind me of my evil past." This last was stated with a measure of relief.

"Well, if we could take justice into our own hands we might take pleasure in beating you to a pulp, but we know justice belongs to Christ. If we were allowed to do that, we would be preempting countless others from having the same pleasure we might have in killing you. There is no possibility of our hurting you. You know that, too, don't you? We have come to hear how you can live with yourself now. How can you look in the mirror in the morning? How can you go to the chapel where prayer is made to God? How do you lift up your eyes to heaven with bloodstained hands?"

A Guilty Plea

"Oh, yes, indeed, I am guilty of unspeakable crimes. In the day of my power I would occasionally have some pangs of guilt from my conscience, but I never let my emotions interfere with what I convinced myself was science. I had to rationalize that the information I was gathering would help some of our Luftwaffe pilots who had to ditch their planes in icy waters. I, after all, was not like Frau Ilse Kach, who selected those with tattoos to have them killed for their tattooed skin so she could make lampshades of them. That only served her trivial liking for human skin lampshades with artwork on them. There was no redeeming value there.

I carried out equally ruthless experiments, putting men in altitude chambers and either increasing or reducing the atmospheric pressure. We watched them die in unbearable pain.

"Yes, I did such terrible things. I could go on and on telling you of the horror I inflicted on people. None of those scenes have left me, especially now that I am growing in mental alertness and my mind only gets more capable of detailed memory. However, not one Nazi ever suggested that I cease from those awful experiments. After the war the whole medical community in the world sought to collect the data from my experiments. The world was a very evil world. I was tarred with the same evil that covered the whole Nazi party. We were absolutely mad.

"Even when we knew the war was lost, the gas chambers continued unabated until almost the hour before the Allied armies overrode our camps. We were in a killing frenzy unparalleled in history. Mercy, kindness—what was that? We had become savage beasts and our bloodlust was running high. Do the lions pity the prey as they savagely tear flesh from its quivering body? We were worse than lions. The lions dined on meat. They killed to assuage their hunger. We killed to assuage our madness. It was madness that drove us to betray every last vestige of humanity and gentleness.

"Gentlemen, how often I wish that I had remained in the grave. Then I would not lie awake at night breaking out in a cold sweat, praying to God to remove this pain and guilt from me. It does not go away. Now you are relaxed and rejoicing in life. You have friends and family who shared your pain and the injustice done to you. Most people would condemn me if they could, and I am worthy of such treatment. I was a monster in every sense of the word.

"What can I do now to fix it?" he implored. "I cannot take away the pain I caused you. It is there forever embedded in your mind. Can you ever forgive me? I don't know. I have no right to ask for your forgiveness. I don't deserve it, I really don't. I have in my past life dug a pit so deep and so wide for myself that I fear I can never climb out of it. If it weren't for Lev, I would not even try.

"Yes, Lev, a Jew no less; it is he that has encouraged me to believe that somehow and some way Christ will forgive me and then maybe others may do so to follow his example. Gentlemen, what can I do now? I cannot kill myself. I have thought of that over and over, but spiritual powers would prevent me from this easy way out of my present pain. There is no way for me to go but forward. I must change and become a caring and loving human being. It seems so out of reach that I faint in my mind. How can I be transformed into an image of God? I have been about as far away from God as a man can go."

Stunned by the Doctor's Admissions

The two Russians sat stunned at his frank admission of the heinous crimes he committed. In silence, they occasionally looked at each other but didn't know how to answer. Granting this monster forgiveness was impossible. He could never gain their respect, at least so it seemed, as they realized suddenly that they had to be reconciled to him at some point in time.

One of the gentleman said, "Perhaps Christ can forgive you. He forgave those who crucified him. He was, however, the Son of God who came to forgive sin and reconcile mankind to God. We are just Russian soldiers returned to life who fought and killed Germans before we were captured. We killed on the battlefield; but you not only killed, you almost had pleasure in human suffering. You were Satan's child if there ever was one. I can forgive many things, but I cannot forgive the pain and agony you caused not only us, but countless others."

His voice rose and he screamed, "You are a monster. I hate you, I detest you, and I loathe you."

Poor Dr. Raschor; he cringed in his seat. He felt this man's anger and outrage that he so justly deserved. There was nowhere to hide and no way to undo the pain and the agony he had caused. He sat there limply, shaking while contemplating those moments he so callously stood over his victims. Now he was the one being tormented. He knew that hundreds of others would seek him out, and he despaired of this. If he had only known then that all men would live again and with them all past evil and good deeds.

The doctor had seen the joy of those coming to life again who loved and sacrificed on behalf of their fellow men. He could not remember any good that he had done. He was a selfish and ambitious man and now his shallow life seemed to have no redeeming value. What were all his experiments worth now in this world of love and kindness? No one could bear to consider them, let alone commend him for them.

Lev saw it was time to get involved.

"Gentlemen, as difficult as this may seem to you, your hating, detesting and loathing will not benefit you or the doctor. We have had six thousand years of selfishness and hatred. Left to ourselves, we would have destroyed the whole human race. Fortunately, Christ intervened and showed us a higher way. What does sin bring forth? Death. Remember the story Jesus told of the man who owed a great debt that he could not pay? He pleaded for mercy from his creditor and received it. Then what did he do? He found the man who owed him a small amount and grabbed him by the throat demanding his money and would not show him mercy. Christ has forgiven us all a great debt. That is why we are all alive again. Here you are gentlemen grabbing for the doctor's throat, demanding he pay his relatively small debt. Does something sound wrong here?"

Lev continued, "The judgment of death was upon all men. While the evil brought upon you was deliberate and pernicious, it is only a part of the total suffering mankind has endured. There were plagues, famine, flood, fire and wars that never seemed to end. Then there were the accidents that blinded, maimed and paralyzed countless millions. There were people born with painful infirmities, with twisted and contorted bodies, and insanity—the list could go on and on. Think of the lepers who endured a living death. They were just unfortunate victims of the things that have befallen mankind. This we accept because no one bore direct responsibility for these things. Admittedly, when pain is precipitated deliberately, it is especially evil and harder to endure. Christ will mete out justice—every sin and evil will receive a just punishment. Nobody is getting away with anything, no, not even the doctor here. He must live down his past."

The second Russian had been less vocal and sat listening very carefully. He finally said, "I came here today knowing that nothing the doctor could say would undo the past. I know that somehow I must lay my aggrieved heart at the foot of the cross. I can never forget the pain and helplessness we felt dying of hypothermia. I can never forget the sadistic face of the doctor who probably would have shown more mercy to a dog than to us, and I cannot help but wish we could put him in that ice-cold tank of water for a half hour to let him feel what it was like. However, we cannot do that. I must confess that the doctor's plea at this time does sound sincere. The most we can hope to accomplish today is to have the doctor change and put on human qualities of love, compassion and good works. Will he do it? I don't know, but Christ must know the answer. Every man's work will be revealed."

A Godless Communist Confesses

It was his turn to do some admitting. "I was a godless communist. I know, if the tables had been turned and we had captured the doctor, I would not have hesitated to torture him. His cries for mercy and compassion would have fallen on deaf ears. I hated the Nazis, and those we captured only wished they could die quickly. We beat them and starved them and God only knows what else we did to those poor captured souls. So in many respects, I guess I'm no different from you.

We all need the lessons on compassion that Lev speaks of. If Christ can forgive you, I guess I must do likewise. I would not want to be in your shoes. You must face a lot of angry people yet, and not all will forgive you easily. However, as Lev said, we have all been forgiven the judgment of death that stood against us for over six thousand years. I should be able to forgive someone for three hours of excruciating pain."

The doctor was shocked and pleased with this last response. Here was the first person that was prepared to forgive him, even before he had proven his change of heart. For the first time in many years, tears welled up in his eyes. He could hardly believe what he was hearing! This man whom he had tortured was willing to forgive him. He didn't even try to repress the desire to go over and give this man a hug.

With a shamefaced expression, the second Russian finally said, "My comrade here is right. I can carry my hatred as easily as a hundred pound rock. I carried it to assuage my anger, but it is too heavy to carry any longer. Dr. Raschor, if Christ can forgive you, so will I. We will trouble you no more." And with that, he extended a hand of fellowship.

The doctor's eyes were flooded with tears. He said, "This is the first answer to my prayers. I longed for forgiveness, and your kindness returned for my evil to you is better than I deserve. I thank you from the bottom of my heart. Any favor or kindness I can return to you, any hour of the day or night, I will be at your service. I owe you more than I can ever repay, but Christ will reward your kindness."

Dr. Raschor continued. "I was beginning to think recovery for me was impossible. This is the first gleam of hope strengthening my resolve to become a caring, loving and sacrificing human being. I owe society more than I can ever repay. You now are witnesses of my pledge to do all I can, to show that the love of Christ has reached my heart and is overflowing."

As they stood to leave, the doctor said, "Thank you, thank you, thank you. I dreaded seeing you at first. You were monuments to my cruelty. You reminded me of my merciless past. Yet today's discussion has changed me. I am going to ask Christ to remold me into his image. I was your enemy and now I am your friend. I would gladly die in your service. I say that sincerely."

The two men each gave him a bear hug which he returned before they left. There were tears in everyone's eyes. Lev even hugged them and said, "Shalom."

As soon as they left, the doctor thanked Lev. He said, "Today I have found love for the first time. I lived a life of hatred and meanness to my own hurt. Lev, you have been a legend of love in our time and I envy you. My door is open to you day or night. I will try to be a friend in the truest sense not only to you, but also to all my fellow humans. Today is a new beginning in my life. Let's now have a belated breakfast. I feel like Scrooge on Christmas morning." And he laughed aloud with joy.

"Strengthen ye the weak hands, and confirm the feeble knees"
(Isaiah 35:3).

Chapter Sixteen

While walking home from the doctor's just a few doors from Lev's present abode, he met a man who seemed bursting with happiness. Lev paused to greet him to see if he might share his joy.

"Shalom, my name is Lev and I just live a few doors away, at least for the present. May I share your happiness with you?"

"Yes, by all means, Lev. My name is John and I just heard I might start building homes for my parents. Their assigned lots are not far from here. You see I was afflicted with Down's syndrome in my previous life, and I couldn't live normally with my limited learning abilities. I remember my dad trying to teach me to ride a bicycle. All the other kids in the neighborhood learned how to ride one, but finally my dad realized I could never learn. He was disappointed, but I was very much more so. I soon learned I could not live like other children.

"My mother and father were both wonderful. They loved me and cared for me until the very end. I also had a wonderful sister who took over when my parents died. All I could give my parents and sister was love. Now I am going to love them by helping to build their homes. I am so happy I could dance for joy. At last I am a normal human being able to bless my parents with new homes that I will build with my own hands."

"Oh, how wonderful!" Lev was truly almost as joyful as the young man. "May I help you for a few weeks? I have built many homes. I have a friend, a doctor who lives down the street, who will also be glad to help, I am sure. When can we start?"

"Oh, thank you. I have never done much work before. My sister helped build my home. I have no disabilities now, and I have been taking courses on building. However, we can use all the help we can get. We were told we might start tomorrow. The ground is all prepared and we have planted most of the trees and some other things in the garden. The first shipment of material is being delivered tomorrow. If you could be there after breakfast, my sister and I would appreciate your help. It is about three-quarters of a mile going in this same direction." He gestured down the road. "You will see the freshly prepared place for the foundation to be laid. You have made my day even happier. Thank you."

Lev shook John's hand and congratulated him on his joyous news. "See you tomorrow after breakfast. Shalom."

When Lev reached home, he called Dr. Raschor and told him of the opportunity to help John build a home for his father.

The doctor quickly responded, "Yes, I am definitely available for service starting tomorrow and every day of my life from now on." How glad was the doctor for his first opportunity of service!

For the first time in many months, Lev felt satisfied that progress was made in dealing with people who committed crimes against humanity. At last, he had experienced a positive attitude from one wishing to change from the inside out and willing to commit himself to such a transformation. Others may have liked the idea of change, but couldn't accept the challenges that such change would incur. It would take a true admission of guilt and a desire for willed change. Such change would take enormous courage and fortitude. King David committed enormous sins, but he lived them down in greatness. No wonder he was a man after God's own heart. That kind of greatness was not in all. Some simply wished that God would sweep their past sins away and that everyone would forget them. That wasn't about to happen.

The next morning the doctor was at the chapel unusually happy and eager to meet people and shake hands. Instead of hiding his past, he was prepared to confess it. He asked the chaplain if he could give a testimony that morning. After the opening hymns and prayer the chaplain said, "One of our new members wishes to have a few minutes of testimony. So now I will ask Dr. Raschor to come forward."

Dr. Raschor's Confession

"Thank you for affording me this privilege. Some of you may have remembered my name. Up to now I tried to hide my identity. I have been a cruel and terrible monster. I am here to apologize for what I have done in my past life. Yesterday two Russian visitors tracked me down and wished to interview me. They were two victims I had used in experiments in seeing how long men could live in ice water. I kept them conscious for three hours in excruciating pain and they lived for five hours before they died of hypothermia. Lev was at our meeting together. After I confessed my sin and after a long interchange, they said, if Christ could forgive me, they would too.

"We parted friends and hugged each other. That has been the sweetest moment since I have returned to life. You have no idea how happy that has made me. Two people forgave me for what I had done to them. Now I am determined to live down my sinful past, and I am prepared to give myself to serve humanity in all sincerity. Anyone needing help day or night, please feel free to call me. If I can help I will. I owe humanity and God my entire dedication. I cannot undo the pain and suffering I have caused. I know that. However, God has given me a new life and a new opportunity to love my fellow men, and this I intend to do with God's help. Pray for me, please. Thank you."

His testimony relieved a lot of tension and touched everyone's heart. Here was a man with godly sorrow trying to do the only thing he could do to live down his evil past. After the services, many people flocked around him showing their appreciation for open confession of past sins and his high resolve to step up higher by God's grace. This is what life was all about. The most important word now was reconciliation. That is why Christ was raising everyone to life, so that they might be reconciled to God and be reconciled to each other. Christ's reign would not be completed until that was accomplished.

That lifted the whole membership to higher ground. A warm bond was formed and love was welling up in every heart and was finding love being returned from every heart. It was a day none would forget, especially Lev. He had come on this assignment with an empty feeling, and suddenly his joy was full.

Lev invited the doctor to stop at his house for breakfast after he changed to his work clothes. The doctor accepted with enthusiasm. As they ate the doctor said, "I have played yesterday's conversations over and over in my mind. To have two men forgive me was just the most wonderful experience in my life. I am not worthy of that forgiveness, and that is what makes it so precious to me. It was an act of love from two men who had every reason to loathe me. I didn't earn either Christ's love or theirs. It was freely given and that is the most beautiful thing that has ever happened in my life.

"Suddenly I want that kind of love more than anything in life. And then when you called yesterday offering a work assignment, I could have danced a jig I was so happy. Lev, thank you, you helped make all of this possible. To think that I almost tried to throw you out of my house. Thank God you didn't allow me to crawl back into my shell." The blond man's voice quivered with his fervency. "Your words were like arrows straight into my heart, and I knew that you were right."

Soon, they both strode off to work with John on his father's house.

"Wait until you see how happy this young man is," Lev related. "He was a handicapped boy who could not live a normal life. He knew what a burden he was to his parents, and now that he is back fully normal and able to work, he is overjoyed to show his love for his father by helping to build a house for him. He is so excited that it gives you goose bumps of joy."

When they arrived, Lev introduced the doctor to John and they hit it off immediately. Lev could see that the doctor loved this young man the moment he saw him. Soon the doctor was calling him "son." Both were eager workers. Lev was able to use his experience in building to get everything organized properly. He knew what needed to be done, and these two men were the most eager workers he had ever seen. Soon John's sister, Irma, arrived, marveling to see John able to work so intelligently. She had lived with his tragedy all her life, as did her parents, and now she was overwhelmed at seeing her brother so handsome and bright and so full of love and devotion to his parents.

Neither the doctor nor John was an experienced worker, so occasionally Lev had to correct little mistakes before they could become big mistakes. However, they were eager to learn and always thanked him for helping to get the job done right. Irma had a little experience in building her brother's house, so she was better prepared. However, never was there a happier group of workers on the job.

The doctor loved John's spirit of love and devotion. Every parent would love to have such a child. How happy his dad would be to see him! As they worked, they were all astonished with their happiness. The music of their laughter kept time with the percussion of the hammers. This was a tonic for the doctor, the best medicine for the sad heart and mind that had oppressed him. Now he could endure facing those he had tormented. He could do so with love instead of the meanness that once ruled his heart.

Suddenly the doctor wanted to live, to love and to be happy. Lev could hardly believe his ears when he heard the doctor singing the hymn sung at the chapel that morning. "The cross now covers my sins, the past is under the blood, I am trusting in Jesus for all, my will is the will of my God." Who could have known that this was once the "Dr.

Bluebeard" of such disrepute or that such a man could now rival a lark for his voice or song?

Lev finally had to call them off the job to take a lunch break, or they would not have stopped working.

"Then the eyes of the blind shall be opened"
(Isaiah 35:5).

Chapter Seventeen

Lev had asked for a few months off from working with people who carried enormous guilt because of previous crimes against humanity and general wickedness. He said to Moses, "I need to deal with normal, healthy people who have hearts full of love." He told Moses how refreshing it was to find John who had in his previous life been afflicted with Down's syndrome. Lev mentioned how both he and Dr. Raschor had found this a sweet balm for their hearts. The doctor lived for a few weeks in the overflowing love of John as he prepared for his father's return to life. John's happiness was infectious and the doctor began to see love was missing in his own life. Lev confessed he needed a few months working with normal people, building homes for their beloved dead, so Lev could gain the emotional strength to once again deal with criminals returned to life.

"I will not turn down any assignment from your good offices, however, it is such a relief to be dealing with normal, healthy people who have loved and struggled in their former lives. It is such a reprieve to find them rejoicing now. They have no evil to bring into their new life. Sometimes in dealing with a sequence of people who had warped minds, I lose the perspective of the countless millions and billions who are rejoicing and so happy. That's why I think I need to spend a little time with healthy, good people."

Moses responded, "You certainly are entitled to a few months off from those more difficult assignments. As a matter of fact, we have a woman who was formerly blind, returned to life and needing someone to help her make arrangements to build for her parents. She is only a short distance from you in Hungary. I shall send you your new assignment tomorrow as soon as I get the details. Shalom, Lev. God bless you."

When Lev told both the doctor and John that he was leaving to help someone in Hungary, they both hugged and wished him God's blessing in his new assignment. The doctor once again thanked him.

"I owe you my heartfelt appreciation. I couldn't believe anyone could forgive me or that anyone would accept me as worthy of a place in a righteous society. There was nothing for me but to seek to return to the dark grave from which I was raised. Not that I really wanted to die. It just seemed the only way out of my misery. When those two Russians finally accepted me into the human family again, I couldn't believe it. They returned good for evil just like Jesus did. I resolved then and there that I was going to become loving and caring or die trying."

John, with his bubbly enthusiasm, thanked Lev for his contribution in building skills.

"Just think, in a few more weeks my dad will be back. He was such a wonderful father. He shared my handicap in life, but both he and my mother made my life as beautiful as it could be for me with my limitations. I want them to see me now, without any handicaps, with a bright mind and nimble hands and feet. I can't wait to see their joy. They deserve the best for they were the greatest."

The doctor couldn't hide the tears rolling down his cheeks.

"John, I want to be there as soon as you can stand having me around when your dad comes back. I want you and Irma to have a few days with him alone, but I want to meet your father. I love him already because I know he loved you."

A Son's Devotion to His Father

John embraced the doctor. "Yes, I want you to meet my dad. You will love him, I know. Oh, I can hardly wait to see him again. He will be so proud of me helping to build his house and planting his trees and garden. I used to watch him work and do all the repairs around our house. I was never able to do any of that and all my attempts to help only made it worse. However, Dad was so kind and patient. He always praised me to make me feel good, even though I knew I had made things worse rather than better. Dr. Raschor, you must meet my dad. I have to tell him what a good friend you have been in helping me build this house."

The doctor just stood there with tears in his eyes. Lev saw a different man now from the fiendish doctor. Lev gave the doctor a farewell hug, too, and said to him, "I was about to give up thinking that people who did such terrible things could change into caring human beings.

Doctor, you have made a believer out of me. No one is beyond the power of Christ to wash away their past if they are willing to humble themselves and make a sincere effort to reform. You are a perfect example that I shall use in my further visits with people. Shalom."

With that, Lev left for his journey to Hungary. He drove through the beautiful countryside. It was spring and trees were in bloom with flowers springing up in the coiffured gardens. There were no impatient speeding drivers, but only courteous and thoughtful ones who smiled as they drove by. Everywhere people seemed happy. It was amazing.

There were no obese or skinny people, and no deformed or handicapped persons. There were no old or infirm persons anywhere. There were no funeral processions or marching armies going to war. You could hear children laughing in communities as you passed. There were no slums, no ghettos, no prisons, no police, no crime, no mean or abusive people, no drugs, no alcohol, no hospitals, no nursing homes, no ambulances, no mental institutions, no abusers of themselves or others, no gangs, no riots, no murders or mayhem, no profanity, no sick music, no sick people, no advertisements along the road, no electric or telephone poles and no basis for fear or worry. This was the kind of world that everyone shared under the guidance of the Ancients. While there were people with problems, most of the problems were borrowed from the conditions that previously prevailed because of sin.

Lev arrived in a community once called Miskolc to stay at a newly finished home that was waiting for its occupant to return to life. Everything was new and nicely decorated with the latest amenities. However, he noticed the electrical system did not provide enough voltage to run several appliances at once. With his expertise he immediately checked the system to find some things were not connected properly. Within a matter of minutes he made the adjustments and everything functioned properly.

Lev Meets Christine

The next morning Lev went to the chapel service where to his surprise a young beautiful lady with large blue eyes met him. She inquired if he might be Lev Aron.

"Why yes, how did you know who I was?"

"My name is Christine Schuster. The Ancients told me that you would be helping me build the home for my mother, so I have been looking for you. I thought you would show up here first because they told me a little about you. They gave me a glowing report of all the wonderful things you have done."

"Christine, it's exaggerated I fear. But I am eager to work with you; and, if you know of anyone who might need a little extra help while I am here, I will be at their service also. This is really a vacation for me. I have been dealing with people with enormously difficult backgrounds who are finding unusual difficulty adjusting to a new and righteous world."

"You will have no such trouble with me, Mr. Aron. I'm walking on air these days. Once I was blind, but now I can see. To live in a world of light and beauty is simply breathtaking."

"How did you become blind, Christine?"

"Well, Mr. Aron, when we were little, my sister and I were always getting sick. Sometimes it was a cold—sometimes it was worse. The scary words were 'scarlet fever.' When we were sick, we had to stay in the dark in our bedrooms. We had to take nasty-tasting medicine. They always said, 'If it tastes good, it's probably not good for you.'

"One time, my sister and I had bad headaches—our eyes hurt, we could hardly see. The doctor came to the house and told our mother to put this eye salve on our eyes. He was an old man and had been visiting so many sick kids that he was very, very tired. He hadn't had any sleep for a day or two. He liked people and wanted to help them. He had a family at home whom he seldom saw because he was so busy helping everyone else. He left the salve with our mother.

"My sister was sick of being sick. She was rebellious. She didn't want that smelly stuff on her eyes. They hurt enough already without that. When our mother walked out of the room, she threw her salve away.

"But I was different. I was the obedient one. Of course, the ointment was terrible to smell, but I was told to put it on, and it didn't occur to me to do otherwise. I put it on faithfully, day after day after day.

"My sister got over her sickness. Her eyes grew better, but mine grew worse. And after it was too late, it was determined that the eye salve was not good for my eyes. I had more and more trouble seeing, and finally blindness set in.

"I always had to remind myself that there were blessings from the Lord that resulted from that blindness. I was forced to become more thoughtful, meditating on why I had this experience. The Lord enlightened my mind, although I had to wait for the Kingdom for my vision to return. When I awakened to life again and opened my eyes and could see, I almost danced for joy.

"Not only did I previously not have sight, but also we were very poor and many days had little to eat. We were too poor for me to go to school to learn to read Braille. I lived in a world of darkness with the barest necessities. When I awakened to life and realized I had perfect vision, I thought this was a dream and I would awaken with the same handicaps I always had. As soon as I dressed, I ran out of the room dancing and jumping—I knew this was no dream."

Christine paused and then continued, "This is my friend, Marion."

"Hi, Mr. Aron. I am helping Christine build her house for her mother. I lived my life crippled in a wheelchair. Now I have two legs equal in length and can walk and jump. I helped build Christine's house for her and now am helping her to build her mother's house. It is so wonderful to have a healthy body and to be able to help others in this world. We are so excited to wake up every morning and be able to walk and see!"

"You are both so very happy."

Trying to Understand Those Not Happy

They really could not believe how anyone could not be happy and eager to live. They were filled with uncontainable happiness—how could it be otherwise for anyone under such blessed conditions? How could anyone not be jumping for joy? When Lev was with them, he felt like jumping for joy, too. They were so full of life and love it buoyed him up.

The morning passed quickly and Lev had to make them break for lunch. During lunch, Christine told how she had died.

"Conditions were very severe one winter. My father had died earlier, and so my mother and I lived in a very small, drafty house that was impossible to keep warm except when we stood around the kitchen stove.

"I became ill with the flu that turned into pneumonia. My mother hovered over me and tried to save me, but she couldn't. My sister had died earlier and I was her only child left, so my family was cut off. My mother became ill and died only days later. Marion volunteered to help build a home and make preparations to receive me back to life.

"I owe Marion so much. She is the greatest friend anyone could have. I thank the Lord for such a wonderful friend who loved me enough to work, building my house before she even knew me. Now she is helping build a house for my mother. Can anyone have a better friend?"

The girl seemed to suddenly become aware of something else. "Here you are, a perfect stranger working with us. Why would you spend your time with such nobodies like us? I know you ran large companies and accomplished great things in the business world. We can't repay you anything."

"That's not true, Christine. You've already paid me in love and joy. I've never been happier than working with you two enthusiastic young ladies. Your previous hardships and handicaps have given you beautiful characters."

"The time that I give is so small. If we prove that we love the Lord our God with all our heart, with all our being, with all our strength, and our entire mind, and our neighbor as ourself, then eternity will be ours. So what are a few weeks or months spent in helping our fellow men? In the wonderful love and joy we experience now, we have a taste of what eternity will be like."

"Do you mean that everyone has to demonstrate such a love for God and for man as you expressed, before they will have everlasting life?"

"Yes, that's why the devil will be loosed at the end of the thousand years – to deceive all whose hearts are not in harmony with God and righteousness. The only reason Adam and Eve failed the test they were subjected to was they didn't love God supremely because of lack of experience. Satan deceived Eve. She believed his lie that she would not die. Adam was not deceived, but he loved Eve so much he chose to share her fate rather than live without her. In other words, he loved Eve more than he loved God. So the test upon mankind will be much the same at the end of the Millennium. Some will be deceived as Eve was, and others will go along with the deceived ones because they loved them more than they loved God. The final test will be love for God above all."

Lev then said with a smile, "We better get back to work or we'll never get this job done."

"Charge," Christine cried.

A Stranger Asks if He Might Help

The following day as they began work in the morning, a man walked up to Lev asking if he could help. "Welcome aboard, we need all the help we can get. Tell us about yourself."

"My name is Sigfried. I was a guard at Auschwitz. I helped in the systematic killing of tens of thousands of people. My heart is heavy and I have felt unclean ever since my experiences at the concentration camp. All the faces I sent to their death haunt me. I chose that job rather than going to the front, thinking that I would avoid being butchered on the battlefield. Now I wish I had chosen to go to the front. I was able to hide my occupation before I died; but, since I have returned to life, I have repeatedly been confronted by people who recognize me as the guard who sent thousands of innocent men, women and children to the gas chambers. When I tell them, 'I was following orders,' it sounds so hollow. Now the truth appears that I was working part and parcel with criminal murderers. I was assisting in these murders, so that made me a partner in their crime. I can understand the anger of the people when they recognize me."

Christine and Marion were horrified with Sigfried's confession. They had been spared many of the details of what happened. They had heard only vaguely of the death camps. Now they were learning more about those awful moments through Sigfried.

In all innocence, they asked, "How could you do such things?"

Poor Sigfried thought, how do you tell such innocent young people the horrors of the concentration camps? He really didn't want to go any further. He had only told them his background so that they could refuse his labor if they chose to. Now he feared if he told them the awful things that happened they would ask him to leave.

He finally said, "Perhaps I can tell you more later. Now if you will allow me, I shall be glad to help you. Give me the heaviest tasks for I am very strong. I am determined to do as much good as I can. I must in some way make up for the harm and evil that I have done. You do not have to understand, but please allow me to help you. I'm a good worker and need to engage in good works now. I hated what I did every day when I was involved in that grim business. However, I was weak. I had a family, and I didn't want to leave them as orphans by being killed at the front. So I killed other people and their children to save my own. That was wicked, wasn't it? When I volunteered to work in that concentration camp, I had no idea how evil and degrading it would be. I lost my human heart in the process. I have continual sorrow in my heart now."

Lev responded, "We're glad for your help, Sigfried. You're welcome here in spite of your troubled background. I've dealt with many people guilty of war crimes and only a few have shown true godly sorrow, the kind of sorrow that tries to reform and make good the second time around. Some did evil in their previous life, but can't seem to bring themselves to doing all the good they can now. So I, for one, Sigfried, appreciate your honest confession and your willingness to do whatever it takes to make good now. Working with these two girls will be a tonic for your heavy heart. They are as pure and innocent as you will find anywhere. They are so happy that it will rub off onto you."

True to his word, Sigfried worked very hard, volunteering for all the heavier tasks. He wasn't especially experienced in this type of work, but he was willing to take instruction and learned very quickly. Usually people only worked three or four hours a day, but Christine was eager to finish the house so she could have her mother back. She was so excited about the prospect that they spent the whole day pushing the work along.

Christine wanted to work in the evening as well, but Lev discouraged her.

"I would rather be there with you. If you make a mistake at the ground level, it will take long hours to fix it. Tomorrow is another day and we made terrific progress for one day. We'll have this house up and finished very quickly."

Sigfried Stays with Lev

Lev asked Sigfried if he had a place to stay.

"No, I should have made some arrangements, but I was told of this opportunity to help so I hurried over. I can drive home and be back in the morning."

"There is no need to travel that far. I have an extra room where I am staying, and you're welcome to stay with me. I'd like to hear more of your past. Come home with me. I have plenty of room and food."

"Very well, Lev, if you're willing to have a former criminal stay with you, I'd be very glad to."

They returned to Lev's place. Strange, that as he was trying to catch a breath of fresh air dealing with normal happy people, another war criminal should step into his life.

As they ate, Lev said, "You know I am a Jew, don't you?"

Sigfried stiffened a little when he heard that. "I have heard of your name before, but I didn't realize that you were a Jew. Dear Lord, I killed so many Jews, Lev, I would have it coming if you strangled me. I deserve it."

"No, no," Lev replied with a gentle chuckle. "I have no such feelings or even the faintest wish to do such an evil thing. Christ takes care of punishment, not me. Did you know that I was with Hitler when he came to life? And I was with the prelate of Rome, as well, after he returned to life. I wish I could find the same honesty and willingness in them to live down their evil deeds as I see in you.

"Tell me one thing, Sigfried, did the people in the community know what was taking place at these camps?"

"How could they not know? Trainloads of people were coming in and empty trains were leaving. They didn't want to know. You could smell the awful smoke from the furnaces cremating the dead. It certainly didn't smell like wood burning. Only small trucks brought in what little food there was when they would have needed trainloads of food to feed all those people. It was something no one dared talked about. I never told my family what I did. I was too ashamed to mention it to them. The Nazis tried to hide the fact that these were death camps, and many people later tried to deny these things ever happened. The mind finds it convenient to deny that these things happened. However, now each person one by one is returning to life. There is nowhere to hide and no way to disclaim reality."

If They Only Knew

"If you knew that every person you killed was coming back to life again, would it have made a difference to you?"

"Of course. We believed in the mythology of the immortal soul and that these people at death were going to heaven or hell. Naturally, we knew the Jews did not believe in Christ, so we believed they were going to hell. We didn't think we were that bad. We killed them in a few minutes in the gas chambers, but theology taught they were going to be tortured for eternity. If I'd known all those haunted faces entering the gas chambers were coming to life again to look upon me in a world of righteousness, I probably would have committed suicide rather than do the grim work I was doing. It was so evil. Men were not made to handle such evils. You couldn't believe what was happening—or even worse, that you were engaged in a gigantic killing machine so loathsome that no one wanted to own up to it, even now.

Poor Sigfried seemed depressed at the memory. "You might ask how a person was able to work at something so gruesome. It was not as easy as it seems. I took to drinking. I couldn't tell my wife and family why I was drinking so heavily, but if I didn't drink enough in the evening, I couldn't sleep at night. I kept seeing those poor souls enter that chamber of death, whom we told were going to take a shower. The psychologists had figured out how to prevent mass hysteria before entering the gas chambers. They had a few musicians playing nice music. They thought that surely nothing evil could happen while they were playing a lovely refrain or a lively march. The prisoners guessed they were going to die, but it seemed surreal to them. The truth hit once the doors slammed shut, and they started pouring in the poison gas. It was horrible. Victims piled up by the door trying to get out. In a few minutes it was over and it was time to remove the bodies to the incineration furnaces. Such a smooth operation—I don't think the devil could have devised a better killing machine. Why did people march to their death as lambs to the slaughter? Because the Nazis were so cruel, that's why. Any insubordination brought cruel torture. The people's spirit was broken—they had no way to resist.

"We had the power to murder these innocent victims but not the right to do so. I knew this was evil. It was so evil that I couldn't tell my family the gruesome details of what happened. Groups of people were arbitrarily selected to die at different times of the day. We cleaned out whole barracks of emaciated living people and within hours only ashes were left. So efficient and devilish. The evil that went on in those camps will gradually come back to haunt the Nazis. They were smug in their power and were driven to destroy the Jews from the face of the earth. Even knowing that the war was lost didn't slow down the killing operation. It was pure madness and so grossly evil that those who were in power then don't wish to address it now. They just want it to go away. However, everyone who died in those camps is coming back, one by one. A great cloud of witnesses is standing up to remind us of our sins."

Lev responded, "You see, Sigfried, those in power just received statistics of how many people were processed each day. The Germans were great for statistics. They recorded every detail in facts and figures. The leaders of these atrocities sat with white gloves on, as it were, as though none of that blood would ever be on their hands. All they held were white sheets of paper, while men like you did the dirty work for them. You had to look into those faces of women with their children, and tell them that they were going to have a nice warm shower. You knew you were lying and they did too. What did it matter? No one practiced virtue. You were partners with Satan and as long as you were in the killing business, what did it matter if you told lies as well?"

Looking Back with Angst

His companion nodded sadly. "That's the truth of the matter. I look back at what I did in shame. I wasn't raised to be a killer. I had been a decent person before I became ensnared in this ghastly business. I looked into the faces of my German associates. We never talked about the business we were in. Like machines, we performed our deadly assignments with precision and efficiency. We couldn't show mercy. Our job was to process and eliminate people. Why we were doing it was not our concern. Someone had decided this was the thing to do—that's the way it was.

"It still troubles me, Lev, as to how such a civilized nation as Germany, which under the Weimar Republic had a wonderful rule of law, had turned full circle so that we were totally without the rule of law. The government was run by madmen. No one dared question them. I never could have believed how evil begets evil. We marched like idiots to the music of demons. I knew it was wrong. I hated every moment I spent in this wicked business. But I didn't have the courage to stand up and say, 'No.' They would quickly remove me to the ovens and some other fool would be given my job. Once evil got on the throne, all hope of containing it faded."

Lev responded, "I am very interested in hearing about your experiences. I've met with Hitler twice, trying to get him to accept responsibility for what was done. But despite all my attempts, he can't accept the magnitude of evil that occurred. The people who were responsible cannot accept the facts of what they did. Oh, they're sorry that it happened. Judas also was sorry that he betrayed our Lord and even threw the moneybag on the floor. Then he went out and hanged himself. He found that easier than admitting his wickedness. These people say, 'I didn't ask to be raised from the dead.' That's like saying, 'I didn't ask to be born.' Therefore, because I didn't ask to be here, I can't be held responsible for what I did while here. Isn't it strange, Sigfried, that in the day of their power no one dared challenge their authority, but now in a world of righteousness, they consider themselves the victims who couldn't contain the evil raging under their rule?"

Sigfried replied, "I was very impressed when I learned what the Bible said in Jeremiah 17:9, 'The heart is deceitful above all things, and desperately wicked; who can know it?' When the Allies overran the concentration camps, some of the people survived. I met some of them later and I didn't know what to say. One kind lady confronted me with, 'I forgive you, Sigfried.' That is all she said, and that was the turning point in my life. Tears welled up in my eyes. I couldn't forgive myself, and here this kind person returned good for the evil I was a partner to. I knew people hated us because we were a part of that evil

Nazi regime. I can only dream now that somehow I can be reconciled to all those I murdered and most of all to God. I am willing to do anything to demonstrate my love for God and for mankind now. That is the only hope I have of living down my sins."

"Right," Lev responded. "Just because through Christ we have forgiveness of sins does not mean that previous sins go unrequited. They need to be addressed before reconciliation with our fellow men can take place. We were always free to sin, but never free from the consequences of it. You are blessed, Sigfried, because you're willing to learn the true lessons from your experiences with sin."

Those Who Chafed Under Grievous Assignments

Sigfried had worked very hard that day and had traveled quite a distance to join in the opportunity of helping Christine, so he was exhausted and wanted to turn in early. Lev took this time to digest all he had learned from his new friend. He had dealt with those in authority first, but now he was seeing things from the perspective of a soldier forced to carry out the orders that he despised. It was obviously by divine providence that Lev met Sigfried. He was getting a firsthand education on how such enormous evils were carried out by ordinary men and women.

Before retiring, Lev needed to read the Bible. Evils were recorded there, too. Thank God that the reign of sin and evil was being dealt with now. If the power of God was not being exercised in the world, people would still be trying to hurt each other, and the latent evil in the hearts of men would find expression all over again. Soon Lev also needed to sleep, but he was thankful for the extraordinary experiences of the day. The privilege of working with Christine and Marion, who were pure at heart, was so refreshing. On the other hand, there was the contrast of working with Sigfried and hearing his story of evil so vile that it was incomprehensible. Hopefully, he would be able to put this knowledge to use.

They were up early the next morning and prepared to go to the chapel meeting. Sigfried said, "I used to avoid these services for fear of being recognized and creating an unwanted confrontation. However, having been recognized repeatedly already, I now accept this as a constant reminder of my bloodstained past. I now just contritely face my previous victims expressing my great sorrow for my part in what happened and ask that they forgive me for Christ's sake. It doesn't always work instantly, but usually people do respond in time and do forgive me. I really look forward to the day when I will have accomplished all my work of repentance and can begin to truly enjoy this new order."

They arrived to find Christine and Marion at the chapel already. They were bubbling over with enthusiasm and delightedly greeted them. It was a joy to Sigfried to see that after hearing his confessions yesterday, they still were so warm and friendly to him. Because he loathed his past, he automatically thought everyone would loathe him, as well. What a joy to see it wasn't so.

The services were especially fervent this morning. There were a few new faces today who seemed to be newly returned to life and were singing with extraordinary enthusiasm. Lev introduced Sigfried to some of the chapel members, and he was graciously received. No one seemed to recognize him, or if they did, they chose not to make a scene of it at this meeting. Lev also introduced him to the chaplain, mentioning briefly about his past so that he could be prepared for any confrontation that might erupt.

"Blessed are they that mourn"
(Matthew 5:4).

Chapter Eighteen

When they returned to the work site, they found yet another volunteer waiting. He introduced himself as Mr. Kraup and expressed his desire to help. Christine was delighted for all the extra help to speed the building project along. Lev assigned everyone to work according to his or her abilities. He could tell that Mr. Kraup was an extremely intelligent man who was capable of doing almost any assignment without supervision. He had him work with Christine, Marion and himself. As always, Lev inquired about his background.

"I was CEO at the Kieffer Stahl works in Czechoslovakia."

Christine asked, "Why would a man of your talents be working on such a humble project with a formerly blind girl?"

"Christine, I am here to give back to mankind what I owe. I ran a large operation at a time when production was more important than people. As with all businesses, we had to get as much work from the workers at the least cost. We were given slave labor during World War II. Because there was an endless supply of hapless victims, this money-saving scheme was presented to us. We were told we could feed these slaves a bare minimum of food and work them until they died. We didn't need to give them medical treatment and could house them in factory storage areas. Because of the war, laborers were difficult to come by, so this diabolical plan was offered and I accepted the proposal. I don't know how many hundreds of people died in our factory because of this sadistic arrangement, but I do know that I was responsible for it.

"I have trouble facing these people when I meet them today. They put the blame on the Nazis, and it is true that a lot of the blame rests with them. However, I was to blame as much as anyone for allowing this ill treatment of people. I rationalized that if I didn't employ these slaves they would have been sent to the gas chambers, so why not give them a few more days and weeks to live—maybe they would outlive the war."

Christine asked, "Couldn't you have provided food for them and warm clothing? Why did you have to treat them worse than animals?"

A Pure Heart Is Kind

"You know, Christine, your pure heart is so kind. In the world of that time food was scarce. The Nazis never provided food for their enemies. People were dying by the hundreds and thousands on the battlefields, so who worried about a few Jews or Gypsies? Planes were dropping bombs on our cities. The countryside was not being farmed properly and what food there was first went to the politically connected and then to the Germans. There was hardly anything left over but old stale bread occasionally and a watery soup made from whatever they could find to throw in the pot. This was what our slaves had to eat. Clothing was also scarce, too. The Nazis would take some of the clothing from prisoners who went to the gas chambers. The best of it went to the Germans. Only clothing that nobody else wanted trickled down to factory slaves. Those were awful times, but still we consciously knew what we were doing was evil."

Marion listened intently. Finally she said, "I could never believe people were that horrid. How can you live with yourself knowing how badly you treated so many people?"

"Marion, I carry a heavy load of guilt and shame—it never leaves me day or night. That's why I am here. I owe society so much that if I worked every hour, I could never pay back my debt. Then, too, I thought that when these people died, it would be the end of the matter. I never dreamed that every person who died from our abuse would be back one day standing on my doorstep to look me in the eye and say, 'Mr. Kraup, how could you do that to me?' Now it is all so obvious and there is no way anyone can rationalize it. However, back then we had production quotas to meet. If we didn't meet them, the Germans would threaten to put us on the factory production lines. No one was shown mercy and no one extended mercy.

"Still, Marion, one knows in his heart when he is abusing people and sending them to an early grave. I couldn't talk about this to my wife or family. I had to carry on this situation secretly. I was locked in the vise grip of an evil system that didn't allow anyone to be kind or generous. I was a part of that wicked system, and this is what bothers my conscience. I've had a myriad of sleepless nights and troubled days thinking of my sinful past. Oh, how I hate everything I did. I was raised by kind and loving parents, and certainly I knew what I was doing would cause my parents to disown me, if they knew. All I can say, Marion, is that I was caught in a web and couldn't disentangle myself from it.

"The Nazis made sure that everyone was entangled. That was their plan, to make as many people as possible partners in their crimes. It worked. Who could fault the Nazis when everyone was in partnership with them? No one was righteous, and no one reproved their evil ways."

Christine observed, "Yes, my mother taught me that people have always tried to get Christians to do evil; then, as soon as they did, these same people despised the Christians, saying, 'See, you are no better than we are.' I always remembered that, Mr. Kraup."

Getting an Education

Lev listened with great delight. Everyone was getting an education. The two young ladies were learning how evil spread like a canker in those times, and Mr. Kraup was learning something of the pristine beauty of hearts that were not corrupted with evil. How he longed to have such a pure heart and clean hands again!

Sigfried heard part of the conversations that morning. At lunchtime he informed Mr. Kraup of his past. Mr. Kraup smiled and said, "I guess we are both doing penance, aren't we? Oh, to be as innocent as these two young ladies."

Turning to them, he said, "Your handicaps left you on the sidelines of life, so you were not dragged into the evils of this world. However, maybe you would have been nobler than we were. There were always people who lived on a higher level and didn't let the world defile them. They died instead of violating their consciences. As a matter of fact, I lived near a devout family of Bible-oriented Christians whose son refused to join the army. He was taken to a concentration camp and was never heard from again. I certainly admired that young man. He had the courage to live his convictions. If I had that same courage, I would not be so distressed in mind now."

Lev could see that once the evil influences in the world had ended, people were beginning to think clearly and were able to recognize evil and sin for what they were. In former times it had been easy to blur right and wrong and make everything look gray. Now, everything was right or wrong, white or black. This whole experience of having pure and clean people and sinful and defiled ones rubbing elbows on the job was an excellent education.

At the rate the house was coming together, it would be done in half the time. Mr. Kraup was a take-charge person, but he was careful not to take Lev's place in any decision-making. He'd heard of his successful industrial management abilities and so was careful to get Lev's approval every step of the way. Sigfried was not one to sweat the details, but he was very energetic and needed close watching to make sure nothing was left undone. The two young ladies were good workers but lacked experience, so it was a boon for Christine to have all this needed help.

The afternoon found them making enormous progress on the building. Christine was excited that everything was coming together like clockwork. She was counting the days until her mother's return and they all shared her joy. Sigfried was especially impressed with Christine's purity. She was not stained with evil like he had been, and it was a joy to have someone around that was so innocent in heart and mind. He confessed to Lev that afternoon, "I have asked the Lord to help me to gain such purity as these two ladies. I am stained with ugly sin that I hate. I will do anything to prove my love for God and my fellow men. I don't know how I'm going to secure everyone's forgiveness for my part in their deaths, but I am willing to do anything to prove my love."

"That's the right spirit, Sigfried," Lev encouraged. "I only wish everyone who has done evil would have that same attitude. You can be sure that, having made such a commitment of yourself, your sincerity will be tested. Overcoming is never easy, but it can and must be done."

When at last they finished for the day, they were all happy, but tired. Lev invited Mr. Kraup to stay with him, since he had an extra bed in the house where he lived. He gratefully accepted the offer, avoiding a long drive home.

The next morning at the chapel meeting, Mr. Kraup joined them. He was a little reticent, fearing someone would recognize his name, but Lev encouraged him to come along.

"We all have to be reconciled to those we injured sooner or later. Better to do it sooner and bring peace to our own hearts as well as to the hearts of those we injured." With this encouragement, he decided to go.

Lev introduced him to the chaplain and asked Mr. Kraup to tell a little of his background to him in the event that he should be recognized and a disturbance arise. It was well he did, because someone recognized him and stiffened almost instantly. The individual kept his composure through the services, but Lev could see that he was restless and very angry.

Joe Miskawitz Recognizes His Former Boss

As soon as the services were over, the gentleman who recognized Mr. Kraup came up to him.

"Am I correct in observing that you are Mr. Kraup?"

"Yes, I'm afraid I am, and I suppose you are very angry with me?"

"Angry is not an adequate word. I thought back then, that if I ever met you in some dark alley, I would surely kill you. Now I know I cannot even do that. The Nazis protected you then and now Christ ensures your safety. No one ever protected us." Joe Miskawitz, a Pole, had been picked off the street one day by some Gestapo agents and sent to Mr. Kraup's factory. His wife and children never knew what happened to him. He was forced to labor sixteen hours a day, often cold and always starving.

"We were weak from lack of food, but we had to work, otherwise we were beaten. It was not unusual for one of us to be shot because we didn't work fast enough or because we had dysentery and were incapable of work under those conditions. I was able to last for six weeks before I was too weak and could no longer perform. Then they put a gun to the back of my head and shot me. I still remember the cold steel on my neck and the Gestapo agent who, in a matter of fact way, said, 'I shall put you out of your misery. We can't have you sub-humans slowing down our work.' That's all I remember."

Mr. Kraup was very pale and he shook a little facing this man.

"I know an apology cannot make up for all that befell you. You have every reason to hate me, but I must tell you, I hate myself. The Nazis knew what they were doing. They knew they could get about six weeks of work out of people like you before you were too weak to work and were then shot. To them people were expendable and human life meant nothing. I knew what they were doing, but we needed workers and they were hard to come by. So the Nazis just picked people up at random and said, 'Here are some new workers for you.'

"Not that it's an excuse, but I had to keep production up or I would lose my job. I couldn't produce without the workers. I had little choice. I should have argued for some food for you, but the Nazis weren't generous with food for slaves or prisoners. I'm so very sorry. I hate every memory of my past. I have spent sleepless nights and troubled days over this matter, and it still haunts me today."

"I know you weren't fully responsible for what happened. Yet we saw you sit in your nice comfortable office with fragrant meals carried in to you. We were forced to work with only a crust of moldy bread and some kind of watery soup that tasted horrible. There was no one to pity us. We were treated worse than animals, for they were fed regularly and given a place to stay at night that was comfortable. We slept in cold rooms with only a flimsy blanket. The cots we slept on were infected with lice. You wouldn't even enter that room for fear of the lice. You never stopped to talk to any of us poor slaves, never a kind word—never did you hold out any hope to us."

"You are absolutely right," Mr. Kraup affirmed. "I can't make it right. Everything you say is true, and I confess to my part in your evil treatment.

"The Nazis strictly forbade any contact between the workers and me. They didn't want me to exercise any human feelings by mixing with my fellow men. For that matter, they always had two officers checking on each other, lest at any time either one should start showing human compassion. It was all so devilish. But I accept responsibility. In what way can I make it up to you?"

Living Witnesses

There was a long pause. A crowd had gathered around. People were learning what exactly happened in the past. Dead people could not be witnesses. However, when they returned to life, they brought the whole truth from the past. That which was done in secret was now being shouted from the housetops. There was no hiding place. The waters of truth overflowed the hiding places.

Joe sadly dropped his arms to his side. "Nothing you say can undo the suffering and misery I and my fellows endured. I know you cannot give me back my previous life or restore my dignity. Christ has already done that. At least I find you are honest enough to admit what happened, and I guess you had little control over events of that time. I can forgive you, but not those terrible Germans."

Poor Sigfried just stood there silently listening. He could have remained quiet and no one at that moment would have known his past except Christine, Marion and Lev. However, he cleared his throat and said, "Joe, I am one of those awful Germans. I was a guard at Auschwitz. I sent thousands of innocent people into the gas chambers.

If I could repay those I injured by taking my life, I would gladly do so. However, that is forbidden. I have maddening memories of those haunted faces that looked desperately at me as they entered the gas chambers. I sent men, women and crying children to their death every day. Mr. Kraup doesn't bear the responsibility that I do. He had little to say about those events. If he protested, he would himself have been placed on the factory floor to be worked to death.

"I volunteered to work as a guard at Auschwitz, not knowing what it entailed. I was offered the job instead of going to the Russian front. I took it to save my life. Now I wish I had gone to the front and died liked a man.

"I ended up drinking heavily every night in order to sleep. During the day I was numb and my conscience soon turned to stone. Oh, I heard the cries of despair, but nothing I could do would change it. The biggest mistake I ever made was to volunteer to be a concentration camp guard."

Pitying Those Locked Into Crimes

Joe stood there speechless. He had wished to settle one score and soon found a flood of information coming forth in the form of honest confessions. Finally, he said, "Never did I think I could pity those who were locked into those horrible crimes of the past, but at least I died and that ended my misery. I see you gentlemen have to live with horrible memories that will not easily go away. Thankfully, Christ has forgiven you, but your victims still have to. I for one extend my forgiveness to you, Mr. Kraup, if that means anything to you."

"It means everything to me, Joe. Thank you from the bottom of my heart. If I can do anything for you, any service or labor, I will gladly do it. I owe you and all those who suffered under me a great debt of service and sacrifice. There is no job too menial for me to serve nor will my convenience have any consideration. I am at your service, Joe, and at the service of all who suffered under my responsibility. If there is anything more that I can do, please tell me."

Joe said, "Thank you, I know that nothing can change the past. It is the future that we all have to address."

Christine then spoke up, wanting to cheer everyone by telling something good about her new friends. "You should all know that both Sigfried and Mr. Kraup have been helping me build the house for my mother's return to life. I never knew the same evils that these men were subjected to, but I know one thing. They are trying everything in their power to make up for their past. Isn't that wonderful? Isn't life for reconciliation? These men have both shown true repentance. What more can they do?"

Lev was impressed with the wisdom of Christine's comments. All he could say when she finished was, "Amen!"

Everyone joined in, "Amen!"

The chaplain then said, "Today, we have begun the healing and reconciliation that is going to be needed over and over again until we are all reconciled with Christ and with one another. It cannot be any other way. We have to forgive if we are to receive Christ's forgiveness. Sufficient is the evil of the past. If we do not from the heart forgive one another, then evil will continue to live in our hearts. Saul, who helped to have Stephen martyred, and who was later converted to Christ, carried continual sorrow in his heart for what he had done. He went on to become the great Apostle Paul, but never could he forget the death of Stephen. So it is with those who did these evil things. Even when granted everyone's forgiveness, they will never be able to dismiss the scenes of sorrow sealed in their memory. These memories will be a monument to the forgiveness of Christ."

The Testimony of another Observer

As the chapel members were about to leave, still another person spoke up. He had been very quietly listening to the testimonies of Sigfried and Mr. Kraup. Finally, he cleared his throat. "Before you all leave, I must tell you of my experience. Bear with me one moment. My name is Mack, as many of you know. I have never told you that I lived near Auschwitz during those terrible years. I lived near the railroad tracks going in and coming out of that cursed camp.

"I saw trainloads of boxcars loaded with passengers crunched in together like sardines going into that awful place. I heard the muffled groans and screams of tormented people without water, without food and without sanitary conditions moving systematically to that monstrous place. Of course, I knew what was happening. I saw the same trains return empty. I saw the crematoriums belching black smoke every day. I knew they weren't burning wood. When the wind blew in our direction, the stench would reach us. There was no gas to heat our homes, but they always had plenty of gas to cremate their victims. The Nazis were determined to destroy all the evidence.

"All there was left were piles of ashes with some bone fragments. Sigfried, you stood by day after day supervising this ghastly operation. Your escape from that ghoulish job was to ask to be transferred to the front. You couldn't do that though. You were safe here. Probably the first day you were sick to your stomach. You knew that sinister forces were at work at Auschwitz. Did I know it? Yes, I knew it without a doubt. The only difference between you and me, Sigfried, was that I was an inactive observer. I didn't see the faces of those poor people stripped of their humanity, every vestige of dignity and honor, as well as their clothing, and condemned by insane murderers to such an unconscionable death." Mack seemed almost bitter.

"You were a soldier who eagerly joined the army enamored by your great Fuehrer. You believed his lies of Aryan superiority. While the bands were playing and the war drums were beating, you became a gung-ho follower of this war-crazed company of deceived people. That is where you lost your way.

"You thought that the German army was invincible. When the war was going your way and you were overrunning the smaller countries of Europe, Hitler was the greatest. Being a soldier was heady stuff. You would go goose-stepping around Germany, drinking in the admiration of foolish people. You were a part of that miserable army that terrorized the Jews, Gypsies, yes, and even Germans who did not approve of your lawless behavior.

"You knew of the awful carnage the Germans suffered trying to take Stalingrad. You were no longer the happy marcher through the streets of Germany. You knew that Hitler lost five hundred thousand of his best troops because he wouldn't let them retreat for the winter months from their siege of Stalingrad. He said, 'Germans do not retreat.' Well, they didn't and they died in the cold without food, sufficient clothing or ammunition. They were condemned to a death perhaps more cruel than those who died in Auschwitz by their own Fuehrer. That is why you didn't want to go to the front, isn't it Sigfreid?"

Sigfried Admits His Fears

Poor Sigfried turned pale. He finally said, "Yes, I must admit it. Mack, I have never had anyone analyze my past in a more penetrating way before. You are absolutely right. I messed up by a chain of decisions. It was not just my decision to seek protection of my own life at Auschwitz that marked my demise."

Mack then turned to Mr. Kraup, "You, sir, also knew what you were doing. Your plant was vital to the Nazi war machine. The great Kieffer Stahl works that you were in charge of is what enabled the Nazis to become capable of being the Great War engine of Europe. When the Germans took Czechoslovakia, the great prize they sought was the Kieffer Stahl works. Even before the Germans provided you with slaves, your factory turned over all your industrial resources to feed the German war machine. Nobody dynamited the plant before the Germans took it over. It was fully operational. Nobody wanted to lose any of that costly equipment.

"You became the same efficient CEO for the Nazi war machine that you were before. Perhaps in that time and place nobody knew how mean and vicious the Nazis would become. Yet you knew they were bent on world conquest. As long as you served them well, you remained well taken care of, didn't you? Why make waves? This way your factory would be here long after the war. I don't say this to condemn you. I would have probably done the same thing in your place. We all were trying to get through a difficult time, and we all made choices that cost us the least." All trace of ugliness faded from his face, replaced by a shadow of sorrow.

"I looked at train after train bringing these people in who were marked for death. I wondered what I could do to stop it. I thought of putting something on the tracks to derail the train. Would that result in freeing them? Or maim and kill many of them? I thought about this over and over, but I could think of nothing that could save those poor souls. They were doomed by a sinister power greater than any of us."

Mr. Kraup, looking rather gaunt, said, "Mack, as bad as your observations make me look, I cannot deny a word of them. You are absolutely correct. We had no plans to change what was happening. And we had no will to change it either. I was well provided for, and I was taking good care of all our costly equipment. I wasn't going to change anything. If there is no will to change, nothing will change— it's that simple. I just muddled through those years on a day to day basis, hoping the war would end this carnage."

Lev had quietly listened to this group analysis of the past and was amazed at how profoundly wise they were now, after the fact. They were free to think and analyze. There were no evil consequences to owning the truth. Why was everything so clear today and so muddled before? More importantly in the light of reason, all anger and finger pointing had ceased. No one was angry with anyone. What happened was beyond anyone's personal responsibility, even though human weaknesses made it easy for the Nazis to carry out their nefarious plans without hindrance. The people were weak and not organized for resistance and, therefore, little or none took place.

Lev Admits His Harsh Judgment of Jews Who Did Not Resist

Lev cleared his throat, "If everyone knew beforehand that the Nazis were bent on exterminating the Jews, perhaps they may have made a plan of action. No one ever conceived that the Nazis would have such ironclad designs on destroying an entire race. Who would believe that such an evil plot could exist in the so-called Christian nation of Germany? It was unthinkable, and yet such was their diabolical plan.

"Not only did they plan to kill all the Jews in Europe," he continued, "but also they had General Rommel, the 'Desert Fox,' sweeping eastward across northern Africa. Their plan undoubtedly was to take the Suez Canal, and then take the Holy Land. Had they succeeded, they would have been able to destroy all the Jews in Israel, and also make null and void God's plan to set up his kingdom in Jerusalem as it now is. I think the master strategist of the Nazis was Satan himself. Thankfully, he is in the abyss now and not able to deceive or mislead a single person."

They all had stayed much longer than normal and would be late for their work appointments. However, this was a most profitable discussion, because they were able to understand how step by step they had become hedged in and helpless by reason of the sinister designs of Satan. They were unwittingly made partners to these crimes against humanity.

Lev invited all the workers on Christine's work project to his house for breakfast. Everyone was so keyed up from the conversation that morning that they wanted to continue the discussion. For Christine and Marion it had been a revelation. They had little knowledge of what had happened in the world. They had lived sheltered lives, kept out of the mainstream of life, so they were learning for the first time of the evils that swept over Europe. It was a rude awakening for them. They were so full of love and joy at the moment, and to be exposed to so much evil at one time was overwhelming.

As they ate breakfast together, Sigfried apologized to the two young ladies. "I am sorry to have all this bad history dumped on you in one morning. You're in bad company, I'm afraid."

Marion said, "Don't say that. I got a belated education this morning—there's no need to apologize. You've been through a lot more bitter and painful experiences than we were ever exposed to. Our physical handicaps insulated us from normal life. After this morning's discussion, I can understand how these things happened and how otherwise decent people got swept away in the mad torrent of human emotions and conflict."

"Yes," Christine said. "I'm very thankful for the discussions of this morning. We learned history from people who experienced it firsthand. I knew that bad things happened, but I could never figure out how seemingly good and decent people got entangled in that web of death and destruction. Now I understand what happened, although I know I'll never fully grasp the emotional impact of seeing one person go into the gas chamber, much less wave after wave entering those death chambers. Each life is very precious."

They returned to work again and the house structure would soon be completed. The roof needed to be put on and the windows installed — then the plumbing, heating and cooling. Christine was ecstatic when she saw the actual structure in place. Being blind, she had never seen a house in her previous life, much less helped build one.

Marion Wants to Use Her Legs

Marion wanted to work on the roof to use her newly gained ability to walk with two normal feet. Lev decided they all should work on the roof to best preserve the structure they had just put up.

As they worked, questions kept presenting themselves. Christine said, "I know from what I heard this morning and from previous bits of information something about the Holocaust. Yet, here I am working with one of the guards in that camp who seems to be such a fine person. I could never believe you sent people to the gas chambers, Sigfried. If you didn't tell us, you would be the last person I would suspect of doing such things. How can people be so different?

"My parents were the only people I really knew. They were so good and kind. I can't imagine people being otherwise. As people return to life, we are seeing some of the good and bad in their past life. I always knew that people made mistakes because I made mistakes, as did my loving parents. However, neither they nor I were ever intentionally mean or heartless. When hungry people came to our door for food, my mother always gave them something to eat, even when we had very little food. I thought everyone was like that."

Sigfried replied, "That is how we're all going to be if we are to gain everlasting life. Probably my wife and I would have been that kind to a person who needed food if they came to my home. However, in the camps there was very little food and no one ever got any extra food out of kindness. Prisoners were known to give their rations to others, especially when they knew they were about to die. They would see the barracks next to theirs emptied one day and they figured they would be taken in the afternoon or the next day. They would see new prisoners filing into the adjoining flea-infested quarters. We couldn't show kindness or mercy to anyone. It was forbidden. The guards were required to report on each other. No one could express human compassion or mercy.

"Although, I must tell you, I always felt heartsick when my assignment for the day was to send prisoners into the gas chambers. Perhaps I looked as hard as stone standing there. However, my heart bled for those poor people. What had they done to deserve such cruel treatment? What right did anyone have to take another's life away? They were good, decent people. The devil was the one most responsible for what was happening. I think that some guards became mean and ruthless and enjoyed the power they had over people. We knew some guards that were exceptionally cruel and we never liked them. I know if I sat in the seat of authority, this insane killing would have stopped. I hated what I did and what I saw everyday. Most of the guards felt as I did."

Mr. Kraup spoke up, "You're right, Sigfried. Among the guards there was a big difference. I knew that cruel acts would occur on the days that certain guards were on duty. Some guards would look the other way when people didn't make their quotas, and they would make believe the slaves had done well for the day. Others would kick or punch slaves who were too weak to meet their quotas or too sick to do the job right. When I saw certain guards, I knew a slave or two would be shot that day. I hated those guards so much I would have loved to knock them flat and let them taste how it feels. However, it was the cruelest ones that were always in charge. They had become mean. I am expecting one of those mean guards to show up someday, and I tell you they are going to have to do some tall talking to gain my respect."

"Are You Exaggerating?"

Christine shook her head, "I guess I am naïve. I never knew that people found pleasure in hurting other people. That sounds so gross to me. Are you sure you are not exaggerating?"

"My dear child," Sigfried said, "Make no mistake about it, some people loved to hurt other people. They seemed to get pleasure in abusing others. I saw guards rounding up people for the gas chambers; and, if any of them did not walk fast enough or were a little wobbly from lack of food or dysentery, they would kick them or hit them with their rifle butts. Here these people were going to a painful death and were being abused on the way. Maybe they had sick minds, I don't know. We all hated those guards."

Marion loved climbing up and down the ladder. She volunteered to supply everyone with material. Of course, they had a power lift for the heavier supplies, but they always needed nails and little things, plus in the heat on the roof they always needed something to drink. She appreciated her legs the way those who always had good legs could never imagine. She was listening to all the conversations and would wait to hear what the men were talking about before hopping off on her mission.

They finished half of the roof that day and had waterproofed the other half. If it rained that night, as it often did, everything would be dry inside. They agreed to meet at the chapel in the morning, so Sigfried and Mr. Kraup came to Lev's home for supper and the night.

*"Who can understand his errors?
Cleanse thou me from secret faults"
(Psalm 19:12).*

Chapter Nineteen

In the morning they were at the chapel early. Mr. Kraup stiffened when he saw a man enter the room. Lev could see him tense up.

"Is anything wrong?"

Helmut Appears

"Remember what I said yesterday about some guards being cruel. Well, there is Helmut. He shot more slaves than anyone. I'm going over to talk to him. Please come with me, Lev and Sigfried. Don't let me swing at him."

"Remember me, Helmut?"

He puzzled for a moment. "Why, yes, Mr. Kraup, I remember you very distinctly. You sat up in your ivory tower, far away from all the unpleasantness and our lot to keep production going with a bunch of ill trained, inadequate slaves. Somehow we were expected to keep up production. However, Mr. Kraup, I am a very forgiving man. I know you were under great pressure, and besides, I knew the Nazis were constantly after the bottom line. I know you had done your best."

Mr. Kraup was stunned by his remarks. Helmut made him look like the ugly ogre and himself a victim of personal oppression. By the time Mr. Kraup recovered his composure, the music was starting and he hadn't even introduced Sigfried and Lev to Helmut.

As they sat down Lev whispered to Mr. Kraup, "Things can be made to look quite different than they were with a little ingenuity, can't they?"

He whispered back, "Lev, I am completely flabbergasted by his remarks."

The services were special this morning. Those assembled were singing from their hearts, and all the biblical messages were excellent. Afterwards, Mr. Kraup tried to catch Helmut again, but he had gone directly to the chaplain to thank him for the wonderful service. He had introduced himself and explained to the chaplain that he would be in the area helping to build a house for the return of his aunt.

"I am so happy for the privilege of working to provide for my family members to return. It's such a wonderful privilege to give of oneself freely to help others."

The chaplain was impressed with his comments. Before Mr. Kraup could arrive to catch up with Helmut, he turned and headed toward the exit, saying to the chaplain, "Forgive me, I must hurry to the work cut out for me."

He had seen Mr. Kraup heading his way and was eager to leave before he could be engaged in further conversation.

Lev said to Mr. Kraup, "We'll catch up with him again. He has learned how to project a good image of himself. No godly sorrow evident there. That is the besetting sin of many who were guilty of horrendous war crimes against humanity."

The two gentlemen stopped over for breakfast at Lev's temporary home. Mr. Kraup was especially concerned about meeting Helmut. It awakened old scenes from the past. From his office window he could see the slave laborers, tired, yet desperately trying to keep producing. Their life depended on it. How often he saw Helmut strike workers on their bony backs with his nightstick. If that didn't improve their performance, often it was the cold steel pistol on their necks as a reminder of what awaited them.

No God Watching in Heaven

They tried so hard to produce to save their lives for another day or two, hoping the war would end or some miracle would save them. It was a false hope, and soon he would hear a pistol shot and the slaves would have to carry out their fellow worker. Mercy? No one knew the meaning of the word. There wasn't a shred of human kindness. That was forbidden. If one began to show kindness, one might think of these poor souls as people. No, they were to be considered sub-humans with no feelings or pain. One could beat them, starve them and kill them at will. Surely someone must have concluded there was no God in heaven watching from above.

Now it was so clear that God had been watching all along. Nobody was getting away with anything. Every sin would receive justice and every virtue its due.

Lev said, "I know where he's working. It's less than a mile from here. Someone at the chapel told me where his aunt's house is going up. Perhaps we should stop in for a brief chat with him before starting at our job. We're ahead of schedule already, so if we arrive a half hour late, we can make it up in the afternoon. What would you say, men?"

Both agreed that it might be profitable for all concerned to address the past squarely with Helmut, so on their way to work they stopped to see him. Mr. Kraup was very determined to confront him with his past. He was known as the "butcher" at the factory.

They drove up to see Helmut with two other men standing around. Mr. Kraup was determined to confront him.

"You got away this morning before I could talk to you. You know I sat in my office because I was not allowed in the factory itself. I dreaded the days you were on guard, as did all the workers. Do you know why?"

"Mr. Kraup, I had a job to do. We were not running a rehabilitation center. We had production quotas to meet."

"That was my department. You know that we could never meet the quotas they wanted. Who could with sick and starved workers? Especially workers who were so beaten and bruised that everyone's muscles and bones ached in pain. I only wished I could put you on the work floor and see how well you could do without food and a decent place to sleep. I would like to have seen the slaves beat you with your nightstick and scream at you. As you got sick and weak, how would you like to have a gun put to your head as a reminder of what awaited you the next day or hour? Sir, you were called the 'butcher' at our plant because that is what you were. You were outstanding for your meanness and cruelty."

"You exaggerate, Mr. Kraup. It was my ability to keep everyone working that at least enabled you to come close to your assigned production goals. You seem ungrateful that I saved your skin from the German SS men."

"You imagine that your meanness was my salvation. You are so wrong, Helmut. The Germans knew that no one knew the logistics of running that company better than I. They could fuss and fume, but there was little they could do. I made sure that we never met their quotas. I was no fool. They could not give me sick and starved people and expect them to perform like strong healthy people. They could rant and rave all they wanted, but I would smile and say, 'Get me some healthy people and give me food to feed them.' They would storm out of my office."

A Rationalization

Helmut replied, "I was just doing my job."

"That is what we all said," Sigfried exclaimed. "I was a guard at Auschwitz. I sent hundreds of people into the gas chambers on many more days than I wish to remember. At first I would nearly throw up when they opened the doors to the death chambers. We would see those poor souls piled up by the door, their bodies emaciated from the horrors they were subjected to. I hated that and I hated myself for being a part of it. But I didn't want to die up at the Russian front, so I was granted the job of a guard at Auschwitz. I saved my life, but lost my honor and peace of mind. I knew what I was doing was wicked and intolerable by the standards of all noble men and women everywhere."

"That's where most of our laborers would've gone if we hadn't used them for slave labor," Helmut sneered. "They were given maybe six weeks of extra life. Why do you think that I'm worse than you?"

Mr. Kraup said, "Because you *enjoyed* abusing people. When beating poor hapless workers and shooting them, you felt you were somebody important. You didn't show an ounce of mercy or kindness."

"The war wasn't about mercy and kindness. No war ever is," Helmut declared. "We were fighting the whole world at the time. Saving our nation and our own skin was the business we were in."

"The Germans were fighting the whole world because they made war against the whole world. Germany had visions of world dominance and to secure it they violated every rule of decency, and even more, the rules of God," Mr. Kraup exclaimed. "I don't think you are repentant about what you did. You enjoyed exercising ruthless power over people, didn't you?"

"Look, I was a good father to my children and a good husband to my wife. I know the war was a mistake. After all, everybody in Germany knows that now because we lost the war, we lost millions of our own soldiers and our own citizens. With hindsight we can all look back and say we should not have begun that war because we lost it."

Sigfried said, "Thank God, we lost it. Our reign of terror against the human race was ended. We behaved worse than barbarians. Imagine how much more evil we would have become if we won!"

"Few nations ever murdered more people in cold blood than the Germans did in that war. War breeds cruelty and causes men to do things that they would not have done in normal life. The people who planned this wholesale murder sat in comfortable rooms and engaged top-notch scientists in the gruesome business of killing innocent men, women and children. What we did is an embarrassment to the human race," Mr. Kraup said.

Pleading Innocence

"You don't hear me bragging about what I did," Helmut exclaimed. "But I certainly was glad that I wasn't one of those poor slaves. I didn't control food supplies. It would have been nice to at least feed them and give them a warm place to sleep, but that wasn't a part of the German plan. The only reason they weren't sent to the gas chambers was to get free labor out of them before they died. But we weren't responsible."

"What you are saying is only half true, Helmut," Mr. Kraup asserted. "True, we were in the grips of an evil vise. But we were parties to this crime, because no one stood up against the evil. The Nazis were cruel and relentless, asserting control over everyone. They didn't allow any correction or dissent. They were in power, so they were right. Like all dictatorships, they were obsessed with perpetuating themselves in power. However, they knew our weaknesses. To save our own skin, we would do anything. The difference, Helmut, is that some of us knew in our hearts that we were trapped and we hated it and loathed the evil we were ensnared in. You enjoyed your job, I think."

"Oh, you're just trying to make a monster out of me. I would've been happy to see those slaves fed and properly sheltered. We had to push them to keep up production, and that was my job," Helmut asserted once again. "Anyway, gentlemen, you're keeping me from my work. If you don't mind, I would like to get on with my job."

"Very well, good day," Mr. Kraup said.

They returned to work a bit late. They couldn't help feeling that they hadn't been effective in getting Helmut to take responsibility for his ruthless past. This disturbed them, because the first requirement necessary to correct a wrong condition of heart was to acknowledge that it existed. The power to rationalize was what made those terrible wrongs possible in the first place. The German leaders had risen to power on the pretext that Jews were the cause of Germany's problems. The next step was to destroy the Jews, and then all the problems of the world would be solved. This was absurd thinking, but it got them into power. Scoundrels in history had often used the "scapegoat mentality." Because there had been some latent anti-Semitism in people, no one could have known that prejudices could lead to such cruel fanaticism as seeking the destruction of the Jewish race. However, the unthinkable happened in a supposedly Christian nation that once professed a desire to uphold the Golden Rule.

Christine and Marion, grinning, good-naturedly chided them for being late. Sigfried said with a smile, "We'll do double duty now that we're here."

The following morning at the chapel, Lev met another new person who said he was here to help a relative build a home for his sister. He introduced him to Sigfried and Mr. Kraup. His eyes lit, "You are not the Mr. Kraup of the great Kieffer Stahl works, are you?"

"Indeed I am. I'm so happy to meet you under these wonderful conditions of the present. I can't say that I remember meeting you because I was kept away from the production areas. However, am I right to assume you were a part of the starved and abused slaves that worked there?"

Henry Comes Back to Indict His Tormentor

"Yes, I'm sorry to say that I am. My name is Henry. The last thing I remember was the 'butcher' putting his revolver to my head. He had done that a few times before as threats, but apparently that last time put me out of my misery. I was so weak and sick I just couldn't go on. Maybe being shot was kinder than being kicked and beaten with his nightstick. At least I felt no pain after that."

Lev interrupted, "Here comes Herr Helmut, I think you might remember him."

The music started, but Henry became very tense and Lev could see him shaking. He recognized his old tormenter. Love and hate were such powerful emotions. It took a great character to live above the controlling influences of these two emotions. It was hard to be like our Lord who "loved righteousness and hated iniquity."

Helmut saw Henry when he entered the chapel, but he obviously didn't recognize him. When he had last seen Henry, he was as thin as a rail, weak and emaciated. His face was gaunt and reflected the pain and misery he was experiencing. He knew that he was at death's door, for he could not continue to work. He was weak from hunger and dysentery, and Helmut, the "butcher," must have broken some of his ribs with his nightstick. His rib cage was so painful, he could hardly move. Every effort he made to work created unbearable pain. He was about to tell Helmut, "Just shoot me and be done tormenting me." Perhaps Helmut read his mind, because before he could utter his thoughts, he felt the cold steel revolver at the back of his neck. He said nothing, realizing the moment to die had come. That was all he remembered.

Henry couldn't sing or concentrate on the rest of the service because he was so emotionally upset. He sat there exercising tremendous restraint. His impulse was to take a chair and rap it over Helmut's head. He knew he couldn't do this, but he wished for a free minute so he could give this monster what he deserved for all the pain, misery and death he was responsible for, not only to himself but to countless others.

When the services were over, Helmut was among the first to start for the exit. However, Henry wanted to confront him when he was not carrying a gun and nightstick. He quickly moved ahead of Helmut and stood squarely in his path. "Remember me, Helmut?" he exclaimed, his face red with anger.

"Can't say that I do, my friend. I don't remember faces well, but please refresh my mind," Helmut suavely invited.

"I don't think you would remember my name if I told you. You might remember my number. It was 4560. You were in the habit of beating me with your nightstick, breaking my ribs. It was you who terminated my life in your own illustrious manner. You never counted on the regeneration, when all the dead would come to life again, did you?"

"Well, sir, I am sorry for any grief I may have caused you."

"Sorry! How nice of you to be sorry," Henry exploded. "You are being protected now, and that is the only reason I don't have you by the throat, strangling you. Nothing would relieve my pain better than to see your eyes bulging while I slowly ended your miserable life. That would not be suitable punishment, for you would be paying only for your cruelty to me. How are you going to pay for the cruelty and murder to all the others that seemed to be your daily delight?"

"You seem to attribute all the evil in this world to me," Helmut said defensively. "I was just a small cog in a big wheel. My job was to see that slaves delivered their full capacity of labor. I couldn't help that you weren't fed and sheltered properly. If you were the guard and I were the slave, you would've done the same to me as I did to you. You can't hold me accountable for all the evil in the world."

"Listen carefully, Helmut," Henry said. "You were one of many guards. I know they were there to push us and extract work from us. How is it that you were the only one guilty of breaking bones in our rib cages while beating us with your nightstick? Can you explain why you only had the title of 'the butcher?' How is it that you were always putting your cold steel weapon to our heads, threatening death?"

Methods That Worked

"My methods worked, that's why I used them," Helmut justified himself. "You were only kept from the gas chambers so they could extract some free labor from you. You had several more weeks of life than you would have had if you had gone directly to the gas chambers. I'm not responsible for the sad state of affairs in that time and place."

"You were responsible for being a human being, not a sadistic monster. Actually, I think you were only sorry about killing me because you no longer had me to beat and bully. God made death my way of escape. The moment of death brought peace and freedom from tyranny. I wanted to live, too, but death was the only way out. So it was with all those who went up in the black smoke belching out of the smokestacks. They were then freed from Nazi masters. You overlooked one thing, though. You never thought that I and countless others would be back as witnesses to your brutality."

A crowd of chapel members had gathered around Helmut and Henry. Lev stood by, too, wondering how to diffuse the situation. Certainly Helmut was receiving some of his due. His sins were coming back to haunt him. Lev couldn't help but contrast Sigfried with Helmut. Sigfried was involved in the same grisly business of death. However, Sigfried loathed his involvement in that wickedness from the bottom of his heart; whereas Helmut wished that his accusers would go away or, better yet, that they had not returned to life to haunt him.

Meanwhile, Sigfried joined the fray. "It sounds as if you enjoyed the power you had over people. We had those types in our death camps, too. Most guards would look the other way at small violations. We knew the people were sick and hungry. If they didn't walk fast enough, we just grumbled, but never did we hit or abuse those poor souls. We had to sound gruff, but at heart we loathed the whole killing business. However, it was different with some of the guards. They found pleasure in beating and threatening those poor souls marked for death.

"Had I known how evil it was, I would never have chosen this work over being at the Russian front. I would rather be dead than to have been a partner in the crimes that were being committed at Auschwitz. Once I was there, I admit that I was too weak to protest or to ask to be moved to the front. I became paralyzed out of fear of the awesome power of the Third Reich."

Helmut Denies Being a Monster

"How dare you all try to make some kind of monster out of me. I was good to my children and my wife. However, I had a job to do and I did it because I was a patriot. I wanted Germany to win. I don't think I can receive a fair hearing from this kangaroo court. Believe me, I'm not that bad. I am not proud of my past. Germany certainly behaved as a desperate nation. We lost integrity in the eyes of many people—but the United States didn't hesitate to incinerate Hiroshima and Nagasaki with nuclear bombs. War is mean business. Why don't you admit that?"

Lev responded, "Yes, we all know war is evil. Men were committed to killing and destroying their enemies. That is what war was all about. However, because it was so evil, the Geneva Convention set down rules to limit man's cruelty to their fellow man. There was a way prisoners were to be treated. But Germany broke all the rules. Their leadership had the power to do whatever they wanted, and that's exactly what they did."

Helmut replied, "I certainly agree to that. Our country behaved badly. However, I was just a small player in a big world. I never had any power or position before. Perhaps I became a little heady with my authority. But even Henry admits that death was a peaceful exit from the pain and suffering he was enduring."

Christine said, "Death came to all men. God never gave the authority to you or anyone else to decide who should live and who should die. You know, I was blind in my former life, and I didn't know such evil existed in the world. It's like I just came out of a dark closet to find what horrible crimes were done. I cannot believe that you beat Henry with a club, breaking his ribs. Did you have to do that?"

Suddenly Helmut turned pale. He looked down because he couldn't look into those pure eyes. "Well, maybe I overdid it."

Henry said, "There is no 'maybe' about it. No other guard performed as cruelly as you. There was no reason for it. You certainly couldn't get more production out of a man by cracking his ribs, could you? We were just skin and bones. There was no flesh to absorb the blows of your club. You could hear your nightstick bang on our bones."

"But remember—we had production schedules to meet," Helmut said defensively.

Mr. Kraup said, "Production was my responsibility. Did I ever tell you to beat the workers to get more work out of them? Did I?"

"No, I can't remember your ever saying that."

"You made yourself production chief, Helmut. You were living under a grand illusion. We never met the production levels the Germans wanted. They used to growl and threaten, but I always told them to give me food for the workers and let me give them a warm, comfortable place to sleep. They would say, 'We don't have enough food for the Germans—and now you want to feed these swine,'" Mr. Kraup explained.

Marion finally addressed Helmut saying, "I was a cripple in my former life. A loving father and mother raised me. I cannot understand what I am hearing you say. You were cruel to people who were helplessly under your control."

Then looking at him with her big, beautiful eyes she asked, "Have you no heart? How can you face Henry after what you did to him? You are justifying yourself instead of seeking his forgiveness.'"

The whole assembled body began to nod approvingly at Marion's statement. Helmut had nowhere to turn.

"All right, all right! I'm guilty! I did abuse my power as a guard. How will that relieve the pain that Henry feels? When I admit that I bullied those poor workers, will they forgive me? No, they all hated me then and hate me now. I never asked to be brought back to life. Henry was right. The grave was a peaceful place. Sometimes I wish I had been left there."

The Past Cannot Be Undone

Lev said, "There is no way back. There is only one way to go, and that is forward. You are beginning to feel sorry for yourself because your crimes are greater than you can carry. You must remember you have been brought back to life for a purpose. Christ didn't give you life again to condemn you. You have been given a fresh opportunity to turn your life around. You have to have the will to change if you are going to change. If you indulge in self-pity, you won't change. Great men have sinned but have managed to live down their sins in a remarkable way. You can make good, despite your criminal past, if you will it."

Henry then said, "I could forgive you if I saw you repented of your evil past with godly sorrow. I gain nothing by holding a grudge against you. However, you were mean and evil in what you did to us workers, and I see nothing in your testimony that shows you are truly sorry."

"It is hard to believe that you could forgive me, Henry. I knew you hated me for what I did to you. However, I didn't care, because you were as good as dead. When people hated me, it made it easier for me to kill them. That's an awful confession on my part, but I guess it's true."

Helmut continued, "I guess I did get a certain amount of pleasure of having power over people. Production was my excuse for abusing people. I could make believe that I had a right to beat and abuse people because they were too sick and weak to carry a normal workload. We had orders to shoot people when they could no longer function properly. It's amazing how the will to live drove people to work harder. When I killed someone, the others automatically did a little better for the rest of the day.

"This now must seem so outrageous and unbelievable to pure people like Christine and Marion. Please remember that death was everywhere in those days. Suffering was common; they suffered from hunger, cold, homelessness and deprivations of every kind. Only the rich and those politically connected to the rulers of the Third Reich fared well. The Allied Armies were advancing against Germany and the Allied aircraft were obliterating our cities with bombs. My family members were dying both on the front lines and in the cities. I felt the need to help the sagging fortunes of our country."

Marion said, in her beautiful innocence, "Patriotism I can understand, but to cruelly beat and abuse poor suffering workers, I cannot understand. What you did was loathsome, not only to me, but to every standard of human decency. You did such awful things not because you were patriotic, but because you enjoyed abusing and killing people."

Poor Helmut, he knew his rationalizations and excuses for what he had done were paper-thin. Finally, he crumbled.

"Yes, Marion you are right. I have to admit the real motive for my meanness was not patriotism. I enjoyed having power over people. I abused people because then they had to acknowledge my power. Who would know of my power unless I used it? The Nazis rewarded my meanness too, for they knew I was one of them and I received high marks for my performance. Cruelty begets cruelty, just like love begets love. Saying 'I'm sorry' sounds empty. I am sorry though. I knew what

I was doing, but there was no reason to change. I was locked into evil of overwhelming proportions, but that was what was in power. I had joined in it, and there was no way back. I avoided praying, because I knew I would be a hypocrite in prayer."

Helmut Urged to Renounce His Past

Christine said, "Helmut, you wouldn't have been locked into such evil if an opportunity to do so weren't given you. You might have been a soldier wounded or killed at the front and neither you nor any other person would know how evil you could become. Perhaps there are many people who would have put in a similar performance if they had been placed in a similar position. So we can't assume we are superior to you, because we have not demonstrated what kind of character we would really possess under those circumstances. Perhaps many who hold you in contempt might have done worse than you in such a situation. Christ is the righteous Judge. You must renounce the past, not merely with words, but in your heart. You have the present to demonstrate true godly sorrow and to seek to give back to mankind the love that you did not give before."

Everyone clapped.

Helmut suddenly sat down in the nearest chair. To everyone's stunned amazement, he began to weep. "Thank you, Christine. This is the first time tears of sorrow have genuinely run down my cheeks. You are right, so very right. Not only am I sorry, but also by God's grace I intend in godly sorrow to give back to mankind the love I failed to give in my former life. You are right in saying life might have given me different experiences. Had I died on the front lines, I would never have known what weaknesses of character I possessed."

Henry came up and placed his arm around Helmut.

"I never thought I could do anything but hate you, but I'm here to say I'm willing to forgive what you did to me. Holding anger in my heart will not undo the pain and misery I endured. I desperately wanted to live then and I struggled until I knew I could go no further. However, in spite of what happened to me, here I am living in such a beautiful world and life has never been more sweet or beautiful. I now have the life I so desperately wanted. No one can take it from me either. Yes, Helmut, I forgive you and you should forgive yourself."

Lev looked on speechlessly. These two young innocent ladies seemed to have reached Helmut's heart. They were so sweet, yet so wise that it melted his heart. His defenses collapsed. Helmut seemed ready to start his journey toward attaining love for God and for his fellow man.

When they arrived back on the job that day, Lev knew his purpose in being here was over. He would help finish the house Christine was building for her mother and then seek another assignment. Lev had learned some lessons he would never forget from these two young ladies. They had succeeded in human relations with their purity and innocence better than Lev could have ever hoped to do.

THE END

John Class has written a series of five books to cover the experiences of the regenerated human race under Christ's rule—*Alive Again, From Ashes to Beauty, Fingers Stained with Evil, Adam and Eve Live Again* and *When the Thousand Years Expire.*